SHOO FLY PIE

A BUG MAN NOVEL

TIM DOWNS

Our purpose at Howard Publishing is to:

- *Increase faith* in the hearts of growing Christians
- *Inspire holiness* in the lives of believers
- *Instill hope* in the hearts of struggling people everywhere

Because He's coming again!

Published by Howard Publishing Co., Inc.
3117 North 7th Street, West Monroe, Louisiana 71291-2227

In association with the literary agency of Alive Communications, Inc.
7680 Goddard Street, Suite 200, Colorado Springs, CO 80920

03 04 05 06 07 08 09 10 11 12 10 9 8 7 6 5 4 3 2 1

Cover design by David Carlson Design
Cover images by Getty Images
Interior design by Stephanie Denney

Library of Congress Cataloging-in-Publication Data

Downs, Tim.
Shoofly pie : a Bug Man novel / Tim Downs.
p. cm.
ISBN: 1-58229-308-2
1. Forensic entomology—Fiction. 2. Entomologist—Fiction. I. Title.

PS3604.O696S56 2003
813'.6—dc21

2003050934

For my beautiful Joy,
whose constant love and encouragement
keep the bugs away.
Remember, I can do anything you think I can do.

ACKNOWLEDGMENTS

I would like to thank the following individuals and organizations for their generous contributions to this book: Dr. John Butts, chief medical examiner of North Carolina; Steve Bambara of North Carolina State University for his help with beekeeping; Major Dominic Caraccilo, commander of Headquarters Company, 2d Brigade, 82d Airborne, during Operation Desert Storm; Bill Poston of the North Carolina Department of Correction; Randy Young of Young Guns, Inc., in Apex, North Carolina; Chuck Henley at the Defense POW/Missing Personnel Office; the Department of Entomology, National Museum of Natural History, Smithsonian Institution; the U.S. General Accounting Office; Walter Reed Army Medical Center and Biosystematics Unit; Gulf War Health Center; U.S. Army's *Armor* magazine; U.S. Army Center of Military History; Brown-Wynne Funeral Homes of Cary, North Carolina; the American Beekeeping Federation; and scores of others who took the time to respond to my e-mails, letters, and phone calls.

I would especially like to thank the forensic entomologists who generously gave their time to help me understand their remarkable field: Dr. Boris Kondratieff of Colorado State University, for helping me with the basics of FE; Dr. Robert Hall of the University of Missouri, for introducing me to *Chrysomya megacephala*; and Dr. Neal Haskell, for allowing me to attend his fascinating Forensic Entomology Workshop (a.k.a. Maggot School) in Rensselaer, Indiana. Thanks for assisting me with the science behind what is, in the end, a work of fiction.

I also want to thank the individuals who made the publication of this book possible: literary agent Kathryn Helmers, who was as tenacious as a tick in shopping my manuscript; Jeff Tikson, my longtime advisor and friend; Ed Stackler, for his invaluable skills as an editor and story consultant; and the wonderful people at Howard Publishing, for their creativity, vision, and passion for the written word.

Thanks, too, to the faithful friends whose opinions helped shape this book into its final form: Tim Muehlhoff, Kent Kramer, Joy Downs, Bill and Laura Burns, Jim and Renee Keller, and Dan and Julie Brenton.

And thank God for the Internet.

PROLOGUE

Holcum County, North Carolina, 1975

Zachary Sloan stepped out of the Rayford ABC Package Store and walked to the bed of his primer-gray Ford pickup. Two eager dogs greeted him. The first, Sloan's favorite, was an aging black Labrador, now walleyed and graying at the muzzle; the other was a spotted pup of questionable lineage but unlimited enthusiasm. The dogs nuzzled the paper package in the old man's right hand.

"Get back, mutt. That's for me." He slipped the bottle into the right pocket of his khaki hunting coat and took a crumpled sack from under his arm. "This is for you two no-goods." He tossed a fat pig's knuckle onto the rusty truck bed, then climbed into the cab. He revved the engine, coaxed the transmission into reverse, and backed out on to Highway 29. The dogs took two quick steps back as he accelerated east.

Fifty yards away to his right the tracks of the Norfolk and Southern ran parallel to the road, the side of the towering embankment silhouetted gray-blue by the afternoon sun. Sloan watched the telephone poles click by, each one clipping the hood of his truck with the tip of its shadow. Not far ahead, County Road 42 descended from the left through a vast, open expanse of fledgling corn and tobacco. It dipped down to cross Highway 29, then abruptly rose again to traverse the train tracks fifty yards away. There was no stoplight or sign at the intersection; none was necessary. Sloan could see vehicles approaching for miles in all directions—except from the right on County Road 42, where the Norfolk & Southern shielded the intersection like an ancient fortress wall.

■

Three miles away, a forty-foot flatbed trailer lumbered cautiously down a dirt road and passed beneath a brightly painted sign that hung across the exit to the Good 'N Plenty Orchards. Strapped to the bed of the open trailer was stack after stack of neat, white cabinets, each with a kind of oversize box top that overlapped at the edges. Each cabinet seemed to contain several drawers, expertly dovetailed at the edges. In the lowest drawer of each cabinet was a long horizontal slot stuffed tight with a rag and secured with twine. The drawers could not be opened, yet each cabinet was completely filled...with 40,000 honeybees.

The dirt road ended with a sudden rise to join the county highway just north of the town of Rayford. The teamster cautiously eased the left wheel up onto the roadway. With one great gun of the diesel engine, the right wheel followed. The flatbed behind him rocked right, then lurched left. The beehives flexed and shifted uneasily like tottering stacks of cups and saucers. An angry murmur rose from within the whitewashed columns, then quieted once again as the flatbed settled onto the level roadway of County Road 42. With each grinding shift of gears, the diesel sent a plume of blue smoke into the sky, slowly gathering speed as it headed south toward the tiny town of Rayford.

■

Sloan spotted the long flatbed with the alabaster cargo approaching from far away to his left. He eyed the intersection, then the flatbed, then the intersection again. Their two vehicles seemed to be approaching at equal speeds. Sloan pushed steadily on the accelerator, and the flatbed accelerated in kind.

"Grits-for-brains," the old man muttered. There was a common understanding in Rayford that commercial rigs should always yield to the locals—a common understanding, that is, among locals. Sloan took a different view entirely. His tariffs and duties had *paid* for these roads, thank you, and the meandering locals could get out of the way.

Now Sloan had the accelerator pushed flat against the floor. Behind him, the dogs stood straight and alert, sensing a force of wind and a whine from the engine that they had never felt before. The pup stepped nervously to his left, stopped, then started right again. He began to whimper and pushed his nose into the side of his more experienced companion. The aging Labrador slowly hung his head, circled once, and lay down.

High atop the railroad tracks fifty yards to Sloan's right, three bicycles raced side by side in a dead heat, clattering across the half-buried crossties of the old Norfolk and Southern railway.

Eight-year-old Andy Guilford suddenly veered to the right, forcing Pete St. Clair's bike up against the steel railhead.

"No fair!"

Pete jerked back on the handlebars and jumped the rail altogether. His back wheel spun wide and cut a deep arc in the loose gravel ballast.

"You can whine or you can win," Andy shouted back. He swerved left now and jammed his foot into the rear tire of Jimmy McAllister's rusting red beach cruiser. The bike lurched violently, almost throwing Jimmy onto his handlebars.

The three bicycles simultaneously crunched to a stop at the

crossing of County Road 42. For a while the three boys said nothing; they stood straddling their bikes, panting and mopping their foreheads, staring up the road one way and then down the other.

"We did it!" Jimmy beamed. "We beat her!"

"And I beat the both of *you*," Andy chided.

"Like fun you did!"

Andy glanced to the left. He saw the great white flatbed barreling toward them, still a good mile away, and an old gray pickup streaking down from the left. Now he cupped his hand above his eyes and followed County Road 42 to the right. There was no sign of an automobile as far as the eye could see—no sign of *her* automobile. This is the way she would come—this is the way she came every Saturday afternoon when her father made his weekly drive into Rayford.

"We beat her, all right," Pete said. "But she's bound to be along any minute. Better get ready!"

The three boys tossed their bikes aside and scrambled for position. Jimmy hoisted himself up on top of the big metal signal box beside the tracks. He steadied himself, then slowly stood aright and spread his arms out wide.

"This is where *I'm* going to be," he said. "She'll see me before she sees either one of you!"

Andy stood eyeing the great gleaming crossing signal on the far side of the road.

"No way!" Jimmy shouted over to him.

"Just watch me," Andy called back. He shinnied up the silver post as far as the flashing red target lights, then pulled himself up and over. He climbed past the black-and-yellow Norfolk and Southern sign, up past the great white X formed by the RAILROAD CROSSING signs, until he straddled the post cap like a skull atop crossbones.

"*Now* who's she gonna see first?" he shouted down. "She'll spot me a mile away!"

Pete peered up at Andy, then at Jimmy, then Andy again.

"Hey, Pete!" Andy called down. "Maybe you could wave your hankie!"

"Or drop your drawers!" Jimmy joined in. "She's sure to see that!"

Pete stood gloomily for a full minute, saying nothing. Then he stepped across the railroad tracks onto the pavement.

He lay down in the center of the right lane—*her* lane.

"Are you nuts?" Andy called down. "Get out of the road!"

Pete lay motionless, staring at the sky.

"Pete!" Jimmy shouted. "She'll run right over you!"

"She won't neither. When the car hits the tracks, it leaves the ground. She'll fly right over me."

"What if the car slows down this time? What if you're too far from the tracks?"

Pete said nothing.

"She'll never even see you!" Andy was almost screaming now. "She'll run right over you and squash you like a bug, and she'll never even know it!"

"She'll know," Pete said under his breath. "She'll know I did it for her."

Andy looked up. Far down County Road 42 he saw a tiny blur coming over the horizon.

■

Inside that tiny blur, seven-year-old Kathryn lay on her back, sandwiched between the rear window and backseat of her father's crumbling green '57 Chevy Bel Air. Her left shoulder was wedged tight between the glass and vinyl, and her nose just cleared the window as it curved up toward the roof above her.

She closed her eyes and felt the warmth of the afternoon sun on her full body. The wind from the single open window swirled around her and carried the smell of tobacco from her father's cigarette. She rolled her head to the right and studied the back of her father's head: the sun-furrowed neck, the leathery ears that protruded proudly into space, and the thick shock of auburn hair that always lay carelessly to the left. Last of all, she saw her father's emerald green eyes in the rearview mirror. They were focused directly on her.

"Know what I think?" he said, grinning. "I think you wish you was a big ol' whitetail deer, so's you could ride strapped across the hood."

Her heart raced at the thought that somehow it might be possible—to feel the wind in her hair, to watch the road rushing to meet her instead of always disappearing into the past.

"*Could* I, Daddy?" she asked with childish hope.

He laughed. "Your momma would shoot me dead. Why, she'd tan my hide if she knew I let you ride without a seat belt."

He glanced again in the mirror at Kathryn's body stretched out atop the backseat beneath the rear window.

"You be careful back there, hear?"

He flicked his cigarette out the window and rolled it up, leaving just a hairline crack at the top.

"Are the tracks coming, Daddy? Are we there yet?"

"Almost! Get ready!"

With a squeal, Kathryn wedged herself even tighter against the glass. She was in her favorite place on the best of days, and now she was coming to the best moment of all—when they came to the sudden rise in the road where the Norfolk & Southern crossed County Road 42. When no train was in sight it was agreed—it was *expected*—that her father would accelerate up the rise just as fast as the aging Chevy could possibly go. As they crossed the tracks and the road dropped suddenly away beneath them, the hulking sedan would magically lift from the ground like the pirate ship rising from the Blue Lagoon. Then, for one eternal moment, Kathryn would float weightless above the seat, above the car, above even the gigantic town of Rayford itself. It was the longest two seconds in the universe, an entire world within a world, a glimpse of eternity—and Kathryn was not about to let her father forget about it.

"Faster, Daddy! Faster!"

The signs flashed past like confetti now, and the code of dots and dashes on the pavement blurred together into yellow and white ribbons streaming out behind the car. She heard the growling complaint from the aging engine and the rising pitch of her father's voice.

"Here it comes, sweetheart! Get ready!"

■

Zachary Sloan glared at the center of the intersection and shot defiant glances at the great white blur closing fast from the left.

Two hundred yards...

One hundred yards...

Fifty yards from the intersection, Sloan slammed his hand down on the horn in a final act of anger and defiance and was instantly answered by the shattering bellow of the diesel's great air horn. Both vehicles went raging, shouting, screaming into the center of the intersection.

The Ford arrived a split second before the flatbed. The left headlight of the pickup smashed into the right fender of the diesel just behind the bumper. The hood sprung open and was instantly ripped away in the wind. The pickup spun right across the front of the flatbed, heaved onto its side, and continued through the intersection amid a shower of sparks and the deafening scream of metal on concrete.

The force of the impact spun the diesel cab fully to the left, jackknifed at a right angle to the flatbed behind it. The aging retreads of the diesel skidded, then stretched, then exploded into shards of smoking rubber. The bare metal wheel rims dug into the pavement, and the cab slammed onto its side with astounding force. The flatbed trailer, sheared from its shattered cab, lurched right, then left, then right once again—and then flipped side-over-side down the middle of County Road 42.

The hives that were not strapped down seemed to float in the air for an instant before crashing to the roadway below. Those that were bound to the bed of the trailer were whipped to the pavement as the flatbed began its roll. In both cases, the hives did not seem to simply break or crush or fall apart; they literally exploded. Eighty-five hives had lined that trailer, each weighing almost a hundred pounds. As each hive struck the roadway, the brittle drawer-like supers separated, then splintered into a thousand pieces, vomiting a tangle of wood, wire, wax, and honey. At first, the bees seemed to spill out from the wreckage like pouring gravel. Then, slowly, the million-or-so that survived the crash began to rise into the sky in a black, boiling, living cloud of venom.

■

Pete sat upright in the center of the road.

All three boys stared wild-eyed, gawking at the carnage spewed out on the road behind them and the slowly rising cloud above. Almost simultaneously they remembered—and they turned back again to see the flash of the green Bel Air less than a quarter of a mile away.

Andy and Jimmy dropped to the roadway and Pete scrambled to his feet. All three boys stood jumping, shrieking, and waving their arms in frantic, futile arcs.

■

"There they are!" Kathryn's father called to the backseat. "All three of them, waving their hellos!" He lay on the horn and shoved the accelerator to the floor.

The nose of the sedan tipped upward as they reached the rise. Kathryn heard the whine of the engine as the wheels spun free of the ground, and she felt the lug of the tires as they dropped away below the car. Then at last came the glorious moment when she floated free of the car—or was the car falling away from her? It didn't matter. To Kathryn, it was the sacred moment when she rose from the dead and ascended into heaven.

For an instant, only clouds and sky were visible through the windshield of the airborne sedan. But as the weight of the engine forced the nose of the car back to earth, a hellish landscape rose into view. In the left lane lay a broken and twisted flatbed; to the right, the crushed shell of a diesel cab and the smoldering undercarriage of a gray pickup; straight ahead, a graveyard of crumpled and shattered white bones. And above it all was a massive, swirling black cloud of…

"Holy… *Hold on, Kath!"*

■

Less than a second later the sedan smashed into the first of the hives. The tires lost all traction on the sea of honey and insect parts and spun helplessly to the right. The right fender struck the twisted chassis of the diesel, and the sedan lurched onto its left side. To Kathryn's astonishment she found herself standing perfectly erect, still pressed between the rear window and seat, as if she were suddenly back home standing in front of the storm door, watching the backyard rushing toward her. Just as suddenly, the car flipped onto its rounded top, and Kathryn was thrown face-forward against the window glass. Six inches below her nose she saw a yellow dash streak by, then a dot, then a much longer dash, and then at last the car came to rest.

For a few moments Kathryn lay perfectly still, unable to move but perfectly aware of everything around her. Above and to her right she heard the engine cough and sputter and die. She heard the wheels somewhere above her continue to spin a full minute longer. She detected the acrid stench of burnt rubber, the thick, sweet smell of diesel fuel, and—strangely, more than anything else—an odor like smashed bananas.

She lifted her head a few inches and saw a spatter of blood from her nose on the glass below her. She watched as tears began to fall straight away from her eyes, splash, and run down the window to her right. Out of habit, she rolled her body to the right—but this time she found herself lying on the crumpled ceiling of the car amid paper cups, floor mats, cigarette butts, and coins. She slowly turned to look at the back of her father's head, and through a wash of tears saw his body hanging behind the wheel, suspended by his seat belt. His shoulders sagged against the ceiling with one arm extending straight out, and his head was tucked under like the ducks she had seen on the pond behind her house.

But she had never seen her father's neck bent at an angle like that.

She reached out to touch her father's arm, but then she heard a shout from somewhere outside the passenger side of the car. She turned to the window—all of the glass was still intact. She looked out to see an old man in a khaki jacket standing not more than twenty yards away.

Far beyond him, still atop the rise of the railroad tracks, stood the figures of three helpless boys.

The left side of the man's face was covered with blood, and he stumbled toward a motionless black form on the ground ahead of him. He dropped to his knees and buried his face in the dark fur. Beside him, a mottled gray pup paced anxiously back and forth.

Suddenly the pup started, then spun to its left and snapped at the air. It jumped again and whirled back to the right. In another moment it was leaping, whirling, and kicking like the wild horse Kathryn once saw at the state fair in Raleigh.

The man staggered to his feet. He swung at the air around his face with one hand, then both. He began to duck and weave and flail at the air like a boxer facing some menacing shadow. Now he began to wave his arms frantically around him and pulled his jacket up over his head, running a few steps one way, then the other.

For the first time Kathryn looked up into the sky. She saw a great, swirling black cloud that seemed to be slowly descending around them like a plague, and a single word screamed out in her mind: FIRE! She saw no flames, but she remembered what the fireman once told her class: *The hottest fire is the one you can't see.* It was like watching hell itself. The man and his dog were being tortured by flames but were never consumed.

A wave of panic swept over Kathryn. *"Daddy! Wake up! We have to get out of here!"* She twisted around and put her feet against the window glass. She pulled back and with all of her might kicked out against the glass.

Nothing.

She kicked again and again as the cloud outside grew thicker and darker and closer. She began to weep hysterically, but stopped with a gasp. She saw the man, now barely visible through the whirling cloud, begin to stagger directly toward her. His face looked swollen and blue with patches of black and gray, and his hands clutched at his throat. He bent forward, then straightened and threw his shoulders back and his chest out, as though he were straining to draw each breath through a long tube. He stumbled forward two steps, then suddenly stopped and dropped his arms limp at his sides. For a moment he stood perfectly still, as if somehow at peace with this unexpected fate, and then fell headlong on the pavement not more than ten feet from Kathryn's window. Kathryn screamed and scrambled back from the glass. There were no flames, yet the man's body grew steadily darker—and the black patches seemed to be *moving.*

Kathryn's eyes were fixed in horror on the blackened figure before her. She crawled back, back, until she was flattened against the opposite window glass, her arms frozen down and out to her sides. She felt a tiny tickle on her left wrist and frantically jerked it away. She turned.

Near the ground, her father's window was still open just a hairline crack. The crack was lined with the wriggling heads, legs, and wings of a thousand enraged bees struggling to squeeze through. Behind them, a thousand more pressed forward. Both windows were completely covered with a shifting, throbbing, crawling mass of black-and-yellow insects.

Seven-year-old Kathryn took a deep breath, closed her eyes, and screamed.

Cary, North Carolina, April 21, 1999

Nick Polchak rapped his knuckles on the frame of the open doorway. He glanced back at the Wake County Sheriff's Department police cruiser blocking the driveway, orange and blue lights silently rotating.

"Yo!" Nick called into the house. "Coming in!"

A fresh-faced sheriff's deputy in khaki short sleeves poked his head around the corner and beckoned him in. Nick wondered where they got these kids. He looked younger than some of his students.

Nick stepped into the entryway. Dining room on the right, living room on the left. It was a typical suburban Raleigh home, a colonial five-four-and-a-door with white siding and black shutters. A mahogany bureau stood just inside the door. At its base lay three pair of shoes, one a pair of black patent leathers. Nick shook his head.

He knew the layout by heart: stairway on the left, powder

room on the right, down a short hallway was the kitchen, and the family room beyond that.

Nick paused in the second doorway and took a moment to study the young officer. He stood nervously, awkwardly, constantly checking his watch. His right hand held a handkerchief cupped over his nose and mouth, and he winced as he sucked in each short gulp of air. Nick followed the officer's frozen gaze to the right; the decomposing body of a middle-aged woman lay sprawled across the white Formica island in the center of the kitchen.

Nick knocked again.

"Officer... *Donnelly*, is it? I'm Dr. Nick Polchak. Are you the first one here?"

"I was just a few blocks away, so I took the call." He glanced again at his watch. "Our homicide people ought to be along within the hour."

Nick began to stretch on a pair of latex gloves and stepped around to the victim's head. "The name on the mailbox said 'Allen.'"

"*Stephanie* Allen. That's all I've been able to get so far." The deputy nodded silently toward the family room, where a solitary figure sat slumped forward in a red leather chair with his face buried in his hands. Nick raised his own left hand and wiggled his ring finger. The deputy nodded.

"I didn't get your name—did you say Kolchek?"

"*Polchak*. Nick Polchak."

"You don't sound like you're from around these parts."

"I'm from Pittsburgh," Nick said. "And I'd say you're not."

The deputy grinned. "How'd you know?"

"You left your shoes at the door."

"They don't do that in Pittsburgh? I guess they don't have the red clay."

"The *police* don't do that in Pittsburgh. They figure if you've got a dead body in the kitchen, you've got more to worry about than dirty carpets."

The body lay faceup, stretched out diagonally across the island under the bright kitchen fluorescents.

"Very handy," Nick said. "Too bad I don't find them all like this."

The head rested in one corner, with medium-length blond hair flowing out evenly on all sides. There were deep abrasions and contusions on the neck and lower jaw. The body was in putrefaction, the second major stage of decomposition. The skin was blistered and tight from expanding gases, and the stench was considerable. There were sizable maggot infestations in both eye sockets and in the gaping mouth cavity. She had been dead for several days—maybe a week or more.

"You got here fast, Doc. I thought the medical examiner's office was in Chapel Hill."

Nick shook his head. "I didn't come from Chapel Hill. I came from NC State. I picked up your call on my police scanner."

"From the university? What were you doing there?"

"That's where I work."

Nick removed a pair of slender forceps and a small magnifier from his coat pocket. He bent close to the victim's head and began to carefully sort through the wriggling mass of maggots in the left eye socket.

"Wait a minute. You're not from the medical examiner's office?"

"Never said I was."

"Then who in the—"

"I'm a member of the faculty at NC State. I'm a professor in the department of entomology."

"A professor of what?"

"I'm a forensic entomologist, Deputy. I study the way different necrophilous arthropods inhabit a body during the process of decomposition."

The deputy stood speechless.

Nick plucked a single plump, white larva from the wiggling mass and held it under the magnifier. "I'm the Bug Man."

The deputy began to blink rapidly. "Now just hold on... you're not supposed to...you're not a part of this..."

"Relax," Nick held the forceps aloft. "It's just one bug. There's plenty more where that came from."

"You need to leave, Dr. Polchak."

"Why?"

"Because—you're not a medical examiner, and you're not with the department. You shouldn't be here. It's not procedure."

"Not *procedure*. I have assisted the authorities on seventy-two cases in thirteen different countries. How many homicides did you have in Wake County last year? Five? Ten?"

The deputy shrugged.

"And how many of them did *you* work?"

"I never heard of any *Bug Man*," the deputy muttered.

Nick glanced down at the man's stocking feet. "Now there's a surprise."

Now Nick turned to the motionless figure in the red chair. "Mr. Allen," he called out. "I'm Dr. Nick Polchak. I'd like to ask you a few questions, if you don't mind."

"No," came a whisper from under the hands. "No questions."

"Mr. Allen," the officer broke in. "This man is not a part of the official police investigation. You don't have to answer his questions."

"He's right," Nick said. "But you can if you want to. And when the homicide people get here, Mr. Allen, they're going to ask questions—quite a lot of them. First the police will ask you when you first discovered your wife's body."

The man looked up for the first time. His face was ashen and drawn, and a deep purple crescent cradled each eye.

"It was less than an hour ago," the man said. "I called the police immediately."

"Immediately? Your wife has been dead for quite some time, Mr. Allen."

"I've been out of town. I just got back, just today. And then I found her, like...like this."

Nick nodded. "Next the police will ask you where *you* were during that time."

The man did a double take. "Me? Why me?"

"Because the one who discovers the body is *always* a suspect."

"Like I said, I was out of town. I was in Chicago, on business. For a whole week—they can check it out."

"I'm sure they will," Nick said, "and I'm sure they'll find you're telling the truth. Their next question will be: What day did you leave for Chicago?"

The man thought carefully. "Last Wednesday. The fourteenth."

"That would be...seven days ago exactly. And prior to that time, Mr. Allen, did you see your wife alive and well?"

"We said good-bye right here, on Wednesday morning. She was perfectly healthy."

"You're sure you left that day? On the fourteenth?"

"Of course I'm sure! You think I can't remember a week ago?"

Nick held the specimen up and studied it closely. Then he looked back at Mr. Allen.

"Care to try again?"

Nick dragged a chair from the breakfast nook into the family room and sat down opposite the man, with the tiny white specimen still writhing in the forceps in his right hand. He offered the magnifier to the man. "I want you to take a look at something."

"I can't look at *that*. Get that thing away from me!"

"Oh come now," Nick whispered. "You have a stronger stomach than that—don't you, Mr. Allen?"

The man looked startled; he hesitated, then reluctantly took the magnifier in his left hand.

"Pull up a chair," Nick called back to the deputy. "Learn something." Nick slowly extended the forceps. "Take a look at that end. Tell me what you see."

The magnifier trembled in the man's hand.

"Little lines," he mumbled. "Sort of like slits."

"How many little lines?"

"Three."

"Give the deputy a look, Mr. Allen. Those 'little lines' are called *posterior spiracles*—think of them as 'breathing holes.' The maggot you're holding is the larva of a common blow fly. That fly landed on your wife's body shortly after her death and began to lay eggs in the softest tissues—the eyes, the mouth, and so on. Those eggs hatched into larvae, and the larvae began to feed and grow.

"Now when a larva grows, it passes through three distinct stages of development. Are you following me, Mr. Allen? Because this is the important part: The larva doesn't develop those breathing holes until the third stage. And after many studies, we know exactly how long it takes for this species of fly to reach that third stage of development. Guess what, Mr. Allen? It takes more than a week."

The man began to visibly shake as Nick rocked back in his chair and folded his hands behind his head.

"Let's see what we've got so far. You've been out of town for a week—*exactly* a week. You say that you saw your wife alive one week ago, yet there are insects on her body that prove that she died more than a week ago."

"Well…uh…," the man stammered, "maybe I was gone… longer than I thought."

"The airline's records can clear up that little point. And I'm betting those same records will show that you made your reservations the same day that you traveled—sort of a *last-minute* business trip, you might say. I have just one more question for you, Mr. Allen. The police won't ask you this one, but it's something I've always wondered about…"

Nick leaned forward again.

"When you strangle someone, can you feel the hyoid bone break, or is it all just sort of soft and squishy?"

The man jumped frantically from his chair and lunged toward the door. He ran like a man in a funhouse, stumbling first one way and then the other, throwing himself from wall to wall, ricocheting wildly down the hall toward the open door.

The deputy sat frozen in astonishment, staring wide-eyed at the doorway.

"I think you're supposed to run after him," Nick said. "That's what they always do on TV."

The deputy thrust the magnifier and forceps into Nick's hands and raced barefooted down the hallway. Nick rose slowly from his chair, shook his head, and headed back toward the body. As he passed the hallway he caught a glimpse of the mahogany bureau just inside the front door.

The top drawer was open.

Nick ran to the door and leaped out onto the brick porch. There was no sign of the deputy or his quarry—they had already rounded the house, probably headed for the woods in back.

"He's armed!" Nick shouted. "Your man is armed!"

No response.

Nick looked both directions. He chose left and raced toward the corner of the house. "An amateur cop chasing an amateur murderer," he said aloud. "Someone could get killed this way."

He rounded the corner in a wide arc, expecting to lengthen his stride into a long run for the woods—but there, bracing himself against the far corner of the house, leaned the quivering figure of Mr. Allen. In his right hand a .357 magnum dangled toward the ground.

Nick skidded to a halt. The man saw him, straightened, and wobbled out away from the house. He turned to face Nick and slowly raised the weapon. He couldn't steady it; Nick felt the barrel sweep back and forth across his body again and again.

The man's arm shook so violently that he looked more like he was whitewashing a fence than aiming a firearm. Nick marked the distance between them—fifty feet at least. At this distance, it would take several tries for the man to hit him.

But it only takes one.

"Listen to me, Mr. Allen. You did something stupid. Don't make it worse. You cannot get away, and you know it. You're only running because you're scared."

The gun swept past twice more, marking Nick with a broad X.

"*Think*, Mr. Allen. Maybe you didn't mean to kill your wife—but if you shoot someone else, they'll hang you for sure. Put the gun down. Call a lawyer and see what you can work out."

The gun began to steady…

Over the man's shoulder Nick saw a khaki figure step out silently from behind the house. The deputy drew his own handgun, leveled it, then opened his mouth as if to shout. Nick held up both hands and shook his head violently.

You idiot! I'm in your line of fire!

Too late.

"FREEZE!"

The man spun around, firing wildly before he even faced his foe. The officer fired back; the first shot streaked over the man's left shoulder. Nick could feel it coming, he could sense the air compressing ahead of the bullet as it tore past his left ear.

Nick dove for the ground. The man continued to fire blindly—three shots into the ground, one into the air, two into the side of the house.

The officer fired twice more, shooting for the torso, not trusting his own aim. The first shot caught the man in the lower abdomen and the second hit square in the chest. Nick watched the man take both bullets. It was not at all like the movies—no violent recoil, no sense of impact at all. The man stood motionless for a moment, then his knees suddenly bent in opposite directions, and he sagged to the ground like a crumpling sack.

Nick crawled toward the broken body. He pulled the gun away and tossed it aside; the barrel burned his hand. He placed two fingers on the carotid artery and waited.

Nothing.

Nick looked up at the deputy and shook his head. The officer's knees buckled, and he dropped to the ground, vomiting.

Nick rolled onto his back and stared up into the April sky.

"Seventy-*three* cases," he said.

■

North Carolina State University, April 22, 1999

"Nicholas? A word, if you please."

Nick stepped into the office of Dr. Noah Ellison, chairman of the department of entomology and by far the most senior professor in any department at NC State. Dr. Ellison quietly closed the door behind them.

"Nicholas," he began, wagging a spindly finger, "it has been brought to my attention that you failed to appear for another of your classes yesterday."

"Sorry, Noah, I had to make a house call."

"It is my responsibility as chairman of this department to remind you that your contract involves a certain amount of *teaching*—and your colleagues have reminded me that it is my duty to discipline you appropriately."

Noah picked up Nick's right hand and slapped him on the wrist.

"Consider yourself disciplined. Please do not force me to resort to such extreme measures again."

The old man motioned for Nick to sit.

"I have good news and I have bad news, Nicholas. Which would you like first?"

"Give me both at the same time."

"Very well. The good news is the National Science Foundation has granted funding for your summer research proposal—

continuing study in your beloved field of forensic entomology. The bad news is that the grant is woefully inadequate, hardly more than a one-way ticket out of town."

Noah slid a check across the desk. Nick glanced at it and rolled his eyes.

"Can't we do any better than this, Noah? Aren't there any departmental funds?"

He shook his head. "I control the purse strings, Nicholas, but not the size of the purse. I'm afraid that's it; take it, as they say, or leave it."

Nick studied the check again, hoping to discover a floating decimal point. "What am I supposed to accomplish with *this?*"

"You have the faculty committee's permission to spend the summer at our Extension Research Facility in Holcum County. And you may take your research assistant, Dr. Tedesco, along with you."

"Holcum County? Is that in North Carolina? Please, tell me it's not."

"Forgive me, Nicholas." Noah smiled. "Sometimes I feel like the poet Virgil, leading you to ever deeper levels of hell."

"Holcum County." Nick groaned. "Just the *sound* of it."

"Try not to think of it as a place, but as an opportunity—an opportunity to get away from the university, away from the classroom, away from students...and, I might add, away from the authorities."

"The authorities?"

"I received a rather belligerent phone call this morning from the Wake County Sheriff's Department regarding the way you—how shall I put it—*expedited* one of their investigations. I've spoken with the chancellor; he agrees that this would be a propitious time for you to take an extended leave. Purely in the name of science, of course. May I make a suggestion, Nicholas? As a friend? The next time you desire to assist the authorities, you might consider—just once—*asking* them first."

Nick grinned at the old man, slid the check from the desk, and headed for the door.

"One more thing, Nicholas. This is to be a summer of theoretical research, not applied science. Please…for the sake of the university, the department, and your weary old mentor—for the sake of your *job*—try to stay out of trouble."

"Noah," Nick said yawning, "what kind of trouble can you get into in *Holcum County?*"

Holcum County, North Carolina, June 1999

Sheriff Peter St. Clair stood in the center of the knee-high meadow, staring at the decomposing body of his oldest friend.

The cadaver lay on its back, fully stretched out, both arms extending down and to the sides. It was dressed in khaki pants and a mottled blue corduroy hunting shirt. The torso was bloated and distended, causing the seams of the shirt to split apart between buttons as if the shirt were three sizes too small. The skin was stretched and shiny, and the face was badly decomposed around the eyes and mouth. The only thing that looked at all natural about the corpse was the hair, which still lay neatly and almost comically combed to one side. The left hand was missing almost entirely, thanks to occasional visits by some forest scavenger; the right hand held a gleaming chrome handgun bearing the single engraved word, AIRBORNE, followed by the twin AAs of the All American Division.

The sheriff turned and stepped a few paces from what

remained of his childhood friend and comrade at arms. He stood facing away, staring at the ground and grimly shaking his head.

"It's Jim, all right."

On the other side of the body three hunters stood watching. The first hunter, Ronny, nudged Wayne and nodded silently toward the sheriff; Wayne passed the observation on to Denny, who reached up and slid the bright orange cap from his head. They all stood silently until the sheriff turned back to face the decomposing carcass once again.

"Sorry to have to call you like this, Pete," Denny said. "What with Jim being an old friend of yours and all, we thought you'd want to know straightaway."

"You did the right thing." The sheriff paused. "You boys didn't touch anything, did you?"

"Hey, give us a little credit, Pete. We didn't even move the gun. See? It's still in his hand. He didn't even drop it after he..."

An awkward silence followed. No one wanted to finish the sentence.

"Let's get something straight." The sheriff glared at two of them. "I don't want to hear any more talk about 'suicide' until the coroner has a chance to look things over. All we know for sure is that Jim McAllister is dead."

"I s'pose we know what suicide looks like," Wayne grumbled.

"It's not a suicide until *I* say it's a suicide. That's the law." Sheriff St. Clair folded his arms and kicked at the ground. "As far as we know, it might have been an accident. Maybe even murder."

Ronny and Wayne stood with heads hung low and hands in pockets, looking suitably repentant. Denny, suffering from a lifelong case of what his childhood friends referred to as "diarrhea of the mouth," was the only one foolish enough to respond.

"C'mon, Pete. I know you and Jim went way back and all, but...an accident? Shot in the side of the head? Nobody has an 'accident' like that—least of all an Airborne ex. And who would kill Jim? Nobody *liked* him—but at least he stayed to himself, stayed out of everybody's way. Besides, we just don't have many murders in these parts." Then he added for good measure, "Look who I'm telling."

It was true. The last murder in Holcum County was over a year ago, when old Mrs. Kreger decided to stop feeding her invalid husband. Her attorney got her off on the grounds that she just might have had a touch of Alzheimer's herself, but the people who knew Mrs. Kreger best weren't so sure. In any case, Denny was right; there weren't many murders in Holcum County, but the sheriff was not about to surrender the point. He took a step closer and spoke quietly, as though he might be overheard.

"Look. You boys know what it's like in a town like this when somebody does hisself in. Remember when they found Alvin Rafferty in his garage a few years back? I don't think his family ever got over it—the way people look at you, the way they talk behind your back. Well, Jim's got a sister, remember? I don't want that to happen to her. Let's keep this quiet, okay? Can I count on you? Ronny? Denny? Wayne? For Jim's sake."

Each man nodded gravely. They were a part of the inner circle now, Keepers of the Secret—certainly one of the best secrets in Holcum County for quite some time.

They were interrupted by noise from the edge of the clearing—the heavy, clumsy, crashing footfalls of someone obviously not at home in the woods. From an opening in the small pines emerged the figure of a deputy, a young man of startling stature. He was a full head taller than the sheriff. His shoulders were heavy and rounded, and they hung down over a hulking torso. His arms were shapeless and pale but as thick as an average man's thigh. His blunt-fingered hands swelled into two great drumstick forearms that belied the overall softness of his appearance. His pale blue eyes were set narrow but were large as buckeyes, and he seemed to wear a constant grin. It was the body of a man—an enormous man—but it was the unmistakable face of a child.

He grinned at the sheriff as he approached, and each of the hunters greeted him in turn.

"Hey, Beanie."

"How's it going, Beanie?"

Now there was another sound from the edge of the clearing, and a short, stout, white figure stepped out, panting and mopping his forehead from the early morning humidity. He ran a finger around his collar, peeling it away from his glistening stump of a neck, and stepped toward the already assembled party.

"Mornin', Sheriff. Deputy. Boys. I came as soon as I got your call."

"Mr. Wilkins." The sheriff nodded and extended his hand. "Thanks for coming so quick. I think you know the boys here—Ronny, Denny, Wayne. Boys, you all know Mr. Wilkins, the county coroner."

They all knew Mr. Wilkins, of course, but not as county coroner. They knew him as Mr. Wilkins the drugstore owner or Mr. Wilkins the American Legion coach, but few people knew Mr. Wilkins in his official capacity. There was very little for a coroner to do in a county the size of Holcum.

"Where is the decedent?" Mr. Wilkins asked impatiently.

The four men turned and pointed to a spot at the crest of the meadow where a cloud of black flies hovered in tight circles just above the grass. The group approached cautiously, carefully seeking the upwind side, and formed a line to the left of the body—all except Mr. Wilkins, who, having caught the brunt of the stench, was still ten yards back, doubled over and retching into a stand of foxglove.

They waited awkwardly until Mr. Wilkins recovered and approached again with far more caution. The sheriff and the three seasoned hunters braced themselves against the odor and stood motionless. The deputy pinched his nose and winced in his childlike way, as all of them secretly wished to do, and Mr. Wilkins gagged and covered his mouth and nose with his dripping white handkerchief.

Denny broke the silence. "I'm the one who found him, Mr. Wilkins—that is, we all did. We come through this way a lot in the summer, getting ready for deer season."

"Deer season? That's not till September."

"Georgia Pacific leases out these woods to a group of us to hunt on. They timbered a couple hundred acres last month and they tore the place up real good—and right near where we got our deer stands too. So we were out planting clover and beans, laying out salt blocks, you know—trying to draw the deer back in."

The sheriff nodded.

"To get to our deer stands we got to cross this meadow. Right in the middle we spotted that big cloud of flies. Figured maybe it was a deer carcass, maybe somebody poaching on our lease. Thought we better check it out—and here was Jim McAllister stretched out on the ground. Shot hisself right through the head. At least"—he glanced quickly at the sheriff—"that's what it looks like. Appears he's been dead a long time."

"*I'll* decide how long he's been dead," Mr. Wilkins said in utter misery, still tugging at his collar. As coroner, Mr. Wilkins was not required to visit the death scene—but as it was only his second opportunity in his three-year term as coroner to exercise his official duties, he had gone the extra mile. The sheriff hadn't told him it would be more like a mile-and-a-half, through thick North Carolina woodland on a sweltering summer morning.

Sheriff St. Clair opened a chrome case and pulled out a 35-millimeter Nikon and two rolls of film. He handed a bright yellow roll of barrier tape to the deputy. "Benjamin—secure the perimeter of the death scene." The deputy looked bewildered; he started off one way and then the other and finally just stood staring at the roll of tape as if it might offer some explanation of its own.

"Find some branches," the sheriff said quietly. "Long, straight ones. Stick one there and there and there and over there. Then stretch this tape around 'em."

Beanie smiled gratefully and bounded off toward the woods.

"Take a look, Mr. Wilkins. What do you make of it?"

Mr. Wilkins slowly approached the body for the first time, his handkerchief still clutched tightly over his face. He turned his head away, sucked in a deep breath, then took a few quick steps toward the body. He poked and prodded and probed until his face began to grow red, then took several quick steps away to explode and pant and then once again fill his lungs with air. Wayne began to snicker, but the sheriff shot a burning look his way, and Wayne thought better of it and struck a more solemn pose. Mr. Wilkins repeated this process several times, until it became obvious that he was in danger of fainting dead away. Finally, still facing away from the body, he spoke.

"Suicide. Plain and simple."

"What makes you so sure?"

"Single gunshot wound to the side of the head—two wounds and you might have a murder. Entry wound is on the right—he was right-handed, wasn't he? Exit wound on the left. No chance of ever finding the slug out here, but the angle of entry and exit look about right." He spoke with more and more authority as he continued. "Classic suicide scenario. Most suicides are with handguns, you know, and almost always to the head. Never seen one otherwise." In point of fact he had never seen another suicide at all, and everyone knew it—but they all held their tongues. "The weapon is still present, no signs of struggle or conflict, no indication that the body was moved or disturbed in any way. Yessir, a *classic* suicide."

The sheriff put his hand on Mr. Wilkins's shoulder and turned him aside. They walked several steps away, much to Mr. Wilkins's relief, but they were still easily within earshot of the others.

"I hate to admit it, Will, but I think you're right," the sheriff said. "You know Jimmy McAllister and I go way back. We grew up together here in Rayford. We were both at Fort Bragg, and we served together in the Gulf. But the fact is"—he glanced over to be sure that no one overheard—"things didn't go so well for

Jim after Desert Storm. A lot of chronic fatigue, long bouts of depression. He even made a few trips up to Walter Reed to be treated for Gulf War Syndrome. Nothin' helped for long. He started stickin' to himself more and more, went on hunting trips for weeks at a time. Some of us were beginning to wonder how long it would be before something like this happened."

"That settles it, then," Mr. Wilkins said. "A definite suicide. I'll notify the medical examiner's office in Chapel Hill that no autopsy is necessary."

"You're the expert. What else do you need to do here?"

"In most cases," he said, "we draw a blood sample for a standard toxicology screening. Drugs and alcohol, that sort of thing. But I doubt we could get a sample at this stage. So, I sign the death certificate, and then I call Schroeder's to pick up the body and hold it until we can notify the next of kin. Didn't he have a sister?"

"Amy. I'll make sure she knows."

Mr. Wilkins made a final inquiry of the hunters. "Any of you boys know a reason I shouldn't call this one a suicide?"

Each man solemnly shook his head.

"Then it's uncontested." He paused to look at his wristwatch. "I'm recording the legal time of death as 8:04 A.M. on June 14, 1999. And I'm getting out of this kill-dog humidity just as fast as I can." And wringing out his handkerchief as he went, the Holcum County coroner lumbered back toward the opening in the woods.

Sheriff St. Clair pulled out a cell phone and flipped it open.

"You callin' Amy?" Ronny asked.

"I got one other call to make first." The sheriff paused, waiting for an answer at the other end.

"Good morning, Central Carolina Bank."

"I want to talk to Kathryn Guilford," the sheriff said. "Just tell her it's Peter—and tell her it's important."

CHAPTER 3

Thirty-year-old Kathryn Guilford slowed her car as she approached the small gravel road that cut a hole deep into the woods just outside of Sandridge. Sandridge was the extreme western boundary of Holcum County, a remote area of old abandoned home fields that had been slowly but thoroughly reclaimed first by brush, then by pines, then by the overpowering hardwoods. She turned the nose of her '97 Acura onto the crunching gravel and peered as far as she could down the path. Thirty yards ahead of her, it curved slowly to the right and disappeared behind a gnarled red oak. To her left was a rectangular white sign, too small and with too many letters to be read from the main road. It didn't seem to advertise or welcome, Kathryn thought; it seemed to exist simply to mark a location, like a survey marker or a gravestone. In red gothic letters it stated plainly, NORTH CAROLINA STATE UNIVERSITY—DEPARTMENT OF ENTOMOLOGY—HOLCUM COUNTY RESEARCH STATION. In the center of the sign was the seal of the university, but freshly pasted across the seal was a blue and gold bumper sticker emblazoned, GO NITTANY LIONS.

Kathryn rolled down her window and listened. From the woods came the slow, heavy, rolling chant of the cicadas, already laboring in the rising morning steam. A thousand invisible wood crickets joined the lament, and blunt-bodied beetles, weighed down by the morning haze, buzzed slowly back and forth across the path. The woods were thick and crowded with life, all groaning and complaining in the early summer heat.

Kathryn felt a shudder flutter down her spine. She fastened the top button of her white satin blouse and rolled the window up tight, instinctively glancing in the rearview mirror to make sure that each window had sealed completely. Then, flipping the air conditioning to high, she proceeded slowly down the gravel path.

Thirty yards past the red oak she came to a tall chain-link fence topped by a spiraling roll of razor wire. An unchained gate swung open away from her, and beside the gate was a bright yellow sign bearing a single word: BIOHAZARD. Below the sign was a piece of weathered poster board with a frowning face markered at the top. Below it in rough hand-lettering were the words MR. YUCKY SAYS GO HOME.

"Strange sense of humor," Kathryn whispered, and proceeded through the gate.

The road straightened and widened now, and she relaxed a little and accelerated down the path. Her eyes began to pool with tears when she remembered Peter's phone call, less than three hours ago, with the gut-wrenching news that Jimmy McAllister was dead—and by his own hand. The coroner checked everything out. He was depressed, they had said. It was only a matter of time before something like this would happen. Everything fits; everything is in order; everyone is so sure.

Everyone but me.

Kathryn snapped back to attention at a buzzing sound from under the dashboard. To her utter horror, a single wriggling yellow jacket squeezed from the left floor vent and fanned its cellophane wings. Before she could even scream, the yellow jacket shot forward and landed on her left thigh just below the hemline, then crawled a few quick steps upward. Kathryn found her voice and let loose a scream, snapped both legs straight, and slapped violently at her leg. The car lurched abruptly left, and she jerked the wheel back toward the center of the road. The yellow jacket, now decidedly annoyed, shot upward and buzzed close across her face, then disappeared into the backseat behind her. She threw herself forward and flailed her right arm wildly over, around, behind her head. A venomous hiss sizzled past one ear, retreated, then streaked across the other. With a shriek of terror and rage, Kathryn released the wheel with both hands and swung madly at the air.

In that instant Kathryn Guilford was no longer a thirty-year-old bank executive driving a shining silver Acura. Somehow, one tiny black-and-yellow insect had projected her back through time and space, back to that place that was so long ago and yet never far away… She was once again a seven-year-old girl in an upside-down '57 Chevy Bel Air.

The car weaved from side to side in a widening arc, then abruptly lunged from the road. With a crumple of metal and the dull whump of exploding air bags, it came to a final stop against a massive, smooth-faced silver beech.

She was stunned for only an instant—then she groped frantically for the chrome handle, flung open the door, and bolted out. She spun to face the car and her invisible assailant, her arms still beating at the air, backing away into the center of the road. Exhausted, she began to slow down and then stopped. She stood silently for a moment, panting, then lifted both arms and examined herself. Her navy blue A-line skirt was blotched with a musty white powder. Her blouse hung loose and her silver wire choker was nowhere in sight. She stared in dismay at her shoes, her legs, and her arms; she wiped her face with the back of her forearm and studied her hands.

Finally, she looked at her car.

The gleaming silver hood lay crumpled back, echoing the contour of the stately beech, and steam hissed up through the grill and from under both sides. The driver's door was still open, revealing two limp air bags sagging from the console, and the once-spotless black interior was now blasted with the same white powder that thoroughly covered her.

Kathryn took a deep breath and inched back toward the car, hesitating at the open door; there was her purse, still resting in the center of the passenger seat. She ducked her head, anxiously searching every inch of air space inside. Then, with a lunge, she snatched her purse and scrambled backward, taking one last swing at the air in front of her face.

She dusted her skirt, straightened her blouse and hair, and then stopped. She listened again to the chorus of cicadas, crickets, and beetles that now seemed to completely surround and press in on her. She stood for a moment weighing her options. She glanced back up the road toward the open gate now a quarter of a mile behind her. She could go back—but back to what? Back to ignorance and frustration and doubt? Back to where no one would listen or help? Back to a funeral where the truth would be buried forever along with the body? Along with *Jimmy's* body...

She peered down the road in the direction of the mysterious biohazard, still nowhere in sight. She refastened the top button of her blouse and then, turning toward the invisible research facility somewhere in the distance, Kathryn Guilford continued to do what she came to do.

Ten sweltering minutes later her blue sling-back sandals were coated with gravel dust. Sweat ran freely down her face and neck, and her satin blouse clung heavily to the center of her back. Rounding a bend, she came at last upon a building—a pale green Quonset hut attached to a rectangular outbuilding at the back, forming a large T. The curved, corrugated surface of the roof was broken by a series of large skylights, giving it more the appearance of a greenhouse than a building. The gravel road dead-ended into a small parking lot directly in front of the Quonset.

In the parking lot were two automobiles. On the right was a tidy, silver-blue Camry; on the left was a faded, rusting relic that during some geologic era had been a '64 Dodge Dart. The car slumped decidedly to the left; the original color was anyone's guess. The backseat was split open across the top with puffs of twisted oatmeal poking through. The seat itself was piled with stacks of black and blue vinyl binders and thick stapled papers, accented by a single Papa John's Pizza box on top. In the rear window black-and-gold Pittsburgh Pirates and Pittsburgh Steelers caps posed proudly side by side.

Kathryn stepped up onto the narrow landing, took one last accounting of herself, and knocked. There was no answer. After several moments she knocked again; still nothing. She turned and looked again at the two cars behind her. It occurred to her that the rusting relic on the right may not be in working order. Judging by its appearance, it may not have been driven since Watergate, but the Camry looked in perfect condition. *Someone must be home.*

Just then the screen door began to open, and Kathryn had to step back to make room for it. Behind the door stood a pleasant looking, round-faced little man no more than five feet in height. He was balding down the middle and long strands of chestnut hair were combed strategically from one side to the other. He wore small, round spectacles, which accented perfectly the roundness of his cherubic cheeks and nose. It was an altogether kind and friendly face.

"May I help you?" he asked, self-consciously raking his hand from left to right across the top of his head.

"I'm here to see Dr. Polchak."

"You are?" His eyebrows rose up behind the little spectacles. "Is he expecting you?"

"No... Actually, I was just driving by, and I thought I'd stop in."

He peered over Kathryn's shoulder into the driveway. There was a silver-blue Camry and a Dodge Dart—nothing else.

"I...had a little car trouble."

The little man seemed to come alive at this news. "Where are my manners? Please forgive me. Won't you come in? Please do."

Kathryn gladly stepped into the open doorway, anticipating the cool rush of air conditioning that is the salvation of every home and business in the South. Instead, to her dismay she found that it was just as hot inside the structure as it was outside—but without the breeze.

"Please forgive the appearance of the place—we're not accustomed to receiving visitors here, especially such lovely ones. I am Dr. Tedesco, a research associate of Dr. Polchak," he said, extending his hand. "You look dreadfully hot. Can I get you anything? Water? A cold drink?"

"No, thank you, I'm fine. If you could just tell Dr. Polchak I'm here?"

"Of course, of course." He glanced back into the laboratory doubtfully. "And whom shall I say is calling?"

Kathryn reached into her purse and handed him a card. In green thermographic letters it declared: *Kathryn Guilford, Central Carolina Bank & Trust, Commercial Mortgage Capital.*

"And please—tell him this is not about banking."

The little man held up one finger, winked, and scurried back into the lab.

The interior of the Quonset was a large, open rectangle. Light from the twin rows of skylights streamed down onto a long, double-sided worktable that occupied the center of the room. Worktables lined all four walls, in fact; stopping only for the doors at either end. The only open space in the room was a narrow aisleway that ran the perimeter of the room, separating the tables along the walls from the one in the center. On the far wall was a door, and the center of the wall was filled with one great, rectangular window looking out into the office beyond.

Kathryn watched the little man disappear through the door

and approach a seated figure in the office beyond. The figure was facing away from Kathryn, bent over a desk, intently occupied by some task before him. The little man began to speak in his effervescent style, holding out the tiny business card and gesturing occasionally in Kathryn's direction. The figure never moved or looked up; he simply continued to focus on the task at hand.

Kathryn's eyes wandered back to the room immediately before her, stopping first on the far worktable just below the great window. It was lined with different sizes and shapes of glass terraria. Her eyes followed the path of the cases around the table to the right; it, too, was completely covered, as was the table on the left and the double-sided counter in the center. The entire room was one vast collection of display cases overhung by long banks of fluorescent lights. She could see that each terrarium contained some kind of plant or rock or limb. Some were lined with sand, others with yellow or gray or chocolate soil. Her eyes came to rest on the terrarium directly before her, not more than twelve inches away. It was covered with glistening sand, with a large flat slab of pink sandstone in the center. It was otherwise empty, except for a shallow dish of water in one corner. Kathryn bent closer to study this strange, lonely landscape. Instinctively, she reached out and tapped on the glass.

From under the stone a brown desert scorpion skittered out, menacing tail aloft, pincers ready.

Kathryn drew a sharp breath and leaped away from the glass. She stumbled backward against the screen door, punching her elbow through the stiff wire mesh as it crashed open. She staggered back to the gravel driveway and stood, trembling.

At the crash, the studious figure in the office at last turned to stare in Kathryn's direction—but the lab was now completely empty. He rose, taking the business card from the little man's hand, and stepped out into the lab.

A moment later Kathryn saw the screen door open. A tall

silhouette in the doorway stood silently studying her, carefully rereading the business card in his right hand, then slowly looking her over once again.

From inside the lab the little man urgently pushed his way past and hurried to her side. "My dear, whatever happened? Are you quite all right? Please, come back inside, out of this dreadful sun."

"If it's all the same to you, could we speak *outside?*"

She turned to look at the figure still standing in the doorway. He was holding her business card at eye level now, still glancing from the card to Kathryn and back again, as if he had been handed the driver's license of a bald-headed man from New Jersey.

It was the little man who broke the silence. "Where are my manners? Ms. Guilford, may I present Dr. Nicholas Polchak. Dr. Polchak, allow me to introduce—"

"Kathryn Guilford," the tall figure interrupted, "Central Carolina Bank and Trust, Commercial…Mortgage…Capital." He said the last three words slowly, as if to emphasize the disparity between the dignified title and the disheveled woman who stood before him.

"As I told Dr. Tedesco, I'm not here about banking."

"What exactly *are* you here about?"

"I've come to talk to you about a matter of *utmost* importance," she said with all the solemnity she could muster, but the words sounded ridiculous even to her.

He glanced at the curling shards of screen wire. "Were you in too big a hurry to open the door?" He looked at the little man beside her. "Teddy, we need to fix this. We don't want any local dermestids paying us a visit."

At last the tall figure stepped from the doorway, and for the first time Kathryn could see him in detail. He was lean and angular, with very large hands and feet. He wore a white ribbed polyester shirt with a large open collar, which hung open over a blue and green Fubu T-shirt. Below, a pair of enormous olive green cargo shorts overshadowed two alabaster limbs that protruded into a pair of ancient leather thongs.

He looked about Kathryn's age. His head was rather large and shaped like an inverted triangle. It narrowed from a wide brow to a strong chin with a deep dimple pressed into the center. His skin was fair and smooth, the skin of a man who spent far too much time under fluorescent light. His hair was dark and straight and his hairline receded slightly on both sides, emphasizing the triangularity of his features. It was a handsome face for the most part, Kathryn thought. She glanced quickly over his features, taking an instant accounting of each, but came abruptly to a halt at his eyes.

He wore the largest, thickest eyeglasses Kathryn had ever seen, which so distorted his eyes that they seemed to float behind the lenses like two soft, colorless orbs. They reminded Kathryn of the pickled eggs that eternally floated in a jar beside the cash register at Wirth's Amoco. She almost laughed aloud at the mental image.

His eyes never seemed to rest and never focused long on a single object. It was impossible to tell exactly where he was looking at any moment. Kathryn watched the eyes moving over her. They darted to one side, then the other. They floated upward, then slowly sank again. They studied her, they analyzed her, they examined her; they saw everything but focused on nothing. Kathryn wished that his eyes would come to rest on hers; she wished that she could make *contact* with them—but the eyes always moved on.

"I came here to make a legitimate business proposition," she said. "If you're not interested, perhaps I should take my business elsewhere."

Nick smiled. "I suspect there is no *elsewhere,* or you wouldn't be here."

She softened her tone. "A friend of mine has died—a very

old and dear friend. The police say it was suicide, but I think they're wrong. I'm *sure* they're wrong," she added, then paused for emphasis. "I think he might have been murdered."

"Mrs. Guilford," Nick cut in. "Dr. Tedesco and I are members of the faculty of North Carolina State University. We were sent here this summer to do research."

"You do research on dead people."

Nick's eyes darted rapidly over Kathryn once more, as if he might have missed some detail in his initial estimation. "I do research on arthropods—specific insects that inhabit dead people."

Kathryn opened her purse and removed a folded photocopy. "From the *Holcum County Courier,*" she said, beginning to read. "'Bug Man Comes to Holcum County.'"

"May I?" he said, taking the photocopy from her hand. "'Dr. Nicholas Polchak'—-that would be me—'Professor of Entomology at NC State University in Raleigh, will spend the summer at the extension research facility here in Holcum County to continue his studies in the emerging field of forensic entomology, the use of insects to solve crimes.'"

He quickly scanned the rest of the document. "Blah blah blah and so on, and—here's the good part—'Dr. Polchak, a *tall, muscular* man...' Now that's outstanding journalism. Yes indeed, very well put."

A faint groan came from Teddy, who stood quietly staring at the pavement, shaking his head slowly from side to side.

"Dr. Polchak, I need your help. And I need it right away."

He handed the photocopy back to her. "Mrs. Guilford, you need to go to the police. If the police won't help you, you need to call the medical examiner's office in Chapel Hill and talk to them. Or you can even hire a private investigator. I'd like to help you—really I would—but this summer I'm under strict orders to stick to research."

He turned back toward the Quonset. "Come on, Teddy," he

said, disappearing through the doorway, "we've got some sarcophagids to pin. Let's not waste any more of the lady's time."

Kathryn watched the door swing shut behind him.

"I'm very sorry," Teddy said, looking truly regretful. "He meant what he said—he really would like to help you. But to tell you the truth, this summer he's been given strict orders to stay out of trouble."

"There won't be any trouble."

"Trust me. With Nicholas, there's *always* trouble." And with a heavy sigh he turned and followed his colleague back into the lab.

Kathryn turned slowly back toward the path to her crumpled car. She stood motionless for several seconds, staring directly ahead.

Suddenly she wheeled around, fists clenched, her face flushed with anger. She marched up to the broken screen door, flung it open hard, and charged through the open doorway—then just as quickly drew back again. There was the same glass case, now occupied by *three* brown scorpions. The terrarium at her left elbow contained a tree branch where black, metallic-shelled beetles swarmed up, then dropped off in clusters like thick blobs of oil. In the terrarium on her right, a gray-and-brown wolf spider held a struggling black cricket in its slender, tapering legs.

Kathryn stared desperately across the lab at the large window into the office beyond. Inside she could see the figure of Dr. Polchak already seated again at his work. Her eyes slowly traced the path of the aisleway to her left, pausing at each glass case to imagine the unspeakable horror it might contain. The aisle seemed so much narrower now than at first sight. She measured the distance from her present location to the doorway beside the large window. It couldn't have been more than fifty feet. Or was it seventy-five? Or a hundred?

It might as well be ten miles.

With her left hand she turned her collar up high and squeezed it tight, completely covering her neck. With her right hand she clutched the front of her blouse, wadding it into a ball. She hunched her shoulders forward and pinned her arms tight against her torso. Her breathing was shallow and rapid, and her legs felt thick and rubbery. She closed her eyes, took a deep breath, and stepped slowly forward like a tightrope walker on a windy day.

She forced herself to stare directly ahead, though the hideous temptation to turn and look directly into each terrarium was almost irresistible. From the corners of her eyes she watched each glass case pass slowly by—nothing more than blurs of brown and green and tan—but in her mind's eye she imagined swarms of wriggling insects sucking up to the glass, pressing up against the terrarium lids, their hairlike antennae protruding through the screened tops, probing the air, stretching toward her, *reaching* for her.

The office door was directly ahead of her now, no more than thirty feet away. She was halfway there, but the thought that kept forcing its way into her mind was that she was now *directly in the center* of this living nightmare. She felt herself begin to lose her balance, and a wave of panic and nausea almost overwhelmed her. She imagined falling suddenly to one side, drawn irresistibly by the darkness behind the glass, reaching out to stop herself. Then she imagined her hands crashing through the glass and reaching helplessly into the black abyss.

The panic swelled up within her like a tidal surge. She commanded her legs to run for the office door, but they seemed to move in slow motion. She felt the glass cases begin to slide toward her, and those behind her seemed to swirl in and pursue her like paper boxes whipped into the draft of a passing car. She looked like a toddler taking its last hurried steps before collapsing into the arms of a waiting parent—but to Kathryn, it felt as though she were running down an endless, windowed hallway for all eternity.

With a crash, the office door flew open and Kathryn burst into the room. Nick looked up from his microscope with a start and saw Kathryn, still tightly clutching her collar and blouse, trembling and panting like a spent mare. He rose from his stool and walked slowly toward her.

"Mrs. Guilford," he said, cocking his head to one side, "are you *cold?*"

"Dr. Polchak," she growled through clenched teeth, "I need your help—and I need it *right now!*"

For a moment he stood perfectly still, observing her. Then he slowly reached out and took hold of the hand still clutching at her collar. He pulled gently but said nothing. She resisted. He pulled again, steadily, until she understood and slowly loosened her grip. With his other hand he tugged at the clenched fist on her blouse. He softly lowered both hands to her sides and then began to straighten and smooth her collar and blouse. As he worked, his eyes began to float over her once again, watching, examining, studying.

"Have a seat," Nick said as he returned to his stool. Kathryn looked around the office for the first time. It was smaller than it looked from the outside, and impossibly crowded. The largest single item in the office was a tall stainless steel unit that looked like a double-wide refrigerator with glass doors. The back wall was covered with particle-board bookcases of various colors and sizes, and each shelf sagged under the weight of endless dull-colored volumes with tiny gold or silver titles. Some books were placed well back on the shelf, others stuck out half-returned, and between every few books a manila file or stack of loose photocopies projected. Under the great window was a long worktable, completely cluttered with binders, tweezers, magnifiers, plastic containers, and a hundred other mysterious tools of the forensic entomologist's dark trade. More than anything there was paper: stacks of articles atop the bookshelves, printouts on the tables, manuscripts on the floor. The only break in the endless clutter was two narrow doorways, one at each end of the room—the only means of escape.

Kathryn stood looking awkwardly about the room. There seemed to be no other place to sit. Nick leaned forward and slid a second stool out from under the worktable, topped with a cascading pile of technical journal articles. With a sweep of his hand he sent the mound of paper back under the table and gestured to the seat.

"Don't you ever put anything away?" Kathryn asked, sliding onto the stool.

"That is away. Away from *me*."

They sat in silence for a few moments as Kathryn gathered her thoughts. Nick spoke first.

"Only one of us knows why you're here. I'll bet it's you."

So much for formalities, Kathryn thought, and plunged ahead. "As I said outside, I have a very dear friend—"

"*Had* a dear friend," Nick interrupted. "When was the body discovered?"

"Early this morning—by some hunters in the woods not far from here."

"And what was the estimated time of death?"

"They said a week ago. Maybe longer."

"Now tell me about the disposition of the body."

She stared at him blankly.

"How it was situated," he explained, "how it was dressed, the position of the arms and legs, the contents of the hands…"

"I don't know a lot of…details," she stammered. "They said he was found lying on his back. He was still holding his pistol in his hand—the one he got in the army. He had…they say he…" She grimaced, made a gun with her right hand and held it to her temple.

"A contact wound to the right temporal region—and no doubt an exit wound on the left. The standard service sidearm is a nine-millimeter, and as they say around these parts, you just can't keep that chicken in the henhouse."

She glared at him hard but said nothing.

"The sheriff's department was satisfied that this was a suicide?"

"Yes, but—"

"And the medical examiner's office—what did they say?"

She looked at the floor. "The coroner said nothing looked suspicious to him either."

"Maybe the autopsy will turn up something."

"There won't be an autopsy."

Nick raised one eyebrow. "No autopsy was ordered?"

"No."

"In cases of unattended death—as in the case of a suicide—an autopsy is usually ordered to verify cause of death. Things must have looked pretty straightforward."

Kathryn had nothing to say in response.

"This dear friend of yours—I assume we're talking about a male? He was about your age, thirty to thirty-five? Caucasian?"

"That's right. How did you—"

"Three-quarters of all suicides are by white males. Two-thirds of them are by gunshot, generally to the head. That fits too. He did it outside, probably standing up—men usually do. Women like the comforts of home and almost always lie down. He used his own gun, which was still in his hand. And there was no note, was there? Nothing to explain his motive or timing?"

She shook her head.

He let out a sigh. "You just can't get men to write, can you?" He paused a full measure for dramatic effect. "So, Mrs. Guilford. What can I do for you?"

Kathryn's face was red and hot. "I knew Jimmy since we were kids together here in Holcum County. We grew up together, like a brother and sister. I knew him better than his parents, better than his own sister—better than anyone. He would not, he *could* not have done this to himself. I don't care what the sheriff or the coroner says, they're wrong about this—and I have to know what happened."

Nick took a deep breath. "Let me see if I understand you. The sheriff's department, drawing on its considerable experience in homicide investigation, closed this investigation almost before it opened. And the county coroner, representing all of the forensic knowledge of the North Carolina State medical examiner's system, verified the cause of death without even a second look. But you're convinced they're both wrong—because you have this *feeling*."

It was fortunate at this moment that the door behind Kathryn opened and Dr. Tedesco stepped into the room, providing a momentary respite from the tension. He was startled to see Kathryn again but said nothing. He stepped quietly to the side, pretending to resume his duties, and waited for the conversation to resume.

"I have to *know*," Kathryn repeated, barely containing her anger. "The sheriff won't help me—he thinks I'm wasting my time. The coroner can't help me either. Since he already signed the death certificate, the body is no longer under his authority. I could hire a private investigator, but not in a town the size of Rayford—and even if I found one, I'm not sure he'd know what to look for. I'm out of options, Dr. Polchak—and I'm out of time. The body is being moved right now to a funeral home, and from there it will be turned over to the immediate family. Soon it will be too late to do anything."

Nick said nothing for a long time.

"You'd be helping the authorities," she added.

"I have a long history of *helping* the authorities," he said. "Trust me, it isn't always welcome."

"Then you'd be helping me."

"I just can't look into every mysterious death that comes along—and to be frank, Mrs. Guilford, this one hardly sounds mysterious."

Kathryn paused. "What about money? Are you motivated by money?"

"Money?"

She leaned forward and stared directly into his imposing spectacles. "I will pay you twenty thousand dollars to look into this for me."

There was an audible gasp from behind Kathryn. Dr. Tedesco did his very best to contain himself, but bits of words and phrases still tittered out: "Twenty thousand...oh my, I...*twenty thousand?"*

"This is why Teddy never plays poker," said Dr. Polchak.

"I know more about you than you think," Kathryn said. "I know that you're a forensic entomologist, and that there are very few of you around. I know that it's almost impossible to make a living at it. I know that most of you are employed by museums and universities, and that means you depend on departmental funding and research grants to survive. In other words," she said, adding her own pause for emphasis, "I know you need that money so bad you can taste it."

Nick slowly smiled. "And you said this visit wasn't about money."

"I said this visit wasn't about *banking*. What would this really require of you, Dr. Polchak? One look at a body? A trip to a funeral home? A little work right here in your own laboratory? Twenty thousand dollars buys a lot of bug food."

From behind them Teddy conducted an elaborate pantomime of hair-pulling, eye-rolling, and desperate pleading. Nick ignored him.

"I don't want to waste your money, Mrs. Guilford. Don't misunderstand me, I *want* your money—but I don't want to waste it. I feel I should tell you that there's a very good chance I'll come up with nothing at all."

"I'm willing to take that chance."

Nick sat silently for a full minute. "Plus expenses," he said at last.

"I beg your pardon?"

"Twenty thousand dollars *plus expenses*."

"What sort of expenses?"

"Travel, if necessary. Meals. Supplies. Valium for Teddy. I don't know what else...*expenses*."

"Done." She extended her hand, and as Nick cautiously reached for it she added, "There is one small condition, Dr. Polchak, and this is not negotiable. I want to work *with* you. I want to be there every step of the way."

Nick pulled back, and Teddy buried his face in his hands.

"That's entirely out of the question."

"It's *not* negotiable," Kathryn repeated. "I'm not a fool, Dr. Polchak. Twenty thousand dollars is a great deal of money. What am I supposed to think if you report back in two weeks and say, 'Sorry, I found nothing'? I want to see what you do. I want to know that nothing was overlooked. I want to know that if we find nothing, it won't be because we didn't look hard enough. I want to *know*."

After another full minute, Nick spoke again. "The investigation will take a full week, perhaps two. And if what you say is true—if the body is already on its way to a funeral home—then we have to begin immediately. That means *right now*."

Kathryn extended her hand again. As Nick took it, he said, "I have one condition of my own, Mrs. Guilford. If you're going to work with me, it has to be—as you said—*every* step of the way."

"Agreed."

"Mrs. Guilford," he said, smiling, "you have no idea what you've gotten yourself into."

The interior of Dr. Polchak's crumbling Dodge Dart was even worse than Kathryn had imagined. The brittle vinyl seats were split apart in sharp ridges, and the dashboard was a canyon of cracked ravines and gullies with rivers of dusty foam flowing beneath. Above her head the roof liner draped and sagged. Below, the floorboard was pockmarked with rust holes that allowed her a more than adequate view of the pavement streaking by beneath her feet. She sat rigidly, legs apart, straddling the cratered floorboard as if it were an open bomb-bay door.

"Watch your skirt," Nick said with a sideways glance. "I'd rather you didn't get that sodium azide powder all over my upholstery."

"What upholstery?"

"I like to take care of my car. For example, I try to keep beech trees out of my engine." He glanced at her again. "Care to tell me what happened back there?"

"No." She pointed up ahead. "Schroeder's is on the left at the next corner. If you don't mind, park on the street."

"There are hundreds of unexplained traffic fatalities every year," Nick said. "No heart attack, no stroke—for some reason the driver just swerved off the road. Some experts—like *me*—think the answer may be insects. A bug flies in the window, the driver panics, there's an accident." He looked at Kathryn. "Entomophobia is one of the more common irrational fears, Mrs. Guilford."

Kathryn glared straight ahead. "You're just a bushel full of interesting information, aren't you?"

Nick stopped the car and pulled up on the emergency brake, which moved without a sound. "I don't think it's actually attached to anything," he said. He turned to the backseat, grabbed a large canvas knapsack and then paused, eyeing the two black-and-gold hats resting side-by-side in the rear window.

"This one," he said, pulling it on tight. "I think this might be a job for a pirate."

Great, Kathryn thought. *Just the final fashion touch he needed.*

"No offense"—she looked him over quickly—"but I wish you had changed."

"I wish I had a dollar for every time a woman told me that."

Schroeder's Funeral Home was a landmark in the town of Rayford. For decades it had been known as the Lampiers' Home, the largest private residence in Holcum County. It was still remembered that way by most of the older residents of Rayford. With its white beveled siding, long black shutters, and green-and-white canvas awnings, it had the perfect image for its current function. Mr. Schroeder simply added the embellishments of his trade: the chapel, the garage, and the tonguelike porte-cochere that jutted out above the circular asphalt driveway.

Kathryn hesitated at the tall black door. "Do me a favor—let *me* do the talking."

Nick shrugged. "It's your money."

As Kathryn stepped through the doorway, a wave of frigid air engulfed her. As sweltering as her morning had been, the air felt much too cold. She shivered—not simply because of the abrupt change in temperature but because of the total change of environment. Everything around her was suddenly dark, cold, heavy, and silent. She had the eerie sensation that she had just stepped on an unmarked grave.

The ancient red oak flooring creaked and groaned as they stepped into the center of the high, arching atrium. The walls were lined with dark cherry paneling that disappeared into the darkness above. Directly ahead, a wide doorway opened into a small chapel lined with short pews. On the far wall a Gothic stained-glass window sent streams of multicolored light to meet them. To their left, a smaller doorway opened into an office.

"Remarkable." Nick's voice shattered the silence. "It's amazing the trappings that your species attaches to a simple biological function like death."

A moment later the figure of Mr. Schroeder appeared in the office doorway. His hands were folded in front of him as he walked, and the floor made no sound, as if he had somehow learned to become a part of the stillness around him. He wore a dark suit with a black-and-silver tie, and a white carnation glowed from his left lapel. His silver hair was combed neatly back, and his face seemed to be frozen in an expression of permanent compassion, deep sorrow, and profound concern.

"Kathryn, Kathryn, Kathryn!" he said in a half-whisper, taking both of her hands in his. "How good it is to see you again. I don't believe we've had a visit from you since…why, since we had the privilege of caring for your mother."

"I assume you mean since her mother *died,*" Nick said, running his hand admiringly over the cherry paneling.

Mr. Schroeder cringed slightly at the sound of the forbidden word, taking note for the first time of the bizarrely clad stranger beside Kathryn. Whatever his thoughts, his expression never faltered; Mr. Schroeder had long ago learned that constant politeness, tolerance, and patience were vital assets in his profession. After all, in a town the size of Rayford, almost everyone was an eventual customer.

"And who might this be?" he smiled warmly to Kathryn.

"Mr. Schroeder, I'd very much like you to meet Dr. Nicholas Polchak."

Nick smiled broadly, folded his hands in front of him, and cocked his head slightly to one side. Mr. Schroeder didn't seem to notice, but the mimicry didn't escape Kathryn. She shot him an angry glare.

"It is an honor, Doctor," Mr. Schroeder said warmly and then turned to Kathryn again. "Tell me, does your visit today concern Andrew? Has there finally been some resolution to the situation? I do hope so, for your sake."

Kathryn winced slightly and looked at the floor. "No, Mr. Schroeder. Nothing has changed. His body has never been recovered. This is not about Andy."

"Ah," he said, sighing deeply, "perhaps one day." There was an appropriate moment of silence—Mr. Schroeder's stock-in-trade—and then he smiled at both of them again. "Well then, how can we be of service to you today?"

"Mr. Schroeder, I understand that you are receiving the body of Jimmy McAllister."

Mr. Schroeder looked suddenly overwhelmed with sorrow. "Oh yes, a very sad affair, very sad. We were happy to make our facility available to the sheriff's department until the immediate family can make their wishes known regarding the final disposition."

"Mr. Schroeder, please—may I see him?"

At this, Mr. Schroeder uttered a deep moan and closed his eyes tightly, shaking his head slowly from side to side. Kathryn thought he looked exactly like the ghost of Jacob Marley; she saw Nick turn away to disguise a smile.

"My dear Kathryn," he intoned, "you must understand the situation. I'm told that Mr. McAllister has been deceased for almost a week now. How can I put this delicately? He will be in no condition to receive visitors—as I'm sure the good doctor can testify."

"The body will be in a stage of decomposition known as putrefaction," Nick said abruptly, "perhaps even black putrefaction, considering the ambient temperature lately. The gut will be bloated by intestinal bacteria—so will the eyes and tongue, if there's anything left of them. The skin will be blistered and loose. There will be major larval infestations here, here, and here"—he pointed casually to Kathryn's temple, eyes, and mouth—"and brother, it will stink to high heaven."

Each additional description seemed to rocket off the walls and violate the solemn atmosphere like an obscenity shouted in a cathedral. Mr. Schroeder looked as though he might never recover.

"Nevertheless," she continued, "I still want to see him."

"Kathryn, please," Mr. Schroeder implored. "This is not how Mr. McAllister would want you to remember him. Don't do this to him. Don't do this to *yourself*."

"Please. It will only be for a few minutes."

"I'm very sorry," he said, sighing. "I'd like to accommodate you, but you must understand my situation. First of all, the deceased has not arrived yet. And even when he does, without direct permission from the next of kin I cannot allow a viewing. Have you such permission?"

"I know Jimmy's sister, but...well...it's kind of complicated..."

"There isn't time," Nick cut in. "When the body arrives, you won't bring it in the house—not in the shape it's in. You'll store it in the garage, and you'll dust it with Formalin powder as fast as you can to control the stench. That will kill every insect on the body."

Mr. Schroeder looked at him closely, as if for the first time.

"Look," Nick said, "we're not asking to do an autopsy here—we just want to collect a few bugs."

A look of astonished realization swept across Mr. Schroeder's face. "I'm *sorry,*" he said firmly, "what you ask is out of the question. You're not requesting a viewing at all, you're intending to conduct some kind of examination. What you suggest is quite unethical and improper—and possibly illegal as well."

"Please," Kathryn pleaded now, "I *have* to see him. If only you knew how important this is to me..."

A prolonged and awkward silence followed—then Nick spoke up abruptly. "Mr. Schroeder, I understand your situation completely. As a fellow professional I can appreciate the awkward position that Mrs. Guilford has put you in. We'll contact the immediate family in the next few days to see what options might be available to us. Thank you for your time."

Kathryn watched open-mouthed as Nick wheeled around and walked quickly out the door. She turned, muttered something incoherent to Mr. Schroeder, and hurried after him. She caught up to him halfway to the car.

"What's the matter with you?" she shouted after him. "Are you out of your mind? What were you thinking back there?" Nick said nothing, but got into the car and started the engine. Kathryn hurried around and climbed in, slamming the door hard behind her.

"Easy on the door," he said, pulling away from the curb in a puff of blue smoke. "It's held together by Bondo."

"I thought you said we don't *have* a few days! What happens if he puts that powder on the body?"

"Then you've got no bugs. No bugs, no Bug Man."

"No Bug Man, no twenty thousand dollars!" she reminded him. "I don't understand why in the world you—"

"This should be far enough." Nick pulled over to the curb again a single block farther down the road, just out of sight of Schroeder's Funeral Home. "You coming?" he said as he climbed from the car. She stared for a moment in utter disbelief, then hurried after him.

"It was obvious we were getting nowhere with Mr. Schroeder," he called back over his shoulder. "But he still helped us out in his own small way, bless his icy little heart. He told us that the body hasn't arrived yet."

"So what?"

"Mr. Schroeder can't show us what Mr. Schroeder doesn't have, so why waste our time on him? Let's go around to the garage and wait for the delivery man."

"But won't the delivery man tell us the same thing?"

"Maybe, maybe not. Funeral directors often contract out to have somebody else do the dirty work of collecting bodies. If the collector is an employee of the funeral home, he'll probably tell us to get lost. But if he's just some local yokel, then what does he care?" Nick turned and winked. "He just might let us take a peek."

The garage was the business end of the stately funeral home, providing direct access to the chrome-and-porcelain preparation rooms inside. Schroeder's Funeral Home was first and foremost a place of comfort and condolence and dignity, so it was prudent to attempt to conceal the true nature of the business—the receiving and processing of dead bodies. The garage and driveway entrance were masked by a screen of tall redbuds.

Nick slung off his knapsack and dropped it on the driveway in front of the garage. He stretched out on the pavement and laid his head against the knapsack, folding his arms across his chest and tipping his Pirates cap down over his spectacled eyes.

"Wake me if you see a car." He yawned. "A big black one."

Kathryn was in no mood for sleep—or for humor. She paced nervously back and forth, looking first down the driveway, then around the side of the house, then at the reclining form of Nick—but mostly at Nick.

"Is this against the law?" she demanded.

"Maybe," he said without moving. "Does it matter? I thought you said you have to know."

"I just like to know what I'm getting myself into. I do have a position in this town, you know. I don't want the headline in tomorrow's *Courier* to read, 'Bank Officer Charged with Breaking and Entering.'"

"We're not breaking and entering," he assured her. "The headline will read more like, 'Woman Charged with Molesting Dead Man.'"

"That's not funny! What if Mr. Schroeder comes out?"

"It's still daylight. I'm sure Mr. Schroeder stays in his coffin until midnight."

Nick peeked out from under his cap and took note of the stone-cold expression on Kathryn's face. "Relax," he said, pulling his cap down once again. "The law is a little fuzzy about this kind of thing. When a body is first discovered it belongs to the local medical examiner until he signs off on the death certificate. Later on the funeral home releases the body to the immediate family, and then *they* own it. But in-between—whose body is it? It's not exactly clear. We're not hurting anyone, Mrs. Guilford—least of all your pal Jim."

"What happens if we get caught?"

Nick sighed heavily and sat up. "Mr. Schroeder will raise the roof, and he'll probably call the next of kin. If he's really mad, he'll call the police too. You'll get a nasty call from the sister, and the police will say, 'Don't make a hobby out of this.' *Finito*."

"What would happen to you?"

"Don't worry about me," Nick said under his breath. "They can't send me anyplace worse than this."

Behind them there was a loud click and the whir of an electric motor, and the garage door suddenly began to rise. Nick jumped to his feet and peered down the driveway. The long Cadillac hearse rolled slowly up the pavement and pulled into the garage. Behind the wheel was a young man of no more than eighteen, with an even younger boy beside him.

"This looks good, *very* good. Tell you what"—he smiled, glancing at Kathryn—"this time, why don't you let *me* do the talking?"

The boys stepped from the car and nodded to their unexpected visitors, then proceeded silently to the rear of the car. The older boy wore baggy denims that hung low on his hips and draped about his feet. He wore a green plaid button-up that hung open over a gray T-shirt beneath, and he sported a pair of silver rings in his left ear. His hair was shaved close on the sides, and his sideburns were thin and long. A tangled tuft of red hair lay atop his head. The younger boy was similarly clad. Both wore bright bandannas around their necks, one red and one blue.

"Can I give you fellas a hand?" Nick asked, taking a position opposite them as they rolled the long gurney from the hearse. "Ready? One, two, *three*." They lifted and pulled, and the stretcher's wheels dropped and locked in place. Atop the stretcher was a black vinyl bag, zippered down the center.

"I'm Dr. Nicholas Polchak." He smiled, extending his hand to each of them. "Call me Nick."

"I'm Casey," said the older boy, returning the handshake.

"Griff," said the second, his voice a full octave higher.

"I'm with the medical examiner's office in Chapel Hill," Nick lied.

Kathryn winced.

"It seems we missed a few things in the initial investigation, and they sent me down to take a final look. Why don't we set up over here?" He guided the gurney into the left side of the garage, out of sight of the driveway.

"You guys know Mrs. Guilford? It seems she knew the deceased here, so I said she could tag along." Both boys looked at Kathryn, but Casey looked a little longer. Kathryn smiled back nervously and waved, not trusting her voice.

"Can we watch?" Casey asked hopefully.

"I could use your help. Tell me what you've got here."

"We picked him up this morning, in the woods off Weyerhaeuser Road. Musta had to carry him a mile, maybe more. A big guy, weighed a ton. He's been dead a week—a real rotter. Another few days and we woulda had to use the straps to bag him."

"Well, let's take a look." As he reached for the zipper, each boy slid his bandanna up over his nose and mouth. Nick stopped, closed his eyes, and took a deep breath through his nose.

"You don't use *anything?*" Griff asked in astonishment.

"Whoa," Casey muttered through his bandanna, "you're the *man.*"

As Nick slowly pulled the zipper, it suddenly dawned on Kathryn that she was about to view the remains of one of her oldest and dearest friends—and it wasn't going to be pretty. "Don't do this to him," Mr. Schroeder's words returned to her. "Don't do this to *yourself.*"

A wave of doubt came over her. Did she really need to do this? Did she really *want* to? Is this the way she wanted to forever remember her friend—not as a handsome, always-smiling companion, but as a decomposing, insect-infested corpse? She had hired Dr. Polchak to do the examination. Why did she need to be here at all? She remembered Dr. Polchak's words: "You have no idea what you've gotten yourself into." Was he really warning her, or were his words just more of his arrogant posturing? She edged closer to the body, then stepped quickly back again. She wanted to *know*—but did she really need to *see?*

Nick spread open the body bag near the head and tucked the flaps under the shoulders. "Mrs. Guilford," he said without looking up, "you might want to watch out for—"

Too late. The stench hit Kathryn like a punch in the gut. It was more than a smell—the word was ridiculously inadequate to describe what Kathryn now experienced. Something had reached deep into the limbic region of her brain and triggered an ancient memory—a memory that every human being possesses yet no one needs to learn—the smell of death.

The three men watched as she lurched for the open doorway and dropped to her knees, convulsing. "Now that," Nick sneered, "is what I call gross."

Casey stooped over Kathryn and slid off his bandanna. "Try this. It's covered with Vicks."

"That's an old gravedigger's trick," Nick said. "They used to use camphor. You guys really know your business."

Both boys grinned from ear to ear.

"Casey, open that backpack. We've got to work fast—I mean, I'm on a tight schedule here. See those plastic containers? Pop off the lids and take out the labels. Griff, you hold the containers for me. Casey, you write what I tell you on the labels." He took out a penlight and a pair of long forceps.

Kathryn was already on her feet again, though both legs fluttered like sparrows. She felt a wretched emptiness inside as though her very soul had been sucked from her body. With her right hand she pressed the life-saving bandanna tight against her face; her left hand clutched her stomach, hoping to prevent it from once again hurtling into the abyss. She staggered around the gurney half-doubled over, slowly regaining her strength, taking in everything she could.

She watched Nick pluck several plump white maggots from the open wound in the right temple and drop them into one of Griff's containers.

"You can close that one," he said. "Put, 'right temporal region, entry wound.'" From the opposite side he selected several more. "'Left temporal region, exit wound.'"

He collected specimens from each ocular region, then used his penlight to prop open the jaw and peered inside. "We've got a cave full of bats," he said, as he stepped aside to allow Casey and Griff to have a look, much to their delight. Kathryn felt her stomach convulse like kneading dough.

From deep within the nasal cavity, Nick slowly removed one fat, wriggling larva that was easily twice the size of any he had collected yet. "Jimmy's been a bad boy." He whistled and held the specimen aloft for all to see. "Would you look at the size of that bugger? Label this big boy 'nasal septum.'"

Casey pointed to a missing hand. Nick gathered a few specimens and scraped away several others to examine the exposed stump. "This is from predator activity. Looks like *everybody* liked Jimmy." He winked at the boys.

He worked quickly now. "The infestation is consistent with the estimated time of death," he noted to Kathryn, "and so is the general condition of the tissues." He pulled the tattered shirt sleeves up and observed the purplish black coloration on the dorsal surface of the arms where the skin lay against the gurney. He moved around to the legs and removed the shoes and socks. The left foot had the same burgundy discoloration along the heel and continuing up the leg—but the right foot was completely purple from heel to toe. He jerked up the right pant leg. The color ended abruptly just above the ankle. The leg above it had no stain at all.

"How did you find the body? How was it lying? Show me." He nodded toward the floor. Griff lay down and stretched out on his back, arms and legs straight out.

"You're sure? Exactly like that?" Both boys nodded confidently.

He moved around to the side of the body and began to search inside the bag itself. "Help me out here, all three of you," he said, pointing to the opposite side of the bag. "I'm looking for late-instar larvae—really big ones—and especially for little brown capsules about this big. Sort of like brown rice. Check the pockets and the folds in the clothing too—quick now."

The boys scrambled over one another to set to the task. Kathryn edged up to the bag herself and pretended to search, but her mind was desperately focused on something else, *anything* else that could block out the horror before her.

Nick came around once again to the head. "I guess this will have to do," he said, glancing back over his shoulder at the door. He reached for the zipper and began to slide it up, but as it approached the head, he abruptly stopped. "Well *hello* there," he said, peering closely at a small, sparsely infested wound in the center of the forehead. "You boys almost missed the party—and you just might be the guests of honor." He plucked a single specimen from the wound and held it up, examining it closely.

At that exact moment the door swung open and Mr. Schroeder stepped into the garage, and with a single sweep of his eyes comprehended the situation. His face began to grow red and to contort, as though he were rapidly trying on a variety of new facial expressions in sizes and styles unfamiliar to him.

"What," he blurted out, "is the meaning of this?"

"Oh no," Kathryn said aloud. It was her worst fear realized; in her mind's eye she could already see the morning headlines...

"Mrs. Guilford," Nick said quietly, still studying his specimen, "I could use a little help here." Kathryn rushed to intercept the furious Mr. Schroeder.

"I distinctly forbade you to conduct this kind of examination!"

"Mr. Schroeder, if you'll just listen to me for a moment, I—"

"You have gone *behind my back* to conduct this *reprehensible procedure* in my *own facility!*"

"If you'll just give me a minute to explain, I'm sure I can—"

Casey leaned over to Nick. "You're not really from the medical examiner's office, are you?"

"Nah." He shrugged. "But we're having a good time, aren't we?"

With each exchange Mr. Schroeder grew more and more livid, and soon he began to spit and splutter accusations and invectives so rapidly that it was impossible to understand him. For her part, Kathryn kept apologizing and explaining, calming and reassuring, all the time keeping herself strategically positioned between Mr. Schroeder and "the good doctor." But she was quickly coming to the end of her diplomatic abilities.

"Griff," Nick said urgently, "toss me another container—*quick.*"

"We're out of containers," Griff said, holding open the knapsack. "See?"

"Hold this!" he commanded, shoving the forceps and its tiny captive into Casey's hand. "*Very* gently!" He hastily searched through the already-filled containers and chose the one marked "left ocular cavity." He popped off the lid and with a flip of his wrist flung its contents across the room. The larvae rebounded like tiny marshmallows off the side of the gleaming hearse. "Sorry, boys," he said, taking the forceps carefully from Casey, "somebody else needs this cab."

Mr. Schroeder was almost on top of him now, shouting and threatening and waving his arms around Kathryn. Nick tossed the last of the containers into the knapsack, cinched it shut, and stood up so abruptly that Mr. Schroeder stopped in midsentence.

"I believe we have everything we require here," Nick announced with great dignity. "Thank you, Mr. Schroeder, it was a lovely service." He rubbed Griff's head, gave Casey a quick thumbs-up, and proceeded out the garage door. Kathryn watched him wide-eyed, then turned back to Mr. Schroeder, as if there might be some appropriate parting words for such a situation. She stood silently with her mouth half open, her eyes darting desperately from side to side. At last she smiled weakly, shrugged, and hurried down the driveway.

They sat in the car a long time, silently staring out the windshield. Kathryn pulled at the sun visor; it came off in her hand. She studied herself in the mirror. She was white as paste, and there were red circles around her eyes that almost matched the red bandanna still stretched across her face. She was panting hard, and with each breath the bandanna fluttered out in front of her like a crimson pennant. She sat slumped in the seat, her arms limp at her sides, and both her legs were trembling uncontrollably.

"I don't know about you," Nick said, "but I'm starving."

Kathryn sat slowly sipping black coffee in a remote corner of the Smithfield Chicken and Barbecue in Rayford. She insisted on a table as far as possible from the All-You-Can-Eat Pig Pickin' Buffet and positioned herself with her back to any possible view of food. She stared blankly at the emergency exit door, not more than ten feet away, while she mentally reviewed the events of the day. She had wrecked her new car, ruined an entire outfit, promised her second mortgage to a man who just might be a raving lunatic—and to top it all off broke into a funeral home to pick bugs off a decomposing corpse. She looked again at the emergency exit. *Does the alarm really go off if you open the door?*

"You're not having anything?" Nick said, returning to the table with three loaded plates balanced on his arms. "How do women do it?" He stooped down and slid the dinner plate forward. It was heaped with pulled pork, potato salad, and a pool of beans with a pallid cube of pork fat bobbing in the center. His salad plate held only a few leaves of lettuce, smothered with a great mound of black olives and bacon bits. His dessert plate was piled high with a thick white ambrosia salad of marshmallows, mandarin oranges, coconut, and whipped cream.

"How in the world can you eat after...*that?*"

"You'll notice I passed on the macaroni and cheese," Nick said through a mouthful of potato salad. Kathryn shut her eyes hard. "Sorry. Inside joke."

"I never felt so useless in my entire life," she muttered.

"I thought you did very well back there."

"I spent half the time on my hands and knees vomiting!"

"Well...you were very good at vomiting."

Kathryn closed her eyes again and dropped her head to the table with a thud.

"Don't take it personally," Nick said. "A decomposing body emits two unique chemicals. One is known as putrescine and the other cadaverine—cute names, don't you think? When they team up, they can reach down your throat and jerk your insides out."

"They didn't seem to bother you."

He shrugged. "It's an acquired taste."

They sat in silence for several minutes. It was all Kathryn could bear to sit and listen to the sounds of her companion munching and crunching his way through plate after plate of vile obscenities. She wanted to ask him if he had been able to learn anything from his hurried investigation, but she knew she couldn't tolerate a detailed evaluation—not yet. She really didn't want to talk at all. More than anything she wanted to go home and take an endless, steaming shower—but anything was better than listening to that *sound.*

"Do you think Mr. Schroeder will call the police?" she asked.

"Probably. We dared to disturb Cerberus, guard dog of the dead," he said in an ominous tone, "though I suspect his bark is worse than his bite. I wouldn't worry about it."

She watched him wipe a bit of marshmallow from the corner of his mouth. "You don't strike me as the kind who worries about much of anything."

"I've found that worrying takes a lot of energy and produces few results."

"Must be nice," she said, picking at the plastic chrome peeling from the top of the salt shaker. "I just hope nobody finds out about all this."

Nick shook his head in disdain.

"You're not from a small town, are you, Dr. Polchak?"

"Not quite. I'm from Pittsburgh."

"In a small town, if one person knows, everybody knows. Then come the funny looks and the whispers behind your back when you pass. 'Did you hear what happened at Schroeder's Funeral Home? Did you hear what she *did?*' But to your face it's always, 'How do,' or, 'Nice day.'"

"And all your friends are thinking, 'Why can't she find herself a nice, *living* man?'"

"I'm serious!"

"Mrs. Guilford," he said, pushing aside the last of his empty plates, "there is a difference between small-town people and small-town minds. The first you can live with, the second you can live without. Just let it go."

"That's easy for you to say."

"Yes," he said, "it is."

The front door opened with a jingle, and Kathryn looked up to see Sheriff Peter St. Clair step inside. He was tall, wide-shouldered, and narrow at the waist, looking like an athlete just barely past his prime. His hair was sandy blond and stiff as wire, cut close, a throwback to his last tour of duty less than a decade ago. Kathryn smiled. Everything about Peter was still army; head to toe he was sharp, tight, lean, and hard.

The sheriff tucked his Ray Bans into his front shirt pocket and refastened the button. The waitress smiled and greeted him from behind the counter. He nodded to her without a word, pointed to the percolating Bunn-O-Matic, and headed directly for Kathryn and Nick.

The sheriff stopped abruptly in front of the table and stood, hands on hips, staring silently at Nick. Then he bent over, kissed Kathryn on the cheek, and sat down.

"So much for your fears of police brutality," Nick said sotto voce.

"Okay, Kath," the sheriff said. "What's going on?"

"Hello, Peter," she said, squeezing his forearm.

"I just got a call from old man Schroeder. He said you came by this afternoon with some guy he'd never seen before—some kind of doctor." He glanced at Nick again. "He accused you two of everything from breaking and entering to burglary to desecrating a graveyard. It sounded like *Invasion of the Body Snatchers*!" He turned back to Kathryn and lowered his voice. "He claims you two did some kind of autopsy on Jimmy's body."

"We did not!" she shouted back just as the waitress arrived with the sheriff's coffee. There was a moment of frozen silence as the waitress clacked the cup and saucer onto the table, and Kathryn was greatly annoyed that she took an extra minute to tidy up the table and wipe the ring of water from under each glass.

As the waitress turned away, Kathryn leaned forward. "We didn't break into anything, we didn't desecrate anything, and we didn't take anything!"

"Well," Nick held up the canvas knapsack, "that's not *exactly* true." Before Kathryn could protest, he dumped the knapsack over and sent its contents clattering onto the table. She watched in horror as a single container rolled slowly toward the sheriff until it stopped against his cup. With each revolution the milk-white passengers rode the plastic wall to the top, dropped off, then began the upward ride again. It was like watching the popcorn machine in the lobby down at the Imperial Theater.

The sheriff looked in astonishment at the assortment of plastic containers. He lifted the one before him and stared at a trio of writhing, white maggots on a folded piece of damp paper towel.

"Peter," Kathryn said quietly, "I want you to meet Dr. Nicholas Polchak of North Carolina State University. Dr. Polchak is a forensic entomologist. I hired him, Peter—to investigate Jimmy's death."

"How do, Sheriff." Nick extended his hand with a flourish.

The sheriff groaned and dropped his head into his hands. "Kath, what have you done? I *told* you not to do anything!"

"You told me there was nothing more *you* could do," she said defiantly. "So I decided to do something myself."

"You," he shook his head in bewilderment, "are the most muley, stiff-necked, bullheaded woman I ever met." He reached out and made a mock strangling gesture at her throat, then placed his hands on hers and squeezed hard. Kathryn smiled faintly in return.

The waitress slowly approached the table once again, uneasily eyeing the pile of transparent containers and their contents.

"You folks got anything you need me to…dispose of for you?"

Nick looked quizzically around the table. He handed her a single crumpled Sweet 'n Low packet.

"By the way, Darlene, do you have any liver back there?"

"Liver?" she said suspiciously. "We got the fried chicken livers over by the chickpeas."

"Yes, but can I have them prepared a different way?"

"How you want 'em?"

"Raw. About a half a pound will do." He held up the largest of the containers. "Your sign says, 'Kids Eat Free.'"

She turned away again, stopping every few paces to glance back at Dr. Polchak. "Her name is *Beverly,*" Kathryn scolded.

"Really? I thought everybody down here was named 'Darlene.'"

Sheriff St. Clair set the container back on the table and slid it well away from him. "Down here? And where might *up there* be, Doc?"

"Pittsburgh."

Kathryn watched uneasily as the sheriff studied Nick. He glanced at the Pirates cap that still sat tight atop Nick's head and the tufts of dark hair that protruded from underneath on both sides. He stared a long time at Nick's colossal eyeglasses and the floating orbs behind them. He cocked his head from side to side, as if he were trying to guess the contents of the Mystery Jar in the sideshow at the Holcum County Fair.

Kathryn kicked him under the table.

"You must be just about blind." The sheriff nodded at Nick's glasses.

"Oh, I don't know. You'd be surprised what I can see."

The sheriff carefully considered each feature of Nick's face, then turned his attention to the bizarre polyester anachronism Nick wore as a shirt. His eyes moved slowly from button to button, and he smiled and shook his head slightly at the fresh barbecue stain on one side. When his eyes reached the table, he slowly pushed his chair back, bent over, and stared under the table for a good long time.

"I really should learn to cross my legs," Nick said to Kathryn.

The sheriff sat upright again and stared silently into the enormous eyes for a full minute.

"Hey Kath," he said, without removing his eyes from Nick, "I saw a bumper sticker the other day on Denny Brewster's truck. It said, 'I don't care *how* you do it up North.'"

"He's had that bumper sticker for ten years," she hissed.

"I know. It just came to mind."

"That's a good one," Nick said, "but my favorite is, 'Dixie: Where the family tree does not fork.'"

The sheriff squinted. "What's with all this Bug Man stuff?"

"True bugs belong to the order Heteroptera. I don't just

study bugs; I study other orders of forensic value as well. *Bug Man* is a misnomer, really—sort of like the term *Law Man*."

"Stop it," Kathryn broke in. "You two hounds can sniff each other all day if you want to. But the fact still remains, Peter"—she leaned forward and looked directly at him—"Dr. Polchak is working for me."

The sheriff opened his mouth to speak twice, but each time seemed to think better of it. He slumped back in his chair and stared at her.

"As a private citizen, you have the right to investigate anything you want—within limits." He turned again to Nick as he said this. "If you were a private investigator, I'd say, 'You could lose your license doing what you did today.' But you don't have a license, do you? So consider your hand slapped—and consider yourself lucky." Now he turned back to Kathryn. "Investigate away. It's your money. But I'm telling you, you're wasting your time."

"You seem very certain of that," Nick said.

"You're a forensic what? Etymologist?"

"No. That would be the study of word origins—not much help in a case like this. I'm a forensic *entomologist*."

"Whatever. I suppose from the *forensic* part that you've investigated a few deaths before."

"Quite a number."

"Then you'll be able to appreciate that there was nothing unusual about this one."

"Convince me."

"Male caucasian, thirty. Military background, lots of firearm experience. Gulf veteran, posttraumatic-stress victim with long-term depressive tendencies. A hunter, a loner, disappeared for weeks at a time. Turns up in the woods flat on his back, shot once through the head. The handgun was still in his hand—*his* handgun. No note, but no indications of struggle or conflict—no indications of *anything*."

"Did you do a gunpowder residue test on the hand?"

The sheriff paused. "Yeah," he said. "It was negative."

Nick raised one eyebrow, and Kathryn looked quickly back at Peter. "When a handgun is fired," the sheriff explained, "it sometimes leaves a residue of gunpowder on the hand that fired it—sometimes. I tested Jim's right hand—no gunpowder."

Kathryn's eyes widened with excitement.

"But," the sheriff interrupted, "the better the weapon, the cleaner it fires. Jim had a Beretta nine-millimeter—a fairly clean gun. I didn't expect to find any gunpowder."

"So you ran a neutron activation analysis to make sure," Nick continued.

The sheriff rolled his eyes and sank back into his chair. "Look, I'm the sheriff of a little county with an even smaller budget, which has to cover everything from crime-scene investigation to printing posters that say, 'Clean up after your dog.' You got any idea what an NAA costs?"

This time Nick turned to Kathryn to explain. "No matter how clean the weapon, it may leave microscopic traces of barium and antimony on the hand—traces that can't be detected by traditional tests. What the sheriff is telling us is that he's very certain about the cause of death—as certain as his budget will allow."

"I would have run that test no matter what it cost," the sheriff protested, "if there had been any indication that something was out of line. The coroner checked everything—he says suicide. I talked to Jim's sister—she buys it too. I asked some questions around town—nobody is surprised, nobody has a doubt—except *one person*." He looked directly at Kathryn as he said it. "I'm telling you, there was nothing out of the ordinary, and there was no reason to do any more than I did."

There was a long silence that followed as the impact of the sheriff's words sunk in. It was Nick who broke the silence.

"How long had Jim McAllister been using cocaine?"

Kathryn's mouth dropped open, and she began to blurt out

an angry and absolute denial—but she was instantly aware of the silence from the chair beside her. She turned to Peter, and one look at his face told her that the unthinkable was quite true. Even worse, it told her that Peter had probably known about it for quite some time—and for some reason had kept it from her.

Peter could not meet Kathryn's eyes. He turned to Nick instead. "How did you—"

"Bubba told me," Nick said, holding up a container with a single plump white maggot within—by far the largest of all the specimens. "Bubba is probably an ordinary blow fly or flesh fly larva, but he is *not* of ordinary size. An average larva at this stage of development should be about ten millimeters in length. Bubba is close to twenty. I removed him from the nasal septum. The only thing that can account for his accelerated growth is the presence of cocaine in the tissues where he was feeding. Your friend must have ingested within several hours of his death—and I think it's safe to assume that it probably wasn't the first time."

Kathryn continued to stare at Peter, searching his face for some excuse, some explanation.

"It...started in the Gulf," he stammered. "It wasn't just Jimmy—it happened to a lot of boys going into combat for the first time. He thought it would stop after the war. It didn't..."

His voice trailed off. He looked up into Kathryn's eyes, but the intensity of her stare drove him away again. Even as a child her pale green eyes could burn like emerald fire when they were fueled by anger or injustice. In this case it was both.

Kathryn sat in stunned silence, feeling her face and neck grow redder by the minute. The entire reason for this investigation, which flew in the face of all the available evidence and expert opinion, was her unshakable conviction that Jimmy McAllister would never take his own life. But two minutes ago, it had also been her unshakable conviction that Jimmy would never have used cocaine. If she was so badly mistaken about one part of his character, could she be wrong about another?

Her car, her clothes, her mortgage; the fear, the exhaustion, the utter humiliation—had it all been for nothing? Was she nothing more than a stupid schoolgirl acting on an emotional impulse, too simple and naive to accept how the world really works? The tears welling up within her made her feel all the more childish and silly, and she drove them back fiercely with anger and contempt.

"I need some time alone," she said quietly, rising from her chair. The sheriff rose with her and reached out to put his hand on her shoulder, but she pulled away.

Nick watched until the door closed with a jingle behind her. The sheriff slowly sat down again to face him.

The waitress returned with a brown paper bag rolled down tight and sealed with a clothespin. She opened her mouth to speak, but noting the look on the sheriff's face, she simply set the bag in the center of the table and backed away.

"That was cute, Doc. Real cute. You remind me of one of those psychic hotline people. You got nothing real to offer so you toss out a bone—that cocaine thing—just to keep her on the line, just to keep her believing—just to keep her *paying*."

"You should have told her."

"Why? What would it have proved? That Jimmy's depression *might* have been chemically induced? That his suicide *might* have been encouraged by the drugs? Let me tell you, his weirdness started a long time before the coke."

"You should have told her."

"What do you know about it? Look"—he lowered his voice, glancing around for listening ears—"we all grew up here together—Jimmy, me, and Kath. We were family—about the only family any of us had. She loved Jim like a brother. What good would it do to drag his memory through the dirt by bringing up a drug problem? But I guess you took care of that."

"So her 'brother' had a serious drug problem, and you kept it from her for almost a decade? That's some family you've got there."

The sheriff looked down at his coffee cup. "Jim made me swear. He would have died before he let her find out."

"Looks like he did."

"He thought he could beat it on his own—and he did, a couple of times. He went through rehab a couple of years after the Gulf. He was clean for a year, maybe two. Then he went on it again. He'd kick it for a while, then go back. After a while even I didn't know how he was doing."

"Now you know."

"The point is"—the sheriff leaned in for emphasis— "I knew Jim McAllister since he was a kid. I *knew* him. He came from one suck-egg family—if you don't believe me, go meet his twisted sister, Amy. Jim started showing signs of depression real early, and I'm telling you, his depression led to his drug problem and not the other way around. He was headed for a sudden stop anyway. Some of us saw it coming a long time ago."

"But not Mrs. Guilford."

"She only saw the good side. That's all she wanted to see. It's a bad habit of hers. I wanted to protect his memory for her, so...I kept the cocaine thing quiet."

"And as a result, she believed that little Jimmy could never have done anything as nasty as suicide. And she hired me to prove it."

"I guess I owe you an apology for that," the sheriff conceded. "But at least we know that all *this* is no longer necessary." He gestured to the pile of containers still scattered across the table.

"How so?"

The sheriff hesitated. "The cocaine. I told you that—"

"You told me that his depression led to his drug problem and not the other way around. That means that the cocaine had nothing to do with his death—so nothing new has been introduced into the equation. Mrs. Guilford will still want to know what happened to her friend."

The sheriff stared blankly at Nick for a long time.

"Don't take her money," he said at last.

"Excuse me?"

"I assume she's offered to pay you. How much? Five thousand? More?"

"That's between me and my client."

"Don't take her money," he said again. "No matter what you may think, Doc, she's not a rich woman. She works at a bank, for crying out loud. If she's offering you that kind of money, she's putting her house in hock, I can tell you that. Don't take it."

Nick leaned back and folded his arms across his chest. "Ten minutes ago she couldn't believe that Jimmy would kill himself, because she *knew* Jimmy. Now—thanks to you—she isn't sure what she knows. Unless I miss my guess, she'll still want to do everything in her power to find out anything she can."

Nick began to carefully place each container back into the knapsack, followed by the wrinkled paper bag.

"You know"—the sheriff nodded toward the knapsack—"I could confiscate all this and put an end to it right now."

"But you won't," Nick said, smiling, "because she might not forgive you for it. And I have a feeling that's a risk you're not willing to take."

"I won't let Kathryn be taken advantage of," the sheriff said without emotion. "I will do everything in my power to protect her."

"Are you sure it's Kathryn you're trying to protect?"

Nick slung the pack over one shoulder and stepped toward the door. He stopped and turned back to the sheriff.

"I intend to take her money," he said. "And I intend to earn it."

CHAPTER 6

From each plastic container Nick selected two or three plump maggots, carefully avoiding both the largest and smallest specimens, and dropped them into a small vial of 70 percent isopropyl alcohol to preserve them. Each died almost instantly and floated softly to the bottom. He capped each vial tightly and labeled the victims exactly as he had designated their living counterparts: left ocular, right temporal, left temporal... He treated the hungry survivors in each plastic container to several strips of raw liver and transferred the lot to the wire shelves of the large chrome and glass unit in the corner of the room.

It was after midnight now, and Nick was still hard at work under the glaring blue fluorescent lights of his office lab. He sat down at the gray-and-white dissecting microscope and maneuvered a glass slide directly under the lens. No sooner had he reached for the focus knob than the exterior door to his left suddenly swung open. There in the darkness stood the exhausted figure of Kathryn Guilford.

"Close the door," Nick said without looking up.

"Are you worried that I might let out some of your precious bugs?"

"I'm worried about the bugs you might let *in*—especially the dermestids. They're dry-tissue eaters, and they'd love to make a snack out of my mounted specimens."

Kathryn stood motionless in the open doorway until he finally glanced up reluctantly from his microscope.

"Pretty please?"

Nick studied the standing form of Kathryn Guilford. She was tall, he observed, about 175 centimeters—maybe more. She was wide in the shoulders, with a very lean body mass—perhaps an athletic background. The thorax tapered tightly toward the abdomen, producing a full, rounded curve of the hips. The legs were long and tanned and very lean. The face was equally lean; the zygomatic arch was prominent, producing a high cheekbone, and the nose was long and straight, ending almost in a chisel point. The eyes were wide and very green. The hair was a deep auburn, and she seemed to make less fuss about it than women typically do. Right now she wore it down, but he could imagine it pulled back in a thick ponytail. Green eyes, auburn hair, and a spray of freckles across the nose. Overall it was a pleasing figure, one that Nick imagined some men would find quite beautiful.

Kathryn stepped inside and pulled the door shut behind her. She rolled out a chair from under the table to her right and sat down across from Dr. Polchak. "You're probably surprised to see me."

"I'm surprised to see anyone at this hour. Don't you ever sleep?"

"I have something for you." She reached into her purse and handed him a folded slip of paper. "It's a check."

"Yes, I've seen one before." He turned the check over and held it up to the light as if it might not be real. "One thousand dollars. That's slightly less than the amount we agreed upon."

"I think a thousand dollars is an adequate fee for a single day's work," she snapped. "I see no reason to continue this investigation after…after tonight."

Without a word Nick turned back to his microscope. He carefully removed the glass specimen slide and slid the edge of Kathryn's check under the chrome holding clips instead. He peered once again into the eyepiece. For several moments he studied it—focusing, shifting, then focusing again.

"For crying out loud," Kathryn said, "it's *good.*"

"Not good enough." He looked at her again. "Give me one good reason why you should drop this investigation."

"One good reason! The only reason I started all this is because I believed that Jimmy could never have taken his own life—and then tonight I learn that he was a user! I never thought *that* could be true of him either. Maybe I was wrong about him…maybe I was wrong about everything."

"The sheriff believes that cocaine had nothing to do with your friend's death—that his drug use was a symptom of his struggle, and not the cause. Do you agree?"

She thought carefully. "Yes," she said slowly, and then with more confidence, "yes, I do."

"Then the cocaine tells us only two things: one, that your friend was indeed troubled—which we already knew—and two, that your friend the sheriff is willing to withhold information from you."

"He did it to protect me."

"So he said." Nick studied her eyes closely. "And you obviously believe him."

Kathryn ignored the remark. "So you think there's good reason to continue the investigation?"

"I don't think there was ever good reason to begin—but

then, this is not about reason, is it? You came to me because you had a *hunch.* Your friend could not have died by suicide, you said, because he was incapable of taking his own life. Nothing has changed about that. I just hate to see you give up a good hunch for a bad reason."

Kathryn gazed at him in confusion, trying to make sense of this strange assortment of riddles. Suddenly it all became clear to her.

"This is all about money, isn't it? Give me back my check!"

Nick reached into his breast pocket with two fingers and removed the folded paper. Straightening his arm, he dropped the paper to the floor in front of him and slowly slid it forward with his left foot. Kathryn snatched up the check and spread it out on the worktable beside her, furiously crossing out numbers and figures and writing new ones in their place.

"There!" She tossed the check back on the floor in front of him. "*Five* thousand! Now is there a good reason to call it off?"

Nick sat motionless, continuing to study Kathryn's eyes.

"The body was moved," he said quietly.

Kathryn was stunned. *Jimmy's body—moved? But who would move it? And why?* Her mind raced with all the possible implications of this revelation—but all that came out of her mouth was an astonished, "What?"

"The blood that circulates in your body is red due to the presence of oxygen. When a body dies, the blood becomes purple—almost black—and it pools in the lowest parts of the body. The blood actually stains the surrounding tissues, and after six to eight hours the stain becomes permanent. This is a condition known as 'fixed lividity.'"

Nick laid his right arm out flat on the table beside him, palm up. "I die. My body falls to the ground—like this." He nodded to the arm. "The blood drains to the dorsal surface—down here—and eight hours later the bottom of my arm is permanently stained. Now if someone comes along after eight hours and flips me over, the blood will no longer pool to the bottom—

the stain will stay on top. I died *this* way"—he flipped his arm over—"but my body was discovered *this* way. Guess what? I was moved."

Kathryn squinted hard.

"At the funeral home, our two young body baggers told us that they found the body like this." He leaned back in his chair and extended his arms and legs straight out. "*Exactly* like this. The sheriff seemed to concur. *Flat on his back* was the way he put it, I believe. But during our little examination I removed your friend's shoes. The left foot was stained along the heel, continuing up the back of the leg—exactly as it should be if the leg lay flat for the first few hours after death. But the right foot was completely purple, top *and* bottom, with the stain ending just above the ankle. That means, Mrs. Guilford, that he may have been found 'flat on his back'—but he didn't die that way."

Kathryn sat more and more erect as the full meaning of his words began to sink in.

"That means," she said excitedly, "that when Jimmy died his leg must have been in a position more like…like…" She dropped to the floor and stretched out, then drew her right foot up tight against her buttock with her knee pointing toward the ceiling. "Something like this."

"Very good, Mrs. Guilford."

"And then later—six to eight hours later—someone must have laid it flat. But if someone was there within hours of his death, then someone may have been *involved* in his death. That means Jimmy didn't kill himself!"

"No, it doesn't."

"But," she said, snapping upright, "somebody moved the body!"

"Not necessarily. All we know is that somebody—or something—moved the *leg*. Suppose your friend shot himself, as the sheriff is convinced, and when he fell the leg was somehow propped up."

"But what would keep the leg in that position?" She lay back again and experimented with her foot in different positions. Each time her leg swung outward and fell. "There's no way," she said. "It won't stay like that."

"Suppose something supported it."

"Like what?"

"A rock. A branch. A bush."

"Was there anything like that around?"

"I have no idea."

"And even if something did support it," she went on, "what would make it lie flat again?"

"The rock shifts. The branch breaks. The bush dies."

"How likely is that?"

"I have no idea."

"Then all we're doing is guessing here. Isn't there any way we can check this out? Can't we go see the spot where the body was found? Can't we look around for dead bushes and broken branches?"

Nick leaned back in his chair and folded his hands in front of him. "You mean, can't we *investigate?*"

Kathryn sat quietly for a moment, then picked herself up from the floor. She walked very slowly around the office, carefully considering the choice she was about to make. She came to the large, glass-doored unit in the corner of the room and stopped. Looking in, she saw the collection of plastic containers. Each contained three or four wiggling white maggots hungrily feeding on strips of raw chicken liver—all except for two containers. One contained the infamous Bubba, who was responsible for beginning the entire brouhaha earlier that evening. The other, containing a single specimen of ordinary size, bore the simple label "?."

"What is this thing?" she asked, running her hand along the polished chrome trim.

"It's a Biotronette—a breeding unit," he said. "It allows us to simulate the precise environment in which the larvae were collected. It allows us to rear them to adult flies."

"Why do we need to do that?"

"When they mature, we'll be able to identify their different species."

"And what will that prove?"

"Everything. Nothing. It all depends on what we find."

Kathryn sat down again across from Dr. Polchak. She sat staring at his frosted glasses, trying somehow to connect with the elusive spheres behind them. It was impossible; they darted and evaded her gaze like startled minnows. She knew that she was at a decided disadvantage in this negotiation. He could peer into *her* thoughts, but she had no access to *his*.

"If this is not about money," she said cautiously, "then why do you want to finish this investigation? You never wanted to start this in the first place—so why do you want to continue now?"

"I have my reasons. The only thing that matters to you is that I'm willing to continue. A more important question—and one that may have a direct bearing on this case—is why *you* want to continue."

"I didn't say I did."

He said nothing in response, but slowly raised one eyebrow; it arched up from behind his glasses like a cat rising from sleep. He leaned forward until his elbows rested on his knees.

"What I want to know," he said slowly, "what I *need* to know—is why this is so important to you. Why do you have to know what happened to Jim McAllister?"

For an instant the elusive eyes came almost to rest on hers. The sudden intensity of his gaze startled her, and she rose so quickly from her chair that she sent it clattering across the linoleum floor. She turned and started for the door—then stopped. A full minute later, without turning, she began to speak.

"My father died when I was seven. For my sixth birthday, he gave me a beautiful sweater. It meant everything to me, especially…after. One day the sweater just disappeared. Gone.

I looked all over town for it. Did I lose it? Was it stolen? I asked everyone I knew, and a lot of people I didn't. You know, I never found it. Never," she said with a shrug. "At first, all I wanted was the sweater back. But the more I searched for it, the more I just wanted to know what happened to it. By the end, I think I would have given up the sweater itself if only I could *know*."

"So this is all about a sweater."

Kathryn wheeled and glared at him. She gave her chair an angry shove and it rocketed across the floor toward Nick. He stopped it with his foot, nudged it a few feet away, and motioned for her to sit down. She stood silently for a moment, carefully weighing the potential benefits versus the definite risks of continuing her story.

She straddled the chair and slowly sat down again.

"I told you that the three of us grew up here—Jimmy, Peter, and me." She paused. "There was a fourth. His name was Andy."

"Ah," he said, recalling Mr. Schroeder's inquiry that afternoon. "That would be Andy whose 'body has never been recovered.'"

"You don't miss much."

"That's what people pay me for."

"The three of them were like brothers—too much like brothers. It was always who is the fastest, who is the toughest, who is the *best*. If one of them went out for football, all of them had to go out for football. And then it was who is the captain, who scores the touchdown, who is first-string." She shook her head. "You know how boys can be."

"I'm familiar with the species."

"They competed for everything."

"Including you?"

Her face reddened slightly but she made no reply. "About ten years ago they all took a drive up to Fort Bragg together—that's where the 82d Airborne is based. One of them decided to sign up and—"

"I've got the picture."

"Andy and Jimmy were assigned to one unit, Peter to another. In the spring of 1990 things were heating up in the Persian Gulf and the U.S. was starting its buildup of forces. The boys got the word that the 82nd Airborne might be deployed to Saudi Arabia—"

"And Andy decided to make sure the cow was tied up before he left the barn," Nick broke in, "as they say in Holcum County."

"We were married in July. Three weeks later they were called up. Andy..." She stopped. She couldn't stand to look at Nick any longer. Even if he really needed to know, she couldn't bear to tell the rest of the story to those eyes—eyes that would flit and hover over her words but never care enough to land on any of them.

"Andy was apparently killed in action near Al Salman Airbase in Iraq."

"*Apparently* killed?"

"Remember Vietnam? By the time it was all over, there were more than eighteen hundred MIAs. It was an unbelievable mess—mothers waiting to hear about their sons, kids praying for Daddy to come home. It's still going on today, thirty-five years later. After Vietnam the Defense Department said 'never again.' They started collecting a DNA sample from every soldier. Now if they find nothing but a *finger* on the battlefield, they still know it's you. No more eternally grieving mothers, no more Tomb of the Unknown Soldier."

She glanced up to check for telltale signs of inattention or indifference, anything that would give her an excuse to protest and bring her story to a premature end. But Nick sat transfixed, waiting patiently for her to continue.

"Do you know how many MIAs there were in the Persian Gulf? None. Zero. But what they don't tell you is that there were thirteen soldiers who just *disappeared*. Oh, they know what happened to them—so they say. A Tomcat missed the net and rolled off the flight deck, there was a direct bomb hit, that sort of thing.

So they came up with a new category to cover those situations: 'Killed in action, body not recovered.'"

"Andy?"

"He was lucky thirteen—only they had no explanation for Andy. No missing Tomcat, no witnesses to the bomb blast—*nothing*. All they could tell me is that they were advancing on Al Salman and Andy got ahead of the rest of the unit—probably trying to be the first one there." She tried to force a smile. "Just before nightfall there was a firestorm with the airbase, and Andy got cut off. When the smoke cleared at daybreak, no Andy. No Andy anywhere."

With these words Kathryn dropped her face into her hands and began to sob softly.

"I'm...sorry," Nick fumbled. The impotent words fell and echoed like marbles on a slate floor. "Was there a search? Were there no...diplomatic channels?"

"It was a little awkward to say to Iraq, 'Can you help us find one of our soldiers?' when they lost a hundred thousand of their own." Kathryn carefully wiped under her eyes with both hands. "So what am I, Dr. Polchak? A widow or a lady in waiting? I've spent eight years wondering. You want to know what's worse than grieving for a dead husband? Not knowing whether to grieve or not. Living every day of your life with an open wound."

She rubbed her eyes hard with both fists now—forget the mascara. She sat silently, staring at the floor, floating in a sea of numbness and exhaustion.

"I can't get my sweater back," she said quietly, "but I'd give anything in the world—*anything*—just to know what happened to it. When Jimmy died, I said 'never again.' I want to know how he died, Dr. Polchak. I want to know why he died. *I have to know.*"

Kathryn picked up the check still lying on the floor between them. She opened it and smoothed it out on the table beside them.

"Five thousand dollars is an incredible fee for a single day's work. My offer still stands; take it now and we'll put an end to this. Of course, if you do, you'll miss out on the other fifteen."

"And if I do," Nick returned, "then you'll never *know.* We can stop now, Mrs. Guilford, but there's only one way to put an end to it."

For the first time that day Kathryn smiled. "I was hoping you'd say that."

CHAPTER 7

"One of these, okay, Ed?"

Sheriff Peter St. Clair leaned across the bar and pointed to a red and gold plastic tap handle.

"You off duty yet, Pete?" a voice called out from behind him. "We can't have the law weavin' all over the road, y'know."

"Somebody's stickin' his nose where it don't belong," the sheriff called back.

He turned to see three grinning hunters seated at their regular table just below the ceiling-mount TV at the Buck Stop Bar and Grill.

"Speakin' of which," the sheriff said with a nod, "you boys might be interested to know that the investigation into Jimmy's death isn't over after all."

"Not over? How so?"

Pete picked up his glass and stepped slowly to their table. He reached up and clicked off the TV, drew out a chair with his toe, and settled himself across from them. He studied each of the hunters in turn.

"You boys heard about this Bug Man character? Down from NC State. Here to do research at the County Extension Station over near Sandridge."

"We heard." Denny snickered. "We heard he tried to swipe a body off old man Schroeder! What was *that* all about?"

The sheriff wasn't smiling. "Seems he's been hired to look into Jimmy's death. Thought it might interest you boys—*especially* you."

Ronny straightened. "Why us?"

"'Cause you're the ones found the body," Pete shrugged. "Naturally, that makes you suspects."

No one was smiling now.

"I knew it," Denny groaned. "I told you we should keep our noses out of it. Just walk away and let somebody else report it, I said."

"Oh, shut up!" Wayne barked back.

"You…you don't believe *we* had anything to do with it?"

Pete shook his head. "Not me—but then, I'm not the one doing the investigating."

"This Bug Man," Ronny repeated. "You said he was hired. Who hired him?"

The sheriff paused. "Kathryn hired him."

"Kathryn? Your Kathryn?"

"She's not *my* Kathryn," Pete shot back. "And she's got a right to investigate Jimmy's death or anything else she wants, as long as she stays within the law. She can waste her money any way she chooses."

"But—didn't you tell her how we found him? About the gun and all? And what about Mr. Wilkins? He checked out the whole thing!"

"She knows all about it. She just doesn't want to believe it. She can't believe that Jimmy would ever do himself in."

"Well, *we* believe it," Wayne growled. "Seeing is believing."

"You say this Bug Man is looking for some *other* explanation?" Ronny asked. "How? What does he do?"

The sheriff slowly rolled the golden liquid around in his glass. "He looks at the bugs," he said quietly. "He looks at the maggots on the body."

The three hunters stared at one another in disbelief.

"This is just great," Wayne moaned. "We stumble onto a dead guy in the middle of nowhere, a mile away from everybody, with his own gun still in his hand—and now a bunch of maggots are somehow gonna prove *we* did it!"

"Nobody said we did anything," Denny said with very little assurance.

"Don't you see what's happening here?" Wayne glared back at him. "This whole thing could blow up in our faces! You let one of these 'experts' loose and there's no telling what he'll manufacture! He's being paid, you know—and by somebody who doesn't want it to be a suicide! You think he's going to side with us or with the one who foots the bill?"

The four men sat together in silence.

"Can't you talk her out of it?" Denny whispered to Pete. "You say, 'She's not *my* Kathryn,' but that's not true. Everybody in town knows she's more yours than anybody else's. She'll listen to you."

Pete pushed his chair back and slowly stood up. He bent over slightly, tucked his thumbs in his belt, and stretched his shirt front tight. "You know Kathryn. She has her own mind about these things."

He tossed a five-dollar bill on the table and nodded to the bartender as he left. At the doorway he looked back at the hunters one last time—first Denny, then Wayne, then Ronny.

"Somebody ought to have a talk with that Bug Man."

Kathryn steered her rented Contour once again into the gravel lot in front of the sea green Quonset, which glowed cobalt blue in the first light of day. The air was still heavy with the night's humidity and the warming hand of the sun had just begun to peel back the thick gauze blankets of morning mist. She rested her head against the steering wheel for a moment. It was much too early to be here, but it had been a long and sleepless night, and she could no longer bear to be alone with her thoughts. She had to go somewhere.

To her left was Dr. Polchak's rusting relic, but Dr. Tedesco's Camry was nowhere in sight. *It figures,* she thought. Dr. Tedesco was probably at home somewhere, sleeping peacefully in neatly ironed percales. Dr. Polchak was probably in the back room curled up in a terrarium with some of his "kids." She laughed out loud at the thought, a reminder of just how exhausted she really was. It suddenly occurred to her that he must remove those enormous glasses of his to sleep.

She shook off the thought. Images of Dr. Polchak unmasked were too much to bear first thing in the morning.

The screen door was unlocked as she supposed it always was. She knocked; no answer. She cupped her hands and peered inside. The office was empty and silent, except for a constant hum from the banks of fluorescent blue lights.

Kathryn walked around the side of the building and spotted Nick seventy-five yards away, standing in the center of an open pasture that sloped off gradually to the right. He looked up as Kathryn waded toward him through the knee-high grass.

"These are not exactly bankers' hours," Nick said, stepping slowly around to the left to reveal a gleaming white monolith jutting out of the purple-green rye like some forgotten monument. It was surrounded by dozens of whizzing, buzzing black-and-gold honeybees.

Even before Kathryn consciously recognized the object, it triggered a memory deep within her. She felt her heart lurch into her throat, and she began to scramble backward through the wet, clinging grass.

"Stop!" Nick commanded in a low, even voice. "Stay as close as you can"—he raised one arm slowly and pointed to an area to her right—"but stand over there."

Kathryn stumbled obediently to her right and stood, jerking her head left and right to constantly scan the air around her for any trace of the black pestilence.

"Have you ever heard of honey from a *jar?*" Her voice trembled.

"Have you ever tried spaghetti sauce from a jar? It's just not the same." As he spoke, to Kathryn's utter horror, he began to carefully remove the cover from the hive.

What is he doing?

He was prying off the lid from Pandora's box itself, and any moment a swirling black cloud of malevolence would spew out to consume him, then her, and then infest the entire world with its evil. She started to cry out—but to her astonishment, nothing came out of the box at all.

"That's something you don't have around here," Nick said, reaching gently into the hive. "Good spaghetti. Oh, the menu *says* 'spaghetti,' but it's not. It's North Carolina spaghetti—noodles and catsup. If you want real spaghetti, you've got to come to Pittsburgh." He carefully grasped the edges of the frame closest to him and lifted it straight up and out, resting it with one hand on the lip of the hive. With his right hand he reached slowly into his pocket and removed a small penknife.

"You know what else you don't have around here? A good Reuben sandwich. A good Reuben is like a symphony, like a work of art." With his bare hand he gently brushed back the black mass of bees from the left side of the frame. "You need really lean, tender corned beef from a good Polish deli—not this horse meat you get around here. You need homemade sauerkraut—*piles* of it—and a really good Russian dressing. Not Thousand Island—*Russian*."

With the point of his knife he carefully carved away a piece of comb about an inch square from the upper left corner and set it beside the knife on the lip of the hive. Then he carefully slid the frame firmly back into place.

"Ouch," he said with no emotion whatsoever. "Now, Shirley, what was that for? That hurt you a lot more than it did me." He slowly replaced the lid on the hive, being very careful not to trap any bees lingering on the edges.

"There's a place in Pittsburgh called 'Poli's,'" he said, gently wiping a bee from the corner of his mouth. "It's up north in Squirrel Hill. Now they've got a Reuben that melts in your mouth like butter." He looked dreamily into the sky. "Yes sir. Now *that's* a Reuben."

He picked up the chunk of comb in one hand and set the knife on top of the hive with the other. "Clean this up for me, will you, ladies? It's a bit sticky." Then he turned toward Kathryn, who was still ashen-faced and trembling.

"I think we've got everything we need," Nick said cheerfully as he passed.

In the lab, Nick removed two cups from the top drawer of a tall file cabinet. "I think this is a morning for Dragon Well Green. The Chinese claim that it banishes fatigue and raises the spirit." He dangled a tea bag into each cup and reached for the steaming carafe of water on a hot plate atop the cabinet.

"So where do we begin today?" Kathryn asked.

"*You* begin by going with Teddy," Nick replied, "to the site where the body was discovered."

"You're not coming? Why not?"

"You'll find Teddy to be very competent at what he does. I have other clients to attend to here. Remember, Mrs. Guilford, I was sent here this summer to do research. I can't go back to school without my homework, now can I?"

Nick moved briskly about the lab, filling his knapsack once again with empty containers, a Nikon equipped with a macro lens, a microcassette recorder, a small notebook, and various other paraphernalia. Then he headed immediately for the opposite door.

"Now wait a minute," she called after him as he stepped out on to a small deck area. "I'm paying you twenty thousand dollars to investigate this case for me. That's a couple of thousand dollars a day. I think I deserve your full time!"

"You're paying for my full *attention,*" he said as the door began to swing shut, "not my full time."

Kathryn was on his heels in an instant, almost running to keep up with his expansive stride. "That's not good enough," she said firmly. "Who are these other clients? How many do you have?"

"Right now? Two. But I'm hoping to pick up another one any day now."

"*Another* one? Am I interfering with your recruiting? I'm so sorry!"

"No need to apologize."

They had crossed a narrow meadow by this time and began to follow a dirt path that curved back into the woods.

"Are these other clients paying you more than I am?"

"They're not paying me at all."

"Then why are you charging me?"

"I'm not charging you. You offered to pay me, remember? Besides, you have the means to pay for my services and they don't."

"So I'm subsidizing them?"

"In a manner of speaking, yes."

"Look," she said, working hard to catch her breath, "I'm the paying customer here, so I come first. That's only fair."

"It's not that simple. My other clients have issues that require my ongoing attention."

Nick stopped suddenly and swung the knapsack from his shoulder. He pointed to the ground. Beside the path in a sparse patch of weeds lay a colossal, pinkish-gray lump—the cadaver of an enormous sow. Its mottled skin was stretched taut and almost shiny, causing each hair to stand out like a tiny flagpole. At one end the swollen black tongue protruded from the mouth; at the other, the intestines bulged partially from the anus. And everywhere there were flies—black, blue, and iridescent green—circling, feeding, mating, and laying eggs on this most sumptuous of feasts.

"It's a *pig!*" Kathryn said in disgust, clapping one hand over her nose and mouth.

"Very good," Nick said. "You know your mammals." He bent down, pulled up a handful of grass and tossed it into the air. "I recommend that you stand *up*wind—over there."

Kathryn needed no urging, remembering the lesson she learned just a day ago at Schroeder's Funeral Home.

Nick walked slowly around the immense form. Beside the head a small white sign had been posted, noting the date of acquisition less than a week ago and bearing the name Porky. Below the name were penciled the words, "That's all, folks!"

"Is this what happens to all of your clients?" Kathryn shivered.

"Only the ones who don't pay. She came to us about a week ago from a small hog farm near here. She's much larger than most of the ones I get—I like them at about fifty pounds, but you take what you can get. Sad story, really. She was getting old, had a lot of pain, but she had become a kind of family pet—so no Pig Pickin' Buffet for her. The farmer couldn't afford to keep her anymore, so I told the family I'd take her. I brought her here to this lovely spot—and then I shot her."

Kathryn grimaced.

"I sedated her first," he said, "if that helps any. Less than a minute after she fell, the first blow fly arrived—less than a *minute*. A gravid female, so heavy she could barely fly, looking desperately for some place to oviposit her eggs. She'd been hovering in the air for hours, head into the wind, sniffing, sensing, *waiting*. Suddenly a cluster of scent molecules from the bullet wound came to her. She found her nursery! She followed the scent cluster by cluster to the source a mile away—maybe more. She landed. She knew she had found the right neighborhood, but now she had to decide on a house. The bullet wound was nice but it was so exposed—no trees, no shade. She checked the anal area. Not bad. She was tempted to stay—but she wanted something better for her kids, so she decided to check out a nostril. It's warm, it's dark, it's moist; impressive entryway, cathedral ceilings, large basement. Perfect! She was home at last, and not a moment too soon. She began to drop her eggs—a long line of tiny white specks, sort of like grated cheese. She did her job well, she fulfilled her biological destiny. She made sure her kids would grow up in a decent neighborhood.

"Within minutes there were dozens more. Soon there were hundreds, then thousands. The first to arrive were all friends and relatives—blow flies and flesh flies like the calliphorids and sarcophagids, maybe even a few Muscidae—common houseflies. But then strangers began to arrive. One day she looked across the street, and her next-door neighbors were Staphylinidae—rove beetles—and rumor has it they feed on the eggs and larvae of other species. Then things really started to go bad; the parasites moved in. Ants came in and carried off her eggs. Wasps laid their eggs among her larvae, and when they hatch, guess who's coming to dinner?

"Soon the place is a ghetto," he said with increasing passion, pacing and gesturing as he spoke. "All the decent housing is taken. There's crowding and tension and fighting everywhere. As time passes the whole place begins to dry up. As the tissues continue to decompose they emit different odors, attracting new and unfamiliar species. Soon all the blow flies will be gone—moved out to the suburbs. A few carrion beetles will stick around to carry off what's left of the tissue and bury it nearby, but soon there will be nothing but dermestids like common clothing moths to feed on the hair and hide. By the time they've all finished and moved on, this body will be reduced to nothing but a pile of bones and barely enough skin to make a football. Less than a week ago dear Porky departed our world—but she has *become* an entire world to thousands of others."

Nick shook his head in wonder. "Planet Porky."

His lecture finished, he looked silently at Kathryn for some response, some indication that she, too, cherished the biological marvel that lay before her.

"You," she said slowly, "are a very sick man."

"Mrs. Guilford"—Nick gestured to the swollen mass before him—"this is how a forensic entomologist learns his trade."

"By shooting helpless pigs?"

"By studying faunal succession—the natural order in which different species of arthropods occupy a decomposing body. From studies like this we know the exact order of succession—and we also know exactly how long it takes each species to lay eggs, hatch, and develop to maturity."

Kathryn shook her head. "This is what you do? You go around dropping dead pigs off everywhere, then come back to watch them rot?"

"The hog farmers lost a hundred thousand of them in the floods after Hurricane Floyd. I can get one for you cheap."

Nick removed the notebook from his knapsack and jotted a few notations while Kathryn glanced at the moldering cadaver in disgust.

"So this is your other client," she grumbled.

"This is one of them." He slung the knapsack over his shoulder again. "Would you like to meet the other?"

As they continued down the path, Kathryn glanced from one side of the road to the other, studying each passing clump of brush or grass for a telltale patch of pink or gray...

"If you're searching for a body, don't look down," Nick said. "Look up."

Kathryn raised her eyes and looked ahead down the path. About twenty yards ahead the path came to a rise and then disappeared. Just over the rise, to the left, a black cloud of flies hovered in silent circles.

The cadaver lay under a tree in a patch of tall grass. As they approached, Kathryn caught a glimpse of the now familiar pinkish-gray skin stretched taut.

"We try to deposit them in different environments to study the effects of temperature and exposure," Nick said as they waded into the grass. "Porky was deposited in full sunlight. This one we placed in the shade. Someday I'd like to study one left in the trunk of a car. That's where many murder victims are discovered."

They stood directly over the cadaver now. It had the same mottled and swollen appearance, but Kathryn noticed it was much smaller and somehow different in proportion. Her eye followed the bloated contour of the body. The right end was partially covered by the tattered remains of a flannel shirt.

Kathryn gasped and stumbled back out of the grass onto the path behind her.

"That… That's a man!"

"That *was* a man." Nick walked around the cadaver, pushing back the tall grass to expose the body to full view. Just like the sow, a small white sign had been posted to the left bearing the date of acquisition, just over two weeks ago. Beneath it was adhered a blue-and-white nametag that read, "HELLO! My name is—" with the name Bob handwritten below. In the corner was a round, black sticker festooned with pink confetti that said, "This is what 50 looks like!"

"How did you…*where* did you…?"

"Igor brings them to me from the graveyard," Nick said casually—then seemed to reconsider his choice of words. "Actually, they're very difficult to obtain."

"But how—"

"I request unclaimed bodies through the medical examiner's office in Chapel Hill. There's tremendous demand and a very limited supply. Sometimes there's an organ donor whose cause of death renders his organs unusable, or a migrant worker whose family never learns of his death. On rare occasions there's an executed criminal. Everybody wants them. You just have to wait in line."

"Thanks. I'll take a number."

Kathryn stood squinting, slowly shaking her head from side to side. What was she to think of this man? A moment ago he was just a perverse and twisted little boy playing with his cameras and containers and tweezers. But with each new revelation he seemed more sordid, more *despicable,* like a spook house that grew more macabre around every bend. This was not just another experiment. This was not just another geriatric sow.

"Look at it this way," Nick said. "Bob here donated his body to science. But science didn't want it—at least, not the traditional sciences. So Bob agreed to join me here to advance the emerging science of forensic entomology."

"Did Bob really agree to join you here? Did you say to Bob before he died, 'I'm going to throw your body on the ground and let insects consume you'?"

"Of course not—no more than a medical school would say to him, 'We're going to let ignorant first-year students cut you apart to see what you're made of.'"

"I just don't think he would have wanted to end up like…*this*."

"Like what?" Nick said in disdain. "Decomposed? Decayed? Rotten, putrid, rancid, and rank? What is this 'thing' your species has about death? Everybody ends up like this, Mrs. Guilford." He swept the tall grass to one side and pointed to the swollen abdomen. "This is what happens when you die. Bacteria in the intestine begin to multiply and consume you from the inside out—first the intestines and the blood and then the surrounding organs. These runaway organisms produce sulfides—*gas*—that bloats the abdomen and stretches the skin until it splits. If you're here at just the right time, you can actually hear it rip." He released the grass and stepped onto the path in front of Kathryn.

"The way I see it, you've got two choices: You can be eaten by little bugs, or you can be eaten by big bugs. Either way, you're just shoofly pie."

"Nobody should end up as—what did you call it? *Shoofly pie.* This man deserved a decent burial."

Nick let out a laugh. "What do you think is different if they place you in a shiny copper coffin with a satin lining? Do you think biology stops if they powder your face and fill you with embalming fluid? Did you know that coffins are designed to burp—to let out the gas that's produced inside? They bury the bugs *with* you, Mrs. Guilford. You can slow things down, but you still end up like this. Insects are just nature's way of speeding things along. The arthropod motto is, 'Don't throw it away—*recycle*.'"

He took out his notebook once again and began to make notes. Kathryn glared at him as he finished his observations and began to repack his bag. It wasn't the *nature* of his study that bothered her most, it was his annoying flippancy, his arrogant callousness toward the *objects* of his study—toward aging sows, and unwanted old men, and Jimmy McAllister, and a young woman with a pathological fear of insects—toward life and death itself.

Nick swung the knapsack over his shoulder and started down the path again. As he passed, Kathryn said, "I just don't think you should treat a human being this way."

He looked around in mock confusion. "What human being?"

"*That* human being."

"That? That's bug food, Mrs. Guilford—nothing more—and the sooner you understand that, the sooner we can get to work."

CHAPTER 9

"Is this the meadow?"

"Yes ma'am," Casey said. "That's the spot where me 'n Griff found him over there." The young man pointed to a rise where a tangle of yellow ribbon fluttered between sticks placed in some unrecognizable geometric pattern. "You need anything else?"

"No thanks," Kathryn said. "We can find our way back from here. Oh, there is one more thing"—She tucked a twenty-dollar bill into his breast pocket and straightened his shirt—"Mr. Schroeder doesn't need to know you helped me today—does he?"

Casey grinned, nodded to Kathryn and Dr. Tedesco, and headed back into the woods.

Dr. Tedesco dropped two bulky black valises and pulled a white handkerchief from his shirt pocket.

"How much farther?" he wheezed, dabbing at his face and forehead with the folded cloth. "It seems like we've been walking for an eternity."

"Why don't you give me one of those?" She picked up one of the black valises and turned toward the open meadow.

"I'm sorry. It's just that I've never truly been a *field* man. I'm really more of a researcher—a taxonomist, to be precise. Give me a collection of third-instar larvae and a dissecting microscope and I'm as happy as—"

"A bug?" Kathryn finished the sentence for him.

"All of *this*—the hiking, the exploring, the collecting—this is really Dr. Polchak's forte."

As they walked easily across the open meadow Kathryn looked at him. "May I call you Teddy?"

"I suppose it's inevitable."

"Would you rather I didn't? It's just that I heard Dr. Polchak call you Teddy. "

"That was his little invention. Nicholas just loves to name things. I suppose there's a little taxonomist in his blood as well."

"What's your real name?"

"Eustatius," he said under his breath.

"I'm sorry?"

"So am I. It means *peaceful.* My family is Pennsylvania Dutch."

"Then you're from Pittsburgh, like Dr. Polchak?"

"What makes you think he's from Pittsburgh?" he said with a wink. "Haven't you noticed? Even his honeybees wear black and gold."

They arrived at the perimeter and set down their equipment. Kathryn wasn't sure what she had expected to find at a death scene, but she was surprised at how completely ordinary everything appeared. In the center of the ring was a small depression where the grass was matted and yellow, indicating the original location of the body—but nothing more to indicate that someone she loved had died here only a week ago.

"Nicholas and I met in graduate school at Penn State," Teddy said, unpacking the first of his valises. "We were both studying entomology, and it was there that we both became interested in the forensic aspects of our field. That's when Nicholas and I became friends."

"Dr. Polchak has a friend?"

Teddy smiled. "Have you ever observed a drone fly? It isn't likely—but if you had, you probably would have thought it was a wasp. A wasp makes a distinctive sound. The buzz of a wasp wing registers at about 150 hertz. The drone fly has learned to mimic the wasp's sound almost exactly—147 hertz, to be precise. Listening to them, you cannot tell them apart. The drone fly sounds like a wasp, and he acts like a wasp—but he is in fact a harmless fly. He has no stinger. If there's one thing I've learned in this field, it's that appearances are often deceiving. That is the first principle of taxonomy: Nevermind what a thing *appears* to be—what is its true nature?"

Kathryn lifted one leg and began to step across the yellow police line.

"Wait! Don't!"

"What's wrong? Aren't we allowed?"

"We are allowed, but it would not be wise."

Teddy walked slowly around the perimeter eyeing the yellow patch carefully. "Here," he said at last, "we'll approach from here. When approaching a death scene the first order of business is to establish a single line of approach. That protects the surrounding area from unnecessary disturbance. See there?" He pointed to a wide area of bent and broken grass that surrounded the yellow. "That's where our foolish hunters trampled the area while they were observing the body. I'm afraid they didn't do us any favors." He stepped gingerly across the line and Kathryn followed behind, feeling as though she had just stepped out onto a tightrope.

Teddy studied the shape of the yellowish impression. "The head was up there, and the legs here. Notice the deeper imprint left by the torso. That's where we'll focus."

Kathryn's eyes followed the faded area to where the right leg must have rested. She saw no signs of branches or rocks or objects of any kind.

"I see it too," Teddy nodded. There's no indication of anything that might have held the knee erect prior to fixed lividity. That is most enigmatic."

They carefully made their way back to the valises, and Teddy began to unpack a bizarre selection of devices and paraphernalia. Most of the space seemed to be reserved for a half-dozen quart-sized containers, much larger than any Kathryn had seen yet. He also removed two small hand trowels, some type of long metallic probe, a magnifying glass, and a strange glass cylinder topped with a black rubber cork and a flexible hose.

"I have absolutely no idea what you're doing," Kathryn said.

"How much has Nicholas told you about this whole process?"

"Dr. Polchak tells me nothing—except that he likes to shoot family pets and collect dead bodies." A twinge of remorse came over her as she remembered who she was talking to. "I'm sorry. It's just that—is Dr. Polchak so annoying to everyone? Is it just me or what?"

"Don't take it personally." Teddy returned to the approach point with an armload of gear, depositing it in a heap just outside the fluttering yellow tape. He selected a trowel and a container and stepped carefully across the barrier once again. "Nicholas is not a cruel man. He simply has difficulty relating to...your species."

"You mean women."

"No. I mean your entire species."

"What species is that?"

"Kingdom Animalia, phylum Chordata, and class Mammalia; of the order Primate, in the family Hominidae, genus *Homo*. The species would be *sapiens*."

"I'm not a taxonomist, but isn't that his species, too?"

"Not if you ask him." He wiggled his fingers in the air as he stretched on a pair of bluish green latex gloves, then gently knelt by the yellow patch and laid down a wooden yardstick with one end positioned at the exact center of the open area. At that spot he began working his fingers deep into the dense thatch.

"What are you looking for?"

"I'm collecting leaf litter." He lifted a handful of decomposing shreds of leaf, bark, and grass and dropped it into an open container. "When a body lies exposed in an open area like this, it is quickly inhabited by a series of arthropods—"

"I've heard this part. First come the momma flies, looking for nice neighborhoods with good schools. But because there's no zoning, the whole place goes to pot and everyone moves out to the suburbs."

Teddy smiled. "I see Nicholas has entrusted you with the *technical* version. Perhaps I can fill in a few details." He measured twelve inches out from the site of his first collection and repeated the sifting and gathering process again. "When the egg of a blow fly or flesh fly hatches—about eight to ten hours after oviposition—a small larva emerges, perhaps only two or three millimeters in length. As that larva engorges itself on the decomposing tissues, it passes through three distinct phases of development, known as *instars*. About a week later—depending entirely on the specific species, of course—the third-instar larva ceases to feed and prepares to pupate into an adult fly. It begins to shrink in size, and its skin thickens and darkens into a puparial capsule—a sort of cocoon. Most importantly, the prepuparial larva becomes restless and wanders away from the corpse, seeking a protected site to await eclosion—emergence as a mature fly. Some of these late-instar larvae and puparia will drop off the body and hide in litter close to the ground surface. And those little vagabonds," he said, gingerly depositing his third handful of humus, "are the ones we seek."

"Can I do anything to help?"

Teddy looked up and studied her face thoughtfully.

"Really," she assured him. "I'd like to do *something.*"

"I hope you understand—I thought it best to wait for you to ask." Teddy handed her a magnifying glass and a pair of light tension larval forceps. "Your eyes are better than mine and certainly a *lot* better than Nicholas's. Let's put them to use."

They both knelt down on all fours near the end of the yardstick. "What am I looking for?"

"Puparia. Tiny brown capsules about the size of a grain of rice."

"Like we did at the funeral home."

"This is a most important part of our investigation. The larvae Nicholas collected from the cadaver were in their third instar. Back at the lab he is attempting to rear those larvae to maturity under the same temperature and humidity conditions we find here. Some of those larvae are now beginning to pupate. We should find specimens here at a similar stage of development."

"And if we don't?"

"Then the infestation of the body is at a more advanced state of development than the infestation of the area where the body was discovered. That raises the possibility—only the possibility, mind you—that the body was placed here sometime after the time of death."

Kathryn's heart raced at the suggestion. "Dr. Polchak told me that the body was moved."

"He told *me* that the *leg* was moved," Teddy replied gently. "At this time, we are unable to account for that phenomenon. We must be very careful not to jump to conclusions. For now we must be content to do our homework."

"How far do I have to look?"

"They do have the wanderlust, these little creatures. They may migrate as far as twenty feet away. But concentrate on the circle defined by the yardstick. If there are any puparia to be found, they will probably be found there."

Kathryn began her search with gusto, moving quickly through the crumpled grass. She felt a hand on her shoulder and looked up into Teddy's face.

"Slowly, and very carefully." He patted her shoulder. "We must be careful to see what we see, not what we *wish* to see."

Kathryn started her work again, reluctantly returning to the place where her search began, carefully separating the twisted blades of grass. She felt like a woman doing a self-examination, searching diligently for any telltale lump or bump while at the same time praying that she would find none. If she found no puparia, that meant Jimmy's body might have been moved. If his body had been moved, then someone else was involved—someone who might have done more than just move the body.

Teddy began to dig small core samples of soil at one-foot intervals along the yardstick and sealed each one in a one-liter cylindrical container.

"Some carrion feeders are burrowers," he explained. "We must look a few inches beneath the soil as well."

Suddenly Kathryn's heart sank. There, lying atop the moldy remains of a red maple leaf, was an unmistakable puparium. Teddy followed her eyes.

"As I expected," he said, "as it *should* be. Is the capsule completely enclosed, or is a cap missing from one end, sort of like an open medicine capsule?"

"It's closed."

"Light in color, or dark?"

"Light brown."

"Then it's a young pupa. A very important discovery. Place him in here." He handed her a small plastic vial.

Kathryn returned to her search with greatly diminished enthusiasm. What was the point? The larvae on the ground were apparently at the same stage of development as those taken from the body. Perhaps the body had not been moved after all. Perhaps the coloration of Jimmy's leg was just some unexplainable anomaly. Perhaps all this was a waste of time...and money.

Teddy seemed to sense her change in mood. "Did you know," he said cheerfully, "that there may be more than thirty *million* insect species in the world? Far more than all other species combined—and only about a million have been described and classified so far."

"That's great news," Kathryn murmured.

"Dr. Polchak has studied hundreds of them. He loves to investigate an unfamiliar species—*any* unfamiliar species. And to do so, he believes that he must remain objective. And how can one be objective if one is a part of the very species he hopes to explore? I believe that is why Nicholas has left our species."

Kathryn looked up. "You're joking."

"Oh, he would admit to being Animalia and to having a backbone—and he's a chordate all right. If he was nursed by his mother, then he certainly can't deny being a mammal. I think he would admit to being a primate—and who knows? On a good day, he might even admit to a common family and genus. But I'm afraid that's where it stops. Nicholas is a man in search of a species."

"I didn't know you could resign from your species."

"Technically you can't, of course. But you can refuse to participate. Yes, that's a very good way to put it. Nicholas has decided that he would rather study our species from outside, as an impartial observer."

"Why? Who hurt him?"

Teddy paused. "Suffice it to say that Nicholas has encountered a number of difficult people in his past. And to be honest, this business tends to acquaint one with the more barbarous tendencies of the human species. Somewhere along the line, Nicholas decided he had more in common with the insect world—and so he has turned the tables on us. Now he holds the magnifying glass, and we are in the terrarium. He studies people; he examines them." He let out a sigh. "Personally, I find that it's much more pleasant if you actually get to know someone."

Kathryn watched this tiny, gentle little man as he worked. The few strands of chestnut hair assigned the duty of covering his balding pate drifted helplessly in the wind, fluttering in rhythm with the yellow police line behind him. His round spectacles continually slid down his nose as he worked on all fours, causing him to pause every few moments and nudge them back into place with the back of his hand. He was an altogether harmless and likeable little fellow. How strange it was to find two men, good friends, both drawn to the same esoteric field of study and yet so completely opposite in nature. One tall, one short; one blind, one seeing; one cold, one caring. Maybe there *was* something to what Dr. Polchak believed. Maybe they were *not* the same species...

Securing the lid on the last of his samples, Teddy inserted the long probe into the ground near the center of the yellow patch and noted the soil temperature in his logbook. He then picked up the eighteen-inch sweep net and stood motionless, his eyes darting from side to side as if tracking the movement of the wind itself. In one fluid and remarkably graceful motion he swept the net downward and to the left, followed by a sudden upturn that flipped the long tip of the net up and over the metal ring. It was a simple action, something a child could do, but Kathryn thought that he somehow imbued the motion with the mystery and beauty of a fly fisherman's cast. With his left hand he seized the net just below the tip, quickly twisting and trapping its tiny victims inside. With his free hand he opened a wide-mouth Ball jar, empty except for a half-dozen cotton balls in the bottom. He placed the tip of the net inside and quickly sealed the jar again.

"Ethyl acetate," he explained. "It's a killing jar, if you'll pardon the expression. In about two minutes we can transfer them to alcohol."

"What are they?"

"Blow flies. Mostly *Calliphora vomitoria,* I would guess—they're very common in rural areas and one of the first to arrive after death. We will examine them to determine their species."

"Why?"

"The larvae back at the lab are being reared to maturity for two reasons. First, by determining exactly how long it takes them to reach adulthood, we can work backwards and determine a very precise time of death."

"How can you tell that?"

"Suppose it takes seven days for our specimens to emerge from their puparia. And suppose we know from past studies that this species requires exactly fifteen days between oviposition and final eclosion—to develop from an egg to a mature fly. If we note the exact moment the adult flies emerge from their puparia and count backward fifteen days, we would know the exact time of death. And we would also know the postmortem interval—the amount of time between the moment of death and the discovery of the body."

"How does that help us?"

"It may not. But there is a second reason we are rearing those larvae to maturity. It's very difficult—sometimes quite impossible—to identify the species of a fly while it's still in its larval form. There are ways to tell—but to be certain, you must wait until adulthood, when species becomes obvious. In this case there seems to be no dispute over the time of death—but the possibility *has* been raised that the body was moved sometime after death."

He held up the killing jar and tipped it from side to side. A small pile of lifeless black dots lay huddled at the tip of the soft, gray netting.

"These mature flies will tell us what species we should expect to find when our larvae mature. If there are any surprises—and especially if we find any species not indigenous to this area—then our suspicions will be confirmed. We will know that the body was moved. We may even be able to identify the actual place of death."

Kathryn's eyes betrayed the glimmer of hope she felt. "I'm not promising," he reminded her, "but one can never tell. We're not finished yet."

Teddy repeated the sweeping motion three more times, each time exposing the specimens to the deadly ethyl acetate, then emptying the contents into a vial of isopropyl alcohol. One group was deposited into an empty vial—"For dry mounting later," he explained.

Down on his knees again, he searched among the blades of grass for other living specimens.

Suddenly Kathryn sensed the hiss of compressed air. The black valise by Teddy's side exploded inward and then spiraled up into the air, dropping again a few feet away. An instant later a faint cracking sound echoed past them from the distant woods.

Teddy straightened and reached out for the shattered valise, its back panel blasted outward in curling strips of black sheet metal.

"The case…my specimens…what—?"

Kathryn lunged for Teddy, knocking him flat. She lay stretched across his body, pinning him to the ground.

"Teddy, stay down! Someone's shooting at us!"

Nick snapped the lens cap back on his Nikon, then bent down and shook the leafy green milkweed. Hundreds of tiny black dots rolled off and disappeared into the grass around the decomposing body. They were teneral blow flies, young adults whose wings were still too moist and fragile to allow them to fly. It was a lucky find; they only remain in this transitional state for a few short hours and are seldom photographed. But despite Dr. Ellison's warning back at NC State, Nick's mind was no longer on theoretical research—it was on applied science.

He looked up to see Teddy and Kathryn hurrying toward him from the parking lot. He met them in the middle of the meadow, not far from his alabaster beehive.

"You're late," Nick said, shoving the camera into his knapsack.

Without a word, Kathryn dropped the shattered valise on the ground before him.

"That was careless," he said. "Equipment is expensive, you know."

"Someone tried to kill us," Kathryn said.

Nick turned to Teddy.

"It is possible." Teddy nodded. "This damage was done by a bullet, fired from some distance away."

Nick knelt down and examined the case. "What about the specimens?"

Kathryn's mouth dropped open. "Did you hear what I said? Someone tried to *kill* us!"

"No one tried to kill anyone, Mrs. Guilford."

"How do you know that?"

"Where did the shot come from? How far away were the woods from your location?"

"A good hundred meters," Teddy said.

"And how far was the case from you when it was hit?"

"Maybe ten feet away," Kathryn said, "on the ground."

"So someone fires at you from a hundred meters and misses you by ten feet? That's pretty bad shooting, Mrs. Guilford. If he wanted to kill you he could have come a lot closer than that. And isn't it coincidental that the bullet would strike the case? What was he shooting at, your ankles? Someone wanted to frighten you, that's all. Now what about the specimens?"

"We were able to replace most of them," Teddy said. "That's why we were late. We had to—"

"Wait a minute!" Kathryn broke in. "Is that *it?* Someone fired a gun at us! Whether they were trying to kill us or just scare us, what difference does it make?"

Nick raised his glasses just enough to rub his temples in slow circles. "Mrs. Guilford," he said, "what do you want us to do? Did you get a license plate number? Did you get a description? Did you see a car, a truck—anything at all?"

Kathryn said nothing.

"Then all we know is that someone doesn't want us to continue this investigation. Now *there's* a surprise. The best thing we can do right now is press ahead with the investigation. Time is critical in our discipline, Mrs. Guilford—so why don't you tell me what you and Teddy learned today?"

Kathryn glowered in silence. "First of all," she began slowly, "you were *wrong*. There was nothing to hold up the leg."

Even before she finished the sentence Nick began to shake his head. "I didn't ask what you *believe*, Mrs. Guilford. Tell me what you *know*."

She stopped and reconsidered her choice of words. "We *know* that there was nothing at the death scene to explain how the leg could have been supported." She paused. "If there was something that once held the knee erect, it must have been removed at a later time."

"Very good, Mrs. Guilford. And if there *was* such an object, who could have moved it?"

"I don't know. Maybe the two boys, when they took away the body to the funeral home."

"No."

"Why not?"

"Because the object would have been there when the sheriff viewed the body earlier, and he said he found the body flat."

"Then who else?"

"Think."

"Wait...how about the hunters who discovered the body?"

"Of course."

"But why would *they* move the object?"

"Perhaps to make the body more comfortable."

Kathryn blinked twice.

"It's a common phenomenon at death scenes—and a great nuisance to investigators. A passerby finds a body sprawled out on the ground, let's say with one arm bent behind its back. The passerby says to himself, 'That's got to hurt,' and he helps the poor stiff out by making him more comfortable—and possibly ruins the investigation in the process."

"So Denny or Ronny or Wayne might have rearranged Jimmy's body to make him more *comfortable?*"

"It happens."

"You're only telling me what *can* happen," Kathryn said, "not what *did* happen. How can we know if they really did reposition the body?"

"We can't. That is, unless we ask them."

"Someone must have moved the body before it was found in the woods. Maybe that someone was responsible for Jimmy's death. Maybe the murderer."

"It's possible," Nick conceded. "But there is another possibility you've overlooked." He paused. "The sheriff could have moved the body."

"But he said he didn't."

"Yes." Nick looked directly at her. "That's what he said."

They turned at the sound of a car crunching to a stop in the gravel fifty yards behind them. A moment later the dust settled to reveal the sheriff's black-and-white Crown Victoria. The door opened and the sheriff emerged. The obedient deputy was not far behind, carefully adjusting his hat as he straightened his massive body. The sheriff was out of uniform; he wore blue jeans, boots, and a tight navy T-shirt that emphasized the leanness of his six-foot-two-inch frame. He slipped on his Ray Bans, and they started across the meadow.

"Is this casual day at the sheriff's office?" Nick called out as he approached.

"Thought I'd dress easy today," the sheriff called back. "Sometimes the uniform gets in the way."

"Uniforms often get in the way," Nick said under his breath.

"Saw the razor wire when I drove in. Nice homey touch."

"We like it," Nick said. "It's mostly symbolic, but we do have a legitimate biohazard here."

"I know about that. You caused me a bit of paperwork, you

know. I had to sign off on your last *acquisition*—that old man from over Kensington way. I knew that man."

"You wouldn't know him now."

The sheriff gave Kathryn a peck on the cheek. "Pete St. Clair," he said to Teddy, extending his hand.

"Peter, this is Dr. Tedesco, Dr. Polchak's research assistant."

"The team keeps growing," the sheriff said. "I'd like you all to meet Mr. Benjamin Bohannon, senior deputy of Holcum County."

"*Only* deputy!" Beanie grinned. He leaned forward and extended his beefy hand, wrapping it around Teddy's slender fingers like a huge catcher's mitt. He took Kathryn's hand gently between his thumb and fingers as he might pick up a rose.

"Hullo, Aunt Kathryn," he said, blushing.

"Hello, Beanie dear." She slipped one arm around his trunk-like waist and hugged.

As the deputy reached for Nick's hand, the sheriff said, "Shake the man's *hand*, Benjamin." The deputy began to tighten his grip, and Nick heard the crack of cartilage and felt a flash of pain shoot up his arm.

"Easy, Barney," he said through clenched teeth, "I need that hand."

The deputy relaxed his grip. "Name's Beanie," he frowned.

The sheriff ducked as a single bee streaked by, narrowly missing him.

"I wouldn't stand there if I were you," Nick said, rubbing the blood back into his hand.

"Too close to that hive?"

"Wrong spot. You've heard the expression, *make a beeline?* Well, you're standing in one."

"You're kidding."

"There's clover on the other side of that rise behind you." Nick pointed with his head. "When a bee finds a good source of pollen, she comes back to the hive and does a little dance. The dance communicates the exact location and distance of the pollen—sort of like a briefing before a bombing run. The bees check it out, determine the most efficient path to the source, and establish a beeline—and they don't like anyone blocking the way."

The sheriff shrugged off Nick's advice and turned instead to Kathryn. "Now what's all this about someone taking a shot at you this morning?"

"We were in the woods. Teddy and I were investigating the spot where Jimmy was…where Jimmy died."

"*You* were investigating?" the sheriff said with an angry glance at Nick.

"The shot was fired from at least a hundred meters away," Nick said. "Tell me something, Sheriff—could you hit a man from a hundred meters?"

"Firing from a stationary position? With a scope? Anybody could."

"But they didn't. They hit *this* instead." Nick bent down to the valise and poked his finger into the gaping hole at the exact point where the bullet must have entered. "Could you hit the center of this case from a hundred meters?"

The sheriff estimated the entry point. It was well left of center and near the bottom of the case. "Easy."

"They were aiming at the case, that's for sure," Nick said. "And anyone would naturally aim for the center of the case. But the bullet dropped a good four inches en route. I'd say he fired from more like *three* hundred yards away."

The sheriff looked at him. "I thought you were a Bug Man."

"I took a ballistics course at Quantico," Nick said. "I'm a big fan of continuing education."

Now the sheriff turned to Kathryn. "The doc is right. Whoever it was wasn't aiming at you."

"Peter, someone wants us to stop this investigation. But who? And why?"

"Now hold on," the sheriff said. "Let's not get paranoid here. It might just have been a prank."

"A *prank?* I don't see how—"

"Look, the two of you go crawling around in the middle of an open meadow. What do you suppose you look like to a man with a rifle three hundred yards away?"

"A man with a *rifle?*" Nick raised one eyebrow. "Why would a man be out there with a rifle this time of year? What's in season right now, Sheriff?"

"Nothing," the sheriff admitted. "But a lot of the boys head out that way to work on their deer stands. And while they're out there, they take a little target practice. They'll fire at anything: a stump, a limb—"

"A person?"

"That's why I said it might've been a prank. Some good ol' boy is out taking potshots in the woods; he sees you two, he sees the case…pretty hard to resist. I'll bet you two just about jumped out of your skins."

"You don't seem very concerned," Nick said.

The sheriff's mood changed in an instant. He turned to Nick with a cold stare. "I'm concerned," he said. "I'm concerned that you'd let her go out there in the first place. I'm concerned that you put her in harm's way."

"Stop it!" Kathryn said. "Nobody *let* me do anything. I wanted to go. And no matter why this happened, it's not going to change my mind about anything."

No one spoke for a full minute. The sheriff was the first to break the silence.

"I got to thinking things over last night, and I reconsidered. I think we should cooperate on this. I still think it's a waste of time, but if you're going to go to the trouble—and the expense," he glanced at Nick, "then I'd like to know what you come up with. That way if you do turn up anything, I can take the ball and run with it."

"Thank you." Kathryn squeezed his arm. "That's very thoughtful."

"Yes," Nick said, "I'm sure a great *deal* of thought went into this. But it has to work both ways, Sheriff."

"How do you mean?"

"I'll be happy to share with you anything I find. But in return I'd like access to some things *you've* got."

"Like what?"

"Like the photos of the death scene. I assume you took some? And a look at any test results. And most importantly"—he leaned forward—"I want permission to interview the major players."

"Who are we talking about?"

"The hunters, the coroner, the sister of the deceased..."

"I already took care of that," the sheriff said. "I can brief you."

"No. *I* want to interview them. I want a clear field to talk to whomever I want, in any way I want. And in return," he said with a smile, "I'll be happy to brief *you*."

The sheriff turned to Kathryn with a look of silent complaint.

"Peter," she said, "we just want to talk to them. You've probably already asked all the same questions. Dr. Polchak just wants to make sure there was nothing they missed."

"You mean nothing *I* missed," he scowled. "Okay, Doc. You're free to ask around—but on one condition." He nodded toward Kathryn. "She goes with you. I want somebody there who knows these people, somebody who knows how far is *too* far."

Nick looked at Kathryn. "I doubt she would have it any other way."

Another honeybee whizzed by close. The sheriff ducked his head again and swatted at the dark streak.

Nick shook his head. "I would definitely *not* do that."

Suddenly the sheriff spit out a curse, slapping the side of his neck and batting at the air around him.

"I warned you not to do that," Nick said. "Quick, let me see it."

"I'm fine," he said angrily, brushing him aside.

"Oh Peter, let him look," Kathryn said. "Don't be such a baby."

"Leave me alone," the sheriff growled, rubbing at his eyes.

Nick watched him.

"Please, Peter," Kathryn said again.

"Oh, for the love of… There." He turned his head to one side.

"Too late now," Nick shrugged.

"Too late for what?"

"When the stinger pulls out of the bee, it's still surrounded by part of the abdominal muscle wall. The muscle acts like a pump," he said, making a squeezing gesture with his fist. "It continues to pump venom into the wound—unless you pull it out within the first five seconds."

"Big deal," the sheriff sneered. "It's just a bee sting."

"Not to you it's not."

Kathryn looked at Peter, then at Nick. "What do you mean?"

"Tell her," Nick said. "Tell her what you're feeling. Your eyes itch and your breathing is labored. Your pulse is racing, your skin is pale, and you've already got a welt the size of a quarter at the injection site. You're experiencing a considerable anaphylactic shock."

Kathryn felt Peter's forehead and face with the back of her hand.

"When is the last time you were stung by a bee?" Nick asked.

"Beats me. Not since I was a kid, I guess."

"Then you're developing a sensitivity to Hymenoptera venom."

"Is that serious?" Kathryn asked.

"It's serious to about four people out of a thousand. They drop dead from a single sting. You're a lucky guy, Sheriff. You found out about your allergy before the Big One hit. If I were you I'd stop by a drugstore and pick up an epinephrine syringe—and I'd carry it with me at all times."

"I'm not walking around with a needle like some…drug addict," he said, glancing sheepishly at Kathryn.

"It's your life. But a little friendly advice. Be careful in the summer, especially on bright, sunny days. I'd stick to the uniform—

bees don't like dark colors. And the next time your friendly neighborhood entomologist tells you to step out of a beeline," he said bluntly, "try *listening*. Ignorance can get you killed—and you've got a bad case."

"Thanks for the friendly advice."

"Now a piece of advice from me," Kathryn scolded. "Go lie down for a while, Peter. You look terrible."

"I got work to do."

"Don't make me pull out your gun and shoot you in the leg."

He cracked a smile. "Okay. But only for you." He kissed her on the forehead, then turned to Nick one last time. "So we're going to *cooperate*. You get what I get, and the other way around."

Nick smiled. "Just think of us as one big family. I know I do."

CHAPTER 11

The door to the Buck Stop Bar and Grill burst open and Peter St. Clair headed straight for the table of the three hunters. The sheriff grabbed Ronny by both lapels, dragged him from his chair, and jammed him up against the wall; the TV hanging overhead dipped and wobbled, and the screen went black. Ronny stood three inches taller than the sheriff and outweighed him by twenty pounds, but there was no mistaking the alpha male here.

The straight-faced man behind the bar set down a glass and reached below the counter.

"Leave it, Eddie," Pete called over his shoulder. "This is official business." The sheriff locked eyes with his paralyzed prey. "What's this I hear about someone taking a shot at Kathryn?"

"Not at Kathryn," Ronny fumbled. "Never at her. At that Bug Man guy, the one with all the nets and bottles and stuff."

Wayne got up from his chair and edged toward the door; the massive deputy filled the doorway, blocking his way. "We didn't fire at anyone, Pete," Wayne said. "We just aimed at a little suitcase. Thought it would—you know—send a message."

"What message?"

"You know—to leave it alone. To go away and stop making trouble."

Pete dropped his head and let out a rumbling growl. "You idiots! Is that the message you think you sent? That's like standing in front of a candy jar with your hands in your pockets! Your little message told them somebody has something to *hide*—now they're twice as determined to see it through."

"But…you said somebody ought to have a talk with that Bug Man."

"That wasn't the Bug Man! That was just his assistant, some little guy who goes around catching butterflies for him."

Two truckers rose from their table at the back of the bar. They glanced up at the broken TV and let out a curse as they passed and headed for the door.

The sheriff released Ronny and stepped away. "Which one of you fired that shot?"

No one answered.

Pete looked at Ronny again. "You're the one with the Leupold scope." He stood across the table, eyeing each one of them. "Okay." The sheriff nodded slowly. "But no more of this. You could have hit Kathryn."

"C'mon, Pete. From that distance?"

"You could have hit Kathryn. What do you think I would do if that happened?"

No one had the slightest doubt.

The first trucker arrived at the doorway, where the deputy still stood transfixed.

"Move," the man growled.

The deputy just smiled.

"Hey, Sheriff," the second trucker called back. "Tell this idiot boy of yours to get his big carcass out of the doorway."

The sheriff turned and looked at him. "Move him yourself."

The man hesitated. "You mean it?"

The sheriff slid off his star, held it up, then dropped it into his shirt pocket. "Be my guest."

The first trucker shoved Beanie hard with both hands, barely budging his immense form.

"I said *move,*" the man grumbled, backhanding the deputy hard with his right hand. Beanie absorbed the blow and turned back to face the man with an expression not of anger but of hurt and confusion.

The trucker took a second swing at Beanie, then a third.

Beanie slowly raised both arms and tucked his head, as if ducking from an unexpected summer shower.

The trucker's hands closed into fists and he began to rain down a hail of blows. He stepped in and landed a left and a right to the torso, with no apparent effect at all. He swung a roundhouse left that glanced off the top of the deputy's head, then an uppercut that just touched the tip of his barely exposed chin. He finally stepped back and paused, panting, and when Beanie lifted his head like an ill-fated bird at a turkey shoot, the man shot a solid right cross to Beanie's left eye, tearing open the skin and sending blood trickling down his cheek.

"Sheriff!" the bartender said. "Help your boy there."

"The boy can take care of himself," Pete replied.

The man's blows were becoming wilder and weaker and much less frequent. Beanie somehow absorbed each blow, peeking out from under his arms and staring patiently at the sheriff.

The first man finally stepped back in exhaustion, and his partner, sensing his opportunity, stepped up. Beanie remained immobile, blood dripping from his cheek to the wooden floor below.

"Benjamin," the sheriff said quietly, and then made one large nod.

The deputy stepped forward and reached for the first trucker with his enormous hands. The man swung a wild right at Beanie's midsection, much slower than before. Beanie took the blow and swallowed the man's wrist with his right hand; with his left hand he seized his forearm just below the elbow and drew him closer. The man struggled uselessly to pull away, as if ensnared by some great white tar baby. Suddenly Beanie's vise-like hands tightened and twisted. There was a crack like the report of a rifle, and then a scream.

Beanie released his hands, and the man stumbled back against his partner, his right forearm dangling at a ninety-degree angle.

The trucker lay sprawled on the barroom floor, clutching his shattered arm across his chest. Beanie stood over him, smiling at the sheriff, no longer aware of the man's existence.

The sheriff glanced at the deputy's bleeding face. "Gonna need a couple of stitches. We better head back to the office and have Agnes take a look at it."

On the way to the door the sheriff poked his toe at the man's dangling hand. The trucker screamed in agony and jerked away.

"Better get *that* fixed too," he said.

The sheriff turned back to the three hunters one last time. "Think about this, you morons: Now the finger's pointed at you more than ever. What are you going to do now?"

The door slammed shut. The men stared at one another in silence.

"He's right," Denny whispered. "What *are* we going to do now?"

CHAPTER 12

What is this stuff?" Nick sneered, licking at the little pink spoon. "It tastes like butyl rubber. That's it—it tastes like surgical tubing."

"That's chocolate mousse royale," the man behind the ice cream counter said with a roll of his eyes. His thick southern accent made the word *royale* sound especially ludicrous.

"What about that green stuff? What's that?"

"Mint chocolate chip," the man said tiredly.

"Okay, give me a sample of that."

The stout little man behind the counter was Hiram Wilkins, known to all but the oldest residents of Rayford as Will, the proprietor of Wilkins's Drug Emporium and the elected coroner of Holcum County. Mr. Wilkins was dressed in his shopkeeper's white shirt and black tie, which he never seemed to change regardless of season or occasion. He had a habit of repeatedly running one finger between his neck and collar and tugging, as if to release the buildup of pressure from his expanding midsection below. He wore a well-stained apron that he donned whenever he stepped behind the ice cream counter, a position he now occupied with diminishing patience.

"Well?" Mr. Wilkins demanded.

"I can't place it," Nick said thoughtfully. "Wait—I've got it. Scope. It tastes like mouthwash."

"Look, you've had five samples. Are you going to buy something or—"

They were interrupted by the jingling of the front door. Kathryn entered and stepped up to the ice cream counter with a smile.

"Hello, Kathryn," Mr. Wilkins beamed. "What can I get for you today?"

"I'll have what he's having." She gestured to Nick.

Mr. Wilkins's face dropped. "He don't *know* what he's having."

"Then I'll just have a scoop of cookie dough."

"What about you?" Mr. Wilkins glowered.

"Nothing for me, thanks—I was just waiting for the lady. What I *would* like is to ask you a few questions. I wonder if you would mind joining us for a few minutes," he glanced around at the empty store, "whenever you can find a free moment."

Nick and Kathryn sat down at a round, red Formica table in front of the store window. The chairs had red vinyl seats to match, and the backs and legs were made of thick black wire that twisted and curved to form the shape of hearts. Mr. Wilkins balanced himself uncomfortably on one of these, opposite Dr. Polchak.

"What's this all about?" he said.

"I understand that you are the coroner of Holcum County."

"That's right. Duly elected."

Nick smiled.

"I wanted to have a chance to meet you. I'm Dr. Nicholas Polchak, research entomologist and diplomate of the American

Board of Forensic Entomologists." He leaned forward and extended his hand. "I understand we're colleagues."

Mr. Wilkins smiled vaguely and shook his hand.

"Haven't we met before?" Nick continued. "Your name is very familiar. Dr. Wilkins...Dr. Wilkins... Did we meet at the American Academy of Forensic Sciences convention last year? Or perhaps it was the National Association of Medical Examiners."

Kathryn kicked him under the table.

"No matter." Nick rubbed his shin. "I wanted to ask you some questions about your examination of the body of James McAllister."

"I can't discuss that," Mr. Wilkins said with a wave of his hand. "That's official business. You understand."

"I do indeed," Nick said, "but as Mrs. Guilford will verify, we're here under the jurisdiction of Sheriff St. Clair. That makes this an official inquiry. You can call him if you like."

Mr. Wilkins tugged again at his collar and shifted awkwardly on his wobbling chair.

"What is it you want to know?"

"Mr. McAllister's death was unwitnessed, which in most cases makes an autopsy mandatory—yet you declined to request an autopsy. Why?"

"Because it was definitely a suicide. No doubt about it."

"*No* doubt?" Nick arched one eyebrow. "In that case, I'd like to ask you to explain something to me. How do you account for the unusual lividity in the right leg? The right foot and ankle were marked, but not the dorsal surface of the leg itself. That indicates that the leg was supported in an upright position at the time of death and then moved several hours later."

Mr. Wilkins blinked hard. "How did you—"

"I had a chance to examine the body—very briefly."

"I never saw that. I never saw the leg."

"Really? Why not?"

"Well...he had clothes on."

Nick looked at him blankly. "Did you make any effort to examine *under* the clothing?"

"The body was in no condition for that sort of thing."

"That's because he was dead. That's sort of the whole point, Mr. Wilkins. As a colleague, may I make an observation? Personally, I find it very difficult to determine the cause of death by looking at someone's *outfit.*"

Mr. Wilkins tugged harder at his collar.

"There's something else you missed," Nick continued. "Something that could be quite important."

Kathryn straightened and looked at Nick.

"The bullet produced two wounds—an entry wound here," he pointed to his right temple,"and an exit wound on the opposite side. But there was a third wound—*here.*" He indicated an area on the forehead just to the left of center.

"That could have happened when the body fell."

"When the body fell *backwards?*"

"What difference does it make? We know that his death was caused by the bullet, so what does it matter if there was another wound?"

"It matters because the wound was infested by larvae. Flies oviposit in traumatized tissues. In other words, they don't lay eggs on unbroken skin—they look for open wounds. It took quite a blow to open that wound—a blow that could cause a man to lose consciousness. The third wound was not caused by the bullet *or* the fall. That means that the wound was probably present at the time of death. Now tell me this, Mr. Wilkins"—he leaned back in his chair—"how do you suppose Mr. McAllister injured his head?"

"How would I know? A body gets pretty banged up lying around in the woods for a week."

"Yes it does, but only in certain ways. As the eggs hatch into larvae, they begin to consume the tissues outward from the place of oviposition. That explains why the eye sockets grew larger and the bullet wounds increased in size—but it does *not* explain how an unrelated wound spontaneously opened in the center of the forehead."

Mr. Wilkins said nothing.

"I'll give you a hint: The wound must have been caused by an *object*."

"But there wasn't no object."

"You see?" Nick smiled at Kathryn. "This is what happens when two *professionals* put their heads together. Mr. Wilkins has rightly deduced that, since no object capable of causing the wound was present at the death scene, then something—or someone—must have taken the object away. Now, who would have had motive to do such a thing? Perhaps the one who employed the object to strike Mr. McAllister—perhaps his killer."

"But he died from a gunshot wound from his own gun!"

"An unconscious man makes an easy target, Mr. Wilkins. The sheriff says the gunpowder residue test on Mr. McAllister's hand proved negative. That can be explained by the clean firing of the gun—but it can also be explained by someone else firing the gun."

Kathryn sat open-mouthed, staring at Mr. Wilkins. The combined effect of her probing eyes and Nick's accusing questions was more than he could bear. His face grew red and hot, and he tugged at his collar until his tie hung low like a noose around his bloated neck.

"You're only guessing," he said. "You don't know any of this."

Nick said nothing for a moment. "You're right," he said quietly. "I *am* guessing. Mr. McAllister could have wounded himself prior to entering the woods. Or perhaps he injured himself *in* the woods—perhaps he bumped his head on a tree limb on the way to the meadow. I don't know, Mr. Wilkins. My point is, you don't know either. Where I come from, we call that doubt."

"And where *I* come from, when a man has a bullet hole through his head and he's holding the gun, that's a suicide."

"No, Mr. Wilkins, that's an *apparent* suicide."

"Nobody had any reason to think otherwise."

"*You* had reason—if you had done your job. You didn't bother to look under the victim's clothing. You overlooked a wound in the center of his forehead. Did you roll the body over? Did you check for indications of other wounds? If you couldn't get a blood or urine sample for toxicology screening, did you take a tissue sample?"

"Don't tell me how to do my job!"

"Mr. Wilkins," Kathryn cut in, "we're not here to criticize you. It's just that the investigation went so quickly, there were some things left—"

"I am the duly elected coroner of Holcum County," he said with all the dignity he could muster. "I work under the authority of the chief medical examiner's office of North Carolina! I submitted my report to the CMEO, and they saw no reason to question my conclusions."

"Your *conclusions?*" Nick almost laughed. "Almost every county in North Carolina has a medical examiner appointed by the CMEO to a three-year term, appointed from a list of licensed physicians. But a tiny handful of counties—like this one—are still on the old coroner system, where a coroner is 'duly elected' from a list of anybody who wants the job."

The front door jingled again, and an older gentleman stepped tentatively inside. He was stooped, and he wore his light gray trousers well above his waist, giving the impression that his black-and-red suspenders exerted tremendous tension. He glanced around the room with a puzzled expression.

"Krispy Kreme Donuts?"

"Down the way!" Mr. Wilkins thundered, and the old man muttered something inaudible and shuffled out again.

The room was ominously silent—the kind of silence that follows the blast of a concussion grenade. Nick spoke first, in a perfectly pleasant tone of voice. "Do you know what item is shoplifted from drugstores more than any other?"

Mr. Wilkins and Kathryn both stared at him, expressionless.

"You'd think it would be candy or condoms. Or aspirin. Maybe infant formula or cold medicine. Nope. Know what it is?" He leaned forward and looked at both of them. "Hemorrhoid cream."

He sat back in his chair, allowing the profundity of this revelation to have its full impact. Kathryn and Mr. Wilkins continued to stare blankly, waiting—for *something*.

Now Nick looked directly at Mr. Wilkins.

"But you knew that, didn't you, Mr. Wilkins? You knew that because you *own* a drugstore. You know all about hemorrhoid cream and insoles and nasal spray and those little foam beverage coolers with NASCAR Racing on the side." As he spoke he leaned steadily forward until he inclined well over the table in Mr. Wilkins's direction.

"But you don't know diddly-squat about forensic pathology, now do you?"

Mr. Wilkins jumped up from his chair and sent it clattering across the linoleum floor. He ripped off his apron and threw it onto the table. His face raged red, and the veins that framed his forehead bulged like purple tree roots.

"I think it's time to go," Kathryn said firmly, grabbing Nick by the arm and pulling him toward the door. In the open doorway Nick turned one last time.

"Is it too late to get a scoop of that butyl rubber royale?"

Kathryn shoved him through the doorway, and the door jingled shut behind them. She hustled him down the sidewalk as the fading roar of obscenities snapped at their heels.

"If there's one thing I can't stand," Nick said, frowning, "it's bad ice cream."

Kathryn turned on him. "Why do you *do* that?"

"Do what?"

"Every time you talk to someone you almost start a fight!"

"That's true. You seem to have a lot of argumentative people down here."

"I don't see what you hope to accomplish this way. What's the good in giving poor Mr. Wilkins a heart attack?"

"It could do a great deal of good, if it allows a competent professional to take over Mr. Wilkins's job. Look, Mrs. Guilford, don't feel too sorry for poor Mr. Wilkins. What we discovered in our little interview is that he completely *botched* the original investigation. If that examination had been conducted by a medical examiner, there's a good chance there would have been an autopsy. They would have noticed the unusual lividity, and they would have taken a good look at that third wound—and you might have gotten the investigation you wanted. As it is, Mr. Wilkins signed off on the death certificate without so much as a second look, and they enbalmed your friend before the ink was dry. I only had time to do a ten-minute examination and to collect a bare handful of specimens. That means that we're trying to conduct an investigation with almost *no* evidence and *no* chance for a second look—all thanks to your 'poor Mr. Wilkins.'"

"Why didn't you tell me before about that third wound? Is there anything *else* you haven't told me?"

"That's the question I keep asking you."

Kathryn folded her arms and scowled.

"Well then," Nick said, "I guess we'll both find out what we want to know when we need to know."

"If we have almost no evidence and no chance for a second look, then what *have* we got?"

"We have doubt," Nick said. "That's a start."

"Okay, we have doubt—but as you would say, what do we *know?*"

"Very good, Mrs. Guilford. You've been listening." He stopped and thought carefully. "We know that the anomalous lividity in the victim's leg suggests that the body was moved—at least, we've been unable to account for it in any other way. We know there was a wound on the victim's head unrelated to the gunshot wounds that may have required the involvement of a second party. And on top of that, we have specimens from all three wounds—specimens that are approaching adulthood right now in their little puparia back at the lab."

"What will *they* tell us?"

"Suppose your friend *was* murdered, with the right leg supported at first in an upright position by some object. Eight hours later, lividity became fixed—and then the body was transported to the site in the woods where it was discovered. That scenario would account for the unusual coloration of the leg."

"Okay..."

"If the body was moved, that means the murder could have been committed anywhere. Across town—in the middle of a city—even in another state. Remember, Mrs. Guilford, different flies are unique to different areas. *Calliphora vicina,* for example, is synanthropic—it lives with people. It's found almost exclusively in large cities and towns. But *Calliphora vomitoria* is found only in rural areas. Now suppose our flies turn out to be *vicinas.* How did a city fly get on a body that supposedly died miles from the nearest town? The presence of *Calliphora vicina* would confirm our suspicion that the body was moved—and that would mean that your friend must have been murdered."

"But how could we prove *who* murdered him?"

"We couldn't—not with what we have now. But we would have enough evidence to compel Mr. Wilkins to request an order of exhumation—and if he refused, we could go over his head. The remains would be sent to the CMEO where a real, live pathologist who doesn't sell ice cream on the side could perform a decent autopsy. Who knows what might turn up?"

"And what if the flies turn out to be normal? What if we only find the species that are *supposed* to be there?"

Nick paused. "Then you spent a great deal of money for nothing, and you raised several more questions about your friend's death that may never be answered."

Kathryn stood quietly for a long time. Nick had warned her from the beginning that their investigation might produce nothing. She had known about this possibility all along—but she had never allowed herself to truly consider it before.

"So what do we do now," she asked glumly, "just sit around and wait for a bunch of bugs to grow up?"

"I'm not very good at sitting around. That's what I've got Teddy for. He checks the pupae every hour, and he'll contact us the moment the adult flies begin to emerge. Our time can be better spent asking some more questions. But essentially, yes—we just sit around and wait for a bunch of bugs to grow up."

"Then it all comes down to the flies."

"In my business, Mrs. Guilford, it *always* comes down to the flies."

Kathryn stared at the ceiling fan that turned slowly and rhythmically above her, slicing a hole through the thick night air. She lay heavy and still, feeling the throb of exhaustion in every limb. She had dropped her things at the front door and headed directly for the bedroom, not even pausing to turn on the lights or check her messages. Why bother? The flashing red light told her there were four, and they would all be from the bank: Margaret wanting to know the whereabouts of some elusive file or Robert John asking exactly how many days she was taking off—though she had told him a half-dozen times—or Anna asking if she could just take a few minutes to review the so-and-so account.

She sprawled on top of the covers exactly as she first lay down, her entire body begging her to just stop moving. And so she lay, feeling the warm woolen blanket of sleep begin to creep up over her, mesmerized by the spinning blades above, spinning around the bright brass hub that gleamed each time it caught the headlights of a passing car through the window. It gleamed and then darkened and then gleamed again. On...and off...and on.

Kathryn saw herself swing open the screen door and step out onto the porch on a sultry July night almost ten years past. She instinctively banged her fist on the wall below the yellow porch light, which responded by flickering on and then off and then on again.

"When are we gonna fix this thing, Momma?" she called back into the house. Behind her she could hear the sound of *Matlock* on the television and the soft hissing sighs of the steam iron.

"Why don't you get one of those boys of yours to fix it?" her mother called back. "Maybe they're not smart enough."

"They're smart enough, all right."

"Maybe they don't *want* that bright ol' porch light shinin' all the time. Maybe they don't mind a little dark out there on the porch. Maybe they're *too* smart to fix it."

"If they're so smart, how come they're all three leaving me alone on a Saturday night?" She flopped down on the porch swing and sulked, watching the ailing porch light as it periodically flickered off and then on.

"Where have those boys been to lately? You think they found themselves a couple of Fayetteville sweethearts what stole their hearts away?"

"Stop it, Momma. Andy says things have been hoppin' at the Fort ever since those Iraqi boys marched into Kuwait. He says the Airborne might have to go over there and take care of it. They could get called up any day now."

"I sure hope not."

"They might could. Andy says he wants to go. Says it might speed up his commission."

"I don't like to hear that," her momma said. "I don't like to hear that one bit."

The screen door opened slowly, and Kathryn's mother stepped out, pulling an afghan tight around her shoulders. She never seemed to step outside without a covering, even on a muggy summer night. "It's the night air," she would always say. She looked older than her forty-five years, and she walked thickly and heavily as if she had physically carried the burden of raising a daughter alone for a decade. She sat down on the porch swing beside Kathryn and began to gently stroke her long, auburn hair.

"You got your daddy's hair," she said, smiling, "and his eyes, too. Thank the Lord, he took those ears of his to the grave." They both laughed.

"Your daddy and I got married just out of high school. Seems like most everybody did back then—that was June of '63. Just a year later his number came up, and he was off to Vietnam. I was worried sick, but he said not to go on about it. They was gonna make short work of it; they was gonna march right up the Ho Chi Minh Trail to China, and he'd be back before I even knew he was gone." She stared vacantly into the darkness as she spoke. "I knew he was gone all right. I was worried sick for three years."

"Andy says we got them outgunned and outmanned and outsmarted. We got the whole United Nations on our side! Andy says it's not like Vietnam."

Her mother smiled and studied her eyes. "Andy says this and Andy says that! How come it's never 'Jimmy says' or 'Peter says' anymore?"

Kathryn grinned and bent forward, flipping her hair up over her head, then straightened again and tossed it back. Her mother leaned forward and kissed her forehead, then stiffly rose, creaking and groaning like the weathered floorboards beneath her feet. She paused at the door and gave the porch light another thump.

On, then off and on, then off again.

"You be smart," her mother said from the darkness. "Most girls don't get to choose."

Kathryn sat rocking in the quiet blackness, pondering her mother's words, when she heard a sharp crack from the woods in front of the house. She stared hard into the darkness, and a moment later a lone figure emerged into the clearing and headed straight for the porch.

"Who's that?" Kathryn called out.

"Who you think?" the figure replied. "Who you expecting?"

"Jimmy!" She bounced down the front porch steps to meet him. "Where you been so long?" she scolded. "I was about to die of loneliness here!"

"Like I believe *that,*" he said, laughing. He slid his arm around her waist, but she pulled away and ran to the porch swing, beckoning him to join her.

"What's goin' on?" she asked eagerly. "I hardly seen *any* of you."

"Miss me?"

"I miss all of you. Now tell me—what's the word at the Fort?"

"It's gonna happen, Kath," he said solemnly. "Word is we're goin' in. Nobody knows for sure, but everybody thinks so."

"When?"

"A month. Maybe less."

She sat in stunned silence. "*All* of you?"

The yellow porch light fizzled and switched on again, and for the first time Kathryn could see clearly into Jimmy's face and eyes. There was something there that she hadn't seen before—something her mother had tried to warn her about, something she had denied, something she secretly dreaded and hoped would never come. But it *had* come. It was here. Jimmy picked up her hand and held it tightly.

"I've known you for a long time, Kath..."

The words made her heart feel suddenly sick, and she longed to pull away and run into the house, to keep the words from ever being spoken. But she knew that if Jimmy could summon the courage to speak them, then she owed it to him to listen. She steeled her eyes against the flood of emotions she felt within and waited for the words that would most certainly follow.

"We been friends for a long time. We been more than friends. *I* been more, that is," he stammered. But there were too many thoughts and too few words, and he jumped up in frustration and slammed the porch post hard with the butt of his hand. The porch light sizzled and went out.

He stood silently in the darkness, then suddenly spun around. "You remember that day we drove way over to Asheville? You was maybe sixteen, no more."

"I remember."

"The day went long, the traffic was bad, we got on the road real late."

"And it was pouring rain. A hurricane, I think. We couldn't see a thing."

"So we pulled under an overpass just outside Greensboro to wait it out."

"And we fell asleep!" She laughed. "We didn't get home till the next morning! Did I ever catch it from Momma," she whistled. "Who knows what she must have thought—what *everybody* thought!"

Jimmy sat down beside her again. "You fell asleep. You put your head back against my shoulder, and you fell asleep. But I watched. I watched you all night long."

They sat in silence.

"I don't know what everybody else thought," he said with gathering momentum, "but I'll tell you what *I* thought."

"Jimmy...wait—"

"I thought it was the best night of my whole life. I thought that for the first time I was that close to what I wanted. And I knew I wanted a whole lifetime of nights like that."

He took her hand again. It was strangely limp.

"I got to go. But I don't want to leave without telling you... I want to...I want to ask you to..."

The porch light suddenly switched on again and in one terrible instant Jimmy saw what was in Kathryn's eyes—he saw *everything:* fear, remorse, compassion, pity—and the unmistakable answer to his unvoiced question. He saw it all, and there could be no more mistake than if it were painted on the side of a barn.

He dropped her hand.

"I want to ask you to write to me," he said softly. "I'd kick myself if I left without reminding you."

Kathryn closed her eyes, knowing that they had surely betrayed her. She prayed for the light to go out again so that she could hide, so that they could both pretend that the words had never been spoken and go back to the way they had always been. A thousand explanations and excuses ran through her mind, but she knew that there was absolutely nothing she could say. Her traitorous eyes had said it all, and now things could never be the same again.

Jimmy slowly rose, his stance less confident than it was just a moment ago.

"Don't go," she pleaded, tugging on his hand.

"I better." He pulled away.

"I *will* write, because I *care* about you." Good words, kind words, but only fossils of the words he'd hoped to hear. They stung him as he turned and headed down the steps toward the woods.

"Jimmy!" she called after him in tears, "you be careful! I'll write to you, and you write back, okay? *Jimmy!*"

The light sputtered out.

Kathryn saw herself back on the porch swing, her legs folded and her face in her hands, crying gently in the darkness. Now she understood her mother's words: *Most girls don't get to choose.* Most girls are lucky, she thought. She didn't want to choose. She only wanted to say yes, but never, ever no. She wanted to be chosen and never have to shatter the hopes of someone who was so close…but not quite close enough.

A moment later Kathryn heard another sound from the woods. Why was he coming back, and what in the world would he say this time? But another silhouette emerged into the clearing with a different manner and a longer gait.

"Who's there?" Kathryn called, but there was no response. "Call out, or I'll set loose the dog!"

"Turn that old cur loose," came the reply. "I haven't had a good laugh all day."

Andy!

Kathryn bounded down the steps and met him halfway, throwing her arms around his neck and almost knocking him over.

"I *have* been away too long." He laughed, pulling back and looking into her emerald eyes.

"Oh, Andy, it's been the worst evening! But I don't want to talk about it—come sit with me." She took him by the hand and led him to the porch swing.

As they passed the porch light, he reached out and gave it a thump. The amber light cast deep shadows across his chiseled face and made his bottomless brown eyes black as the night. Kathryn watched the shadows cut deep rivulets through his wavy bronze hair. His arms were long and muscular, and he was broad-chested. He had the stature and physique of a man, but whenever he faced her he always dropped one shoulder like an awkward boy. His smile was the best of all; when Andy smiled his face lit up like a torch.

"It's happenin', Kath," he said with excitement. "They say the division's gonna be called up any time now—I mean the whole 82d Airborne! They say we're heading for a base in Saudi Arabia."

"I know," she said glumly.

He looked at her. "Who was that I passed coming back through the woods?"

Kathryn said nothing.

"I *see.*" He smiled. "There's been another rooster in the hen-house. Well you know what they say"—he nodded toward the flickering porch light—"where there's light, there's bugs."

"It was just Jimmy."

"And what did Private James McAllister want this evening?"

"Maybe it's none of your business."

"Just wanted to drop by and set a spell with the two old spinsters?"

"He just wanted to *marry* me, that's all. Oh, Andy, it was awful. I love Jimmy—I've always loved Jimmy, but—"

"But not *that* way." He finished the sentence for her, and she was glad, because the words sounded so hollow and cheap. "So he asked you to marry him?"

"Not quite. But he was about to."

"What stopped him?"

"I think he just knew, and he backed off."

"No wonder he had his tail between his legs." Andy whistled.

"I guess he'll get over it."

"Maybe. I know I wouldn't." Andy stepped to the light and gave it a thump. It flicked on. "Guess I can't blame him. He's always loved you—ever since we were kids."

"I never knew that!"

"I knew. Pete knew. Even your momma knew. We could all tell." The light blinked off, and he gave it another tap. "I wonder if they all know about me?"

Kathryn felt a lump in her throat.

"I wonder...," he said, "I just wonder what you'd say if I was to ask you the same question?"

"What question?"

"Jimmy's question. The one he never quite got out."

"Well," Kathryn said indignantly, "you'll never know unless you ask."

"Oh, I don't know. Jimmy knew without asking." He wiggled his finger. "Come here for a minute."

Kathryn sat glaring at him. There was something about his arrogance and overconfidence that infuriated her—but there was something else about it that she couldn't quite explain. She stamped over to him and stood, arms folded, nose turned upward.

He wrapped his arms around her waist and stared deep into her eyes.

"What are you doing?" She arched away from him.

"Looking for my answer—just like Jimmy did."

"How do *you* know what Jimmy did?"

"Something tipped him off, and I'm betting it was your eyes. You say everything with your eyes. Always have. And they never lie."

"So what do you see?"

He pulled her closer and looked again. "I see *yes*."

"Yes, what?"

"*Yes,* you love me. *Yes,* you always have. And *yes,* you'll marry me."

"You just might be mistaken," she scolded.

"I'm not." He smiled.

"What makes you so cocksure?"

"'Cause when I look in your eyes this close I see *my* eyes—and I know what mine are saying."

She looked into his eyes, and he was right. It was all there, and there could be no mistake about it.

He pulled her in tight and they kissed, long and deep.

She slowly opened her eyes again—and Andy's face began to somehow change. It grew longer and more angular. Not less handsome, just…different. She had never noticed it before, but he wore *glasses.* They began as tiny round spectacles like an elf might wear, but as she watched they began to grow to an enormous size, and Andy's beautiful brown eyes began to soften and fade until they floated away like two gray orbs—then they disappeared completely. Still the spectacles continued to grow; now they were the size of windows. In place of the eyes a pair of tiny black-and-gold spots appeared, then two more, then more, until there were thousands crawling and wriggling and pressing against the glass. She frantically struggled to get away, but the arms still held her fast. At last she broke free, but the spectacled figure only laughed and tipped his glasses downward, and the thousands of angry black spots streaked toward her, swarming over her arms and legs, clinging to her face and neck, filling her eyes and nose and mouth…

Kathryn shrieked and threw herself from her bed. The lamp from her nightstand crashed to the ground and shattered in a flash of blue light. She stood in the darkness, flailing at the air, trapped inside the black cloud that always hung so near.

She scraped furiously at her legs and arms—and then stopped, panting, gradually recognizing the familiar walls around her and the fan still spinning overhead.

She sank slowly to her knees and began to weep in long, hopeless sobs.

CHAPTER 14

It was just after dawn when Nick came jogging into the parking lot. He wore a gray Penn State sweatshirt torn off at the shoulders and a pair of sagging black running shorts that hung to his knees. He sported a spotless pair of Nike's, the nicest article of clothing he owned. He stopped beside the Dodge and pulled off his cap—the Steelers this time—and tossed it through the back window.

Parked beside the Dodge was a trim black sedan. Nick checked the license plate; in the upper left corner it bore a Holcum County sticker, and below the cherry red "First in Flight" insignia were stamped the words, PAX DEI. Nick headed for the lab.

As he approached the office, Nick could see a figure seated inside. He was a black man, ancient in years and as thin and brittle as a reed. His head was large and seemed to dominate his body, and his magnificent brow overshadowed his sloe-black eyes like a mahogany cornice. He was dressed immaculately in a blue-black suit and a silver tie. Oversized hands projected from slender wrists and rested gently on either side of a large, open book. There was a profound calmness about him; his hands moved slowly and deliberately, with the beautiful economy of motion that comes only with age.

Nick rapped on the office door and stepped inside. The old man looked up and smiled. "I do hope you'll forgive the intrusion. The door was unlocked, and it was a bit muggy outside."

"No problem," Nick said. "What can I do for you?"

"Dr. Malcom Jameson." He extended his hand. "Pastor of Mount Zion African Methodist Episcopal Church."

"Nick Polchak, NC State University." Nick returned the handshake and glanced down at the massive tome that lay open before him. The text was entirely in Latin. It was Jerome's Vulgate, opened to the Gospel of Matthew.

"Adtendite a falsis prophetis qui veniunt ad vos in vestimentis ovium," Nick read aloud. "Beware of false prophets who come to you in sheep's clothing."

Dr. Jameson's eyes brightened. "You read Latin? I can't say I'm surprised. I was admiring some of your specimens in the outer office—especially the *Pandinus imperator Koch.*"

"My Emperor Scorpion."

"A magnificent specimen, with an imperial name to match. But then, you know the old saying: *Quidquid latine dictum sit altum viditur.*"

Nick smiled. "'Anything said in Latin sounds profound.' No offense, Dr. Jameson, but what's a smart guy like you doing in a town like this?"

Now the old man smiled. "I am a fisher of men. The biggest fish is not always found in the largest pond."

Nick nodded. "I've caught a few in small towns myself."

A look of recognition spread across the old man's face. "You are that Bug Man fellow, are you not? I believe I read about you in the papers. A fascinating discipline, this fo-ren-sic en-to-mol-o-gy of yours." He pronounced the words slowly, delighting in each syllable. "I'm afraid a man of your—how shall I put it—breadth of experience may find life a little dull in a town such as ours."

"Things are picking up," Nick replied. "I've been hired to investigate the death of Jim McAllister."

Dr. Jameson seemed taken aback. "I understood that the young man took his own life. Do you have reason to believe otherwise?"

"Let's just say I'm looking for reasons. How did you hear about his death?"

"I have been requested to preside at Mr. McAllister's memorial service." The old man pulled a folded piece of paper from his coat pocket. "I received a call from a Kathryn Guilford asking me to meet her here today, to arrange any necessary details."

"We had a long day yesterday," Nick said. "It might be best if I had her call you. Did Mr. McAllister attend your church?"

"Mr. McAllister was unchurched," the old man said. "That is, he was not a member of any local congregation. In situations such as this, I am often called upon to perform the services."

"In other words, you get the white trash."

Dr. Jameson looked at him sternly. "There is no such thing. Will you be attending the funeral, Dr. Polchak?"

"Never had much use for them."

"Oh yes, I see. You only handle the *clinical* side of death. I suppose there's nothing clinical about a funeral."

"Just a lot of fuss over a little shoofly pie."

"Shoofly pie," the old man repeated thoughtfully. "An interesting euphemism. The body dies, it starts to decompose. What remains becomes food for other living things. And what happens after?"

"After what?"

"After you die."

"Your question has no meaning," Nick said. "*After you die* is like saying *after the end*. If it's the end, there is no 'after.'"

"You believe there is nothing after?"

"What I believe is irrelevant. I'm telling you what I *know.* I see a body; it ceases to function; it decomposes. That's what I know."

"Sometimes knowing is not enough, my young friend. Sometimes you have to believe. That is *my* business."

"Different lines of work," Nick shrugged.

The older man studied Nick. "Perhaps. Perhaps not. We have more in common than you may think, Dr. Polchak. You seek guilty men to administer justice; I seek guilty men to offer grace and forgiveness. But it seems to me that, in our own way, we are *both* fishers of men."

He closed his book and slowly rose to his feet. He extended his hand to Nick once more.

"I will pray that you find what you are looking for. Much more importantly," he said with a penetrating gaze, "I will pray that you discover what it is that remains when even the shoofly pie is gone."

Nick walked the old man to his car. Just as the black sedan disappeared from view, Kathryn's silver Contour rounded the corner and came to a stop directly in front of the Quonset.

"Was that Dr. Jameson?" she said.

"I told him you'd call. Oversleep?"

"*Didn't* sleep." She followed Nick to the front door, where she hesitated. "Aren't we doing another interview this morning? What do we need to go in *there* for?"

"Dr. Jameson wanted me to show you something," Nick said.

Kathryn followed him cautiously, stepping only as far through the doorway as was absolutely necessary. "What is it?" she asked, eyeing the glass cases on either side.

Nick stepped around to the right and removed the lid from a terrarium. He reached in and slid his right hand under something that looked like a black leather glove. He returned to

Kathryn with a smile on his face, holding his hand in front of him like a waiter with a dessert tray.

It was not a glove, but it was black—black as coal tar. Two bulbous arms extended before it like the claws of a lobster and a thick knotted tail curved up behind it like a whip—a whip with a *very* sharp tip.

"This is Lord Vader."

Kathryn began to back away. "Dr. Jameson wanted me to see *that?*"

"He was quite impressed with him. 'A magnificent specimen,' I believe he said. 'Be sure to show it to my dear friend Kathryn.'"

"I've never *met* Dr. Jameson."

"Lord Vader is an Emperor Scorpion. He's quite impressive, don't you think? A good eight inches if he's an inch." Nick held his hand at eye level and stepped forward, smiling. Kathryn stepped back.

"I can see it just fine from here."

"From way over there?"

Another step forward, another step back.

"Emperors are very unusual—first, of course, because of their enormous size. But they're also unusual in that they're social. You can keep several together in one tank, like I do, and they get along just fine. But they do like to be alone every now and then, so from time to time I allow Lord Vader to go for a stroll here in the lab."

"You let that thing run loose? It could kill someone!"

"Don't be ridiculous. Lord Vader rarely stings—only in self-defense. He doesn't need to, really, because of these." He stepped forward and pointed to the enormous black projections the scorpion held menacingly aloft.

"Are those pincers?"

"They're called pedipalps. They're remarkably powerful. I feed him mostly crickets and giant mealworms, but every now and then... See that metal box under the table? That's a rodent trap—a *live* rodent trap. Whenever an unfortunate Muridae tries to invade our sanctuary, he must face the wrath of Lord Vader. It is his *destiny*. It's an amazing battle—arachnid against mammal, invertebrate against vertebrate."

"You let that thing loose on a helpless mouse?"

"A mouse isn't defenseless, Mrs. Guilford. It has teeth and claws. It can crack through a kernel of corn or gnaw its way through a floorboard. But it's no match for Lord Vader, I'm afraid. Would you like to hold him?"

"No. *Thank* you." She retreated a step farther.

"You'd think Lord Vader would use his stinger. After all, a mouse is the size of a *cow* to him. But he doesn't. He just grabs hold of Mickey with those pedipalps and tears him limb from limb."

As he spoke, Nick continued to inch forward. He held his hand out to one side and gestured to it as he sidled closer to Kathryn, then swung his hand back slowly in her direction. Each time she would back away, and they would repeat this maneuver, over and over like a kind of waltz, both of them moving slowly down the aisle toward the office door.

"The fact is, his sting is no worse than a wasp's. There's a rule of thumb in the scorpion world: the bigger the pedipalps, the more harmless the scorpion. The little brown ones with the long, slender pedipalps—now those are the ones to watch out for."

"Do you have any of those?"

"Of course. The entire row of cases just inside the door is my Scorpionidae collection. On the right, Lord Vader and his Imperial Stormtroopers. In the middle, common southwestern U.S. species. But on the left, watch out—those are my North Africans."

"For heaven's sake, what do you keep them for?"

"It's a hobby," he said, placing Lord Vader on the floor and nudging him forward until he skittered away. "I think from time to time everybody needs a bit of distraction. Don't you?"

He reached past Kathryn, opened the office door, and stepped inside.

She stood motionless for a moment, realizing in amazement her current location; then she quickly slipped into the office and slammed the door, eyeing the floor behind her as it closed.

"You look much less wrinkled today," Nick said. "Now how about that interview?"

CHAPTER 15

The Dodge rolled to a stop on the shoulder of the dirt road about fifty yards away from the decaying farmhouse. Kathryn heard two completely different hissing sounds emanating from somewhere under the hood, then a mysterious clicking noise followed by a kind of groan. She shifted to keep water from dripping onto her shoes from under the dash.

"We'd have been a lot more comfortable in that rental of yours," Nick said. "Why did you insist on taking my car?"

"I just thought it might be a good idea."

"You know, it's customary to call ahead and set up an appointment before doing an interview. I don't usually just drop by. 'Hello, I'm a forensic entomologist. I collected some maggots from your brother's corpse, and I'd like to ask you a few questions.'"

Kathryn rolled her eyes.

"What if Mr. McAllister's sister isn't home?"

"She's home. She's always home."

Several minutes passed.

"What exactly are we waiting for?" Nick asked.

"I'm just not sure this is a good idea." Kathryn shook her head doubtfully. "I don't see why we need to talk to her."

"Because the difference between a suicide and a murder is one of *motive.* Motive is everything, Mrs. Guilford—and who might understand the motives of the deceased better than his own kin?"

Kathryn continued to shake her head.

"If I didn't know better, Mrs. Guilford, I'd think you didn't want the lady to see you."

"Amy McAllister and I don't exactly—what I mean is, we have a history."

"Really? I love history."

Kathryn took a deep breath. "Jimmy and Amy came from a…troubled family."

"Troubled in what sense?"

"*Troubled* is a small-town term. It covers everything from minor neglect to outright cruelty and abuse. It's the polite way to say it, and polite is very important in a small town."

"Well, I'm from Pittsburgh. Was Amy abused?"

"In every way imaginable. You could say that she's…not quite right. Growing up, Jimmy and Amy kept each other sane. Jimmy was all she had in the world—no mom, no dad, no real friends—she had Jimmy."

"And Jimmy had you."

Kathryn winced. "Jimmy…*wanted* to have me. Nine years ago Jimmy asked me to marry him—the same night that Andy proposed to me."

"Two in one night. Boy, you were on a roll."

"This is not a joke! I had to turn him down, and it broke his heart. Jimmy always walked the line, and I think—*Amy* thinks—that my rejection is what started him over the edge. He went into a depression after that and started disappearing for long periods without explanation."

"And sometime during that period his drug abuse began."

"Sometimes I wish I had married him," Kathryn said under her breath.

"A rescue marriage." Nick nodded. "Very common. Very noble. Very stupid."

Kathryn glared at him. "Everything is so easy for you, isn't it? It must be so much simpler working with insects that have legs and wings but no feelings!"

"You have no idea how much simpler."

Kathryn closed her eyes and massaged her temples in slow circles. "Amy blames me for Jimmy's depression, for his withdrawal from her, for his anger and isolation. Amy blames me for everything."

"For his death?"

"Especially for his death."

"In other words, one of your motives for this investigation is to prove to Amy that it wasn't your fault. If it was suicide, then you're to blame; if it was murder, you're off the hook."

"Does that matter?"

"As I said, Mrs. Guilford—motive is everything."

Nick peered down the road at the crumbling farmhouse.

"And I thought this was going to be just another boring interview." He smiled, opening his door. "This could be downright interesting."

The dirt road disappeared into the mottled front yard of the aging house. Two Leghorns wandered aimlessly across the grass and one misshapen ligustrum thrived beside the sagging porch stoop. Four wooden columns, each rotted away at the base, supported a rumpled and pockmarked tin roof. The floorboards of the porch were cupped and twisted, long ago worn bare, and the brittle glazing around each window pane curled in like yellow parentheses. The curtains were thin and worn and pulled tight across each window. It was a dark and tired and withered house that had long ago given up hope.

Nick knocked gently at the door.

"No answer," he said.

"She's home."

Nick knocked again, a sharp, rapping, annoying barrage that continued until the curtain jerked to one side and an ashen face suddenly appeared, startling both of them. Kathryn stared at the floorboards and stepped slightly behind Nick.

The door opened, and a woman of almost undiscernable age stepped out. Her features were still young and rounded, but her skin was sallow and pasty, drawn into tiny canyons that drained into the eyes and mouth. Her hair was pulled back in a thoughtless manner, and her dark eyes bore a constant glare. She was still dressed in a faded blue housecoat. She studied Nick, starting with his feet and working her way up, recoiling when she came to his enormous spectacles. She leaned forward and glared harder, as if trying to grab hold of the elusive eyes darting beneath.

"What you want?" she barked.

"Are you Amy McAllister?"

"Depends on who *you* are."

"I'm Dr. Nicholas Polchak. I'd like to ask you a few questions."

"Don't need no doctor." She dismissed him with a wave of her hand, retreating back into the house. "You tell Family Services I ain't crazy, I just like my privacy."

"I like my privacy, too, Miss McAllister. I'm not that kind of doctor."

She turned as Kathryn reluctantly slid out from behind Nick.

"Hello, Amy," Kathryn said softly.

Amy's eyes widened and then narrowed again until they were only slits. Her mouth began to form a dozen different words, but the only one that emerged was a guttural, *"You!"* And with that she stormed back into the house and slammed the door behind her.

Kathryn hung her head and muttered, "I told you she still blames me. I told you there was no use in trying to—" But in the middle of her protests, Nick casually opened the door and stepped in.

He walked briskly from room to room, stopping in each room just long enough to make a quick appraisal. On the left was a dining room; the table was thick with dust, and a vase of long-dead flowers sat crumbling in the center. On the right was a kind of sitting room dominated by the smell of mildew and an aging Queen Anne sofa covered in a slick and barren red velour.

But the most noticeable feature of every room was the candles. Tall ones, short ones, on saucers and coasters and tins, lining bookshelves and furniture and dotting the floor like tiny fireflies. Candles smoldered everywhere, scenting the air oppressively and giving the entire house the look of a mausoleum.

At the end of the hall a double doorway opened into a small room completely devoid of furniture. The drapes were drawn tight, and the room would have been black as night if not for the candles. On the far wall was a stone fireplace. On the center of the mantel stood an Olan Mills portrait of James McAllister in full-dress uniform, framed by a pair of thin, white, flickering tapers.

Kathryn was right behind Nick, glancing nervously about as she tiptoed from room to room.

"You can't do this! You can't just march into a person's house and—"

Nick ignored her, continuing on until he finally rounded a corner to find Amy McAllister, squatting on the kitchen floor among several more candles, peacefully stroking a yellow cat. She had let her hair down, and it draped raggedly around her face. Her housecoat spread open at the waist and her pale legs jutted out to both sides. She looked like an alabaster gargoyle as she squatted and stared, mesmerized by the undulating movements of the cat.

She looked up at Nick and Kathryn with no expression at all. Then, slowly, a look of recognition came over her face. She snapped to her feet and opened her mouth to speak, but before she could get a word out, Nick cut her off.

"Miss McAllister, I am investigating the death of your brother. There are some questions that need to be answered—and I need your help to answer them."

Amy glared furiously at Kathryn.

"Why not ask *her?*" She pointed accusingly. "*She* knows why Jimmy died!"

"Amy," Kathryn said with a groan, "that was nine years ago!"

"You killed him!" Amy hissed. "You killed him just as sure as if *you* put that gun to his head! *You* was the one…the one who…"

Amy's voice suddenly trailed off, silenced by the sound of pleasant humming and cabinets quietly opening and closing again. Both women stood dumbfounded, watching Nick as he casually searched through the kitchen cupboards and pantry. He pulled out a faded tin of almond mocha, sniffed at it, and with a look of disgust, slid it back in place again. He turned a tall jar with his thumb and finger to peer at the label—instant Nestea, decaf. He shivered and wiped his hands on his pants. On the top shelf he spotted a half-empty box of Celestial Seasonings.

"This will have to do. Miss McAllister," he said, placing the box in her hand, "do you believe your brother took his own life? I'm not sure I do. If you want to talk about it, I'll be in the parlor." He tapped on the box. "I take mine with honey."

He turned and walked out of the room, leaving Amy staring open-mouthed after him. Kathryn glanced at Amy, then lowered her eyes and walked quickly after him. Nick was already stretching out on the Queen Anne sofa when Kathryn entered the parlor.

"I love what she's done with the place." He nodded approvingly. "The candles are a nice touch—sort of a Stephen King motif. I wonder if she decorated Schroeder's Funeral Home."

"Be quiet! Are you out of your mind?"

"You keep asking me that."

"Is this how you conduct an interview?"

"You were doing so well, I hated to interrupt."

"I tried to tell you about her. Amy hasn't been quite right for a long time."

"Quite right? Take a look at this place, Mrs. Guilford—the lady is skating on the other side of the ice."

"She's had a lot on her mind."

"She's had *you* on her mind, that's for sure."

Kathryn glanced nervously back down the hallway. "I think you had better do the talking this time."

"Gosh. I just hope I can handle it."

The clinking of metal against ceramic brought their conversation to an abrupt halt. Amy cautiously rounded the corner carrying a tarnished metal tray bearing two china cups with mismatched saucers. A single tea bag floated in each; one was still in its package. She stopped in the middle of the doorway, as if uncertain whether to enter or not. Her eyes went immediately to Kathryn. She stepped around to Nick and offered him a cup, then set the tray down on the coffee table and pulled a chair up close. She sat silently, her black eyes darting from the remaining cup to Kathryn and back again.

Kathryn slowly reached to take the cup. Amy immediately snatched it up for herself and redoubled the intensity of her glare. She sat silently sipping her cup of cold water, her eyes never shifting from Kathryn's face. Kathryn drew back, red-faced, and stared fixedly at her hands in her lap.

They all sat in silence for several minutes. Kathryn could feel the heat from Amy's eyes, as if she were being prodded with a fire iron.

"Miss McAllister," Nick said at last. Kathryn almost let out an audible sigh of relief. "I am a forensic entomologist from North Carolina State University. I specialize in the investigation of unwitnessed deaths and the analysis of their possible causes." As he spoke he saw Amy begin to shake her head slightly, like a mare trying to force her eyes into focus. Nick paused, set down his cup, and began again.

"Miss McAllister. Do you really believe your brother killed himself?"

She shrugged and shook her head several times before finally speaking.

"*They* say he did."

"Who says he did? Who are *they?*"

She shrugged again. "Peter. Peter says everybody thinks so."

"Do you think so?"

Amy's eyes grew darker and more confused. It was obvious to Nick that she had little ability to form her own opinions; those she had could easily have been given to her by someone else. Her only contribution would be her knowledge of her brother's past.

"Miss McAllister, I'm told your brother had a history of depression. Is that right?"

She nodded.

"When did it begin? Do you remember?"

"I remember, all right." She turned her glare to Kathryn again. "It started after *her! She's* the one who—"

Nick interrupted. "When Mrs. Guilford rejected your brother, I'm sure he was hurt. He was disappointed and angry—that's not the same as *depressed.* Think carefully. When did he begin to sleep longer hours? When did small tasks begin to seem overwhelming to him? When did he begin to stay to himself and disappear for long periods of time?"

"He always did some of that. But it got worse after the Gulf—*lots* worse. He went up to Walter Reed for a spell. Didn't help much."

"Walter Reed Army Medical Center? In Washington?"

She nodded.

"Was that the Gulf War Syndrome treatment program?"

"He went for a couple weeks at a time. Didn't do no good."

"Did he have any other symptoms besides depression? Weakness? Fatigue? Memory loss, neurological disorders?"

"None of that." She shook her head. "He just got down on hisself."

"Did your brother see action in the Gulf? Did you ever talk to him about what happened there?"

"I tried—but when I asked about it he just clammed up. Sometimes *he* brung it up. Sometimes he'd start to talk about what he done or what it was like in the desert or some tight spot him and Andy was in—but then he'd just as soon get quiet again, and no matter what I did, I couldn't bring him out of it. That's when he'd head off by hisself—sometimes for weeks."

"Where did he go during those periods? Do you know?"

"Off in the woods, mostly. To hunt. Jimmy loved to hunt."

"Mostly around here?"

"All over. You go where the game is, where the season is."

Nick paused. "Who did your brother hunt with?"

"Most everybody in town."

"The three hunters who found him? Ronny, Denny, Wayne?"

"Sure, lots o' times."

"Did he ever mention a problem with any of them? One of them he didn't seem to get along with?"

"None in particular. Jimmy didn't take to nobody too well."

"What about the sheriff? Did your brother hunt with the sheriff?"

"Peter, sure. Most of all Peter. Peter got hisself an old hunting cabin just outside of Valdosta. Hunt turkey and hog there."

"Valdosta, Georgia?"

She nodded.

"Miss McAllister, I want you to think very carefully. Who was the last person to see your brother alive?"

Her eyes took on a distant look. "Me, I guess."

"The last time you saw him, how did he act? Was there anything unusual about his behavior? Can you remember anything he said?"

Amy squinted hard, as if staring into a deep darkness. "He was mad as mud—even more than usual. Said he was going to make things right."

"*Make things right*—what do you think he meant by that?"

She shrugged. "Jimmy said a lot of things didn't make no sense."

"And when he went to 'make things right,' where did he go? Any idea what he did, who he spoke with?"

No answer.

Nick sat quietly for a minute, his searching eyes darting rapidly behind their glass enclosures. Amy's eyes sank to the floor, and Kathryn ventured her first glance up at Amy's face. She looked so tired, so much older than her twenty-five years. Her entire childhood had been a walking death, and now death surrounded her, suffocated her—perhaps as it had Jimmy.

"Miss McAllister," Nick spoke again, "I'd like to ask you one last question—one that I asked you before: Do you really believe your brother killed himself?"

Amy's face began to twist and contort. Half a dozen times she seemed as if she would speak, only to shake her head or shrug and start again. At last she managed just a single word.

"No."

"Why not?"

"Because *I'm* still here," she whispered. "And Jimmy wouldn't leave without me."

Kathryn let a single sob escape.

Amy slowly rose from her chair and silently left the room.

It was all Kathryn could do to contain herself. The utter wretchedness of it all almost swallowed her alive.

Nick slapped his hands on the sofa and stood up. "I think our interview is over," he said, stretching. "She gave us a lot to think about." He headed for the door, and Kathryn slowly followed. A part of her wanted to stay behind, to find Amy and hold her, to stay with her.

At the door a quiet voice stopped her.

"Wait."

Kathryn turned to see Amy holding a small Bible and a faded cigar box bound together with a cracked and brittle rubber band.

"These are Jimmy's things," she said. "His personal things. They might as well go with you." She held out the bundle, and Kathryn saw the briefest flicker of light in Amy's eyes—then darkness again.

"I can't see you again," Amy whispered. "I can't."

"Amy—I want you to know—" Kathryn stopped midsentence.

Over Amy's shoulder Kathryn saw thick gray smoke rolling toward them down the hallway ceiling from the back of the house. She spun around. Nick was already halfway back to the car.

"Nick! *Fire!*"

By the time she turned back again, Amy was halfway down the hall. She ducked into the living room just long enough to grab her brother's portrait, then raced toward the kitchen.

"Ariel! Here, Ariel!"

"Amy! Leave the cat! We've got to get out of here *now!*"

Amy hesitated in the doorway, silhouetted against a rising amber glow, then disappeared into the roiling cloud.

"Amy!"

Kathryn started forward when she felt a powerful hand grab her by the arm and jerk back. "We've got to get out of here!" Nick shouted, dragging her back toward the open doorway. "We can't find her this way, the smoke's already too thick! We've got to head around back and find a shorter way in!"

They raced across the porch and around the left side of the house. Flames were visible from three windows, and individual panes cracked and exploded outward from the expanding gases. The vinyl siding began to brown and curl like frying bacon.

The end of the house was already engulfed in fire. Flame belched out from the kitchen window like a blowtorch. Less than a yard from the house, in the very center of the inferno, was a hulking silver capsule.

A propane tank.

They both saw it simultaneously.

"Back the other way!" Nick shouted. "Go, go!"

They raced back down the side of the house through blasts of flying glass and heat, around to the front of the house where the raging remains of the house might shelter them from shrapnel. Above the flames they could hear a shrill whistle that steadily rose to a deafening shriek.

"The ditch!" Kathryn screamed. "Into the ditch!"

They both dove headlong into the shallow water of the drainage ditch and threw their arms over their heads and necks.

There was a thundering roar, and a great orange fireball rolled into the sky.

CHAPTER 16

Nick and Kathryn clutched coarse woolen blankets around their shoulders and watched the Holcum County Fire and Rescue team kick apart the remaining embers that an hour ago formed the house of Amy McAllister. Somewhere in the smoldering ashes lay the remains of Amy herself.

Sheriff Peter St. Clair stood with his arm around Kathryn as the fire chief approached.

"What can you tell us?" the sheriff called out. "How did it start?"

"Are you kidding?" the fire chief said. "You tell *me*. All I can tell you is what you already know: It hit the propane tank. There isn't enough left of the house to tell us anything else. Man, the heat inside that fireball must have been like a hog roast on the Fourth of July."

Nick felt the stubble on the back of his left arm, where the heat from the blast had singed it almost to the skin. "My guess is she started the fire herself. She went to make us some tea—

probably left the gas on. The woman wasn't dealing off the top of the deck."

"I can tell you how the fire started," Kathryn grumbled. "Somebody *set* it."

Both men looked at her.

"What makes you think that?"

"First somebody takes a shot at us in the woods; now they try to burn us alive."

The sheriff squeezed Kathryn a little tighter and shook his head to the fire chief, who turned and headed back toward the EMT truck.

"Kath," Peter said softly, "they were two separate things."

Kathryn twisted away from him. "Are you going to tell me that *this* was just a prank too?"

"No. I'm going to tell you it was an accident. C'mon, you saw the condition of the place—the bare wood, the brush, the debris piled next to the house. You saw how many candles she had burning in there, like it was some kind of shrine. It's a wonder the whole place didn't go up a long time ago. Like the Doc said, she probably set the fire herself."

"But it *didn't* go up a long time ago, Peter. It went up while *we were in it.*"

"That is a bit coincidental," Nick joined in. "The fire started in the back of the house, probably in the kitchen. But we were *in* the kitchen less than half an hour before we saw smoke, and the place went up in minutes. It's hard to see how a spontaneous fire could spread that fast."

The sheriff glared at him. "So now you're the Fire Man too?"

"Okay, so I'm out of my league here. All I'm saying is it seems a little odd."

"You said it yourself, everything about the place was odd. Including Amy."

Kathryn turned to face Peter. "Someone wants us to stop this investigation, Peter. If Jimmy's death was such an obvious suicide, why would anyone care if we take a closer look? It looks to me like someone has something to hide."

"Now wait a minute. Slow down—"

"Maybe this *was* an accident. Maybe Amy burned her own house down. Maybe she decided to set fire to it herself when she first saw me at the front door! But Amy didn't take a shot at us in the woods. And when you put the two together..."

"Hold on," the sheriff began—and then he stopped abruptly. He kicked at a piece of charred debris and smothered a curse. "I know who fired on you in the woods."

Nick poked his head around Kathryn and stared at the sheriff. "Excuse me?"

"It was Ronny. Or maybe Denny or Wayne—one of those three."

"The three hunters? The ones who discovered the body in the meadow?"

Peter nodded. "I had a hunch about it, so I stopped by the Buck Stop the other night—it's a bar over in Elkhorn where some of the boys like to hang out."

"And?"

"Look, put yourself in their place. Three good ol' boys stumble across a body in the woods. They know the man's problems, they see the gun in his hand, they put two and two together. So they do their civic duty and call the authorities. Next thing they know, some witch doctor comes to town saying he's gonna find out what *really* happened. And the boys get worried that somebody's gonna point the finger at them. So they fired a shot to try to scare you off. They weren't trying to hurt anybody."

"That's it?" Nick said.

"That's it," the sheriff said. "Now you know. Don't worry, I put the fear of God in all three of 'em. There won't be any more of *that* nonsense."

Kathryn looked at the charred remains of the house and wondered.

Nick turned to the sheriff. "Do you believe their motive? That they were only trying to protect themselves from false accusation?"

"They saw the O. J. trial, Doc. They know how screwed up the law can get."

"Did it ever occur to you that they might be covering up a deeper motive? They discovered the body, Sheriff; they certainly had the opportunity to manipulate it before you saw it. Any one of them could have played a role in Mr. McAllister's death."

"Maybe. But you're forgetting something, Doc—something you can't understand because you're not from around here. I *know* those boys—and I knew Jimmy. That plays a big part in knowing what did and didn't happen."

"*You're* forgetting something," Nick responded. "Mrs. Guilford knew Jimmy too—but she holds a different opinion. You put a lot of faith in your knowledge of people, Sheriff."

"Jimmy was an accident waiting to happen," the sheriff said.

"You're sure about that? Absolutely positive?"

"You see a blind man walking toward a hole, you watch him walk right up to the edge, then you turn away for a split second—and when you look back, he's lying at the bottom of the hole. Do you ask who pushed him?"

"No," Nick said. "I ask, 'Who's the blind man here?' "

Kathryn could contain herself no longer. "Why didn't you tell us this before, Peter? Yesterday or the night before? You said you were going to cooperate!"

Peter pointed to the smoldering ruins of the house. "Because *that's you*. You're a fire out of control. First you thought somebody was tryin' to kill you in the woods, and it was just a couple of boys tryin' to cover their own backsides. Now you think somebody wants to burn you alive. Pretty soon you'll be finding conspiracies under every rock! Jimmy killed himself, Kath—I'm sorry you can't accept that. I just don't want to see you wasting any more of your time and money. I don't want to fuel the fire."

"If I'm wrong," Kathryn seethed, "then I'm only wasting my own time and money. But if *you're* wrong"—she pointed to the house—"then *that* was another murder!"

Kathryn picked up the small pile of Jimmy's personal belongings and began to brush off the dried mud and soot.

"What's that?"

"Jimmy's personal things—what's left of them anyway. Amy thought I should have them."

"Mind if I have a look?"

The sheriff slid the crumbling Macanudo cigar box out from under the rubber band and handed the Bible back to Kathryn. He flipped open the lid. Inside was a scattering of personal items: Jimmy's Airborne insignia and campaign ribbon, a small Buck pocketknife, a pair of shiny onyx cuff links, and a banded deck of Aviator playing cards. There were also a half-dozen letters and papers of various shapes and sizes.

"Mind if I hang on to this for awhile? I'll go through the papers, see if I find anything that might help." He leaned toward Kathryn. "I don't expect to."

"If you don't expect to find anything, then give them back," Kathryn said.

"We said we'd cooperate," the sheriff said gently. "You got to let me do *something*."

Kathryn shrugged the blanket from her shoulders and dropped it at Peter's feet. She spun around and stormed away toward the car.

Nick let the embers cool for a few moments before saying, "It is her time, you know. Why don't you just humor her?"

The sheriff glared at him. "It's time that could be better spent."

"Better spent…on you?"

The sheriff leaned in close and spoke in a low, rumbling voice. "There are *lines*, Doc." He turned and stomped off toward the waiting patrol car.

"There *are* lines," Nick whistled. "And I think I just found one."

Ten o'clock, hon. League play just ended; it's open lanes now."

"Thanks." Nick sat at the snack bar at the Strike 'N Spare Lanes, watching three men in matching gray Loungemaster shirts with the name *Buck Stop* chainstitched in red across the back.

"Can you give me lane twelve? The one beside those three there."

"Sure thing. Friends of yours?"

Nick shook his head. "What can you tell me about them?"

The waitress eyed him suspiciously. "Why you asking?"

"I'd like to do a little business with them."

"Ronny, Denny, and Wayne," the waitress said, pointing. "Three peas in a pod, those boys."

"What do they do—for a living, I mean?"

"Denny—he's the little one—still works for his daddy at the Feed & Supply. Don't worry, he'll tell you more'n you want to know. Never stops talkin', that one. Wayne—the one that used to have hair—he drives a truck for Ferrellgas. Ronny's the big, quiet fella. He's got hisself an office over on Dalrymple. He's the success of the three."

"What's his business?"

"Insurance, I think. Something like that. Always seems to have money anyway." She glanced up just in time to see Denny chest-thump Wayne after picking an easy split. "If you ask me, none of 'em's a bargain."

Nick picked up his plate of pork ribs and potato salad and headed for the alleys, stopping by a rack of multicolored spheres just long enough to fit his fingers into a coal black, sixteen-pound Ebonite.

"You need shoes?" the waitress called after him.

Nick shook his head. "Not for this game."

The three men recognized him even before he sat down. They had never seen Nick before, but they had no doubts about his identity; his massive spectacles were already legendary in the little town of Rayford. They watched as Nick silently added his ball to the return rack and set his plate down on the scoring table.

"Mind if I join you?"

"Can you bowl?" Wayne snickered. "I mean, can you see the *pins?"*

Nick lifted his ball and turned to the alley. He held the ball chest high, paused, then took three quick steps forward. His backswing rose above his head, and the black shape floated weightless for an instant before arcing down again. The ball met the alley without a sound and rocketed forward along the right gutter, spinning like a gyroscope on its side. Two-thirds of the way to the target lateral rotation overcame forward momentum, and the ball broke, curling in perfectly just behind the headpin. Ten pins exploded and ricocheted inside their black frame.

Nick turned to the three hunters. "Did I get any?"

"You're that Bug Man," Denny said. "Settle a bet for us. What's the deadliest insect in the world?"

"Who are the nominees?" Nick asked.

"I say it's the female black widow spider."

"A naughty lady, but not even in the running."

"Your turn, Wayne. Tell the doc what *you* said."

"It's a definite fact," Wayne stated with all the authority he could summon, "that the daddy-longlegs, if eaten, is the deadliest spider in the world."

"Anyone stupid enough to eat spiders isn't likely to live very long, but he won't die from the Phalangida. That's an urban legend. Any other votes?"

The third and largest of the three cleared his throat and spoke a single word. "Scorpions."

"That's right," Denny said, "I hear there are scorpions that can kill a man in less than a minute!"

"Not *that* fast." Nick shook his head. "But you're getting closer."

"Okay then," Wayne said with a generous dose of contempt, "what *is* the deadliest insect in the world?"

"You've got one on your arm."

All three men jumped back, and Wayne wiped frantically at both arms, sending a single black fly buzzing back toward the snack bar. Ronny and Denny erupted into laughter. Not Wayne.

"That was *close*," Denny hooted. "Good thing we got a doctor nearby!"

"Funny," Wayne grumbled. "Real funny."

"I wasn't joking. Less than 3 percent of insects can harm a human being, but that little *Musca domestica*—a common housefly—is at the top of the list."

Nick raised his plate up to eye level. There sat a second fly, motionless, leisurely feeding atop a heaping mound of creamy white potato salad.

"Flies can't chew. They can only suck up liquid. So when

they land on solid food, they spit. They eject saliva, and the saliva dissolves the food—dinnertime. The problem is, the fly always leaves a little saliva behind wherever he goes. Now if this fly *only* visited potato salad it might be okay—but the fact is, he was raised in a manure pile, and he stopped off for lunch on a decomposing rat."

He carefully lifted a hefty forkful of potato salad, fly included, and brought it to his open mouth. He paused.

"Or maybe he stopped on one of the cadavers over at my place." The fly buzzed away at the last possible moment before its meal disappeared down the dark, gaping cavern.

"Flies carry cholera, typhoid, leprosy, and polio," Nick said through his generous mouthful. "They've killed millions." He held out his plate to the four men. "Say, this is really good. Try some?"

"You really got *cadavers* over at your place? What for?"

"I'm a forensic entomologist. I study the way necrophilous insects can indicate the time and the manner in which someone died."

"What kind of insects?"

"*Necrophilous.* Dead flesh eaters."

"What these scientists won't come up with," Denny said.

"What I do is nothing new. The first book on the subject was written seven hundred years ago by a Chinese investigator named Sung Tz'u. He called his book *The Washing Away of Wrongs.*" Nick cocked his head to one side. "Great title, don't you think?

"Back in 1235 some good ol' boy got angry with one of his drinking buddies and decided to express himself with a sickle. The authorities questioned everyone in the village but got nowhere, so they sent for Sung Tz'u—the local Bug Man. Sung Tz'u didn't bother with questions; he just had all the villagers bring their sickles and lay them side by side in the hot sun. Then he waited."

Nick casually took another bite of potato salad. "Mmm. You're sure you don't want to try this?"

"Waited for what?"

"Flies."

"What flies?"

"On the sickle. Necrophilous flies were attracted to traces of blood and tissue left on the killer's sickle."

"What did they do to him?" Denny asked.

Nick shrugged. "I suppose they *Washed Away the Wrong*. So you see, I'm part of an ancient tradition. There's only one way to learn about death, fellas—you have to study the dead."

"Disgusting," Wayne muttered.

Nick arched one eyebrow. "Oh, come now. I thought you boys were hunters. Surely you're not squeamish about seeing something dead."

"Animals," Denny said. "Not people."

"That's not what I heard. Weren't you the three that found Jimmy McAllister's body in the woods?"

Nick looked down and picked at his plate just long enough to allow each of the men to exchange awkward glances. Then he casually set his plate down on the scoring table and wiped his hands on his shirt.

"I answered your questions—how about answering a couple of mine?" Nick smiled at each of them. "I'm investigating the murder of James McAllister."

No one smiled back.

"You got to be kidding," Denny said. "It was an obvious suicide."

"Oh? How so?"

"The gun was still in his hand—his own gun."

"And the way we found him," Wayne joined in, "flat on his back. All his stuff was there. No sign of a fight, no struggle."

"And his history," Denny added. "You know, the cocaine thing and all."

Nick stopped. "What cocaine thing?"

"Didn't you know? It turns out Jimmy'd been doing the stuff. For a long time—since back in the Gulf. That stuff can make a man do things he might not do in his right mind."

"It can indeed," Nick nodded. "Where did you hear about this?"

"From Ronny."

Nick turned to Ronny.

"Pete told me," he said with his usual economy of words. "I told these two."

"When did Pete tell you? How long ago?"

"A few days."

Nick paused.

Denny suddenly felt the weight of two sets of eyes. He glanced awkwardly at Ronny and Wayne; one rolled his eyes, the other shook his head and turned away.

"Okay," Denny grumbled. "Maybe I wasn't supposed to tell anyone."

"And maybe you *were,*" Nick said quietly. "Where do you suppose Jimmy got his cocaine?" There was no response. Nick smiled. "Maybe it's not so hard to keep a secret in a small town after all… Let's change the subject. Tell me how you found the body. How was it lying?"

"Sort of like…this," Wayne pantomimed, standing with his arms and legs spread wide.

"Show me." Nick pointed to the maple floor.

"What—*here?*"

"Why not? Who's going to notice?"

Wayne looked around cautiously, then spread out uneasily on the glossy surface. "Like this," he said, and quickly started to rise again.

"Not yet." Nick knelt at his side. "Think carefully. Could one of the arms have been like…this?" He lifted Wayne's right arm and dropped it across his chest.

"Uh-uh." Wayne shook his head. "It was definitely out to the side." Ronny nodded his agreement. Denny kept silent, still smarting from his earlier indiscretion.

"How about the legs?" He lifted Wayne's right knee and pulled his foot in tight against his buttock. "Could the right leg have been more like…this?" He let go, and Wayne's leg flopped out to the side.

"How could it? It won't stay up like that."

"No, it won't," Nick said. "Not without help. Were there any objects around the body, anything that might have temporarily supported a limb in a position like that?"

They all shook their heads.

"Did you boys move anything? Take anything? Did the three of you adjust the body in any way?"

There was a long pause, then Wayne jumped to his feet. "I don't like this," he snapped. "Are you saying we did something wrong? 'Cause if you are, say so."

"I'm not saying you *did*. I'm saying you *could* have. Let's be honest. You three came across the body in the meadow. You could have put it there."

"Now why would we do that?" Denny growled.

"You tell me."

"Jimmy'd been dead a week when we found him!"

"When the *three* of you found him, yes. But any *one* of you could have put him there the week before, then accidentally 'discovered' him a week later with the other two. By the way—which one of you suggested that you work on your deer stands that day?"

The three men looked at each other nervously.

"It was Denny, wasn't it?"

"*Me?* I'm the one who said to go have a beer and wait for better weather!"

"Now I remember," Wayne said. "It was *Ronny…*"

Nick picked up his ball again and stepped up to the line. This time, the ball hit the headpin square-on and left the seven and ten pins standing.

The hunters stared warily at Nick. They were downwind now, heads held high, straight and alert and ready to run.

"Settle a bet for me," Nick said. "Which one of you is the best shot?"

No one dared to answer at first—then Denny spoke up unexpectedly. "Probably Ronny. He's got a Weatherby Mark V Crown Custom. It's got a Leupold scope on it, and—"

"Shut up, Denny!" Ronny roared. "Can't you ever keep your mouth closed?"

Nick turned to Ronny. "A Weatherby Crown Custom? Business *must* be good. Then I assume you're the one who tried to kill my assistant?"

"We didn't try to kill anybody!" Wayne spluttered. "We only wanted to scare you off!"

"That's what the sheriff thinks," Nick said. "He said you boys only did it to protect yourselves. To protect yourselves from what?"

"From this!" Denny shouted. "From some long-nose trying to make out like we had something to do with Jimmy's death!"

"How could anyone get that idea? Did any of you have any reason to *want* Mr. McAllister dead?"

Silence again—but now the air between them was electric.

"Did you boys hear about Amy McAllister? Just this afternoon. I was there, did you know that? Quite a close call—I barely made it out of the house in time. There was a fire, and the fire hit the propane tank. It went off like a bomb. Would you believe her propane tank was right against the back of the house? But you knew that, didn't you, Wayne? You work for Ferrellgas, don't you?"

Wayne scrambled to his feet and charged at Nick. Nick spun to face him. Wayne drew back his right arm, then glanced at Nick's huge spectacles and hesitated.

In that instant Nick swung a roundhouse left. It was smooth and sure, and it came from the floor. It caught Wayne square on the jaw; there was a click and a dull smack, and Wayne crumpled to the floor like a stringless puppet.

Denny jumped to his feet, while Ronny sat and watched. Nick glared at both of them. "Anyone else want to try?"

Wayne lay on his back on the hardwood floor, just as he had done a few minutes ago; this time, his imitation of the dead was much more convincing. Nick reached down with one hand and grabbed Wayne's belt where it curved around his side. With one smooth motion he flipped him over onto his face, a skill he had mastered by rotating the decomposing carcasses of countless swine.

He reached into Wayne's back pocket and pulled out his wallet. He flipped it open, took out two twentys, and tossed the empty billfold at Ronny's feet. "To cover the cost of my equipment," Nick said. "You boys can work it out between you."

He glanced down at Wayne's motionless form. "When he wakes up, tell him I don't believe the three of you are responsible for Jim McAllister's death. But *one* of you might be—and one of you just might know who it is. Think it over—all three of you don't have to take the blame. If you want to talk, you know where to find me."

Nick backed slowly away toward the exit. He glanced one last time down the alley at the two remaining pins.

"A split," he whistled. "Tough one to pick."

"You did what? You *punched* him?"

"It seemed the thing to do at the time," Nick said.

"You can't go around getting into fistfights," Kathryn scolded. "You of *all* people!"

"Why is that?"

She cocked her head and stared at his enormous spectacles.

"What, these? Actually, I've found them very helpful. I find that most people hesitate to take a swing at a man wearing glasses." Nick smiled. "I don't have that problem."

She shook her head. "You'd think a blind man would have learned not to go around throwing punches."

Nick shrugged. "Where I grew up, you learned to swing first."

Kathryn glanced around the cavernous room; the Idle Hour Café looked more like a hunting lodge than a nightclub. A score of pedestal tables were scattered randomly across a floor half the size of a skating rink, and a handful of couples eagerly spun and two-stepped among them. On the table sat a half-dozen empty brown bottles, courtesy of the Carolina Brewing Company of Holly Springs, North Carolina.

"So you beat up Wayne just to get the money back for your equipment? I guess I'd better be careful to pay you on time."

"We know the hunters want this investigation to stop," Nick said. "What we don't know is *why.* The sheriff thinks they were just covering their backsides. Maybe—or maybe they're trying to cover something more. I wanted to divide them, Mrs. Guilford. Three peas in a pod—that's what the waitress at the bowling alley called them. They're a team, and as long as they act as a team they'll protect each other. I wanted them to know they're all in danger so each of them will start looking after his own backside. Now we'll find out if they have anything to hide or not."

Kathryn rubbed at her face with both hands. "I can't stop thinking about poor Amy. Peter said it was just an accident."

"Could be. She could have caused the fire herself—she was capable of it. But I find the timing a little too coincidental, and the fire spread awfully fast. No way to check for arson though. The propane took care of that."

"Do you think it was one of the hunters again?"

"Hard to say; this was more than just a warning shot. What can you tell me about Ronny?"

"Why Ronny?"

"He's the one who fired at you in the woods. What business is he in?"

"Investments, I think."

"The waitress said insurance."

"I'm not sure. But he seems to do pretty well."

Nick paused. "The waitress said the same thing—and Ronny owns a very high-end weapon. Don't you find it a little strange that a man could be so successful in a town this size and no one is sure what he does?"

Kathryn shrugged. "People don't know everything in a small town."

"Really? I wonder." Nick flagged down a passing waitress. "I'm a little new around here," he said. "Everybody's talking about this *Jimmy McAllister* character. What's the story?"

The waitress glanced over her shoulder. "Jimmy was a home boy, grew up right here in Rayford. Shot hisself in the woods just a week ago. And no *wonder*—turns out he been doin' a little..." She held her little finger up to her nose. "For years, they say. Guess it finally caught up with him." A man at another table signaled her, and she moved away.

Kathryn was stunned.

Nick looked at her. "Who did you tell about Mr. McAllister's cocaine habit?"

"Are you kidding? Why would I tell anyone?"

"The three hunters knew," Nick said. "The sheriff told Ronny a few days ago. Ronny told Denny and Wayne. By now the whole town knows."

"But—why would Peter tell anyone? Why *those* three, especially a loudmouth like Denny?"

"There's an old saying, Mrs. Guilford. If you want a secret kept, keep it yourself."

Several minutes passed. Suddenly, for the first time that evening, Kathryn became aware of the intimacy of the couples around them. A young couple to her right leaned together across a table with no more than a handbreadth between their faces. On the dance floor a man and woman were entwined like kudzu, swaying eagerly with very little regard for the rhythm of the music.

"I'm not going to call you 'Dr. Polchak' anymore," she said abruptly. "It takes too much energy. From now on I'm going to call you Nick."

Dr. Polchak—*Nick*—said nothing.

"Okay?"

"Are you asking for my approval?"

"For twenty thousand dollars I think I should be able to call you Nick."

"For twenty thousand dollars you can call me Queen Latifah."

She looked at Nick, who sat quietly rapping the rim of his bottle on the table in time with the music.

"Would you like to dance?" Kathryn blurted out—then quickly glanced around as though the words might have come from another table.

Nick looked over both shoulders, wondering if he had accidentally intercepted a message intended for someone else.

"I really don't dance—except at weddings."

"How often do you go to a wedding?"

"Never."

They sat in awkward silence again. Nick inspected the roof trusses and ventilation shafts that lined the ceiling while Kathryn carefully removed the paper labels from four of the empty bottles.

"Dancing is a strange phenomenon," Nick said suddenly.

"Excuse me?"

"Dancing. It's one of the ways your species and mine are very much alike."

"This I've got to hear."

"Look at those two women standing at the bar. They're dressed in bright colors; they're wearing makeup—too much makeup—and probably perfume. Those are their *attractants.* Watch...they seem to be friends, don't they? They're not. They have to compete with one another for the available males, just as members of my species do. Watch their movements. The one on the left keeps tossing her hair back—see? Each woman knows what her most desirable feature is and tries to draw attention to it. This allows her to choose between better males."

"Why does everything have to be about *males?* Did you ever think that maybe she did it for her own self-esteem?"

Nick rolled his eyes. "Look at her, Mrs. Guilford. See the way she swings her hips as she talks? I'm sure that enhances her *self-esteem.* And look at the way they both smile and laugh and try to look as animated as possible. No, this is typical courtship behavior."

"You seem to be an expert on female behavior."

"I am. Did you know that in one study a caged female pine sawfly attracted more than *eleven thousand* males? Now that's what I call perfume."

"I thought we were talking about females of *my* species."

"I've studied a few of them too—purely in the name of science, of course."

Suddenly Kathryn noticed that Nick's elusive eyes had come to rest on some object behind her, just across her left shoulder. She turned. At the jukebox stood a young woman with a body as sleek as a hornet, swaying seductively from side to side as she studied the selections. Kathryn turned slowly back to Nick with a broad smile.

"Aha."

"Aha what?'

"Nothing." She raised one eyebrow. "Just 'Aha.'"

"Don't be annoying, Mrs. Guilford."

"You seem to have taken more than a clinical interest in a member of *my* species. Down here, that's what we call *eye-eatin'*."

"Nonsense," he said casually. "I was merely observing."

Kathryn leaned forward. "Liar."

"Well," he took a second glance,"it's hard not to appreciate an outstanding example of any species."

Kathryn watched as Nick's floating eyes turned back to her again, studying, analyzing, searching for something. She had the distinct impression she wasn't going to like what came next.

"I suppose your attraction to someone can keep you from seeing things clearly," he began. "Sometimes it takes a third party to help you see what's going on."

Kathryn hesitated. "Who are we talking about?"

Nick rocked back in his chair and folded his hands in front of him.

"Let me ask you a question. It appears quite possible that your friend's body was moved—and if it was moved, he was most likely murdered. The body could have been moved just a few feet—or many miles. The murder could have occurred anywhere—in another county, even in another state. Suppose the murder occurred far away; why would the killer choose to return the body to Holcum County? After all, an apparent suicide could be staged anywhere."

Kathryn shrugged.

"The killer would return the body here because Holcum County is one of the only counties in North Carolina that still operates under the old coroner system—where the death investigation would be conducted by the ice cream man. Here he would have the best chance of faking a suicide and fooling the authorities. Now—who would know such a thing? Not the hunters. The coroner would know, of course—and anyone else who is familiar with medico-legal procedures in your county. Now, who might that be?"

The hair began to stand up on Kathryn's neck.

"Of course, even if the killer fooled the coroner, the *police* might figure it out." Nick looked directly at Kathryn now. "Unless for some reason the police didn't *want* to figure it out..."

Kathryn's eyes narrowed to a fiery glare. She brought both fists down hard on the table and sent two bottles clinking to the floor. The couple on her right stopped and turned. She glanced awkwardly over at them, then turned back to Nick and lowered her voice to a growl.

"Are you saying you suspect Peter? You think *he* might have done it?"

"*Could* have done it," Nick corrected. "Of course, there is one other possible suspect..."

"Who?"

"You."

Kathryn slumped back in her chair and threw both hands in the air.

"Me? You think I would pay you twenty thousand dollars to investigate a murder I committed *myself*? Are you out of your mind?"

"You know your problem, Mrs. Guilford? You're *naive*—and in this business that can be a fatal error. This sort of thing happens all the time. Here's the scenario: A beautiful young woman decides to do away with her friend, or boyfriend, or lover—whatever—and then she comes to me to investigate the death for her. She knows that there's little chance I'll be able to find anything, but her eagerness to investigate and her willingness to sacrifice her hard-earned money convinces everyone in town of her innocence. Twenty thousand dollars is a small price to pay for that kind of public support."

Kathryn sat in stunned silence, shaking her head in disbelief. "Do you actually suspect *me?*"

Nick paused. "No. I don't."

"Then why—"

"Because I want you to open your eyes. No, I don't suspect you of murdering your friend—but I'm *willing* to suspect you. I'm willing to suspect you and the hunters and the Sunday school teacher and the president of the PTA. I'm willing to suspect anyone—including your old friend the sheriff. My concern is that *you're not.*"

"Peter offered to cooperate with us in this investigation."

"I believe his words were, 'I'd like to know what *you* come up with.'"

"And in return, he said he'd give us everything *he* has."

"Which is nothing. An interesting form of cooperation."

"Then why did you agree to go along with him?"

"First, because like it or not your friend is the law, and it's within his power to demand our cooperation. Second, because I'd rather keep him where I can see him. And third," he said with a tilt of his head, "because I have no choice, do I? This is *your* investigation—and wherever *you* are, I have a feeling the sheriff won't be far away."

Kathryn could barely contain herself. "Let me tell you something about Peter," she seethed. "When I lost Andy he was the first one there. He stayed with me. He held me while I cried."

"What a terrible burden for him."

"He helped settle Andy's affairs. He fought with the Department of Defense about searching for Andy's body. He took care of the finances. He washed my car, he cut my grass, he did my shopping for me—he kept me from losing my mind."

"That reminds me of a joke," Nick said. "A man lies dying on his bed with his faithful wife sitting beside him. He says to her, 'You've always been there, Margaret. When I lost the business, you were there. When I had the accident, you were there. When I suffered the nervous breakdown, you were there. And now that I'm dying, you're still there. It just occurred to me—*you're bad luck.*"

"That's not funny," Kathryn glared. "I owe Peter everything."

"Apparently not."

"What's that supposed to mean?"

"You don't love him."

"How do you know? Maybe I do."

Nick raised both eyebrows and peered at her over the top of his glasses. "You're a very poor liar. Take it from an expert."

"What makes you so sure Peter loves me anyway?"

"Oh, come on," he groaned. "Mother bears are less protective."

"Oh, really. It just so happens Peter has a girlfriend, you know."

Nick stopped. "Now *that's* interesting. And what might her name be?"

"Oh no you don't," Kathryn shook her head. "The last thing I want to do is turn you loose on Peter's girlfriend."

"I'm not going to *eat* her, Mrs. Guilford. I'd just like to ask her a few questions."

"What kind of questions?"

"Like, 'When the sheriff holds you, are you aware that he's thinking about someone else?'"

"You are *way* out of line!"

"In my business, Mrs. Guilford, there are no lines."

"I am *not* paying you to suspect Peter!"

"Oh? Who *are* you paying me to suspect?"

"Anyone else, but not him!"

"Why? Because he's not capable of killing anyone? You know better, Mrs. Guilford. Because he had no reason to? Take another look behind you."

Kathryn turned to see the woman with the hornetlike body still smiling and swinging hypnotically from side to side. Two eager young drones now circled around her, vying for her attention and flashing increasingly angry glances at one another.

"She could settle this right now if she wanted to—but she won't. She'll let them fight over her. In another ten minutes they'll be out in the parking lot. If it goes badly, one of them may even die. That's why your species kills, Mrs. Guilford. That's all the reason they need."

"Not Peter."

Nick adjusted his glasses. "And you thought *I* was blind."

Kathryn jumped to her feet. "Why don't you drop this 'your species' and 'my species' routine? Like it or not you're a part of this species, mister! You can withdraw if you like—you can hole up in that perverse little laboratory of yours and spend your life staring at bugs, but you're still one of us. You can look down your nose at everyone and distrust everyone and pick fights with everyone—but that doesn't make you more of a bug, it just makes you less of a human! You say I'm naive—well maybe I am, but you're a *cynic!* You think you're above it all, standing outside and staring in the window at the rest of us—but you're not! You're just the pathetic little boy with the big funny glasses who got tired of being hurt and ran to his room and slammed the door!"

Kathryn suddenly realized that she was standing and that her voice had inadvertently risen to a shout. Half the room had grown silent, watching, and several couples now stood motionless on the dance floor. As if in response to the change of atmosphere, the music segued to a slower beat.

She sank awkwardly into her chair again and sat staring at her reflection in the amber bottle closest to her. There was a long, long silence—so long that Kathryn began to wish that Nick would shout or scream or even throw something—*anything* would be better than the awful silence.

"You know," Nick said suddenly, "I believe I'd like to dance after all."

He rose and stepped a few paces away from the table, then turned and held his arms out for Kathryn. She sat stunned, blinking in disbelief, her mouth gaping open—until she noticed her reflection in the bottle. She slowly rose from her chair and stepped toward him. She stopped a few feet away and held her own arms out, almost with a shrug, as if to say, "It's your move."

Nick stepped forward and slid his right arm around her waist, pulling her closer than she expected. He held her right hand against his chest and put his cheek almost against hers, his lips just a few inches from her right ear. They began to move with the music, far more smoothly than Kathryn would have imagined possible—for someone of his species.

Minutes passed.

"So you're convinced that the sheriff couldn't have done it," Nick said softly.

"I'm absolutely sure."

"Then the next time you see him, will you ask him something? Ask him why, after nine years of silence, he suddenly chose to make your friend's cocaine habit public knowledge."

"He only told one person," she reminded him.

"Yes. But he told the *right* person."

Kathryn thought about his words. "All right. I'll ask him."

Nick spotted the waitress working her way toward them across the dance floor. He stopped and looked into Kathryn's eyes. At this distance, his eyes seemed truly enormous.

"Promise? The next time you see him?"

"I promise."

"Your ride is here," the waitress said to Kathryn.

"Hope you don't mind," Nick said. "I have a few things to take care of."

"Thanks for thinking of me." She patted him on the chest.

She turned and headed toward the door. Halfway there she recognized the figure of Peter St. Clair standing by the entrance, grinning, holding a handwritten sign that said, KATHRYN GUILFORD.

Kathryn spun around and glared back at Nick, but Nick had already turned away, busily studying two angry young men hustling one another out the side door.

CHAPTER 19

"Looked like quite a party back there." Peter smiled without taking his eyes from the road. A burst of static and an indistinguishable voice broke through momentarily on the police scanner. He reached down and switched it off.

"It wasn't a party," Kathryn said, her eyes transfixed by the endless telephone poles blinking past her window. "It was work."

"You needed a ride home from *work?* You got a better job than I do."

"I didn't need a ride home," she said irritably. "This was Nick's idea."

"So now it's *Nick.*"

Kathryn looked at him for the first time since she got in the car. His face flashed lean and angular in the stark headlights of each passing car, and his eyes sparkled like blue ice in the glare of the cold halogen beams.

"How is Jenny?" she asked softly. "You never say."

Peter paused. "She's fine."

"She's *fine*," Kathryn repeated. "That's all men ever say. This is *fine*. That's *fine*. *I'm* fine, thank you very much. 'She's fine' just means, 'I don't want to talk about it.'" Kathryn paused and looked at him again. "How are you two doing?"

Peter turned and looked at her. "Fine."

She shook her head, and they sat in silence for several minutes.

"Do you love her?"

Peter said nothing.

"I saw you dancing with the doc," he said lightly. "Looks like you're keeping your employees happy."

"That was his idea," she lied. "We had an argument, and I think he was trying to patch things up."

"An argument about what?"

This time Kathryn said nothing.

"I thought we were going to *cooperate* on this investigation of yours. How come I'm not invited to these 'work sessions'?"

"It's Nick. He likes to work alone."

"He didn't seem to want to work alone tonight."

Kathryn winced.

"So when am I going to hear something? After all the hours you two have spent together, you must have come up with something."

Kathryn hesitated. "Nick says he wants to wait until he's sure."

"C'mon, Kath, this is me. I know when I'm being stonewalled. I expect that kind of runaround from the doc, but not from you." He reached over and squeezed her arm.

Kathryn looked out the window again.

What's wrong with me? Why am I hesitating? Nick suspects everyone—he said it himself. Why am I allowing him to plant doubts in my mind about Peter, of all people?

"Peter, I need to ask you something."

"Go for it."

"Why didn't you tell me about Jimmy's cocaine habit?"

Peter sighed. "Put yourself in his place, Kath. Life isn't going the way you wanted. You got baggage from the past, you got a sister who belongs in the loony bin, you even got dumped by the girl you wanted to marry."

"Thanks."

"One day you find yourself in the middle of some nameless desert, about to fight the Mother of All Battles. They say you could get nuked or gassed or infected with who-knows-what. You could use a little confidence. I suppose that's how it started for Jim."

"But the war wasn't as bad as everyone thought it would be."

"That's right—so when it's over, you feel a little silly about the whole thing. *Never again,* you tell yourself. You'll just stop—nobody has to know—you'll beat this thing all by yourself. So you quit. But then you do it just one more time—in a moment of weakness, maybe on a bad day. So what? You beat it before, you can do it again. And you do—until the next time. You beat it for a couple of years, and you tell yourself it's over. Then you can only hold out for a few months. Pretty soon you can only go a week, but every time you tell yourself that you're in charge, you can handle it. Fact is, you *can't* handle it—but you're not about to admit it to anyone. You won't even admit it to yourself."

"I don't get it. I would have told someone. I would have asked for help."

"You're not Jim," he said. "Call it a guy thing."

"Then how did *you* find out?"

"From Andy. They were in the same unit, remember? Andy walked in on Jim one day. Caught him in the act. If he hadn't, believe me, Jim would never have told anyone."

"But why didn't you tell anyone else?"

"I did what Jim wanted me to do. I did what I would have wanted him to do for me."

"Couldn't you have at least told *me?*"

Peter glanced at her. "Think about it, Kath. He asks you to marry him. You say no—so he figures for some reason he doesn't quite measure up in your eyes. But maybe he can do better, maybe he can make you wish you had said yes—and then you hear that he's got this little drug problem? I couldn't do that to him. The thought of having a second chance with you is what kept him alive."

Kathryn smiled at him and took his hand. "You're always protecting someone, aren't you, Peter? Andy and Jimmy and now me. Most of all me."

"Just doin' my duty, ma'am." He smiled. "We aim to serve."

Kathryn hesitated. She felt foolish, she felt *faithless* asking her next question—but she had to ask. A promise is a promise.

"You didn't even want *me* to know," she said softly. "So why did you tell Ronny? Ronny told Denny—Denny, of all people. Now everybody knows."

Peter slowly shook his head. "You don't believe Jim killed himself. I do. All the evidence points that way, especially when you figure in the cocaine—but nobody knew about the cocaine. So along comes your Bug Man friend, and he starts to stir things up, starts people talking. Maybe Jim *didn't* kill himself, maybe it was murder, he says. He talks to Amy, he talks to Ronny and Denny and Wayne. He tells the coroner he didn't do his job—next thing you know, maybe I didn't do *my* job. I wanted to put an end to it—so I let people know the rest of the equation." He paused. "Maybe I shouldn't have."

"No, you shouldn't have—not until we find out the truth."

"The truth." Peter rolled his eyes. "Is that what you and the doc are finding? Admit it, Kath, all you've got is questions. You've got no *answers.*"

Kathryn studied his face carefully and took a deep breath.

"Peter," she whispered. "Jimmy's body was moved."

She waited for his reaction…there was none. Not a word, not

a questioning glance, not even the rapid blink of a startled eye. He sat rigid, staring straight ahead, as if the words had never been spoken. They *had* been spoken, and he had certainly heard them—but whatever Peter St. Clair thought of those words he was not about to reveal it.

"What do you mean *moved?*" he said slowly. "Moved how?"

"Do you know what 'fixed lividity' is? Do you know about that?"

Peter nodded, then glanced at her. "Do *you?*"

"I do now. Jimmy's right leg was different—not the way it was supposed to be. Nick says he died with his leg like this." She lifted her foot onto the seat and pulled it tight against her thigh. "But everyone agrees that when they found him, his leg was flat out again. That means that somebody moved him." She longed to add, "And that means somebody killed him"—but she remembered Nick's constant admonition to say only what you know.

Peter groaned. "That could be explained a hundred ways."

"For instance."

"Maybe the leg just stayed up on its own."

"It can't do that." She shook her head. "Try it yourself."

"Then maybe something *held* it up."

"What? Did you find anything? Everybody else says there wasn't anything around. If there was, somebody had to move it. Who would do that?"

Peter grew more impatient with each of Kathryn's questions.

"Do you know about rigor mortis?" he said irritably. "Where the body stiffens up? Did the doc tell you about that too?"

Kathryn frowned. "I've heard of it."

"It usually takes a few hours to set in—but there's a thing called 'instant rigor mortis' too. It happens when the victim is exhausted just before death, and when the death is real sudden—like in a suicide," he said pointedly. "The whole body goes into an instant spasm—it locks up on the spot. I've seen it happen on the battlefield. A guy takes a bullet to the head and you have to *pry* his fingers off his rifle."

"That can't be it."

"Why not? Tell me."

"I don't know why. It just can't, that's all!"

Peter pulled the car into Kathryn's driveway, shifted into park, and turned off the ignition. They sat side by side in the silent shadows for an eternity. Kathryn performed the crucial task of wiping dust from the creases of the dashboard while Peter squeezed and relaxed his grip on the steering wheel in rhythm with his pulse.

Peter turned and reached into the backseat. "You'll want these," he said, handing Kathryn the crumpled cigar box. "Jimmy's things."

"Did you find anything?"

"Just what I thought I'd find," he said. "Just what you see there."

She opened the lid and removed a small bundle of paper. There was a torn and ragged birth certificate, a Social Security card, and a few outdated and irrelevant financial records. There was a yellowed clipping from the *Courier* proudly announcing that no less than three of Rayford's finest had enlisted together at Fort Bragg, and that the world was sure to be a safer place as a result. There were faded letters from Amy during the deployment in the Gulf. There were two letters from Kathryn as well—just two—and the sight of her own handwriting stabbed her through the heart. It seemed pathetic that a human life could be ultimately reduced to such a tiny collection of memorabilia.

She looked at Peter. "What are you thinking?"

"You don't want to know."

"Yes I do."

"I was wondering why you always seem to prefer the dead to the living."

Kathryn turned away.

"First it was Andy," he said. "I know you loved him—I mean, I know how hard it must have been to lose your husband."

"No you don't. You *can't* know."

"Maybe not. But I tried to help in every way I could think of. I was there for you every day—in person, in the flesh. I'm the soldier who came *home,*" he said, "but you wanted the one who didn't. I knew it would take time for you to get over Andy—but I hoped that...over time..."

"We talked about this, Peter," she said awkwardly. "It was hard to let go—not knowing what *happened* to Andy. It's like he was never really gone. I never felt free."

"That was almost ten years ago, Kath. Aren't you free *yet?"*

She said nothing.

"Now it's Jimmy. Now you spend all your time trying to figure out what happened to *him.* I think I got sore about this investigation of yours because it started to look like Andy all over again! I was sorry about Andy—and now I'm sorry about Jim. But life goes on, Kath. They're dead—we're alive. It's time to stop living in the past and start looking ahead."

Kathryn tried to look at him but couldn't.

"It's true. I know it is. I couldn't let go of Andy—and now I can't let go of Jimmy either. I can't let go because they're all I ever had."

"You've still got me."

"I know, but...it's like that story in the Bible, remember? If you lose one sheep, you leave the other ninety-nine and go look for the one you lost."

"You don't leave the ninety-nine forever," he muttered. "Sooner or later you come back. Sometimes I think the only way to get any attention from you is to *die.*"

"Don't say that! Not even joking."

They sat in silence again. Kathryn leaned back against the headrest and searched carefully for her next words.

"I know you won't believe this," she said, "but I do love you."

"Then why—"

"I don't *know* why—and I know it's not fair to you." She looked at him hopelessly. "Why don't you marry that nice Jenny McIntyre and start a family? She *deserves* you."

"And I deserve *you.* But that doesn't seem to matter."

A car rolled by behind them. The sweep of the headlights lit Peter's face for a few seconds, and Kathryn caught a glimpse of his gray-blue eyes. She had always thought that his eyes were the color of deep river ice or perhaps winter fog. To her amazement, she suddenly realized that Peter's eyes were very much like Nick's—both seemed somehow elusive and unapproachable; both seemed to hide behind a thick wall of glass. Somewhere behind that flat gray wall, a soul floated and darted but never really came to rest.

Peter spoke quietly now. "You say you love me. For me, it's more than that. Have you ever felt like you were *made* for someone? Like you were meant to be together? I don't know how to explain it, but that's how I feel—that's how I've always felt about you. So far things have gotten in the way—but those have only been delays. It has to happen, Kath. I know that we're supposed to be together—now, always, forever."

They were the most endearing words Kathryn had ever heard. Once again she dredged the depths of her heart for some token of longing or passion for Peter. She found none. She had done the exercise a thousand times, and each time that she hauled the net to the surface she found only the scattered debris of gratitude or pity. She hated herself for her coldness, for her inability to respond to such a loving, loyal, and patient man. He was right—he *deserved* her love. He had earned it. She ought to love him. And yet...

Kathryn looked at Peter with tears in her eyes.

"Was it my fault?" she whispered.

"What?"

"Jimmy's death. Was Amy right? Did I send him over the edge? Did he kill himself because of me?"

"It wasn't you," he said. "It took more than that."

"How do you know?"

Peter smiled and took her hand. "He was disappointed over you. But if disappointment was enough to kill a man, I would have been dead a long time ago."

Kathryn put her face in her hands and began to weep, and Peter began to softly stroke her hair.

CHAPTER 20

"Lay it over there on the grass, upside down." Nick turned from the hive and handed the lid to Kathryn, who took it with her thick, gloved hands.

Kathryn watched as Nick picked up a tin smoker and sent a single blue puff from the smoldering pine straw into the hive opening, then two more puffs across the open top. He lifted off the entire top super, a drawerlike unit laden with more than forty pounds of amber honey. Row after row of thin wooden frames projected down into it like air filters in a furnace. Each frame was spanned by a section of chicken wire, and the wire was almost obscured by thick golden comb in a quilt of hexagonal cells. On each frame hundreds of bustling bees raced about, darting into empty cells and out again.

"The bees don't look...angry," she said in wonder.

"Bees don't *get* angry—or jealous or cruel or spiteful. Those are qualities of *your* species, Mrs. Guilford, qualities you project on other species to justify your own irrational fears. They do share one quality with you, however. They will fight to protect their home, just as you would."

Nick followed Kathryn to the selected site and gently placed the super on top of the inverted lid, then returned to the hive and prepared to remove the second super. Kathryn studied this strange ritual in silence.

"You've barely said two words all morning," Nick said. "Something on your mind?"

"I'm mad at you," Kathryn said.

Nick peered deep inside the hive. "I think I've got varroa mites," he said. "That's bad."

"Don't you want to know why?"

"You expect me to *ask?* That's like volunteering to be shot. You'll tell me when you're ready."

"You called Peter to drive me home last night. You set me up."

"I arranged an interview for you. As I said, it's customary to call first."

"I thought you were concerned about me. I should have known better."

"I'm *concerned* about completing this investigation. I thought that was your concern too."

Kathryn said nothing.

Nick peered at her over the top of his glasses. "So…did you have a nice drive?"

The third super was about ten inches deep. Nick carefully hoisted it and lugged it to the growing stack of supers just a few yards away.

"I told him," Kathryn said. "I told Peter that the body was moved."

Nick said nothing for a few moments but continued about his work. "The point of an interview," he muttered, "is to *gain* information, not to give it away."

"He deserved to know. We said we would cooperate. Fair is fair."

"By all means let's be *fair,*" Nick said under his breath. "So tell me, how did the sheriff react?"

"I told him about the leg and he said—"

"No—how did he *react?* What did he do in the first five seconds after you told him the body had been moved?"

"Nothing."

"Nothing at all? No exclamation, no look of surprise, no comment of any kind?"

"No. He just…sat there."

"Did he turn to look at you?"

"He just stared straight ahead. I don't see what difference it makes."

"I know you don't. Now tell me what he said about the leg."

"He told me about something called 'instant rigor mortis.' He said the body might have locked up instantly, and that might have frozen the leg in place."

"Very clever." Nick smiled. "It's actually called 'cadaveric response.' It happens because adenosine triphosphate disappears from the muscles. ATP is the compound that allows muscles to contract—without it, the muscles stiffen until decomposition accelerates about a day later. Rigor first appears in the jaw and neck and works its way toward the feet. That means it might take several hours to affect the right leg under normal conditions. But if there's been violent exertion just before death—as in the case of a struggle, for example—the ATP is already depleted and the muscles stiffen rapidly. In the case of sudden death, rigidity may occur instantaneously. That's a 'cadaveric response.'"

"Peter said that can happen in a suicide."

"It can—but it didn't happen to your friend."

"How do you know?"

"Because we have to account for the bent position of one leg, not two. Remember, the spasm is instantaneous. Was your friend standing or lying down at the time of death?"

"There's no way to tell."

"Then let's suppose he was standing. To stand, both legs have to be straight; to crouch, both legs must be bent—but you can't have one straight and one bent. For a cadaveric response to leave your friend's leg in the position we're looking for, he would first have had to somehow exhaust himself, then stand on one leg and raise the other one like a whooping crane—then put the gun to his head and pull the trigger. Very strange behavior, even for a manic depressive like Jimmy."

"What if he was lying down?"

"It's a similar situation. Your friend runs all the way to the woods, thus exhausting himself; then he lies down, raises one knee in an uncomfortable position, takes out his gun and fires. Do you believe that? Besides, if he was lying down we might have found some blood spatter on the grass around the exit wound. Teddy found none. I'm afraid the sheriff's theory doesn't hold up to scrutiny. The best explanation for the leg continues to be that the body was moved."

The look of relief was evident on Kathryn's face. Nick studied her closely.

"What else did the sheriff have to say? What about *my* question?"

Kathryn looked back at him awkwardly. "It's a little complicated..."

"Translation: *I find it embarrassing to talk about.* Look, Mrs. Guilford, can't we get past this 'it's too personal' thing? Repeat after me: 'Peter loves me. I don't love him. He won't give up. He wishes Jimmy and everyone else would get out of the way so he can have me all to himself. He wants this investigation to be over—so he purposely spread the word about Jimmy's drug addiction to put an end to the rumors and help seal the verdict of suicide.'"

"He wants the investigation to be *over,*" she said, "because he thinks I'm obsessed with Jimmy's death."

"And he foolishly assumes that when Jimmy's death is behind you, your attention will turn to him."

Kathryn glared at him. "He answered your question. Now do you understand why he told Denny about the cocaine?"

"I understand that he wants the investigation to be over," Nick said. "And I understand the reason—the reason he gave *you* anyway. But there may be another reason he wants things wrapped up so quickly. That's a possibility we still have to explore." He leaned toward her. "That is, if you're willing."

Kathryn shook her head in exasperation. She looked at the shrinking hive, which now had only two deep supers remaining.

"What in the world are you doing?" she asked.

"I thought we'd do something very special today—and something even more special next time. Come over here."

Kathryn didn't like the sound of his invitation, but she also knew by now that it wasn't really an invitation anyway. Nick slid one of the frames from the exposed super and studied it closely, then carefully plucked a single wriggling insect from among the swirling masses. It was slightly thicker and darker in color, with eyes much larger than the rest.

"There are three kinds of honeybees in a hive," he said. "The vast majority are infertile females—*workers.* Their job is to build and maintain the comb and to care for the brood of young bees. They provide, they nurture, and they defend—they're the ones who can sting you. Then there's the queen, the only sexually productive female in the hive. Her only job is to lay eggs—one every twenty seconds, about fifteen hundred a day. But for those eggs to produce new workers, you need one of these." He held up the wriggling creature between his thumb and forefinger. "This is a drone—a male."

"Why doesn't it sting you?" Kathryn shuddered.

"Because it has no stinger. He's helpless—he has to be fed and cared for by the females."

"Just like in *my* species."

"In many ways bees are very much like your species—and in other ways they're different. The male's single goal in life is to mate with the queen. He has to compete with other males for the privilege, and he often dies in the act of mating."

"How are they different?"

Nick smiled. "There are only a couple hundred of them in the hive. The ladies will keep him around until autumn and then drive him away. There's nothing more useless than a tired old stud." He turned to Kathryn. "Hold out your hand."

Kathryn hesitated, then slowly extended her gloved left hand.

"Good," he said. "Now—take off the glove."

Kathryn began to pull away, but Nick quickly caught her hand in a firm handshake. He loosened his grip and began to pull—slowly, gently, all the time smiling and looking into Kathryn's eyes. The glove began to slip away. She stared wide-eyed at the growing patch of soft, pink flesh at the end of her sleeve.

"I…I can't…"

"You *can*," he said firmly. "This is just a little bit of yarn—a piece of carpet fuzz."

"With *legs*."

"With legs, yes, but *no stinger*. He can't hurt you. He likes you—after all, he's a male. He's thinking to himself, 'That's the most remarkable female I've ever seen! I'd sure like to mate with *that!*' Very much like the males in your species."

"Don't make me laugh!" she said nervously. "What do I do?"

"You do nothing. You just hold still."

Nick held her by the wrist and gently set the drone on the palm of her hand. It had six fragile, finely haired legs. The twin forelegs seemed to pat their way along as the tiny creature crept a few steps, fanned its wings, then moved on. She could see the individual mouthparts, the threadlike veining of the cellophane wings, and the bulbous compound eyes that protruded on either side. The striped abdomen waggled from side to side as it moved.

"It…tickles." Kathryn stared at the tiny life form in her hand

and marveled at its complexity—but even more she marveled at the experience itself. She was actually holding an *insect*—and not just any insect, but the ancient demon from the pit of all her fears. For an instant she allowed her memory to slither back to that day in the Chevy long ago—then she looked again at the tiny bee in the palm of her hand. Her fingers trembled slightly, not from fear but from the rush of pure adrenaline. She felt exultant, she felt redeemed—for the first time since she could remember she felt *free.*

The drone lifted off from her hand and buzzed away, and Nick released her wrist. Kathryn continued to stare at her bare hand, astonished at its vulnerability and at her simultaneous absence of fear. A moment later the bee returned and landed once again on her open palm.

"I guess he *does* like me." She grinned broadly.

"By the way," Nick said, bracing himself to hoist the fourth super, "you might be interested to know that I did a little interview of my own last night."

"Who did you punch this time?"

"I was at the Glam-O-Rama Coin Laundry, and who do you suppose I happened to run across? Jenny McIntyre."

"That *is* a coincidence."

"I think she's in the market for a new relationship," Nick said, looking directly at Kathryn. "Things don't seem to be going well with her current boyfriend."

"Oh?"

"It's very odd. She says he seems distant, distracted—as if his mind is always someplace else. He takes her to public places, but doesn't care to spend time with her alone—as though he were only interested in the *appearance* of a relationship. And she said, 'He never touches me.' That's very strange with such an attractive woman, don't you think?"

"So you find her attractive?" Kathryn said casually. "Do you think you'll be seeing her again?"

"I doubt it. She already told me everything I need to know."

"And what did you need to know?"

"Why a man who loves *you* so single-mindedly would dabble in another relationship."

Nick waited, but Kathryn said nothing. She stood silently, arms folded, looking as indifferent as possible.

"Well?" he said. "Don't you want to know why?"

"You'll tell me when you're ready."

Nick smiled. "Have you ever seen a reduviid? It's commonly known as an assassin bug. It carries a long, curved beak underneath its abdomen like a sheathed sword. It stalks its victim with incredible patience. Sometimes it will run after its prey and then suddenly stop, almost as if it lost interest. And that's what the victim thinks, too, until the assassin bug slowly raises that beak and—"

"I'm getting fed up with all these bug analogies," she broke in. "We're talking about *my* species, remember?"

"The sheriff is not interested in Jenny McIntyre," Nick said. "He's interested in you. Jenny knows it—and according to her, so does everybody else in town—except, apparently, *you.* My bet is that he was pressing in on you, and he sensed you were getting nervous—*why* is your business—so he decided to take the pressure off by acting disinterested. And what better way than by appearing to have another relationship?"

"That's what you believe," she said crossly.

"That's what you believe too—if you'll open your eyes."

"Why are you so suspicious of Peter?"

Nick shrugged. "He smells funny."

"He what?"

He turned and looked at her. "Did you know that a male lasiocampid moth can detect a female from more than two miles away? *Two miles.* Do you know how he does that? By smell, Mrs. Guilford. Insects navigate the world by smell. Only a few of the so-called 'higher life forms' are limited to sight and reason."

"So you have no real reason? This is nothing more than a *hunch?*"

Nick smiled at her. "Maybe we're not so different after all."

By now, the hive was reduced to a single super covered by a thin sheet of metal perforated with small holes.

"Are you having fun playing with your blocks?" she said. "One more and you'll have a brand-new hive over there."

"We're not moving this last one," he said, lifting away the sheet of metal. "We're looking for something."

"What?"

"Her royal highness, the queen."

Kathryn looked again at the tiny piece of fuzz that wandered harmlessly over her hand. "What does the queen look like?"

"She's huge," he said ominously. "Didn't you see *Alien*?"

"How do you know she's in there?"

"Because of this," he said, leaning the sheet of metal against the base of the hive. "This is a *queen excluder.* The small holes allow the workers to pass between the supers, but keep the larger queen below in the brood chamber. That restricts her egg laying to the lower level and reserves the top ones for honey. That makes it a lot easier for the keeper."

He removed the outermost frame and set it aside, then began to work his way toward the center, examining each frame carefully and moving it toward the outside.

"These are the brood frames. The comb is exactly the same, but instead of honey each cell contains a single egg. Take a look." He held one of the frames up for Kathryn. Some of the cells appeared empty, some contained a single plump, white larva, and still others were capped off with wax.

"This is the queen's domain. Her job is to wander over the comb looking for open cells. When she finds one she inserts her abdomen and deposits an egg. All we have to do is search these frames carefully, and…bingo."

There in the center of the frame was one bee that was clearly different. She was larger overall than the surrounding workers and her egg-producing abdomen was twice as long as any other.

"Watch her for a minute," he whispered. "She even *moves* differently."

The queen wandered quickly from cell to cell, searching determinedly for the empty nursery she would require in the next few seconds. Her wings, long unused, were folded back along the top of her thorax. Nick reached down and gently pinched her wings together, plucking her from the comb.

"Can she sting?" Kathryn shivered.

"As many times as she wants. Her stinger is straight, not barbed like the workers. But she only uses it to kill other queens. We can't have anyone usurping the throne, now, can we?"

Nick picked up a piece of screen wire rolled into the shape of a tube about the size of a roll of quarters. A wooden plug sealed each end, and in one plug was a hole no wider than a pencil. He started the queen into the hole headfirst. She seized the edges with her forelegs and willingly proceeded inside. Nick sealed the hole behind her with a rubber cork, then held the contraption and its prisoner aloft by a string attached to each end like a kind of living necklace.

"No thanks." Kathryn shook her head. "It's not exactly my style."

"It *is* a necklace," Nick said, "but it's not for you. It's for me."

He turned to a small cage about the size of a thick briefcase. It was framed in thin cypress, but the sides were covered with fine screen wire. In the top panel was a hole a baseball could just fit through.

"This is a bee crate. This is how bees are shipped—you can order them by mail, in case you're interested. Now, the first thing we do is put in the queen." He dangled the queen's wire cage into the bee crate until she hung suspended, halfway to the bottom, like an ousted ruler condemned to the gibbet. He secured the shoestring with a thumbtack, then inserted into the hole a large funnel rolled from galvanized sheet metal. From the stack of relocated supers he selected a frame thick with workers and held it above the funnel. With one well-practiced flip of the wrist he shook off a fist-sized clump of bees into the funnel and down into the throne room below.

"Will they just *stay* there?" Kathryn asked.

"They'll stay. That's where the queen is. The queen constantly emits a pheromone from her mandible. It's sort of like a powerful perfume that tells the workers, 'I'm the queen. You're safe here. This is where you belong.' For a honeybee, the hive is not home; the *queen* is home. Wherever the queen is, that's where they belong—and they'll follow her anywhere."

Nick continued to fill the bee crate with the inhabitants of a second frame, then a third, continuing on until several thousand honeybees huddled around the queen in her tiny cage and wandered over the wire sides of the box. Satisfied with the size of his collection, Nick removed the funnel and sealed off the hole with a simple wooden plug. Then he picked up a plastic spray bottle and began to wet the screened faces of the box with a clear, viscid liquid.

"Sugar syrup," he said. "Bees love any source of sugar. For the next day or so the bees will engorge themselves on it. It makes them fat and happy, and when they're fat and happy they forget about little things—like stinging you."

"I still don't get it. What exactly are we going to do?"

"We're going to make a bee beard, of course."

Bee beard. Kathryn remembered hearing the phrase only once before, at the age of nine, when her mother took her to the state fair in Raleigh. She had accidentally wandered into a demonstration by the North Carolina Beekeepers Association where a man had purposely covered his face and neck with thousands of wriggling bees—and she had to be carried screaming from the pavilion.

"*You're* going to make a bee beard," she corrected him. "Look, Nick, I know what you're trying to do. And I appreciate it, really I do—"

"No, you don't."

"And I've already got the message: *Insects are your friend.* I believe you, okay?"

"No, you don't. Mrs. Guilford, you don't just have a fear of insects, you have a *pathological* fear of insects. The most effective form of therapy for that kind of phobia is immersion therapy."

"You want me to immerse myself in bees? You're out of your mind."

"No, I'm going to immerse *myself* in bees. I just want you to watch—and maybe help a little. It's a remarkable experience. It's a *therapeutic* experience."

Kathryn looked at him doubtfully. "How exactly does this bee beard work?"

"You've probably guessed most of it. We've removed the queen from the hive and placed her in a kind of collar. We've gathered two or three pounds of workers around her and we'll sedate them for a day or two on sugar water. The bees have been removed from the hive so they have no honey to protect or brood to defend. Their instincts will tell them to stick to the queen. So in a couple of days I'll pull out the queen and I'll tie the collar around my neck—and then all the bees come to Mama."

"And you won't get stung? Not at all?"

"Maybe once or twice, but only by accident. You have to be careful, of course."

She looked down again at the single bee that still clung tenaciously to her hand. She slowly rotated her wrist this way and that. Each time the bee simply crawled to the upper surface and remained.

"I think I've made a friend."

Nick reached out and gently took Kathryn by the wrist again.

"I wouldn't get too attached," he said. "You've been holding a female."

Before Kathryn could jerk her hand away Nick clamped a paralyzing grip on her arm.

"Or is it? Maybe it's a male, too, just like the first bee. Or maybe I was lying to you all the time—maybe there never was a male. Maybe they're impossible to tell apart. Or maybe *this* is the queen, and she can sting you as many times as she wants. Think about it, Mrs. Guilford. A moment ago you thought you had made a new friend, and now you feel that old bogeyman crawling up your spine again. What changed? Your enemy is not out here," he said, pointing to her hand. "It's in your *head*."

He gave her wrist a quick flip and the bee soared away, back to what remained of the hive.

Nick began to reassemble the hive from the nearby stack of supers, while Kathryn stood rubbing the white imprints of his fingers from her wrist. He picked up the lid and began to reposition it atop the hive. At the last moment the lid slipped from his fingers and dropped, crushing two workers lingering on the edge. The faint smell of smashed bananas floated up to Kathryn, triggering an ancient, haunting memory.

"We'd better wrap things up," Nick said. "That alarm pheromone will make them more aggressive, and I'm a wee bit underdressed for *that* party."

He collected the smoker, the funnel, and the other tools of their morning's work, then headed back toward the lab.

"Well?" Kathryn called after him. "Aren't you going to tell me what it was? Was it a drone or a worker? A male or a female?"

Nick stopped. "What do you think it was?"

"It doesn't matter what I *think* it was," she said irritably. "What was it?"

"On the contrary, Mrs. Guilford. It makes no difference what it was; it only matters what you *perceived* it to be."

Kathryn watched as he turned and walked away.

"Meet you at the car," he called back. "We've got a long drive ahead of us."

We need gas." Nick nodded toward his fuel gauge. He draped his left arm out the window in a halfhearted signal as Exit 83 approached.

"How can you tell?" Kathryn shouted above the hot afternoon wind that rumpled past the open windows. She pointed to the bottom of the fuel gauge where the red needle indicator had long ago fallen and lain to rest.

"It's an intuitive thing for me. You live with someone long enough, you get to know their needs."

"You two make a great couple."

He turned off I-95 just north of Richmond, Virginia, and steered the smoking Dodge into the Parham Road Texaco. Kathryn was glad for the break. They had been on the road for over three hours now, and she felt half-beaten by the combination of pummeling wind, stifling heat, and bone-jarring vibration. The thirty-five-year-old Dodge had no suspension left at all and handled each dip and pothole like a bowling ball on a stairway. The wind constantly whipped wisps of auburn hair across her face where it clung to her lipstick. She took a tissue from her purse and wiped her face clean, then pulled her hair back in a thick ponytail.

The car shuddered several times and lurched to a stop at the pump, followed by an angry complaint of hisses, clicks, and groans. Nick turned and looked at Kathryn.

"You expect *me* to pump the gas?" she asked.

"Of course not." He tossed aside his seat belt. "I expect you to pay. 'Plus expenses,' remember?"

Kathryn enthusiastically slammed the door and flashed a look of mock remorse back at Nick before heading toward the service center. She set a Mountain Dew and a convenience pack of Extra-Strength Tylenol on the counter.

"Pump six," she muttered to the cashier, who glanced out the window and slid a quart of 10W-40 and a paper funnel across the counter.

"It's on the house," he said with a note of genuine sympathy in his voice.

"How far to D.C.?" she asked, tearing through the foil of her Tylenol.

"An hour and a half—that's just to the Beltline. Where you headed?"

"Walter Reed Hospital." She rolled the capsules to the back of her tongue. "On the north side—almost to Maryland."

"Then add forty-five minutes. Double if you hit the traffic."

As they pulled back onto I-95 North, Kathryn slid a yellow foil-wrapped sausage biscuit across the seat to Nick. He peeled back the foil with his teeth and took a bite.

"What's this?"

"*Plus expenses.* Eat hearty."

Nick reached down by his feet and took a chocolate chip cookie from a plastic bag. "They're from Teddy," he said through a mouthful. "He made them for you."

"How am I enjoying them?"

The Dodge slowly accelerated to cruising speed like a jet

approaching the sound barrier. It vibrated and shook until Kathryn was sure the frame would come apart beneath her—but then it somehow settled into a relatively smooth and even ride.

"She just has to hit her stride," Nick said, and Kathryn wondered silently why unreliable equipment is always referred to in the female gender.

They had passed most of the journey in silence, neither one wanting to expend the energy to shout above the constant roar of the wind, but by this point the ennui was becoming more stifling than the heat. Kathryn stopped rubbing her temples and glanced up at Nick.

"We could have taken my car, you know. It has this new thing called 'air conditioning.'"

"I thought my car would fit the image better."

"What image?"

"The image of a down-and-out Desert Storm veteran and his poor wife, their lives plagued by his lingering Gulf War Syndrome—mysterious rashes, fibromyalgic symptoms, chronic fatigue, and memory loss."

"How long have we been married?"

"You're asking me? I'm the one with memory loss."

Kathryn smiled in spite of herself. "And why is this little charade necessary?"

"I've been doing a little research. It seems Walter Reed Army Medical Center is the premier treatment unit for Gulf War Syndrome in the entire U.S. Several years ago they opened a Specialized Care Program for Gulf veterans and their families. It's a three-week outpatient program. According to Amy, her brother took part a couple of times."

"What are we looking for?"

"Our interview with Amy raised some interesting questions. Who was the last one to see Jim McAllister alive? Amy didn't know—no one in Rayford seems to know. It may have been someone up at Walter Reed."

"Is there some prize for being last in line?"

"The last one to see your friend alive may be able to give us some insight into his state of mind just before the time of death. Was he angry again? Did he seem out of control? Did he say where he was going or what he planned to do? Did he appear in any way suicidal?"

Kathryn felt a knot tightening in her stomach. "I don't like all this pretending. Can't we just request Jimmy's medical records or something?"

"Sure, if you're the next of kin. I suppose you could tell them you *almost* married him..."

Kathryn shot him a look. "I just don't want this to turn into another Schroeder's Funeral Home. All right? Okay?"

Nick smiled. "Did you bring the things I asked for?"

"I packed an overnight bag, if that's what you mean."

He paused. "Does the sheriff know we're making this trip together?"

"Yes. Why?"

"Does he know we're staying overnight?"

She narrowed her eyes to tiny slits. "Why *shouldn't* he know?"

"Good," he whistled. "Good, good, good."

Kathryn turned to the backseat. "I brought you this." She held up a faded gray T-shirt with the words '82d AIRBORNE' in black block letters across the top with Master Parachutist's wings beneath. "It's the only thing of Andy's that I thought would fit you."

"It might be a little tight in the chest."

"You wish."

"What else have you got for me?"

Kathryn hesitated.

"Come on, Mrs. Guilford, let's see them."

She turned slowly to the backseat once more and removed an accordion letter file with a brown shoestring wrapped around it. She opened it and carefully removed a small stack of well-worn envelopes, each bearing her name and address in a coarse handwritten script. Some bore large and foreign-looking stamps; some had no stamps, but several different postmarks; some were so badly worn that the pages within poked through the crumbling corners of the envelope.

"There aren't many of them," she said. "Not as many as I would have liked—not many at all before September of '90, when the postmaster announced that the soldiers could send letters home for free. Andy said he'd go to mail a letter but the whole book of stamps would stick together because of the heat. The truth is, he wasn't much of a writer."

She flipped through the crumbling papers like a rabbi handling the Torah. She turned to Nick.

"I'm not sure I want you to touch them."

"I don't want to touch them. I want you to read them to me."

Kathryn looked aghast. The words of these few letters were more than personal; they were sacred. Was she supposed to casually recite each one as though it were nothing more than an interesting tidbit from this morning's *Holcum County Courier*? And how was she supposed to read them? Should she simply relay each word, or should she make a real performance out of it—should she put some *feeling* into it? The worst part was that she knew this Bug Man was oblivious to all of these concerns. To him these sacred writings were nothing more than miscellaneous bits of evidence—perhaps *insignificant* bits of evidence—to be tagged and filed away for possible use. Her blood ran cold at the very idea. She felt incensed; she felt insulted; she felt *violated.*

Nick interrupted her thoughts.

"Mrs. Guilford, we're trying to understand the cause of your friend's depression. Your husband and Jim McAllister were in the same unit—that means they camped together, they ate together, they probably fought together. Jim's depression may have been triggered by a specific event in the Gulf, and that event may have taken place before your husband was killed. If so, his letters may provide some clue as to what it was. I'm sure you've read them a hundred times; maybe there's something you overlooked."

"Maybe what killed Jimmy *was* my husband's death," she snapped. "Did you ever think of that?"

"I doubt it."

"Why?"

"Because *you* survived it, and no one felt his loss more than you."

It was a minor acknowledgment of her feelings, no more than a nod in her direction, but Kathryn appreciated it nonetheless.

Nick began to slowly shake his head. "There had to be something else—something more. Mr. McAllister felt that there was something wrong that needed to be made right. Maybe your husband knew what it was."

Kathryn slowly picked up the first of the precious envelopes and carefully removed the letter within. With the first glimpse of her husband's handwriting a wave of grief overtook her. These were more than words, they were strokes made by Andy's hand—a hand that no longer existed anywhere in the universe. The script was rough and uneven, and the left margin of his letters was never straight. He dotted every "i" with a tiny circle because Walt Disney did, and he liked that. Whenever her name appeared—always as "Kath," never "Kathryn"—it began with a printed "K" simply because he had never mastered the cursive letterform. Every jot and loop and curve reminded Kathryn of the man. It was almost like hearing his voice again, and she longed to weep. Instead she felt sick to her stomach.

She turned to Nick. "Roll your window up," she said. "I'm not going to shout this."

He took one look at her and complied without question. She began to read clearly and evenly.

August 8, 1990

Dear Kath,

Well, by now you know it wasn't just another alert. Got to the base just before midnight—it was pouring rain. Most of the boys were betting that this was just another emergency deployment exercise and after a day in the woods we'd be back home. Then a Red Line came down from brigade HQ and we found out the whole 82d was called out! That's when I knew it had to be the Middle East.

Spent the night at the Corps Marshalling Area. Slept on the concrete floor—sure wished I was back in bed with you. Most of the unit made it for lock-in but I bet they had to search all the bars in Fayetteville to round up some of the boys. Pete and Jim both made it in, but I was in first. The 2d Battalion split off and that's the last we saw of Pete.

The next day was just squat and hold. Tried to find out what we could about the mission, but nobody knew much of anything except that we're headed for someplace called DARAN (can't spell it) and we're not jumping in. Then we got the word that the 2d Brigade would be first to deploy and Jim and me were on the first chalk out. We were slotted to leave on a DC-10 but we drew a C-141 instead. It was crowded—forty boys, two Hummers, and a M-105 trailer. We had wheels-up less than fourteen hours from call-in—good thing we were the DRB. Stopped to refuel in Goose Bay, Canada, then again here at Torrejon AFB in Spain. I'm mailing this from the USO post. Free mail!

Can't tell you much about the mission except nobody thinks we'll be here long. Sorry I didn't get to say a proper good-bye—you were sleeping sound and I didn't want to wake you. Wish you hadn't been too tired when we went to bed! NOW how long do I have to wait? When I get home let's set the day aside and—

Kathryn looked away. She folded the letter and gently returned it to its envelope.

"I followed most of that," Nick said. "What's the 'DRB'?"

"The Division Ready Brigade. The 82d Airborne is the army's rapid-reaction force, and they have to be ready to deploy anywhere in the world in just a few hours' time. The division is made up of three infantry brigades. They take turns being the

DRB, each one for six to eight weeks at a time. It's like a doctor on call. When you're the DRB, you're on two-hour recall and you have to be ready to have wheels up on the lead aircraft within eighteen hours of call-in. Andy and Pete and Jimmy were all in the 2d Brigade, and they were the DRB when the call came in."

"They were all in the same unit?"

"Not exactly. You were never in the army, were you? A brigade is broken up into battalions. Andy and Jimmy were in the 4th Battalion, Peter was in the 2d. The 4th Battalion was designated DRF-1—Division Ready Force 1—that's why Andy and Jimmy were the first ones out."

"Two-hour recall—that's pretty short notice."

"Andy left so fast he took the car keys with him. I couldn't drive because the keys were in Saudi Arabia." Kathryn stared out the window. "I never even woke up," she whispered. "Maybe that's why I never sleep now."

Without looking down she opened the second envelope. "The next one's dated two weeks later."

August 24, 1990

Dear Kath,

We made it into Dhahran. Me and Jim marched out the back of the Starlifter in full combat gear and camo paint ready to go to war. It was the middle of the night and there was nobody around anywhere. We felt like idiots! Some buses met us on the tarmac and took us to our command post out in the middle of nowhere, an old Saudi air-defense base near a place called al-Jubayl.

Got your first letter last week along with three more. Jim was jealous as a jay—write more! Took a while for the mail to catch up with us here. Thanks for the picture but guess what? The Saudis blackened out your arms and legs. Seems that's pornography around these parts, young lady! I'll have to fill in the rest from memory. Thanks for the County Courier. It's a few days old, but the papers are our only source of news around here. Send a Fayetteville Times if you can.

You wouldn't believe how hot it is here! We picked a great time to fight with Iraq. Yesterday we deployed into the desert for the first time, mostly to start getting used to the heat. By 0800 it was 95 degrees—it can hit 130 in the afternoon. We started NBC training—nuclear, biological, and chemical—and we're learning to spot Iraqi land mines.

Most of all we're learning how to see. Sounds crazy, doesn't it? In the desert, distances are really tough to judge. That's risky when you're trying to call in fire. Sometimes the rocks heat up and they look like enemy patrols through our thermal sights. We got a lot to learn fast—the 82d's last deployment was in the jungle in Panama!

Nobody knows when the enemy might come. We keep hearing about terrorist threats but we haven't seen a single wog since we've been in country—but they tell us there are 250,000 of them just a hundred miles north! We have to wear our helmets and carry our weapons and masks at all times, even at mess. Got to be ready when the balloon goes up.

You'd love it here, Kath. They've got the biggest black flies you ever seen! The joke around here is that this is where the army's helicopters are born—the flies are really baby Chinooks. They love our food so we have to eat fast. Had our first scorpion casualty too. Your kind of place—wish you were here.

Word is we might redeploy soon. Rumors everywhere—none of them reliable. I'll write when I can. Jim says hello.

Miss me?
Andy

"I know those flies," Nick whistled. "They're tabanids—probably *Tabanus arabicus*. Very large, very nasty."

"Is that all you're getting out of this? Observations about the local insects?"

"Not at all," he said calmly. "So far we have a lonely soldier eight thousand miles from home, uprooted on a no-notice call-out, adjusting to a strange and hostile desert environment, and living under the constant threat of enemy attack."

"*Two* lonely soldiers," Kathryn corrected.

"But only one with a loving wife waiting for him back home."

The traffic began to slow and came almost to a standstill where the HOV lanes had been closed after the morning rush. With the windows rolled up and the breeze no longer forcing its way through the vents, the car became more and more unbearable.

Kathryn resisted the urge to wipe a bead of sweat rolling down her forehead.

"The next letter didn't come for over a month."

October 15, 1990

Dear Kath,

Sorry it's taken so long to write—you know me. The first of the month we redeployed to a place called Ab Qaiq. It's the home of a huge ARAMCO oil complex and we're here to protect the pumping station from attack—a ton of Arab oil flows through here to the Gulf.

It's about a hundred miles farther away from the enemy—bet you're glad to hear that, but I can't say I am. We were the first troops into Saudi Arabia and now it seems like we're being told to move over and let the heavy forces do their stuff. I didn't come here to squat and hold, Kath. I want a front-row seat when the show gets started. It looks like we could be at Ab Qaiq for a long time and nobody likes it.

The 4-325 is in an area called Camp Gold, nothing but a huge piece of desert surrounded by concertina wire. We've built a tent city there—it's really something to see. Pretty rough—no lights, no mess facility, no wash basins, no laundry. We shower together outside—no stalls. It's okay now but they say it gets cold in December! There's no privacy at all. We each have a small corner we call our own and everybody's starting to stockpile stuff sent from home. We stash it in our MRE boxes we keep under our cots. That's my whole world right now—one cot and the stash underneath.

Caught a glimpse of Pete yesterday. 2d Battalion is in Camp White, an old warehouse across the way behind the motor pool. I waved but I don't think he saw me.

Three weeks ago we lost our first man—a truck overturned on a paratrooper from the 505. Somebody wasn't paying attention. Last week some grunt gave himself the "million dollar wound"—shot himself in the foot just to get back to the States. The waiting and the crowding are starting to wear on all of us. I think the cracks are starting to show. I'm handling it okay but I think it's driving Jim nuts. You know he likes to get alone sometimes, and there is no alone here—not anywhere. No alcohol either—that was one of the Saudi's rules. I'd give a week's pay to be able to take Jim out for a couple of brews. He looks like he could use it.

Write to him, Kath. The mail comes in every day on two or three forty-foot tractor trailers. Some of the guys get piles of letters and all Jim gets is some hen scratchings from that sister of his begging him not to get killed. He's taken to reading the unopened "To Any Soldier" mail—stuff from some grade-school class from who-knows-where. I think it's getting him down. I used to show him all the great stuff you send, but not anymore—it just makes him angry. Write to him.

I miss you.
Andy

"So did you?" Nick asked.

"Did I what?"

"Write to him."

Kathryn shifted uneasily.

"Why not?"

"I did a couple of times, but I didn't want to give him—you know—the wrong idea. So I kept writing, 'Andy and I this,' and 'Andy and I that.' But Andy said it only seemed to make things worse, so I just stopped."

They sat in silence for a few minutes before Kathryn reached for the next letter.

"So we know that Jimmy's getting discouraged," she said.

"Yes," Nick said under his breath, "and we know that he's getting *angry.*"

"The next letter wasn't until January. Andy called home at Christmas—both MCI and AT&T offered free three-minute phone calls to all the troops. It was wonderful to hear from him, except that an NCO was listening in the whole time to make sure we didn't pass along anything confidential. I got a video from Andy too—every soldier got a free videotape and the chance to record a fifteen-minute message for the folks back home."

"Did you bring it along?"

"Of course not."

"Too bad. I guess it's ESPN tonight."

There was a long pause that followed.

"I got a video from Peter too. I suppose you'd love to see *that* one."

Another pause.

"It was nothing." She shrugged. "Really. It was just about where he'd been and what he'd done and how he hoped he'd be home soon—that sort of thing."

"What could be more harmless than that?" Nick intoned.

"Exactly."

"So why did it make you feel uncomfortable?"

"Who said it made me feel uncomfortable?"

Nick slowly turned and looked at her.

At last they began to move again, slowly and relentlessly gathering speed as they approached the Capital Beltway. The traffic didn't open up, it simply began to accelerate together in one vast, irresistible herd. Kathryn had visited Washington several times, and she always felt as she approached the city that there was a kind of suction, a vortex that seemed to draw her toward some mysterious end of its own.

January 25, 1991

Dear Kath,

I know you've been following the news so you know where things are going. Some UN bigwig went to Baghdad on the fourteenth to try to get Iraq to pull out by the deadline the next day—no luck. Iraq's got the fourth largest army in the world and they're itching to try it out. For our part, the 82d is happy to oblige them.

Now the air war has started and that means more waiting—but at least we got our marching orders. The entire brigade has moved into attack position. I can't say where, and you won't hear about it on the news, but I'll tell you this—I can see the border from here. At night I can hear the bombers pass overhead and when the strike zone is close enough I can hear the bombs. On the way back home they dump their excess ordnance in the desert not far from here, and I can feel the ground rumble. The Iraqis fired their first SCUD at us but a Patriot brought it down. We started taking our PB pills every eight hours—they're supposed to stop anthrax and nerve gas, but nobody knows for sure. They make some of the boys sick.

Two soldiers from the 3rd ACR were wounded yesterday in a firefight across the border. The Iraqis are only six miles away. They know we're here and they can reach us with artillery if they want to. The pressure's building. Everybody knows we're going in but nobody knows when. Not much time to talk to Jim—everybody's busy digging in.

I plan to write again before G-Day. The mail caught up with us here so you can still write to me.

Andy

They took the exit for 495 North to Rockville, Maryland, where I-95 dumps into the Capital Beltway in a violent confluence of horns, engines, radios, and tires. Hulking gray rigs and flatbeds lumbered along belching puffs of smoke, while Porsches and BMWs honked and darted between them like angry mosquitoes. They all pushed, shoved, and jammed their way toward their destinations, some chatting on phones or dabbing at makeup as casually as if they were still parked at home.

The next envelope was a medium-sized manila padded mailer. Kathryn squeezed it open and peered deep within, as if she were searching for a bucket in the bottom of a well. She reached in with two fingers and removed a folded letter on ordinary notebook paper, then carefully tipped the mailer over. A golden band rolled out into her left hand.

She sat silently staring at the ring for several minutes. The folded letter still lay on her lap.

"May I?" Nick said gently.

She barely nodded.

He propped the letter against the steering wheel and began to read.

February 17, 1991

Dear Kath,

I can write this now because by the time you get it everyone will know anyway. A few days from now the ground war begins. G-Day.

The 82d has been attached to the French 6th Light Armor Division. We'll be under their command when the battle begins. Our job is to do what the Airborne always does—push in fast and deep, secure a foothold, and clear the way for the heavy forces behind us. Our objective is to seize Al Salman Airbase about 90 miles north of here. At Al Salman we'll go up against the Iraqi 45th Division—three infantry brigades and two artillery battalions. They got a tank battalion, too, if there's anything left of it. They're not the Republican Guard, but they're no pushovers.

The French will lead the way in AMX-10RCs—small, fast six-wheeled tanks with 105mm guns. Our boys will follow in five-ton trucks, stopping to clear enemy positions along the way. We'll wear our NBC suits—they're awkward, but nobody knows what to expect from the Iraqis. At Al Salman the real party begins.

The 4-325 was the first to deploy, the first in country, and now we have the honor of being the first into Iraq. I tell you the truth, Kath, I can't wait. I'm sick and tired of being a target—I want to do what I came to do—what I joined the Airborne to do. Try not to worry—I won't do anything stupid—but they don't give battlefield promotions to the ones who sit on their hands. I plan to do the deed. I'll make you proud.

I'm enclosing a little something for you. What with the heat and sweat and all I was afraid I might lose it in the desert. It might be a good idea if you hung on to it for me. Don't worry, I'll tell all the Iraqi girls I'm married.

Went over to the 2-325 to see Pete today. Wanted to wish him luck—and I needed to talk to him about Jim. We had a big blowup the other day—can't tell you about it now. I guess everybody's been a little nuts lately. All I can say is, he better straighten himself out fast. We sure need to be on the same team in a few days.

I'm not going to say good-bye—by the time you read this it will all be over and I'll be writing you another letter. But I want you to know how much I—

"Don't," Kathryn snatched the letter back again. "Don't read that part."

He looked down at her hand. "That's the ring?"

"A lot of the boys mailed them home. The wives all panicked, of course. The Family Support Group at Fort Bragg had to call us in and assure us that this was perfectly normal and that we'd all be slipping them back on our husbands' fingers in no time at all."

She held up the ring and slowly examined it. "I've still got mine."

Nick let several minutes go by before he spoke again. "Andy said he had a 'big blowup with Jim'—something he didn't want to talk about."

"Something he didn't want to *write* about. Until the ground war began, all the letters home were read by censors."

"So you think that's when your husband discovered Jim's drug habit?"

She nodded. "He wouldn't take a chance on putting that in print."

"So—what happened on G-Day?"

Kathryn removed the last envelope, the only official-looking document among them. The letterhead bore the address of the United States General Accounting Office.

B-260898
April 7, 1995
The Honorable Jesse Helms
United States Senate

Dear Senator Helms:

In response to your request, this report presents the results of the GAO's investigation of events leading to the apparent death of PFC Andrew Guilford of the 82d Airborne Division; and an assessment of the adequacy of U.S. Army investigations following the incident.

On the night of February 26, 1991, PFC Guilford's unit, under OPCON of the French 6th LAD, encountered heavy resistance at the Al Salman Airbase. In pursuit of the enemy PFC Guilford became separated from his unit in a position exposed to both friendly and hostile fire. Hostilities ceased near daybreak, at which time a search was immediately conducted for PFC Guilford. Despite considerable effort, no identifiable trace of his body or equipment was discovered.

Two soldiers of the 6th LAD were killed in the same hostilities, and ten were wounded. It is assumed that PFC Guilford was the victim of indirect fire of either friendly or hostile origin. Within hours the 82d Airborne began an AR 15-6 fratricide investigation of the incident. No disciplinary action was recommended.

Supplemental investigations yielded no further evidence; all available diplomatic channels with the Iraqis were exhausted. The Forces Command Staff Judge Advocate recommended that PFC Guilford be officially listed as Killed in Action, Body Not Recovered. He was posthumously awarded the Bronze Star for his actions.

GAO has briefed U.S. Army representatives and the deceased serviceman's immediate family on the content of this investigation.

Yours,
Richard C. Stiener
Director

Kathryn carefully returned the file of letters to the backseat, then rolled her window down again. She leaned her head back on the seat and let the wind engulf her, washing away the stinging words and the broken promises and the haunting memories—lifting her out of the past and setting her gently back in her own world again.

"What about Jim?" Nick said. "Did he have anything to add to the official account?"

"Jimmy said nothing. He could never bring himself to talk about Andy. I think it hurt him almost as much as it hurt me."

She looked at Nick, who sat motionless behind the wheel. She knew by now that even when his body was at rest, his mind was in constant motion. "I'll probably hate myself for asking this, but...what are you thinking?"

"Nothing you haven't thought of before."

"What does that mean?"

Nick glanced over at her. "Jim McAllister asked you to marry him. You not only turned him down but accepted another man's proposal the *same night*. Think about it, Mrs. Guilford. How does that make a man feel?"

"I don't know," she mumbled. "Hurt, I suppose."

"No. How does that make a *man* feel?"

She said nothing.

"Come on. You know the answer to this one."

"Angry," she said slowly. "It makes him feel angry."

"Angry at *whom?*"

"At me, of course."

"Wrong. He loved you."

Kathryn looked at him. "Where are you going with this?"

"You spurned Jim McAllister for another man, Mrs. Guilford. What do you suppose Jimmy told himself—that you didn't love *him* or that you loved another man *more?* Jim McAllister had every reason to resent your husband, even hate him. He had everything to gain if your husband was removed from the picture."

"That's ridiculous."

"Is it? Who was the last one to see your husband alive, Mrs. Guilford? Odds are it was someone on the battlefield—someone in his unit. Why is it that Jim McAllister could never bring himself to talk about what happened in the Gulf? Sounds like a man wrestling with his conscience to me."

"Stop it!" she shouted. "You didn't know Jimmy *or* Andy, and you have no idea what they felt or what they might have done! You have no right to accuse Jimmy this way! I am not hiring you to investigate the death of my *husband!*"

They drove on in silence. It was several minutes before Nick glanced over at her again.

"Like I said," he whispered. "It's nothing you haven't thought of before."

CHAPTER 22

"What can we do for you, Mr...?"

"Call me Nick. And this is my wife, Darlene."

Kathryn glared at Nick as hard as she dared, then turned and smiled at the man and woman before them.

"Nick, Darlene—welcome to the Specialized Care Program."

Kathryn sat beside Nick in a comfortable reception room on Ward 64 of the Main Hospital at Walter Reed Army Medical Center. The man across the desk from her was the program administrator, a pleasant-looking man in his midfifties, himself a veteran of over thirty years in the infantry who traded in his uniform for a pair of comfortable khakis and a navy button-down. The trim woman who leaned against the desk to his right was the social worker, who said she always sat in on the initial interviews.

"Exactly what kind of information are you looking for?" the man asked, folding his hands before him.

"I heard about this program from a friend, another Gulf War vet. He came here a couple of times, and he said it did him a world of good. He said I should check into it myself, so here we are."

"You really should have made an appointment, Nick. To tell you the truth, I shouldn't be talking to you at all, but the receptionist said you were very...persistent."

"I appreciate that, I really do," Nick nodded. "It was a last-minute thing—call it a whim. The little woman dragged me up here to see the Gowns of the First Ladies exhibit over at the American History Museum, so I said what the hey! It's just a stone's throw to Walter Reed. Might as well drop by."

He smiled at Kathryn and put his hand on her knee. She smiled back, lifted his hand, and put it in hers while the social worker watched.

"I need to ask you for a last name, Nick, and what branch of the service you were in. We need to verify that you are in fact a Gulf War veteran. Just a formality."

"Well now, that's the thing," Nick said uneasily. "I'd rather not say. Not just yet."

"Why not?"

"It's my job. I've been calling in sick a lot at the factory, and people are starting to wonder. I get these joint pains and headaches, and I'm tired all the time. And I have trouble remembering things. If word gets back to them that I have some kind of 'syndrome' or something, it could be bad for me."

"Nick—your employer cannot legally discriminate against you just because you have Gulf War Syndrome."

"Not *legally*—but you and I know it happens in other ways. They forget to ask you if you want overtime, you get passed over for a promotion, whatever. There's always some other explanation, but *you* know why."

The social worker stepped in. "Nick, you mentioned pain and fatigue and memory loss. Are there any other symptoms?" She glanced at Kathryn. "What about your relationship with Darlene?"

Nick looked forlorn. "I don't mind telling you it's not what it used to be. I mean, Darlene used to be a regular ball of fire...*you* know. But lately—"

"We don't like to talk about it," Kathryn cut in abruptly. "It's very personal."

"But we *need* to talk about it, Darlene," Nick implored. "If we can't talk to these nice people, who can we talk to?"

Kathryn glowered at him hard, since it was appropriate to the part she played, hoping that her deeper meaning would come through. But it was obvious that Nick was enjoying his little game and that he was not about to give it up for something as insignificant as her dignity.

"Perhaps some general information about the program would be helpful," the administrator offered, sliding an information packet across the desk. "The Specialized Care Program serves Gulf War veterans of all branches of the military. It's a three-week outpatient program that runs continuously throughout the year. At any given time there are from seven to ten personnel joining us—spouses are welcome too." He smiled at Kathryn.

"On the first day we take the group on a tour of the hospital. After that they're introduced to the program staff. Each patient works closely with an internist and our staff psychologist. The rest of the team includes myself, Mrs. Andino here, a physiatrist, an occupational therapist, a physical therapist, a fitness trainer, a wellness coordinator, and a nutritionist. We meet Monday through Friday, 7:30 to 4:30."

"How long has your psychologist been here?" Kathryn asked.

"Ten or eleven years. I assure you, Darlene, he's very experienced."

"I'm sure all conversations with your psychologist are *confidential,*" Nick said with emphasis, glancing over at Kathryn.

"Absolutely. All of our clinical records are confidential. You need have no fears about that."

"Tell me more about the group," Nick said. "I imagine they get to know each other pretty well after three weeks together."

"They become very close," the social worker said warmly. "They spend a lot of time discussing their experiences in the Gulf, the impact of their symptoms, areas of personal struggle—what we call 'life stressors.'"

"Do you find that some of them stay in touch after the program has ended?"

"Some of them become lifelong friends."

Nick nodded thoughtfully. "What if three weeks doesn't do it? Can I come back?"

"As many times as you like," the administrator said. "We teach vets how to manage a chronic illness. Some of them have returned several times over the years."

"Do groups ever return—together, I mean?"

"We've never had a whole group return. But we sometimes find that two or three group members become so close that they agree to return together from time to time to sort of renew their friendship."

Nick leaned forward. "That friend," he said quietly, "the one who told me I should check you out? The last time he came here he met some other fellows—well, they really hit it off. He never stopped talking about them, and the more he talked the more I realized those are just the kind of guys *I'd* like to get together with."

"I'm sure you'll have just as much luck with the group *you're* assigned to, Nick." The social worker smiled reassuringly.

"I don't put much faith in luck," Nick said. "What I want to know is, can I meet with those fellows? Can you put me in touch with any of them so I can see if they'd like to meet together?"

The administrator shook his head. "Can't do that, Nick. It's a privacy issue—you understand. I can't reveal the names of any past members of our program. I'm sure you can appreciate that."

"Suppose I gave you my number and you passed it on to the fellows in that group. All you'd have to do is say, 'If you're interested, give Nick a call.'"

"Sorry, Nick. The groups are formed randomly, and we facilitate no outside meetings between group members. That's our policy."

Kathryn squeezed Nick's hand hard. She knew they had reached a dead end; if Nick pushed any harder it would only generate suspicion.

"You said the day ends at 4:30. What do people do in the evenings?"

"Whatever they wish. Some of them take the Metro downtown and see the Capitol. Most of them just hang around the Mologne House and talk further."

"The Mologne House?"

"We have a wonderful hotel right here on the base," the social worker beamed. "The Mologne House is open to all military personnel, active and retired, and to their extended family as well."

"That's where all the group members stay?"

"Unless they live close enough to commute from home. If you'd like to check it out, it's just a five-minute walk from here—just past the Institute of Research on Fourteenth Street."

"We don't have accommodations for tonight yet—any chance of us getting a room there?"

"I can call over for you and find out," the administrator said. He reached for the phone while the social worker turned to Kathryn.

"Our couples often use the evening hours to work on their *relationships.*" She winked, and Kathryn managed a faint smile in return. "Do you two have children?"

Kathryn shook her head, "No," while Nick nodded, "Yes."

There was a pause.

"None at home," Nick explained. "Military school."

"Then you should have an uninterrupted evening." The social worker winked again. "Trust me, Darlene—that can make a world of difference."

"I'm not sure we're ready for that," Kathryn said. "I'm not sure *Nick* is ready—if you know what I mean." *Two can play at this game.*

The administrator interrupted. "They have one room left with a queen-sized bed."

"No!" Kathryn shouted.

There was an awkward silence from all parties. Nick turned to Kathryn and took both her hands.

"You know how I feel about you, Darlene—and I know how you feel about me. If we just had this one night—*at the Mologne House*—I think it could make a big difference for us. A *big* difference..."

Kathryn flashed her most compassionate smile and dug her fingernails into the back of Nick's hand.

"We'll take it," she smiled to the administrator.

"They want to know how you'll be paying."

"She'll be paying in cash," Nick said.

CHAPTER 23

The Mologne House was a four-story structure of the same Georgian brick and stone that comprised all the original buildings at Walter Reed. Off the main lobby was a restaurant—the Rose Room—and there Nick and Kathryn sat at a table in the exact center of the room.

"I could move you to a nice booth," the waitress offered, "if this is a little too public for you."

"This is perfect," Nick replied. "Do you have any kind of buffet? Something where you have to get up and get your own food?"

"Don't you army boys ever get tired of the chow line?"

"What makes you think I'm an army boy?"

The waitress rolled her eyes and pointed her pencil at his gray 82d Airborne T-shirt.

"Oh yeah," he said. "Forgot I had that on."

Kathryn ordered a dinner salad, and the waitress left them

alone. A handful of other couples filled most of the booths while servicemen in twos and threes dotted the rest of the room.

"Did you have fun back there?" Kathryn asked with more than a little sarcasm.

"I did. I enjoyed myself very much. But," he said as he leaned forward and put his left hand on hers, "the night is still young, Darlene."

Kathryn tapped his ring finger, now bearing Andy's gold wedding band. "Lose this and you die."

"Lose it? It's like part of my hand."

Kathryn paused. "Ever wear one before?"

"Briefly," he said.

"You seem to have lost that one."

Now it was Nick's turn to hesitate. "I lost *her.*"

"Different species?"

"That's as good a way as any to explain it."

"Don't tell me she was from the *South!*"

"Be reasonable, Mrs. Guilford. We were both from Pittsburgh. I grew up in a hill town on the north side called Tarentum. She was from across the river in New Kensington."

He ended the sentence as though the story was finished, but Kathryn's insistent gaze told him she was not yet satisfied. He took a deep breath and continued.

"Where I grew up you went to high school, you got a job, you got married, you had babies—not always in that order."

"But you decided you wanted something more."

"No. She did."

He took a roll and tore it in half and reached for a pat of butter. Kathryn felt suddenly ashamed. It had never occurred to her that the Bug Man could at one time have been just a human being. This man who caused her so much frustration and embarrassment could have been—could *still* be—hurt by someone else. She wondered what the woman looked like, what qualities she possessed that actually caused him to *love*—maybe for the one and only time. She watched him as he ate, head down, his huge spectacles hanging from his ears like a pair of glass scales weighing in the balance everything that passed before them. She wondered how long he had worn those glasses and how much pain they had caused him.

"Plus twenty diopter," he said without looking up.

Kathryn started. "What?"

"Plus twenty diopter. You were looking at my glasses."

Kathryn opened her mouth to deny it but quickly realized how silly and unconvincing the words would sound. Nick was right—she was a very bad liar.

"Don't let it bother you," he said. "There comes a time in every relationship when I know they're looking at my glasses. It was just your time."

"What does 'plus twenty diopter' mean?"

"I'm hyperopic. I'm *farsighted.* I see things better at a distance—not good, just better. 'Plus twenty' means that up close I'm blind as an earthworm."

Kathryn wondered what the world looked like through those massive lenses. She wished she could try them on, but she couldn't bring herself to ask. *How do you ask a blind man if you can try out his cane?*

"You may," he said, and carefully removed the spectacles from his head.

Kathryn started again. "I hope you use these psychic powers wisely."

"I'm not psychic. I just know your species."

As he held out the spectacles, she saw his face for the first time whole and complete. She had imagined that his real eyes would be tiny, molelike dots; in fact, they were larger than normal and very dark. They were beautiful eyes, really, and it seemed very sad that such eyes could only be viewed in a mirror dimly.

"How do I look?" She smiled.

"I have no idea. Go across the street and let's have a look at you."

Kathryn's mouth dropped open. Looking through the bulky lenses was like staring into a cloud through wax paper. She raised her right hand and flexed her fingers; she saw a pink feather boa curl across her field of vision, undulate at one end, and then disappear. She looked at Nick; she saw nothing but amorphous blobs where features should be, as though a painter had roughed in areas of color where a final portrait would follow. It was a world without particulars of any kind, and Kathryn felt her own eyes darting back and forth just as Nick's did, searching through the mists like a rock climber groping for a solid grip.

She handed the glasses back, placing them carefully in Nick's open hands. "How long have you worn these?"

"Forever. When I was in first grade my teacher thought I was an idiot. Numbers, letters, they were all just blurs to me. I thought that's just the way the world looked. Then one day my mother took me to an optometrist. When I walked out I was wearing these, and for the first time in my life I saw *details.* I looked down at the ground and saw an ant mound." He shook his head. "I must have sat there for an hour. Then my mother thought I was an idiot."

"And you've been staring at ant mounds ever since."

"My folks both worked for Allegheny Ludlum Steel. Pittsburgh was a steel town when they were growing up, and they always figured their boy would grow up to work at the plant just like they did—just like everyone in Tarentum did. But then the Japanese started dumping cheap steel in the '60s, and the mills all started to close down. No one knew if Pittsburgh would even survive. That's when my folks decided they'd better save up and send their baby boy to college."

"And you decided to study entomology. What did they think of that?"

"They didn't even know what it was," he shrugged. "So I graduated with a B.S., and the only job I could get was driving a pickup truck with a big cockroach on top. That's when I decided to go to graduate school. My folks were thrilled. The only thing they heard is that their son was going to be a *doctor.* So I finally came home—*Doctor* Polchak—and all the relatives start dropping by. My Aunt Edna said her hip was bothering her. What should she do? I told her, come back and see me when you're dead."

Kathryn laughed out loud—a genuine belly laugh. It was the first time she had made that sound around Nick, and she stopped a little short. But she couldn't help herself. Images of a grade-school Bug Man and exterminator trucks and an ailing Aunt Edna were more than she could contain.

At that moment three men in civilian clothes passed by on their way to the buffet line.

"Excuse me," Nick said. "It's been fun, but I'm late for work."

He stood up from the table and stretched, rotating left and right from the waist to display his T-shirt to the widest possible audience. He walked slowly around the entire restaurant, occasionally bumping into a chair and stopping to excuse himself. He finally arrived at the buffet line, picked up a plate, and nodded a greeting to the enlisted man across from him. A few minutes later he returned to the table with one small plate of food.

"It looks like the Gulf War Syndrome has affected your appetite," Kathryn said.

"I plan to go back several times."

"Why?"

"To show off this T-shirt. Somewhere in this hotel there may be a man who knew Jim McAllister—or knew someone who did. We have exactly one night to find him."

CHAPTER 24

It was just after midnight when Sheriff Peter St. Clair stepped through the screen door into the darkened lab. The bright light glowing from the office beyond cast streaks of blue fire across the faces and edges of glass throughout the room, but still left the inhabitants of each terrarium a dark mystery. The sheriff walked slowly down the aisle, stopping to peer uselessly into each shadowy case. He tapped on the face of one and heard a quick skittering sound. He ran his fingernails across the screen wire atop another and a menacing hiss shot back.

What in the…

He avoided the rest of the cases and made his way to the office door, stopping for a moment to observe the excited little man with the cell phone pressed against his ear. The sheriff rapped sharply on the window.

Teddy looked startled; then his face erupted into a broad smile. He folded the cell phone and set it on the counter.

"Thank you for hurrying," he spluttered, shaking the sheriff's hand and pulling him into the room. "I'm sorry to call you so late. I hope I didn't catch you at an inopportune moment."

"What have you got back there, some kind of snake?" The sheriff nodded back toward the darkness.

"Ah! You must have disturbed our giant hissing cockroaches—they let out a loud hiss when they sense danger. Impressive, aren't they?"

"Impressive," the sheriff muttered.

Teddy stopped abruptly. "You didn't reach into any of the cases, did you?"

He shook his head.

"Thank heavens," Teddy whistled. "That could be serious—quite serious indeed."

"So"—the sheriff glanced around disdainfully at the incredible disarray of paper and equipment—"what's this big news?"

Teddy grinned from ear to ear and held up one finger, then turned to the Biotronette environmental unit and removed a single plastic container. He held it with both hands as one might hold a bulging water balloon.

"The big news," Teddy beamed, "is this!"

The sheriff bent down and peered into the container. Inside was a single black fly clinging to the plastic wall, motionless except for the sporadic fanning of its tiny wings.

"It emerged less than fifteen minutes ago. We expected it to be a *Calliphora vomitoria* or a sarcophagid—perhaps even a stray Muscidae—but I'm fairly certain that it's a *Chrysomya megacephala,* a species not indigenous to the Carolina piedmont at all."

"Whoa!" The sheriff interrupted with a wave of his hands. "Slow down! What are you talking about? Is all the excitement over one lousy fly?"

Teddy turned and set the container carefully on the worktable, then took a few moments to calm himself and collect his thoughts.

"When Mr. McAllister died, certain species of flies deposited eggs on his body. We call these necrophilous flies—flies whose larvae feed on the tissues of decaying animals. Now certain flies are indigenous to certain areas," he said slowly and precisely. "That means if an animal dies in one area, its body will be infested by one species of fly; but if it dies in another area, it may be a different species of fly entirely. Dr. Polchak collected specimens from all of the observable wounds on Mr. McAllister's body, and we have been rearing them here in our environmental chamber, waiting for them to mature so that we could accurately identify each species. Over the last several days each specimen has reached eclosion—the moment when the adult fly emerges from its puparium—and each has turned out to be precisely the species one would expect in this area. That is," he said with a grin and a nod toward the worktable," all except that one. That specimen emerged just a few hours ago, and I am quite certain that it is a *Chrysomya megacephala*—a species not found anywhere in North Carolina."

"Where does that one come from?" the sheriff asked.

"From a place with warmer winters. This species is found only in Florida and southern Georgia."

The sheriff said nothing.

"That means," Teddy continued, "that Dr. Polchak was correct in his suspicions about the unusual lividity of the left leg. The body must have been deposited here—but death actually occurred somewhere in Florida or southern Georgia. And if the body was transported"—his eyes widened—"then in all likelihood you have a murder on your hands."

The sheriff turned away and began to slowly pace around the office. He stopped and stood motionless, staring at the floor. He took a few steps more and put his hands on his hips, staring at the bare wall ahead of him. After a few moments he turned back to Teddy again.

"You're saying that Jim's death was not a suicide at all. You're saying he was murdered—in another state—and his body was only dumped here."

"Precisely!" Teddy said with obvious satisfaction.

"But the coroner's report—"

"The coroner's report indicated that it was an apparent suicide, and so no autopsy was ordered to verify the cause of death. But now that we have contravening evidence, we have every reason to obtain an order of exhumation to examine the body in detail. Further forensic study may provide any number of clues to the manner of death—and perhaps even to the killer."

The sheriff nodded slowly. "We got to be careful here—this could rock a lot of boats. You're sure you can prove all this?"

"Oh yes," Teddy assured him. "Forensic entomological evidence is considered quite reliable by our courts, and species identification is my specialty."

The sheriff turned away again. "Does the doc know yet?"

"I haven't been able to reach him," Teddy said. "They're up in Washington, you know, but they never checked into the hotel where they made reservations. I asked the front desk to check under other names, and I asked them to check with their other hotels in the area, but no luck. That's why I called you, Sheriff. You must have some connections, some way of tracking him down."

"What about his cell phone?"

"I just tried it—no answer. Maybe his phone is off, or maybe he's outside of a digital area. I was just about to leave him a voice mail when you came in."

The sheriff stepped to the worktable and gently lifted the plastic container. "This is the one? The *only* one?"

Teddy nodded. "We must be very careful. Its wings will be dry soon, and it will be capable of flight. In the morning I'll kill it and prepare it for positive identification."

"Identification? I thought you said you already knew."

"I do; I mean, there are ways I can already tell—but legally it's not considered a positive identification until certain procedures are followed."

The sheriff carefully set the container down again. "Then let's wait till morning to fill in the doc. No sense getting his hopes up if this whole thing turns out to be smoke. They oughtta be back first thing, and you'll know for sure by then."

"Is there anything else I can do?" Teddy offered. "Any way I can help?"

"There is something you can do. You can go home and get some rest. I need you alert. Come tomorrow, I have a feeling it's all gonna hit the fan."

"You must be Nick," a tired voice said. "I'm Vincent—Vincent Arranzio."

Nick looked up from his lukewarm tea to see a tall, gaunt figure wearing an open fatigue jacket over a sagging gray T-shirt. His clothing seemed loose and ill fitted, as though he had lost a considerable amount of weight. Nick extended his hand and then motioned for the man to sit down opposite him. The man slid into the booth and sat quietly, moving only occasionally to scratch at both arms.

"I wish I could offer you something"—Nick gestured to his tea—"but the place closed down a long time ago."

The man shrugged. "Looks like you don't sleep any better than I do."

Nick glanced at his watch—2:45 A.M. "I appreciate you meeting me here. I know it's a bit late."

"It was either this or stare at the ceiling for another couple of hours." The man leaned forward. "How did you say you got my name?"

"From a marine I met in the lobby a couple of hours ago. He was with the 4th Marine Expeditionary Brigade in the Gulf. Said he knew you from a group you were in together a couple of years ago. He said we might have a friend in common—Jim McAllister."

The man nodded. "How is Jim?"

Nick paused. "He's dead, Mr. Arranzio."

The man slumped back against the booth. "How?"

"I was hoping you could help me find out."

The man glanced at Nick's 82d Airborne T-shirt again, then glared at him suspiciously.

"You were never in the Airborne," he said, nodding at Nick's enormous spectacles. "Not with *those.* Now what's this all about?"

"Mr. Arranzio, I am a forensic entomologist—a kind of investigator—and I am helping a very dear friend of Mr. McAllister look into the circumstances surrounding his death."

"How did he die?"

"According to the coroner's report, he shot himself in the right temple with his own service sidearm. Do you believe that?"

"What do you mean do I believe it? If that's what happened, I believe it."

Nick looked at him. "I understand you knew Mr. McAllister quite well."

"We were in a couple of groups here together. He was with the 82d Airborne—I was with the 101st. The 82d attacked on foot with the French at Al Salman—we went in by air in Apaches on their right flank. You could say we had a lot to talk about."

"Mr. Arranzio, do you believe Jim McAllister was *capable* of taking his own life?"

The man paused and scratched at both arms again. "How much do you know about Gulf War Syndrome?"

"A little. In the Gulf our forces were subjected to a series of potentially toxic substances—petroleum smoke, depleted uranium, nerve agents—no one knows what long-range effects those substances might have, especially in combination."

The man leaned toward Nick.

"Want to hear an interesting fact? Since the Gulf War ended, about three-quarters of 1 percent of all Gulf War veterans have died. If you compare that to all the troops who didn't deploy to the Gulf, it's less. The vets are doing better than everyone else! We're not dying from Gulf War Syndrome—we're just going *nuts.*" He stopped scratching at his arm and pulled up his sleeve. "Look. I've got a rash that never goes away. Why? I get headaches, night sweats, swollen glands. From what? I forget things—and I don't know whether I was gassed by the Iraqis or I'm just getting old. It can get you down, Nick—it got Jimmy down—and believe me, it gets pretty dark always looking up from the bottom of the well."

"Mr. Arranzio, did you ever talk with Mr. McAllister about his experiences in the Gulf? I don't mean actions and troop movements—I mean the way things *affected* him."

"That was a big part of the group. Some people think the Gulf was a cakewalk just because our side didn't suffer many casualties. I saw men starved, fried, shot to pieces, and blown all over the countryside. It was no picnic."

"Did Mr. McAllister ever single out any special event—anything that seemed to cause him special anguish or remorse?"

The man dropped his head and began to rub his temples in slow circles as if he were trying to coax an elusive thought up to the surface of his mind.

"Sometimes the group would swap stories about what we saw. One guy kept talking about Khafji. The Iraqi tanks rolled in with their turrets backward like they were going to surrender—

we lost twelve marines that day. Another fella lost a buddy to friendly fire. Remember the Apache that fired a Hellfire at one of our own trucks? Another guy kept talking about Highway 8, where we trapped the Iraqis retreating from Kuwait and it turned into a shooting gallery. They called it the Highway of Death."

"And Jim?"

"Jim had a few stories, too, but he kept coming back to this one. There was this guy—what was his name? Something happened with this one fella. His name was... Man, I've got holes in my head like a Swiss cheese."

"Did he say what happened?"

"Funny thing. It got pretty nasty over there, but Jim could always talk about it, he could *describe* it—except when it came to his problem with this one guy. He'd always start into it and just shut down. I figured whatever it was, it must have been a pretty serious business."

"You said he would 'start into it,' as if he wanted to talk about it, but couldn't. What did he say at those times? Did he give you any idea what had happened between them?"

The man continued to massage his temples in long, slow circles.

"Mr. Arranzio, did he ever mention anyone named Andy?"

Arranzio squinted hard.

Nick looked down into his teacup and noticed the small flecks of black leaf resting on the bottom. The Chinese believed that the remains of tea leaves formed symbols that could reveal hidden knowledge. The rim of the cup foretold the immediate future, the sides of the cup revealed more distant knowledge, and the bottom of the cup contained the darkest secrets of all.

"Mr. Arranzio," Nick said without looking up, "did you know that Jim McAllister used cocaine?"

Silence.

Nick leaned forward. "I'm not with the DEA, if that's what you're thinking."

The man shook his head slowly. "You must think I'm some kind of idiot to ask me a question like that."

Nick raised both hands. "You're right—I apologize. Let me put it another way. I *know* Jim McAllister used cocaine—I examined his body shortly after death. And I know his cocaine use started in the Gulf. What I want to know is, do you think it had anything to do with this problem he kept talking about?"

Mr. Arranzio sat quietly for a moment, glaring at Nick. He took a long, slow, backward glance over both shoulders, then leaned in again.

"It was part of it," he said quietly, and when Nick opened his mouth to speak again the man added sharply, "and that's all I'm going to say about it. Clear?"

Both men sat back in their seats and studied each other for a moment. Mr. Arranzio shook his head and made a kind of snorting sound.

"What kind of an investigator did you say you are?"

"A forensic entomologist."

He sneered. "Seems to me you're asking the wrong questions."

"I'm listening."

"When did Jim die?"

"Less than two weeks ago."

"And Desert Storm was over eight years ago. You keep asking about what happened in the Gulf. I'd be a lot more interested in what happened *after*."

"Go on."

"What's the street price of cocaine these days?"

Nick shrugged. "I suppose a hundred, a hundred-and-fifty bucks a gram. Why?"

"What do you suppose a moderate user like Jim would consume in a week—four, five grams? Well, the last time I saw Jim he was flat busted—not a dime to his name, no job, no prospects. Now where does a guy like that come up with seven-hundred-and-fifty bucks a week for flake?"

"You tell me."

"You beg, you borrow, or you steal. It's as simple as that."

Mr. Arranzio slid to the edge of the booth and stood up. "I hope you find what you're looking for. Answers are pretty scarce these days."

Nick handed him his card. "That guy you mentioned—the one that Jim McAllister had the big problem with. If his name ever comes back to you, drop me a line, will you?"

Nick looked down once again at his teacup and the random bits of stem and leaf that still clung to the bottom. He stared long and hard—and then a pattern began to emerge.

■

Kathryn heard the key in the lock and opened her eyes. The door opened and Nick entered, stopping to observe her motionless form before stepping into the bathroom.

"Too much tea," he said. "Did you get any sleep?"

Kathryn raised her head and looked at the clock—4 A.M. She lay diagonally across the queen-sized bed with the bedspread pulled roughly over her, exactly as she lay down three short hours ago. She heard the sound of rushing water, and Nick stepped out, wiping his hands on a coarse white towel. He dropped it on the carpet and looked at her again. He stepped slowly to the bed and sat down, his hip touching hers. He said nothing for a moment, watching, then leaned forward and gently straightened the bedspread stretched across her. His eyes were truly enormous at this distance, and they hung above her like chestnut moons.

"Mrs. Guilford," he said quietly. "I want to ask you something."

"Yes?"

"Did your bank ever grant a substantial loan to Jim McAllister?"

Kathryn blinked hard and worked to clear her mind.

"Are you asking me if *I* ever approved a loan to Jimmy?"

Nick nodded.

"No. Never."

"If I checked the bank's records, is that what I would find?"

Kathryn paused. "Did you just ask me if I'm lying?"

"I've been wondering how your friend managed to come up with several hundred dollars a week to finance his drug habit."

"I work in *commercial* lending," she reminded him. "Jimmy would never have qualified for a personal loan either—he had no income, no collateral..."

"If you don't beg, and you don't borrow," he said thoughtfully, "then you *steal*. Did your friend have any criminal record? Burglary, breaking and entering, assault?"

"Absolutely not."

Nick raised one eyebrow and Kathryn rolled her eyes.

"None that I *know* of." She sighed. "If he did, Peter would have to know."

"Yes," he said. "That's what I keep telling myself—*Peter would have to know.*"

He sat for another minute staring straight ahead at the wall, then slapped his hands down on the mattress.

"Let's go."

"Go? Go where?"

"Home, of course."

Kathryn glanced back at the clock. "Right now? It's four o'clock in the morning!"

"Okay." Nick shrugged. "Then roll over."

Kathryn sat upright. "I'll get my things."

■

As Teddy turned his Camry down the secluded dirt road, his headlights flashed across a pickup truck half-hidden by a grove of trees, then onto a single-wide trailer a hundred yards ahead. The trailer was long and roomy enough but it was mud-ugly. Despite Teddy's best efforts to add a touch of decoration or landscaping here and there, it was still essentially a tin shoebox with a propane tank attached. Its one redeeming virtue was that it was cheap, and that made it the perfect residence for a research assistant on temporary assignment.

He parked in front of the trash cans, which had been plundered for the third night in a row by the local raccoons—that was the problem with living so far from the main road. He tidied up and fastened the lids down securely, took two sacks of groceries from the backseat, and headed for the door. A single cinder block step led up to the doorway, which was covered by a twisted aluminum screen door that long ago ceased to serve any useful purpose. He went through the gesture of entering the key in the lock, though the door fit so loosely in its frame that all it really needed was a good push to open it. He stepped in and fumbled for the light switch.

He flicked it on.

Nothing.

He turned left into the shadows, feeling his way carefully toward the kitchen counter. The sagging plywood floor creaked with every step. He stopped to hoist the paper sacks higher, and the floor creaked behind him—a deep, groaning sigh—and Teddy stood erect, straining to extend his senses out into the darkness. He felt exactly like the Blattidae, the cockroaches that lined his cupboards and pantry, whose tiny hairs search the air for the slightest vibration and allow them to react ten times faster than the human eye can blink. Teddy saw nothing, he heard nothing, but he *sensed* something—a weight, a presence, a shifting shape in the blackness behind him.

He felt something cold touch the base of his skull and through the back of his eyes saw a blinding white flash of fire.

CHAPTER 26

"We're here." Nick gently nudged Kathryn's shoulder. "You slept like a brick."

She shook her head and felt the deep mists of sleep begin to evaporate from her mind. They were back in Rayford, parked directly in front of her house. She looked at her watch: 9:30 A.M.

"I feel like I slept *on* a brick," she groaned, stretching and rubbing her backside.

"I thought I'd drop you off." He nodded toward the house.

"What are you going to do?"

"I've got one quick stop to make, then I'm headed to the lab to check in with Teddy. That last specimen should be ready to pop any time. I should have heard from him by now. I checked my cell phone just outside of Raleigh; it said *ONE CALL MISSED* from Teddy's cell phone, but there was no message. I called the lab—no answer."

"I should go with you."

"No need," he said firmly. "You get some rest. I'll call you as soon as I know anything."

Kathryn reluctantly walked to the house. At the door she turned back.

"As soon as you know *anything,*" she called after him as he pulled away in a billow of blue smoke.

He drove less than a mile and parked again on Dalrymple Street, two full blocks from the sheriff's office where he could clearly see the Crown Victoria patrol car parked in front. It was almost an hour before the figure of the sheriff emerged from the office, followed closely by a second and much larger figure ambling behind. The patrol car pulled slowly away from the curb, and Nick reached for his door.

■

"Excuse me, is Sheriff St. Clair here?"

A stout-legged woman about fifty years of age sat staring intently at a glowing computer monitor. A shapeless blue dress hung haphazardly over her trunk, and short, tight curls hugged her head like a salt-and-pepper shower cap. Her left hand held open an instruction manual while the thick, blunt fingers of her right hand occasionally pecked at a key.

"Just missed him." She nodded toward the door without breaking her concentration. "He went on rounds—should be back in about an hour."

Nick cocked his head to one side and looked at her.

"Wait a minute. You must be Agnes, the one Pete talks so much about."

She glanced up from the flickering screen.

"I'm Dr. Nicholas Polchak." He rolled up a chair across from her and casually straddled it. "But you can call me Nick. I'm working with your boss on an investigation. Has he mentioned me?"

"Can't say he has."

"Well, he talks about *you* all the time. It's always, 'Agnes does this,' or 'Agnes takes care of that.' Sounds to me like you do most everything around here."

"You name it, I do it," she said with increasing enthusiasm. "I'm the secretary, accountant, and dispatcher. I'm the first one here every morning and the last one out at night. See this?" She pointed to a cheap wood-burned plaque above her desk that proclaimed, "IDEA girl." "That's me—the IDEA girl. That stands for *I Do Everything Almost*."

"I can tell you one thing. They sure don't pay you enough."

"Who you tellin'?" she said with a backward glance. "I swear sometimes I'm nursemaid and mother to those two boys!"

Nick nodded sympathetically. "What about time off? Do you ever get a vacation around here?"

"It's just the three of us. I take vacation when they take vacation. I can't make rounds or take calls without them, and they can't do *nothin'* without me—so we just close up shop for a few days. The Harnett County boys come over and take our calls."

"When *was* your last vacation, Agnes?"

"I got three days back in February—no, January. Went to see my sister—she lives up Edenton way, you know? She got this disk problem, gets laid up real bad, pain shoots all down her legs and—"

"Six months ago? Six months with *no* vacation?"

"Till a couple weeks ago, that is."

Nick leaned forward and smiled. "Well, it's about time. So—the whole office shut down just a couple of weeks ago?"

"I went back again to see Rayleen—not that it did much good, not *this* time. That disk of hers, it just pops out on her one day and then right back in the next. She never—"

"And the boys," he cut in. "Where did they head off to?"

"Down to Myrtle Beach. Spent a few days in the sun."

Nick paused. "That's funny. I thought Pete said he did a little hunting—down in Georgia. You're sure they didn't go to that place of his in Valdosta?"

"It was Myrtle Beach all right. See? They brought me this." From the corner of her desk she slid a small, paste gray sand dollar.

Nick turned the sand dollar over slowly.

"I guess it must have been the beach then. Where else could you get one of these?" He handed it back to her. "Did they bring you any pictures?'

"Can't say as they did."

"No pictures?"

"Do you take pictures on vacation?"

He smiled. "You must have had a couple of sunburned boys to take care of when they got back."

She paused. "That's funny..."

Nick rose from his chair. "Agnes, you've been a big help—and I'm glad to hear your sister is doing better."

"Want me to tell Pete you stopped by?"

"No need. He'll know soon enough."

■

Nick slumped a little lower in his seat as he turned onto County Road 42, headed back toward the lab. He was tired—bone tired—but he was not about to rest. This was the way he preferred to work, driving himself day and night, never stopping to rest until his mind was no longer able to focus—and his mind was clearer than it had been in days.

The sheriff and his deputy were out of town just a week ago, contemporaneous with the death of James McAllister. They went to Myrtle Beach—or so they told their secretary. They brought her back a sand dollar—maybe from the beach, maybe from any gift shop between there and Miami—but no other evidence of their stay. And no tan. A few days at the beach and no sun?

Got to check the meteorological records for Myrtle Beach last week.

Nick began to drum his fingers on the steering wheel in time with some imaginary tune. Behind the great glasses, his dark eyes darted from thought to thought like worker bees.

He rolled to a crunching stop in front of the green Quonset.

That's odd. Teddy's car is not here.

Nick headed straight for the office. He opened the door—and then froze. The left exit door stood wide open.

He glanced quickly around the office. Nothing seemed to be missing, nothing was broken, but the exit door had been left open—an error that Teddy would *never* make. Too many predacious species could be allowed in, or…

Allowed *out.*

He ran to the Biotronette and began to search through the specimens. *Left ocular…thoracic…right temporal…right ocular…* They were there. They were all there.

Wait. Where is… Where could it possibly…

He searched desperately around the room. There in the center of the worktable was a single plastic container—with the lid removed.

Nick ripped a cardboard box from a shelf and dumped its contents onto the floor, fumbling frantically for another lid. He found one and slammed it down on top of the open container.

Too late.

Inside the container was nothing but a tiny, empty capsule about the size of a grain of rice.

He lunged for the open door and jerked it shut. He stood silently, his eyes searching every inch of the ceiling and walls in the desperate hope that the fly had not yet escaped the lab. He began to step slowly around the office, waving his arms in great circles over every table and shelf, straining every sense to detect a quick streak of black or a telltale buzz.

Nothing.

Nothing but a handful of moths drawn to the stark fluorescent ceiling lights the night before.

The door was left open last night.

Nick searched the worktable near the Biotronette and found Teddy's log, the one he used to record changes in the specimens at fifteen-minute intervals. He fanned through the pages, scanning the entries—almost nothing had been entered for more than a day now, when the rest of the specimens had emerged from their puparia.

1515 Left ocular specimen reaches eclosion

1530 No change

1545 Second temoral specimen reaches eclosion

1600 No change

He flipped forward to yesterday's entries—it was an endless list of "No change" notations penned in Teddy's flawless script. He ran his finger down the list, turned the page, and continued until he came to the final entry:

2356 inal specimen eclosion

He closed the book. At 11:56 last night the final specimen emerged from its puparium, and Teddy faithfully noted the event in his log—but what happened next? How did the specimen come to be left out of the Biotronette and allowed to escape? Why was the lab left open and unsecured?

Nick glanced down again at the cluttered counter.

Teddy's cell phone.

Nick flipped it open and jabbed the *TALK* button twice; the auto-redial activated, and a number appeared on the tiny LCD screen—Nick's number. Teddy *did* try to call—but if he couldn't get through, why didn't he leave a message? Nick pulled out his own phone and checked again: *NO NEW MESSAGES.*

It never occurred to Nick for even an instant that these events could be accidental. Teddy was a consummate professional who took pains with the slightest details of his work. The idea that he would leave a door open or allow a critical specimen to escape was more than impossible, it was *unthinkable*. No, someone else had been here, someone who had purposely left the office door open—someone who had an interest in allowing this specific specimen to escape. But how did they get in? How did they get around Teddy? And why was Teddy's cell phone still there?

Where is Teddy?

Nick grabbed the logbook, threw open the lab door, and ran for the parking lot.

CHAPTER 27

Kathryn sat cross-legged in front of the coffee table, working her way through accumulated junk mail and stopping to pay an occasional bill. She hadn't been able to "get some rest" as Nick had suggested, but that came as no surprise. Sleep was a rare and delicate bubble for Kathryn, and once disturbed it was impossible to restore. Her night's rest consisted of the few moments of sweet oblivion she had managed to snatch between bone-jarring potholes on I-95 South.

The muted television in front of her flashed images of chatty news anchors exchanging smiles and nods. Kathryn stared at it blankly for a few minutes, then reached for the remote and switched to channel four. The screen turned bright blue. From the bottom drawer of the entertainment center she took a videotape marked OUR WEDDING and slid it into the machine. She sat back down on the floor and pulled her legs up tight against her chest, resting her chin on her knees.

The church custodian had reluctantly agreed to shoot the video, and he seemed to spend the first fifteen minutes learning to work the camera. A random shot of the church ceiling was followed by a shot of his own shoes, followed by a series of nauseating pans and zooms to nothing in particular. There were broken sound bites of music and laughter interspersed with a few colorful words from the custodian himself. The cinematography slowly began to improve, however, and soon a shot of the front of the sanctuary revealed two bridesmaids and the groom—with Peter and Jimmy at his side.

Finally the bride herself appeared in the double doorway leading down the center aisle. A crude facsimile of the "Wedding March" began to blare from the organ—even worse than she remembered it—and the dozen-or-so guests scattered throughout the pews rose and turned toward Kathryn as she entered the sanctuary. She walked alone, no father to give her away.

She arrived at Andy's side and turned to face him. Words were spoken—the sound was indistinguishable—then the camera jostled, cut off, and started again several yards closer to the bridal couple. It was a tight shot on their faces, and at the sight of Andy's smile her tears began to flow.

From somewhere beyond the wedding party a voice began, "Dearly beloved, we are gathered together today in the sight of God and man..." Kathryn watched her own face, then his, then hers again. She saw nothing in their eyes but hopes and dreams and possibilities.

How long ago was this? It seems like forever.

"Repeat after me," the voice continued. "I take you, Kathryn, to be my lawfully wedded wife, knowing in my heart that you will be my constant friend, my faithful partner in life, and my one true love."

"I take you, Kathryn, to be my lawfully wedded wife..."

For some inexplicable reason the custodian chose this moment to pan slowly across the members of the bridal party.

There was Amelia on the left, who constantly hitched up her slip throughout the service, followed by dear cousin Rose who married shortly thereafter and moved away to… *Where was it? Colorado?*

The voice boomed out again: "I affirm to you in the presence of God and these witnesses my sacred promise to stay by your side as your faithful husband for better or for worse, in joy and in sorrow, in sickness and in health."

"…my sacred promise to stay by your side…," Andy repeated, while the camera suddenly jumped to the other end of the row and settled on Jimmy. Smiling Jimmy, always happy—*maybe not so happy,* Kathryn thought, *but always a smile on his face.* The camera panned slowly to the left, stopped briefly on Peter, and finally came to rest on the groom once again.

Kathryn suddenly stopped. She reached for the remote and backed the tape up to the image of Jimmy, then watched again as the camera rolled past Peter. What was that? What was he doing? She rewound the tape again and let it go, moving closer to the screen this time.

"I promise to love you without reservation," said the preacher, and after each phrase Andy repeated his words. "To honor and respect you, to provide for your needs, to protect you from harm, and to cherish you for as long as we both shall live." Was it just her imagination? No—there it was again! Each time Andy spoke, *Peter's* lips also moved. He was repeating the vows himself, but in silence.

"…for as long as we both shall live," Andy finished solemnly, and Peter ended at precisely the same instant.

Kathryn turned off the tape. What did she just see—and why had she never noticed it before? Was Peter simply empathizing with Andy, willing him to remember his lines like a bowler urging a ball back into the center of the lane? Or was it something else…something more?

She got up and angrily ejected the tape. Why was she even wondering about this? What was so unusual about Peter's behavior? Peter hadn't done anything a thousand other best men hadn't done before him. The only reason she found herself considering some deeper motive was the ridiculous suspicions Nick had planted in her mind.

But somewhere inside her a voice whispered: *Is it really so ridiculous?*

She tossed the tape back in the drawer and kicked it shut, then flopped down on the sofa and reached for a paper. Her life was complicated enough right now without searching for hidden meanings.

The phone rang and Kathryn unconsciously reached for it.

"Hello," she said absently.

"Mrs. Guilford."

The voice on the other end was thin and hollow, almost a whisper. It sounded strangely distant, as though it came from somewhere very dark and very far away.

"Who is this?"

"Nick."

Kathryn sat up in alarm. Something was wrong—terribly wrong. Whatever it was had produced a tone of voice that she never dreamed she would hear from the unflappable Nick Polchak—and it terrified her.

"Where are you? What's happened?"

There was a long pause on the other end. "Do you know where Teddy lives?"

"He lives in a trailer, doesn't he? Off Lead Mine Road?"

"How soon can you be here?"

"Fifteen minutes. Why? Nick, what is it?"

"It's Teddy," came the whisper. "He's dead."

CHAPTER 28

The bullet had entered at the base of Teddy's skull and passed easily through the soft tissues of the brain, exiting through the left eye with sufficient velocity to penetrate the flimsy trailer wall and escape. Death was instantaneous. He fell headlong, his arms still curled around the two crumpled sacks of groceries. The bags still seeped a variety of liquids, but none was as horribly stark and vivid as the red-black pool that lay directly beneath his face.

Kathryn sat on the cool trailer floor with her legs drawn up tight and her head down on her knees, staring at the curled and yellowed linoleum beneath her. She had wept until her soul was empty, and now there was nothing to do but sit and nurse the pounding ache inside her head. Each time she glanced up at Teddy's body sprawled before her, she felt another wave of grief. It angered her that already each wave had begun to diminish a little, like the wake of a distant boat.

Teddy had fallen facedown. The force of the fall shattered the nose and incisors and forced the jaw back into the skull. He lay in this grotesquely comical position with a bag tucked neatly under each arm, looking somehow trim and tidy even in death.

Kathryn raised her eyes and looked across at Nick, who sat opposite her in exactly the same position—arms wrapped around legs and head resting on knees—except that his eyes never left Teddy's body. It was the first time Kathryn had ever seen his huge, dark eyes completely motionless, almost lifeless. They no longer darted and evaluated and analyzed; they just gaped open like two black sewers, draining the image before him of all horror and misery and pain. Kathryn wanted to say something, but she knew from experience that sometimes sorrow is so profound that speech is blasphemous. She just looked at him, using her eyes as best she could to comfort and soothe and hold.

"I did this," Nick said in an almost inaudible voice. "This is the result of my foolishness—my sloppiness—my *stupidity.*"

Kathryn shook her head. "You couldn't possibly have—"

"I should have seen it coming. I should have recognized the danger. I should have warned him to be careful."

"Nick, this is not your fault."

Nick met her gaze. "You haven't asked me how I happened to discover Teddy's body."

Kathryn said nothing.

"This morning I went to the lab. Teddy wasn't there, and the door was open. The *office* door. The final specimen, the one we were waiting for—it was allowed to escape. Someone removed the container from the Biotronette and took the lid off. It's gone, Mrs. Guilford, along with any hope of proving that Jim McAllister was murdered. Who left that door open? Who took the lid off that container?"

"It had to have been Teddy."

"Never."

"But it's possible that he—"

"Listen to me!" he shouted. "You came to me to investigate

the death of Jim McAllister because you believed he would not take his own life—and you believed this in the complete absence of any evidence or witnesses to support your opinion. You believed not because of logic, but because you *knew* him—and you knew this was something he would never do."

Kathryn nodded sadly. "I also found out that sometimes people don't act the way you expect them to."

"Then why are you still here, Mrs. Guilford? Why did you choose to continue this investigation? Have you changed your mind? Have you decided that suicide is something your snow-blowing friend just *might* have done?"

"No. Never."

"And I'm telling you, Teddy would never have made such amateurish mistakes. When I saw that open container I knew—I knew to come *here*—and I knew what had happened to Teddy before I ever opened the door to this trailer."

Kathryn paused. "You think someone released the fly on purpose? And you think Teddy was murdered to cover it up? But why?"

"Because Teddy saw the fly before it was released." He held up the brown leather logbook. "Teddy's log. His last entry indicated eclosion at 11:56 last night—that's when the mature fly emerged from its puparium. Teddy saw it. I'm betting he knew what it was—and where it *came* from. Someone wanted to make sure he didn't tell anyone else."

"Who?"

"You already know the answer to that question—we *both* know—you just don't want to believe it."

Kathryn closed her eyes and began to slowly shake her head.

"We have some very expensive equipment in that lab," Nick said. "But nothing was stolen. In fact, the only thing disturbed in the entire building was *one plastic container.* Whoever opened it had to know what it was and why it was significant. Who else does that leave but Peter St. Clair?"

"Nick, that makes no sense."

"He left the door open to make it appear that the fly had escaped by accident. But Teddy would never have left the container uncovered and he would never have left that door open—and at that hour of the night the fly would never have left the lab on its own. It would have remained inside, attracted to the light. Your friend released the fly outside, then left the door open to make it look like it was all an accident."

"If Teddy saw the fly, why in the world would he call Peter?" Kathryn asked. "Peter wouldn't understand what it was *or* why it mattered. You had your cell phone with you last night—why wouldn't Teddy call *you?*"

"He did try to call—but he didn't leave a message."

"And even if Peter did drop by the lab for some reason late last night, why in the world would he want to let the fly escape?"

Nick looked at her. "There's only one possible reason, Mrs. Guilford—because your friend Peter has something to protect. Because he was in some way involved in Jim McAllister's death."

She opened her mouth to protest, but he cut her off.

"Look. Andy, Jimmy, and Peter all loved you—but Andy won the prize. Then they all went off to war. Andy was killed; that left just two. Both of them came home hoping to fill Andy's shoes, but only one could win. Two men vying for the love of the same woman, Mrs. Guilford—that's called *motive.* And in my world, motive has a powerful smell."

"He didn't have a motive to commit murder."

"Didn't he? In Jim McAllister's mind something was terribly wrong, something that his sister said he wanted to make right, remember? Maybe he found out Peter was about to propose, maybe he felt that *he* should be next in line. Maybe what Jim wanted to make right was *Peter*—but maybe Peter made it right first."

Kathryn looked at him sadly. "You say *I'm* unwilling to believe—it sounds to me like there's something *you're* not willing to believe."

"What's that?"

"That Teddy—dear, wonderful Teddy—was only human, and that he might have just made a *mistake*. That his murder has nothing to do with the fly or the lab or the Gulf—or with Peter. Admit it, Nick—it's possible."

Less than five feet away was the brain that could answer all of their questions—but it was not a brain anymore. It was just a lump of convoluted tissue with a black tunnel torn through the center, three hundred billion lifeless cells already shrunken and ashen gray since the life-giving blood had ceased to flow. His extremities were blue, and lividity was evident in the face and arms where the purplish blood had already settled.

Nick reached out to press the skin to see if it would blanch.

"Did you know that a body begins to cool at a rate of one-and-a-half degrees per hour?" he said in a distant voice.

"Nick..."

"The sphincters relax, and the bowel and bladder void. The skin becomes waxy and translucent, and the head begins to turn a greenish-red. The eyes begin to flatten and the corneas become milky and opaque. Rigor mortis begins in the face and lower jaw and then spreads lower and lower and—"

"Nick. Stop it."

Nick suddenly noticed a sound above him. He lifted his head; in the air above Teddy's body a single black-and-gray fly drifted. It slowly descended in an erratic pattern until it came to rest on the moist tissues of the entry wound at the base of Teddy's skull.

Nick lunged forward and swung at the fly. It darted away and hovered momentarily, then began its erratic descent again. He swung a second time, then a third, each time with growing rage—and each time the gravid female waited patiently for this minor annoyance to subside before pursuing her biological destiny.

Nick jumped to his feet swinging wildly, chasing the black speck higher and higher into the air. He whirled to the right and grabbed a wooden chair from the dinette.

"Nick...don't!" Kathryn screamed, rolling onto her side and shielding her head with both arms.

The first wild arc caught nothing but air. The second tore off a cabinet door and sent plastic plates and cups clattering across the floor. The dazed fly, disoriented by the cyclonic winds, tumbled to the ground—and Nick was on top of it in an instant. He swung the chair high overhead and brought it down with a deafening crash again, and again, and again, until he was left holding nothing but a single splintered spindle.

He dropped to his knees, panting, the adrenaline slowly beginning to withdraw its talons. Kathryn lay on her side, staring at him wide-eyed, her arms still covering her head.

"Go ahead," he muttered. "Say it."

"Say what?"

"That's a lot of fuss over a little shoofly pie."

From outside the trailer came the sound of an approaching engine. Nick glanced up to see the black-and-white patrol car and a bronze Ford LTD crunch to a stop, followed by a rolling cloud of dust. A moment later the screen door opened, and in stepped the sheriff, followed by Mr. Wilkins. The tiny trailer suddenly seemed impossibly crowded.

"Thanks for hurrying." Nick glowered at the sheriff. "Stop for donuts?"

"It's been a busy morning."

The sheriff surveyed the trailer quickly, stopping abruptly when he noticed Kathryn crouching in the corner and the dark, red circles under her eyes.

"Did you have to bring her in on this?"

"I came because I wanted to," Kathryn said angrily. "I came for Teddy's sake."

The sheriff looked down at the pile of kindling at Nick's feet and the broken spindle still in his hand.

"I shouldn't have to tell you this, Doc; this is a *crime scene.* Until Mr. Wilkins here is finished with it—until *I'm* finished with it—you don't touch anything."

Nick looked at the coroner. "I see you brought the ice cream man. I didn't know you deliver, Mr. Wilkins."

Mr. Wilkins looked as indignant as possible and turned to the sheriff. "Sheriff, do I have to conduct my investigation in this unprofessional atmosphere?"

"I'm afraid so," Nick said, "unless you leave."

"You are *way* out of line," the sheriff said. "Mr. Wilkins is the official coroner of Holcum County. Now step aside and let the man do his work."

Nick stood up and dusted himself off. "Before you proceed with your evaluation of the crime scene, may I make a couple of observations? I think you may find them helpful."

The sheriff nodded doubtfully, while Mr. Wilkins folded his arms and said nothing.

"This is Teddy's laboratory log," he said, handing the brown journal to the sheriff. "His last entry was made at 11:56 last night, placing the time of death sometime in the last eleven hours. You'll notice there is some lividity, which takes about three hours to begin, narrowing the window somewhat more."

He knelt down and pointed carefully to the entry wound at the back of Teddy's skull. "Probably *not* a suicide," he said in the general direction of Mr. Wilkins. "The entry wound is star shaped, indicating a contact wound. That means the gun was in contact with Teddy's head when it fired. The gases escaping from the barrel ripped the skin open in a star-shaped pattern. Someone stepped up behind Teddy and fired execution-style. That indicates to me that someone was *waiting* for Teddy."

Kathryn interrupted. "But how could anyone have gotten that close without Teddy seeing?"

Nick stepped to the wall switch and flipped it on. Nothing happened. He stepped around Teddy's body to the single light fixture that hung in the center of the ceiling. The white glass bowl had been removed and one bare bulb stood out like a pearl thumb. He picked up a dishtowel and covered his hand, then reached up and gave the bulb a quarter-turn to the right. The brightness of the light caused all of them to wince and turn away.

"That's how," Nick replied. "It looks to me like someone made sure the room was dark and then stepped out behind Teddy when he first entered the trailer." He pointed to the two crumpled grocery sacks. "He never even made it to the counter."

"I don't buy it." The sheriff shook his head. "The way I see it, your friend just picked the wrong place to live. This is the cheapest part of town all right—it's also the *worst* part of town. We get a lot of lowlifes passing through this way looking for a quick buck. Did your friend own a TV? A VCR?"

"No," Nick said, "but he did own an exceptional sound system."

"Where?"

In the corner of the room a small particle-board cabinet lay overturned, and a bare extension cord snaked across the floor.

"Looks like a drug-related murder to me," the sheriff continued. "Some pothead breaks in and grabs the first big-ticket item he can find—but before he can run, your friend comes to the door. The killer backs into the corner and waits for him to step inside. Your friend goes to set his bags down before he hits the lights—the killer steps in behind him, and..." He formed a gun with his right hand and made a recoiling motion. "If your friend had gone for the lights first, he'd still be dead. He just would have got it from the *front*—like old Mrs. Gallagher did."

Kathryn spun around. "Mrs. Gallagher? What happened to Mrs. Gallagher?"

"Like I said, it was a busy morning." He looked at Nick. "Mrs. Gallagher lived just a quarter-mile from here, on the other side of that windbreak. Lived in a trailer just about like this one. Last night somebody walked in and put a bullet through *her* head too—the *front* of her head—and then walked off with the TV and VCR. Her boy stopped by to look in on her. Found her early this morning."

No one said anything for a few moments. They had all known Mrs. Gallagher for years—for *decades.* She was a kind and gentle woman who had outlived her beloved husband by thirty years and quietly and patiently awaited their reunion in the seclusion of her little trailer.

"Was there any sign of forced entry?" Nick asked.

The sheriff looked around at the flimsy trailer. "In these things? There is no forced entry—just *entry.* Anybody can walk in who wants to."

"Or who is *asked* to," Nick said. "What about the light bulb? How do you explain that?"

"I can explain that"—the sheriff looked at him—"but I don't think you want to hear it."

"Try me."

"Okay. I think *you* did it."

Nick slowly smiled.

"You know," the sheriff said, nodding to the floor, "your boy here called me last night."

The smile disappeared from Nick's face. "What time was that?"

"About midnight. He was all excited, said he had some big news for you—but he couldn't find you. You two left a hotel number for him, but apparently you never showed up. Find better accommodations?"

Kathryn flushed. "We were at the Mologne House at Walter Reed, not that it's any of your business. It was a last-minute change of—"

"Did you go over to the lab?" Nick broke in.

"At midnight? I got better things to do. I told your boy to let it wait till morning. I told him the two of you would be back then, if you hadn't run off together."

"Shut up, Peter."

The sheriff turned to Kathryn. "If your friend here had a little more company last night, he might still be alive. Ever think of that?"

Kathryn glared at him hard. "I don't deserve that."

"I've tried to humor you as long as I can, Kath, but it's time to wise up. Have the two of you come up with any answers yet—any *real* answers? 'Cause if you have, I haven't seen 'em. I think what you've got here is one desperate Bug Man. He's on your payroll; he knows he's got to produce something, so he leads you around on a wild goose chase. Says you need to do research, collect evidence, conduct interviews—but where are the answers, Kath? Now he loses his friend—and he still doesn't have any answers—so he makes his friend's murder part of the story, part of the *conspiracy.* Only he needs things to look a little more sinister, so he unscrews the light bulb. Now he's got an *execution,* not just some senseless killing."

"I don't believe it," Kathryn said. "I don't believe Nick would do that."

"Really?" the sheriff looked at her. "Did the two of you arrive together or did the doc get here before you did?"

He turned back to Nick now. "That's how I explain the light bulb. Now here's a question for you: If your friend was executed, if someone purposely waited here for him, then how do you explain Mrs. Gallagher? How does she fit into all this?"

Nick said nothing. There *was* an explanation for Mrs. Gallagher's death—a simple and obvious explanation—but it was so monstrous that it would have sounded absurd. There were only two possible explanations for Mrs. Gallagher's death: Either it was nothing more than a random and unrelated act of violence, or the sheriff had committed a *double* murder last night. He had chosen a second victim, an innocent old woman, for no more reason than to draw attention away from Teddy's death. It was possible—but Nick knew he could never give voice to such a possibility. Even to him it sounded almost unthinkable...

Almost.

Nick slowly turned to Kathryn again, studying her anew as though he had never looked at her before. Here was a woman who had led one man to the altar, another to depression, and a third to pathological devotion—and possibly murder. One loved her, one lost his mind over her, and one killed for her. What was the power this woman possessed? Nick suddenly felt like Odysseus, longing to understand the seduction of the Sirens' song, begging his shipmates to unlash him from the mast. He looked again at the graceful curves of her hips and thighs, the thick mane of fiery auburn hair, the glistening emerald eyes—but there was something different about her eyes now, something he had never seen before. For the first time there was a strange darkness—it was a look of confusion or hesitation or uncertainty. Then her eyes met his, and he knew in an instant what it was.

It was doubt.

"I should go," Nick said quietly, "and leave you two *professionals* to your work." He stepped to the door and pushed it open, passing Kathryn without a word.

"Don't go far, Doc," the sheriff called after him. "I'll need to ask you a few questions about all this."

Well done, thought Nick as he slid into his car and started the engine. *You not only got away with murder, you managed to shift the suspicion to me. Not even Mrs. Guilford knows who to trust now.*

Well done, Sheriff. Well done indeed.

CHAPTER 30

The memorial service of James and Amy McAllister was held on an unusually pleasant June morning. An unexpected cold front had driven out the two-headed monster of Carolina summer—the oppressive heat and the clinging humidity—and had left in its place a flawless spring day.

Kathryn felt cheated. She didn't expect everything to *stop* for Jimmy and Amy, but it would have been nice if the world had at least tipped its hat in the form of a drizzling rain, or perhaps a dramatic haze over the cemetery grounds. Instead, the skies were a crystalline azure blue.

The change of climate was not overlooked by the people at Mount Zion A. M. E. Church, who all seemed a bit more cordial and cheerful than usual—and in Kathryn's view, a good deal less mournful than the occasion required.

Long folding tables hauled from the church fellowship hall were now draped in white and lined up in long fluttering rows. People stood for the most part, while the older folks sat on folding garden chairs and picked halfheartedly at sagging paper plates. The adults mingled in small groups and did their best to shush the smaller children, who found it impossible to contain themselves on such a day.

Kathryn worked her way through the considerable crowd, patting a shoulder here and accepting a heartfelt condolence there. Conversations seemed to center on the spectacular nature of Amy's demise or the dark curse that hung like a shroud over the McAllister family. And did you hear about old Mrs. Gallagher? Shot through the head just two nights ago—and in her own trailer!

Not a single soul mentioned the death of Dr. Eustatius Tedesco.

Kathryn looked up to see Nick slowly approaching from across the yard, dressed exactly as he was the last time she saw him at Teddy's trailer the day before. She hurried to meet him halfway. He seemed stooped and disheveled and profoundly tired, but there was still an unquestionable alertness in his eyes.

"I wasn't sure you'd come," she said.

"Why not?"

"I know you're not big on funerals. A body ceases to function, it decomposes—what's the point, right?"

Nick smiled faintly. "A wise man once told me: Sometimes, you have to *believe*."

"I wish all this was for Teddy. I wish there was *something*—"

"He's on his way back to Lancaster County," Nick said quietly. "Back to family. Ever been there? It's beautiful country."

Kathryn reached up to straighten his collar. "When was the last time you slept?"

"My species doesn't require much sleep," he said. As he spoke his eyes searched across the sea of heads until he located one familiar face.

"Come on," he said to Kathryn, "I feel like mingling."

The sheriff and deputy stood together near the center of the throng. As they approached, Kathryn flashed Peter a lukewarm smile; the two men exchanged no greeting of any kind. Kathryn reached up and hugged Beanie, then brushed back his wild brown hair and straightened his tie. He hardly seemed to notice; his eyes were fixed longingly on a half-dozen children playing at a picnic table thirty yards away.

Kathryn looked at Peter. He nodded his reluctant approval, and Beanie frolicked off to join his waiting friends.

"I was wondering," Nick spoke up, "now that the investigation is over, would you mind if I asked you a couple of questions? Just out of curiosity."

The sheriff glanced at Kathryn. "Why not?" he said pleasantly. "Fire away."

Nick rubbed hard at his chin. "What was Jim McAllister's problem anyway?"

"What problem is that?"

"You know—in the Gulf. Everybody says he had some kind of problem—it seemed to bug him constantly. He never got over it—thought it was worse than anything that happened to him in the war. Imagine that—worse than the war! What was the problem anyway?"

The sheriff folded his arms and looked at the ground. "The 82d was based at a place called Ab Qaiq," he said. "Andy and Jim were in the 4-325, assigned to Camp Gold. It was a temporary deployment, a tent city. Everybody got packages from home, and we used to stash the good stuff under our cots—and we'd raid each other's stuff from time to time. One day Andy was digging through Jim's stuff, and he found a little container of white powder. Got it?"

Nick squinted hard. "I ran across an old friend of Jim's up in Washington. He seemed to think Jim's big problem was with some guy."

"Jim was afraid Andy was going to turn him in."

Kathryn broke in. "Andy would never have turned Jimmy in!"

"Of course not," the sheriff grumbled. "But Jim was afraid he *might*. That stuff can make you a little paranoid, you know."

"You know what they say about paranoia," Nick said. "Just because you're paranoid, that doesn't mean someone's not out to get you."

The sheriff rolled his eyes.

"How do you know all this?" Nick asked. "Did Jim tell you?"

"I never saw Jim in the Gulf. We were assigned to separate units, remember? Andy came to see me a few days before the ground war began. He wanted me to know."

Nick stared thoughtfully into the sky. "So this *big problem* was that his old friend found out he had a nasty habit—and that was worse than the war? Worse than bombs and tanks and dead people? So bad that he could never even talk about it—even years later?"

The sheriff shrugged. "You'd have to ask Jim about all that."

"Yes," Nick nodded. "And that's not easy to do."

The sheriff grew impatient. "Anything else?"

"Yes," Nick said. "Where did Jim McAllister get all his cocaine? In a small town like this, for all those years?"

"Beats me."

Nick did a double take. "You don't *know*? You knew your friend was a user when he came back from the Gulf. You knew he must have had a supplier. You mean there were drugs being sold in your nice little town for all those years, and you never even knew about it?"

"Not in *my* town. Maybe his connection was up Fayetteville way. That's a rough town, an army town. There'd be plenty of connections up there."

"You knew your friend was a user, and you didn't like it. Didn't you ever think about cutting him off from his source?"

"I didn't know the source, okay?" the sheriff said angrily. "Jim stuck to himself a lot. Disappeared for weeks at a time. Nobody knew what kind of people he was hanging around with—*nobody,*" he said with a glance at Kathryn, then turned back to Nick again. "Any more questions, Doc?"

"Just one more." He paused. "The night before last—the night Teddy was murdered—where were you? I checked the phone records. Teddy didn't call your office, and he didn't call your home; he called your cell phone. Where were you when he called?"

The sheriff shoved his hands deep into his pockets and kicked furiously at the dirt. He muttered something to himself and glanced quickly up at Kathryn—but it was a full minute before he finally answered.

"I was...with Jenny McIntyre," he grumbled.

"After midnight?"

"After midnight."

"How long were you there?"

"Most of the night."

"All night?"

"*All night,* okay?"

Nick smiled.

Kathryn stared at Peter in embarrassment and confusion, and Peter did everything he could to avoid her gaze. "Will you excuse me?" she said awkwardly, and the two men watched in silence as she walked away.

■

"Okay, Doc." The sheriff turned to Nick. "It's just the two of us now, just you and me—so why don't you drop the act and tell me what's on your mind? I'd like to know how you've got this whole thing figured."

Nick studied the sheriff's face carefully.

"I figure you're in love with Kathryn. It's not really love, of course—it's more like a pathological obsession—but it's the closest thing *you've* got. It must have really popped your cork when she decided to marry Andy. But then you got a lucky break when he was killed in the Gulf, and you had a second chance. You played the knight in shining armor to the grieving widow—you were her savior, her deliverer. You couldn't win her love, so you tried to earn it—but it didn't quite work, did it? I think she *wants* to love you, but for some reason she can't—maybe because deep down inside she sees through you, just like I do. You kept pursuing her, but somewhere along the line she started to feel the heat, so you backed off. Like they say in these parts: *If you send in the dog too fast, you flush the bird.* That's where Jenny McIntyre comes in. The sheriff got himself a girlfriend—in name only, of course—and that took the pressure off Kathryn. Now you two could be buddies again. That was a neat bit about spending the night with Jenny. Boy, I would have loved to be a Diptera on that ceiling. You should have seen the look on Kathryn's face when you told her—but then, you were staring at the ground at the time, weren't you?"

The sheriff stared at Nick with the eyes of a shark—eyes gray and flat and impenetrable; eyes capable of masking an entire ocean of rage and wrath with utter, absolute coldness.

"You seem to enjoy pushing me, Doc," he said with no hint of emotion. "Why is that?"

"It's hard to say," Nick said thoughtfully. "You seem to bring out the worst in people."

"I'm not a fool, Doc."

"Believe me," Nick said, "I never took you for one."

There was a long, icy silence.

"Something really bothered Jim McAllister after the Gulf," Nick went on. "I call it *guilt.* I think ol' Jimmy knew more about what happened to Andy than he let on. They served in the same unit, went into battle side by side… I think Jimmy saw an opportunity to have a second chance at Kathryn—and I think he took it.

"So he wrestled with his conscience—but it wasn't bad enough to stop him. He still had to deal with *you*—after all, only one of you could have her. That's where you come into the picture. I'll bet the two of you had a very interesting competition going over the years—vying for position, trying to outdo one another in service to the grieving widow.

"About a week ago it finally came to a head, and that's when you murdered him. I'm not so sure you planned to. Maybe the two of you had an argument, and it got out of hand. Maybe he wanted to kill *you;* after all, he had his gun with him. Maybe you just meant to hit him, and he fell backward—with his right leg propped up. Then you saw your opportunity, so you shot him in the head with his own sidearm and then placed the gun in his hand. No gunpowder residue, remember?

"Not very sophisticated, was it—a phony suicide? I mean, for a professional like you who's seen enough murders to know how to do it right. So sloppy, so many potential questions. Now what do you do? How would you ever get away with it? It took you several hours to figure that one out—time enough for the lividity in the left leg to become fixed. Then it suddenly dawned on you—what better place to bring the body than your own backyard, where the county coroner is the ice cream man! You knew that Mr. Wilkins's incompetence would allow you to avoid an autopsy and all the nasty questions that would go with it. So you dumped the body here—with the leg flat this time—in a meadow where you knew hunters would stumble across it in just a day or two. Very neat. But the ironic thing—the *funny* thing—is that your plan was spoiled by the only person in the world you care anything about."

The sheriff shook his head. "You're in the wrong business, Doc. You should be writing those detective stories."

"Truth is stranger than fiction, Sheriff. Two nights ago the final specimen emerged from its puparium, and Teddy called to let you know; the poor guy was actually naive enough to *cooperate* with you. There could only be one reason to make a fuss over that last specimen—it must have been indigenous to some other area, verifying our suspicions that the body had been moved. But there was only one fly, and Teddy was the only one who knew about it. So you sent poor Teddy home, then released the fly—and left the door open to make it look like an accident. And then, for the *coup de grâce,* you somehow made it to Teddy's trailer ahead of him and waited. Very tidy; no evidence, and now no witness."

Nick began to slowly shake his head. "But the thing I find incredible—the one real shining moment in all of your pathology—is when you put a bullet in the face of an innocent old woman just to help cover your tracks. Her death wasn't even essential. You could have gotten away with Teddy's murder without it. It was that extra little touch that shows what a truly demented individual you are."

The sheriff said nothing at all for a moment. Then he began to smile and finally laughed outright.

"So that's your story?" he said through his laughter. "If I spent all that time at your lab that night, how could I beat your partner to his trailer? And how could I murder your partner *and* poor old Mrs. Gallagher if I was with Jenny the whole night? And most of all, why would I want to kill my own best friend? Why would I *need* to? To win Kath? I've been first in line for Kath ever since Andy. It was never about Jimmy, Doc."

"There are still a few missing pieces to the story," Nick said. "I don't suppose you'd care to help me with the details?"

"What are you going to do with a cockamamie story like that? You've got no evidence or witnesses at all. You think you can take a fairytale like that to the law?"

Nick smiled and leaned forward. "I'm not a fool either, Sheriff. The evidence is gone—you're in no danger from the law. The only way I can hurt you, the only thing that *really* matters to you, is if I can sell my story to Mrs. Guilford."

The sheriff stopped abruptly. He stood silently for several moments, expressionless once again, and then he began to smile once more.

"You hang on like a tick. I got to give you that. She must be paying you a fortune."

Nick shook his head. "This isn't about money. This is for Teddy."

"Go ahead," the sheriff shrugged. "Try to sell your story to Kath. There's one piece of the equation you're overlooking, Doc: *You're the outsider here.* She's known you for, what—a week now? Kath and I grew up together. She loves me."

"Like a brother," Nick needled.

"Maybe so—but that still makes me the brother and you the blind geek from Pittsburgh. Who do you think she's going to believe?"

"You, of course. Unless."

"Unless what?"

"Unless one of those missing pieces turns up."

"So long, Doc." The sheriff waved. "I'll be seeing you around."

Nick gazed after him as he moved away. "I'll be watching for you."

As Nick headed slowly across the churchyard, the sheriff's questions kept returning to him.

How could the sheriff murder Teddy and Mrs. Gallagher if he was with Jenny McIntyre all night? Was he really at Jenny's, or was it just an empty alibi? He must have been there at least part of the night—the story would be too easy to check out. But if the sheriff came and went during the night, Jenny would certainly know. Would she lie to protect him—maybe to win him away from Kathryn?

He approached the picnic table lost in thought when the glint of sunlight from something on the table caught his eye. Beanie stood beside the table like a towering totem with a band of tiny worshipers gathered about him. The deputy held them back from the table with his trunklike arms. The children were oohing and aahing over Beanie's police sidearm, shining in the hot afternoon sun.

"Don't touch," Beanie said with great authority. "Everybody look, but don't touch."

Nick stepped closer and peered over the heads of the solemn assembly. "What kind of gun do you have there, Deputy?"

"A *police* gun," Beanie said proudly.

"It looks a little like the sheriff's gun."

"'*Zactly* like Unca Pete's gun."

It *was* exactly like the sheriff's weapon—a 9 millimeter Beretta 92F, the civilian equivalent of the standard army sidearm. They were identical except for the absence of the engraved emblem of the All American Division.

"I think Uncle Pete's gun is bigger."

"'*Zactly* the same!" Beanie repeated with obvious irritation.

Fifty yards away and thirty feet in the sky, a single black *Calliphora vomitoria* hovered in the breeze, head into the wind, sensing and sampling the air as it rushed past. Suddenly, the blow fly detected an airborne cluster of blood molecules—and then another. She eagerly followed the elusive scent forward, drifting down from cluster to cluster, the scent leading it irresistibly onward until it finally came to rest on the handgrip of the deputy's gun.

Nick spotted the fly even before it landed. "That's enough," Beanie said. "I got to put it away now."

"No!" Nick grabbed his arm as he reached for the gun. "Tell me more about your gun, Beanie. Do you ever get to use it?"

The fly wandered over the serrated grip, its extended proboscis in constant motion—probing, sensing, *tasting*.

"Can't talk about that." Beanie shook his head.

"Do you ever clean it? You can tell me that."

"I wipe it off sometimes."

The sun bore down on the gleaming chrome pistol, and the metal grew steadily warmer. The fly worked its way slowly over the Beretta, first to the trigger guard, then the frame, then the slide, its senses leading it inerrantly toward the muzzle of the gun.

"But do you ever really clean it? Take it apart? Clean the *barrel?*"

Beanie shook his head. "Wipe it off, mostly. Makes it shiny."

Nick held his breath as the fly hesitated for a moment at the very tip of the muzzle—then disappeared into the deep blackness of the barrel.

Nick stood paralyzed, watching as Beanie carefully picked up the weapon and slid it neatly back into its leather holster—exactly as he had done two nights ago after firing a bullet into the base of Teddy's skull.

Nick turned and drove his right fist into the center of Beanie's face. The nasal bone shattered beneath the blow, and blood spurted from both nostrils. The children scattered like startled doves. Beanie staggered backward from the force of the blow, and Nick was on him like a spider on a fly, driving his massive body to the ground with a thundering whump. With his left hand he grabbed for Beanie's bulbous throat, and he brought his right fist back for a crushing blow—and then he stopped. For one split second he met Beanie's eyes, and there he saw…*nothing.* There was neither malice nor anger nor cruelty of any kind. There was nothing but confusion and sorrow and pain. They were not the eyes of a killer—they were the eyes of a little child. Nick lowered his fist. In his rage at the puppet master, he had attacked the puppet.

He felt an explosion of pain in his left side, and the force of the blow threw him off of Beanie and onto his back. His wind was completely gone, and he writhed on the ground in agony, staring into the searing white sky above. The figure of the sheriff stood towering over him, the blinding sun flashing out from behind him like light from the face of Moses. An instant later he felt Kathryn's body drop across his like an interceding angel—covering him, protecting him.

"Stop it, Peter!" she screamed. "You didn't have to kick him that hard!"

"Look at Beanie!" he shouted back. "I should have shot him!"

Beanie stood calmly a few feet away, hands on knees, blood draining freely from his nose.

"Nick doesn't know what he's doing! He hasn't slept for days!"

"He knows what he's doing, all right. He knows exactly what he's doing!"

The sheriff circled menacingly around Nick's body while Kathryn stretched out over him, keeping her body between him and the avenging angel above.

"He's under arrest!" he jabbed his finger at Nick's body.

"Leave him alone! He's had enough!"

"He assaulted an officer of the law!"

"He hit *Beanie.* Don't be so stupid, Peter! Whose side are you on?"

"Not his!"

Kathryn rose up to her knees now and put her hands on her hips. There was an unmistakable fire in her emerald eyes. "Then how about *my* side? You always say you're on my side, Peter, well how about it? For me?"

Peter scowled at her and cursed under his breath. "Get him out of here," he growled, "and keep him away from me!" He turned and stormed off, leaving the deputy still doubled over behind him.

Kathryn immediately began to drag Nick to his feet. "We'd better get out of here before he changes his mind."

He put his right arm around her shoulders and braced his left hand against his aching ribs, and they staggered off together toward the parking lot. She deposited him against the hood of his car, then carefully lifted his shirt.

"Let me see that," she said. "You may have some broken ribs."

The site was already turning a greenish shade of purple. She began to feel gingerly along the contour of each rib. He winced and pulled away.

"Don't be a baby," she snapped. "You're lucky you're not

dead. What in the world got into you back there? Why did you hit poor Beanie?"

"Because 'poor Beanie' murdered Teddy."

Kathryn stared at him in utter astonishment.

"The entry wound on the back of Teddy's skull was a *contact wound,* remember? That means the gun was placed against his skin and then discharged. In a contact wound, the gases escape the muzzle at such tremendous velocity that they create a temporary vacuum in the barrel—and that vacuum sucks blood back into the barrel. It's known as *blowback.* I watched a *Calliphora vomitoria* land on Beanie's gun and crawl into the barrel. That fly is attracted to blood, Mrs. Guilford; fresh blood. It found some."

Kathryn shook her head in disbelief. "There must be some other explanation."

"Give me an explanation. Tell me any other way the deputy could have gotten blood into the barrel of his gun."

"Nick, this is *Beanie* we're talking about. Beanie isn't capable of killing anyone."

"He isn't capable of *hating* anyone, Mrs. Guilford—I'm not even sure he's capable of anger. You still want to believe that the deputy is a gigantic Pinocchio, and your friend the sheriff is just kindly old Gepetto. But *this* Pinocchio is capable of crushing a man's hand or firing a bullet into a man's brain or anything else Gepetto *tells* him to do."

Kathryn's legs felt weak, and her head began to swim.

"Didn't you find it interesting that the sheriff suddenly developed a passion for Jenny McIntyre the other night? Didn't you find it a little surprising? I'll bet Jenny was surprised."

"That's none of my business."

"It is your business, Mrs. Guilford. Don't you see? When the sheriff told you he spent the night with Jenny McIntyre, he was telling the truth. He *couldn't* have murdered Teddy and Mrs. Gallagher, but that doesn't mean he couldn't send someone else to do the errands for him."

"Nick—do you know what you're saying?"

"I'm saying that it wasn't passion that led the sheriff to Jenny's door. He needed an *alibi.* The sheriff was in some way involved in Jim McAllister's death. When that last specimen emerged, it proved that the body was moved—and maybe it proved more than that. The sheriff had to intervene, but he knew that I would suspect him—so he sent his boy around to murder Teddy *and* to knock off Mrs. Gallagher just to throw us off the scent.

"I know exactly what I'm saying, Mrs. Guilford, and so do you. I'm saying that if your friend the sheriff wasn't a murderer before, *he is now.*"

CHAPTER 32

The crowd at Mount Zion A. M. E. had long ago dispersed. All that remained from the morning's elaborate funeral reception were two folding tables draped unevenly in stained and wrinkled linens.

Nick sat by himself on a sagging picnic bench. He picked at the splinters of decomposing wood; it was made of cedar, a wood whose natural resins were supposed to protect it from decay. Everything decomposes, Nick thought. Some get a little more time than others, but sooner or later everything breaks down.

He lifted his shirt and gently tested his aching ribs. He was lucky; they were bruised, but not broken. A scarlet hematoma the size of his fist throbbed an angry reminder of how the world works: Blood vessels rupture under the skin. The blood pours into the surrounding tissues, and the stranded blood cells begin to die. The skin turns purple or blue or black. Black, the color of death; your own little piece of death to carry around with you.

His thoughts were interrupted by the closing of a car door. He looked up to see Kathryn remove a small casserole dish from the backseat and turn in his direction. Her gait was slow and halting; it was obvious that she was very much preoccupied with thoughts of her own.

"I have no idea why I brought this," she said absently, setting the casserole down to secure the edge of a fluttering tablecloth.

"Because there's nothing else to do," Nick said. "People have been bringing food to funerals for centuries." He lifted the foil from the edge of the dish. "Tuna puffs…I love these things."

"I've been thinking about what you said this morning—about Beanie and Teddy. About Peter."

"And?"

"Nick, you've got to try to see all this from my perspective. We're talking about Beanie—a little boy in a man's body. And Peter, a man I've known and trusted all my life. You come to me with eggs and maggots and flies that can smell blood from miles away, and you ask me to weigh those things against the things I *know*."

Nick leaned his head back and drew a long, deep breath through his nose. "Smell the air," he said to Kathryn. "Go ahead, give it a try. What do you smell?"

She sniffed at the air. "Not much. Tuna, mostly."

"Come on, you can do better than that."

She sniffed again. "I can smell the pines. And the asphalt heating up in the driveway. And…I don't know…some flowers, maybe."

"Amazing, isn't it?" Nick said. "Here we are, supposedly the highest form of life on the planet, and yet the only odors we can detect are so powerful that they would *overwhelm* a lower life form. We're thinking beings," he said, "but our senses have grown dull."

"Where are you going with all this?"

"I find that sometimes a situation becomes clearer when you do *more* than think—when you use all of your senses. You say that the evidence I've shown you seems unconvincing compared with what you know about the sheriff—but what do your other senses tell you? How does he *smell?* How does the whole situation *feel?* What do your *instincts* tell you?"

"You're asking me to weigh what I smell against things I know?"

"There are different ways of knowing," Nick said. "Sometimes what we call 'knowing' is just a form of prejudice."

"So now I'm prejudiced?"

"Of course you are. Look at it from my perspective, Mrs. Guilford. I see three men who all fell in love with you—and in your own way, you loved all three of them. You lost the one you loved the most; a week ago, you lost the second. Now you have only one left."

"And if I accept what you're telling me, then I've lost Peter too. I've lost everything."

"You said you had to *know,* Mrs. Guilford. The truth doesn't care."

"Well, I care," Kathryn said, "and I still have to *know.* Before I give up on Peter, I have to be absolutely sure. I'm not like you, Nick. I can't just smell things."

"Can't you? While we were interviewing Amy McAllister, her house just happened to burn to the ground. Then Teddy committed an unthinkable blunder, and that same night was murdered in a random act of violence. A day later, I watched a fly in search of blood enter the barrel of the deputy's gun. Come on, Mrs. Guilford—if you can smell asphalt, you can smell this."

"Can you tell me for certain—*absolutely for certain*—that there's no other reason that fly might have crawled into Beanie's gun? Did you ever stop to think that if you hadn't *hit* Beanie, we might have found a way to get hold of his gun? We might have been able to have it tested to see if there really was any blood—and if it was Teddy's?"

Nick said nothing.

"And there's something else, Nick—if Peter spent the night with Jenny, how did Beanie get to Teddy's trailer? He can't drive, Nick—Beanie can't drive. I'm sorry," she said, "I need proof."

"Wish I could help you," Nick shrugged. "But the only proof we might have had is gone—flying around somewhere, looking for a body of its own."

A small white door at the back door of the church opened, and the figure of Dr. Malcolm Jameson emerged, carrying a familiar black book at his side. Nick turned to Kathryn as he approached.

"About all this," Nick said with a wave of his hand.

"You're welcome. I just wish more people could be here."

"I wish *Teddy* could be here."

Dr. Jameson greeted them both with a solemn nod. "This seems an inappropriate location," he said with a frown at the littered surroundings. "Perhaps Dr. Polchak could suggest something more apropos."

Nick quickly scanned the terrain; at the edge of the church property, through a break in the tree line a golden green meadow rose up and away from them, brilliant in the full noon sun.

"There," Nick said. "Teddy would like that spot."

The three of them walked toward the meadow together. Dr. Jameson's pace was slow and deliberate, and Nick had to rein himself in to stay in step.

"So tell me," Dr. Jameson said, "how is the fishing?"

"Not good," Nick shook his head. "I had a big one on the line, but he got away."

"Nonsense. No one gets away, my friend. As the apostle said, 'Some men's sins go before them, and some follow after.' If your fish needs to be caught, he will be caught—sooner or later."

"I was hoping for sooner," Nick said.

"Patience. You are still a young man, and young men do not make good fishermen. Young men discourage too easily; they give up after the first false strike. The old fisherman knows he must wait."

"Wait for what?"

"For Providence." The old man smiled. "There is more to fishing than meets the eye."

At the crest of the meadow they halted. Nick and Kathryn stood side by side, and Dr. Jameson turned to face them. He opened the great book and slowly searched through the fragile pages; then he stopped, closed his eyes, and raised his face to the June sun.

"God our Father," he began, "Maker of heaven and earth—we gather today to deliver into Your hands the soul and memory of Dr. Eustatius Tedesco…"

He said the name without fumbling—no moment's hesitation, no awkward glance at a written reminder. He said the name as though it was worth knowing, and Nick was grateful for the offer of dignity and respect.

"We remember today the life of a man well-loved, a man who spent his life in the service of others and in the pursuit of justice. This man has been cruelly taken from us, O Lord, and our hearts are darkened—Your *world* is darkened by his loss! 'Help, Lord, for the godly man ceases to be, for the faithful disappear from among the sons of men.'"

The old man spoke in slow, thundering waves. He began almost in a whisper; then his voice swelled to a rumbling crescendo, then broke, receded, and slowly rose again. Almost a song, Nick thought, just like the cicadas in the woods.

"We bring our complaint before you today, for our friend was taken from us by murder most foul. Our hearts cry out for justice, O Lord—and our brother cries out to You from the grave! Nothing is hidden from Your sight, O God, 'For there is nothing covered that will not be revealed, and hidden that will not be known.'"

The deputy can't drive, Nick thought. Then how did he get

to Teddy's trailer and back again? The sheriff couldn't have dropped him off, there wasn't time. He had to take care of things at the lab, and then he had to get to Jenny's to establish his alibi. Then how did the deputy get there?

"You are no stranger to killing, O Lord. You have witnessed the taking of countless innocent lives. You were there at the first, at the slaying of righteous Abel. You looked down upon wicked Cain; You knew the burning jealousy in his heart. 'Why are you angry?' You said to him. 'And why has your countenance fallen? If you do well, will not your countenance be lifted up? And if you do not do well, sin is crouching at the door; but you must master it.'" The old man glanced down at the ancient text and translated the Latin effortlessly as he read.

Would the fly have gone into the barrel for any other reason? Not likely—not that species of fly. The deputy killed Teddy, Nick thought. He could smell it. But that's not enough for Mrs. Guilford—she wants proof.

"But Cain did not master his jealousy; he did not contain his rage. He slew his own brother and thought he could hide his sin from You... From You, who sees all the inward workings of the heart! 'And the Lord said to Cain, "What have you done? The voice of your brother's blood is crying to me from the ground."'"

Nick stopped. "What did you say?"

The old man slowly looked up from his text.

Nick snatched the book from his hand and scanned the facing pages. "Where were you reading?"

"The Book of Genesis," Dr. Jameson said quietly, "chapter four."

Nick ran his finger down the text, searching. "Here it is," he said. "*Vox sanguinis fratris tui clamat ad me de terra*... The voice of your brother's blood cries out to me from the ground."

"What is it?" Kathryn asked.

Nick turned and raced toward the parking lot. "I'll be back

in a few hours," he called back. "If everything goes well, you'll have all the proof you need!"

"Nick! Where are you going? *Nick!*"

Kathryn watched the Dodge belch out of the driveway. She turned back to Dr. Jameson and stared at the leather-bound volume in his hands. "What was it? What did he find?"

The old man smiled. "I believe the young man is going fishing."

Nick steered his Dodge into the impossibly crowded parking lot at North Carolina State University and double parked behind two university service vehicles. His faculty parking permit had long ago expired, and he had long ago ceased to care. He had come to enjoy this ongoing game of eluding the University Safety Patrol—or the "Parking Gestapo," as he referred to them. He plucked a small, clear plastic vial from the passenger seat and held it up to the light. He tipped it gently from side to side, searching for its tiny occupant.

He walked briskly across the Brickyard, the central plaza of the North Campus, an acre-wide mosaic of rose-and-cream masonry punctured intermittently by an ancient red oak or a stately wax-leafed magnolia. The western end of the Brickyard was bordered by Gardner Hall, a nondescript monolith of red Carolina brick and limestone-ledged windows, each choked with its own pulsing air conditioner. The second, third, and fourth floors are home to the NCSU Department of Entomology—and on friendlier days, home to Dr. Nick Polchak as well.

The meandering summer students seemed to sense the urgency in his gait and stepped aside as he strode through the entry door and swung left into the open doorway of the departmental office. A middle-aged woman looked up at him from behind an almond steel-case reception desk.

"Where is Noah?" Nick demanded.

The woman smiled politely. "Why, Nick! It's been quite a while since—"

"Where is *Noah?* Does he have a class? Do you have his teaching schedule?"

The smile quickly disappeared from her face. She glanced at the summer schedule tacked to the bulletin board in front of her. "He has ENT 502," she said dully. "It's in 3214. Do you want your mail? You've got several letters."

Nick turned without a word and headed for the doorway.

"Nice to see you again," she called after him.

He stopped in the doorway and turned back, staring at her curiously.

"Who are you?" he asked, and without waiting for an answer he wheeled around again and was gone.

The heels of his loafers clacked and echoed down the hollow corridors of Gardner Hall, largely empty during the hot summer months except for the ever-present graduate students who slumped lethargically in front of computers and laboratory tables. Nick sprinted up a flight of stairs, then down a long, white hallway veined with pipes and ducts and electrical conduit. The floor was a glossy checkerboard of aging brown and black linoleum, and a single row of rectangular fluorescent dashes lined the center of the ceiling. It was an altogether quiet and sterile environment in the summer, and Nick preferred it that way. He enjoyed the teaching profession most when he wasn't saddled with the annoying distraction of students.

He paused before the door to room 3214 and peered through the translucent glass at the silhouette of a single figure standing motionless behind a lectern. He rapped sharply on the glass, and without waiting for a response, he invited himself in.

The door crashed open, and a half-dozen startled students awakened from their heat-induced torpor. The ancient figure behind the lectern stood oblivious, completely immune to interruption after more than fifty years of teaching—but as he continued with his lecture on Insect Systematics he gradually became aware that his students' focus had been thoroughly diverted. He rapped his knuckles sharply on the wooden lectern and flashed his sternest look. A student in the first row helpfully gestured toward the door. The old man reluctantly turned and studied Nick without any sign of recognition whatsoever—and then a light went on somewhere in the vast, endless library of his mind.

He smiled.

"Why Nicholas," he said with delight.

"Noah." Nick extended his hand. "I need your help."

Dr. Noah Ellison was one of the most venerated entomologists in the world. His research on the systematics of medically important arthropod species was legendary. During World War II, Lieutenant Ellison pioneered mosquito-control strategies for the Allied forces in the jungles of the South Pacific, and he almost single-handedly tripled the specimen collection of the Smithsonian Museum of Natural History, where he was now one of only three curators emeritus. After major field studies and surveys on five continents, he was a veritable encyclopedia of knowledge on the 85,000 species that constitute the order Diptera: mosquitoes, gnats, midges, and—most important to Nick—*flies.*

Despite the summer heat Noah was dressed as always in a crisp white button-down and scarlet bow tie. Regardless of temperature or humidity, he always dressed the same. He never seemed to chill or sweat; he was timeless, changeless, a mathematical constant in a universe of variables. But age was beginning to take its inevitable toll on Noah Ellison, and in the last few years his colleagues had sadly noticed the first decline in his remarkable intellectual powers. Nick had consulted him many times in his investigations and had always thought of Noah as a kind of timeless reference work that would forever stand on ready reserve. Now Nick thought of him more as a priceless, ancient manuscript, filled with wonders of knowledge and wisdom but rapidly crumbling to dust—which fueled all the more Nick's sense of urgency in seeking his assistance.

"Class," Dr. Ellison said warmly, "allow me to introduce Dr. Nicholas Polchak, a colleague and member of our faculty. His face may be unfamiliar to you because he was recently exiled to the wilderness for dabbling in the black arts. Dr. Polchak, you see, is a *forensic* entomologist. So be on your guard"—he glowered at the most sleepy-eyed of the students—"or you may turn up as one of Dr. Polchak's field studies."

The students smiled and nodded their greeting. Nick ignored them and reached into his pocket for the precious plastic vial.

"Noah, I need your help—with *this*."

Noah adjusted his glasses and peered at the impossibly small occupant of the vial.

"Nicholas"—he nodded slightly toward the students—"I'm in the middle of something right now—"

"Noah, Dr. Tedesco is dead. Teddy was murdered, Noah, and I'm after the man who did it. I need you to make a species identification for me—I need to be *absolutely certain*—and all I can give you to work with is this."

Nick held up the vial containing a single brown speck the size of a grain of rice—the puparial capsule left behind when the final specimen was released.

As they headed down the hallway toward the stairwell, Nick had to double back twice to keep pace with Noah's ambling shuffle.

"Let's take the elevator, Noah—just this once."

"Nonsense," Dr. Ellison grumbled and began his slow ascent of the twenty-four steps leading to the fourth floor. The Gardner Hall elevator bore a bronze plaque officially denoting it the "Noah Ellison Memorial Elevator," in honor of the fact that Noah Ellison had never once in more than fifty years employed it.

Room 4321 housed the Insect Collection, a warehouse of gray metal specimen cabinets and shelves that always smelled of mothballs, necessary to protect the thousands of dried specimens from dermestid attack. Noah seated himself with a sigh at a laboratory table bearing a single gleaming microscope. He removed a neatly folded handkerchief from his shirt pocket and spread it on the table before him.

"Now then"—he turned to Nick—"let's have the little fellow."

Nick carefully inverted the plastic vial and the tiny brown speck rolled out into the center of the handkerchief. Noah selected a pair of light tension forceps and turned to the specimen, widening his eyes and craning his head forward and back in an attempt to bring the diminutive object into focus. His hand shook like the tremens of an alcoholic; it seemed laughable that he would ever be able to pinpoint the single elusive speck. Nick held his breath, with visions of the precious specimen flipping onto the floor and disappearing into a vent or crack. To his astonishment, Noah seized the puparium on his very first attempt.

"You seem nervous, Nicholas," he said acidly, somehow managing to place the puparium in the exact center of a glass specimen slide. "You must learn to relax if you ever wish to reach *my* age. Now—tell me about Dr. Tedesco," he said as he adjusted the microscope.

"A body turned up in the woods near our research station just over a week ago. The local coroner botched the examination completely, and I was hired to do an independent investigation—without the permission of the authorities."

Noah glanced up. "Nicholas, is this your idea of staying out of trouble?"

"I only had time to collect a handful of specimens. We've been rearing them in the lab to identify the species. This one came from an isolated wound above the left eye—the kind of wound a good right cross might make. I have reason to believe that the body was moved postmortem, and I was hoping this specimen might confirm that suspicion."

"And the mature fly?" Noah peered into the lens again.

"Teddy was on watch. He indicated in his log that eclosion occurred the night before last at about midnight. I arrived at the lab several hours later. The back door was open and the fly was gone. I went straight to Teddy's trailer—"

"Tragic," Noah said solemnly. "Dr. Tedesco was a fine systematist and an even better human being. I shall miss him."

"I believe Teddy identified the species, and I think he made the mistake of notifying the wrong person—someone with a motive to cover it up."

"Someone quite ignorant of our discipline," Noah murmured. "Someone under the assumption that species can only be determined by the mature specimen and not by the puparial sac it leaves behind." He rocked back from the microscope. "Take a look, Nicholas. Tell me what you see."

Nick groaned. "Noah, please. I'm in a hurry here."

"Nicholas," he repeated sternly, "tell me what you *see*."

It was Noah Ellison's most endearing habit, and his most annoying as well. He was, above all, a teacher—and he never gave a simple or direct answer when he could invite the student to learn for himself. Neatly framed above his office desk were the words of E. M. Forster: "Spoon feeding in the long run teaches us nothing but the shape of the spoon." Nick knew it was useless to resist. Noah moved aside, and the student took his place at the master's knee.

"Now then. As you know, the puparium is formed by the skin of the third-instar larva. This means that the puparium is a kind of shrink-wrap around the maturing fly which retains many of its identifying features—and some of its own morphological uniquenesses as well. Notice first of all the microsculpturing on the cuticle—quite characteristic for this species."

"I see it."

"Look at the bubble membrane. Do you see the little globules? Now examine the dorsal lateral surface of segment five."

"What about this rupture?"

"It is caused by the aversion of the pupal respiratory horn—its location is significant. Now notice some of the other structural features: the scalelike texturing, the tiny projections and processes—"

"I see it." Nick looked up. "I see it all, Noah—but I need an *identification.* What species are we looking at here? Can you tell me?"

The old man closed his eyes for several moments and then slowly began to shake his head.

"I cannot," he said sadly.

Nick's heart sank.

Noah leaned forward and spoke almost in a whisper. "It shames me to say this, but—" He stopped and glanced back over his shoulder toward the door. "I am going to have to refer to a *book.*" He stood up without a word and shuffled out into the hallway, with Nick on his heels.

Three doors down Noah rounded the corner into the tiny room that served as his office. It was sparsely decorated, almost empty except for the tidy metal desk and the vinyl visitor's armchair resting beside it. The one remarkable feature about the room was the complete absence of paper. It was impossibly neat for the office of a scientist—but that was simply because, over the years, Dr. Ellison had carefully transferred the contents of each book and monograph into his formidable memory.

"Now where did I put that book," he mumbled, wandering about the office. "Ah!" He spotted a single green volume atop the lone filing cabinet. Nick wasn't sure the old man could even lift the massive tome; he stepped over and took it down for him, wiped the dusty cover against his shirt, and spread it open on Noah's desk.

Nick agonized as Noah slowly leafed through page after page of crowded text.

"Now *this* is interesting," he would say from time to time—and then point out some obscure tidbit of entomological trivia that had nothing at all to do with their quest. Nick's impatience grew more and more obvious, but Noah was unflappable.

"You must learn to enjoy the journey, Nicholas," he said without interrupting his reading. "You must learn not to weary the soul by longing only for the destination."

Endless, agonizing minutes passed.

"Here it is," he said at last. "Exactly as I suspected. These references are organized very poorly, very poorly indeed. There really should be a cross-index of morphological features. I must speak to the publisher about this, I—"

"Noah!"

Dr. Ellison looked at him implacably. "It is a *Chrysomya megacephala,* Nicholas—commonly known as the Oriental Blow Fly."

"I know that species," Nick said. "It has anterior spiracles. It's greenish blue with purple highlights, and the posterior margin of the second and third abdominal segments is jet black."

"Precisely. *Megacephala* is an immigrant species that was introduced into Florida sometime in the eighties. It prefers the warmer winters, and so its range is limited—but it seems to be adapting and slowly moving north."

"How *far* north?"

"Central Georgia. No farther."

"Not North Carolina?"

Noah looked at him with disdain. "The last time I consulted an atlas, Nicholas, Central Georgia was about eight hours from North Carolina."

"And you're positive?"

Noah raised a single eyebrow. His meaning was unmistakable.

Nick extended his hand. The old man took it and gripped it tightly until they both made eye contact.

"I wasn't joking about the black arts, you know. Be careful, Nicholas. I've lost one colleague this week—I wouldn't care to lose another."

Nick hurried down the hall, stopping at the insect collection just long enough to retrieve the crucial specimen.

"Your mail!" the secretary yelled to him as he raced past the doorway of the departmental office. "Don't you want your mail?"

Nick snatched the rubber-banded stack of envelopes without a word and sprinted across the Brickyard to his car. He pulled the pink square of paper from under his windshield wiper, crumpled it, and threw it into the car, then roared out of the parking lot with a clatter of valves and a trademark puff of blue smoke.

Nick picked up his cell phone and punched in Kathryn's number.

"Mrs. Guilford," he said. "I need you to do something for me. I need you to call the sheriff and invite him over to your house. That's right, your house. Because I need to take a look at his patrol car, that's why; and I can't very well do it while it's parked in front of the sheriff's office. I figure I need about thirty minutes—thirty *uninterrupted* minutes, Mrs. Guilford—I don't think my ribs can stand another encounter with the sheriff just yet. Whatever you do, keep him in the house for thirty minutes. Got it?

"What? I don't know. Tell him you want to talk. Tell him you want to cry on his shoulder. Tell him you're having second thoughts about him—that should do it. And once he's inside, well…you think of something.

"I've got to stop at the lab first, but I can be at your place by a quarter to four. Tell him to meet you at four o'clock. I'll park down the street and watch for his car. What? There's no time now, I'll explain everything when I… Hello? Mrs. Guilford, are you there?"

Nick looked down at the phone. The green LCD panel flashed the words, *SEARCHING FOR SERVICE*. He looked out the window; he was east of I-95 now, well outside the city. He thought about Walter Reed and its location at the northern tip of Washington, almost to the Maryland border.

Nick reached over for the stack of mail and tugged off the rubber band with his teeth. He pinned the rumpled envelopes against the steering wheel and rifled through them: a departmental notice, a schedule of summer classes, a past-due notice from the University Safety Patrol…

Mr. Vincent Arranzio, Washington D.C. PERSONAL.

He tore off the end of the envelope and fumbled open the single sheet of paper inside. In large letters was scribbled a single sentence:

THE GUY'S NAME WAS PETE.

Nick slammed the pedal to the floor.

"I'll see you at four then. Thank you, Peter."

Even before Kathryn hung up the phone, she felt a familiar tightening in her stomach. Nick said Beanie must have killed Teddy. Could it be true? Was it even possible? If Beanie really did it, then Peter had to be behind it. But why would Peter want Teddy dead, unless…

Did I just invite a murderer over to my house?

There was no evidence. There was no proof. She had no way to *know*—but Nick was right. Somehow, there was the strangest smell.

The knot in her gut began to grow.

What was she supposed to do with Peter for thirty minutes? She told him she wanted to talk—about what? What would she say to him, "I invited you over to tell you again that I don't love you?"

She checked her watch: 3:15. Forty-five minutes until Peter would arrive. What was she supposed to do until then? She glanced around the house: The coffee table was stacked with unread newspapers and unpaid bills, the kitchen counter was dotted with spills and stains and articles of glass and plastic, and the carpet was cluttered with everything dropped there in the last week and a half.

She decided to clean up. It was a lesson she had learned from her mother, which her mother had gleaned from her mother before her and so on back to the beginning of humankind: When the world makes no sense, *clean up*. Sometimes the truth is simply buried beneath the clutter.

She started with the paper: the magazines, the flyers, the junk mail that seemed to accumulate like falling leaves. She dumped a mound of unfolded laundry onto the bed, then made a sweep of the house with the laundry basket gathering shoes and books and a score of other wayward items.

She picked up the ancient Macanudo cigar box from the coffee table and carried it into the kitchen. There on the kitchen table sat Jimmy's black leather King James Bible, still bound by an ancient rubber band and stamped in gold by the Gideons International. Kathryn smiled. It was just like Jimmy to include among his possessions a copy of the Book of Righteousness—one that he had stolen from a motel room.

She set the Bible on top of the cigar box and stretched the rubber band around them both—but the brittle rubber band snapped, and the Bible fell to the floor. When she lifted it, the leather cover came loose and slipped away. To her surprise, the text within was not Scripture at all; it was some kind of diary in Jimmy's own broken handwriting. The first entry was dated August 3, 1990—the week before the 82d Airborne was called to active duty. It was more than just a personal diary—it was Jimmy's war journal, his own record of what happened to him in the Gulf. What went wrong, what depressed him, what he could never bring himself to say aloud.

Kathryn scolded her imagination for running ahead of her, and with trembling hands turned the first fragile page.

August 3, 1990

2d Brigade had inspection today. In a few days we start our rotation as DRB. Six weeks on two-hour recall. So what—I got no place to go anyway.

Lots of talk about Iraq and Kuwait and all. Where IS Kuwait anyway? Word is the 82d might get called in to clean things up just like in Grenada and Panama. If the balloon goes up on our shift, 2d Brigade will be first to go.

Can't stop thinking about Kathryn, but I got to try—she's married and gone now. If it couldn't be me, I'm glad it was Andy. Better Andy than Pete. What's the difference? Pete, Andy, either way she's gone. Gone for good.

Can't believe I ever had the guts to ask her. What was I thinking—that she'd take me just because I was first in line? Who am I anyway? Nobody, that's who. I'm nobody and I got nothing. Hi Kathryn, I'm nobody. Will you marry me? You can have half of my nothing. Now you're Mrs. Nobody, with nothing.

Kathryn could hardly bear to read on. She knew that she had hurt Jimmy, but she had only experienced his heartache through the protective buffer of others: through a letter from Andy or a comment from an acquaintance or a scathing look from Amy. But here were Jimmy's own words, the distilled putrescence of all his anger and pain. It was almost too much to endure.

Almost.

August 28, 1990

Arrived in Saudi Arabia, someplace called Dhahran. Lots to do, lots going on. Desert training, trying out our biological suits. Hot as Hades in those suits, but I guess we'll be glad enough if the Iraqis try to gas us like they done to Iran.

Tough schedule. First call at 0430. Hot, crowded, grunts everywhere. 1500 of us so far, twice that many soon. Food stinks. Burgers and fries from Hardees today, twice last week too. They got Hardees over here! Everything was cold.

Some of the boys get mail by the truckload. I get nothing. Tough to watch Andy get so much from Kathryn—cookies, boxes, good-smelling letters. Pictures too. Look at me in my swimsuit, look at me with my hair up. Makes me crazy sometimes. I guess if you win the chicken you get the eggs.

Kathryn began to read faster now. The words seemed to fly from the pages, and the pages seemed to turn by themselves. She felt like a little girl careening downhill on a bicycle, out of control, thrilled by the ride but terrified of what might await her at the end.

October 12, 1990

Redeployed to Ab Qaiq 80 miles southeast—80 miles farther away from the action. Started drawing imminent-danger pay two weeks ago, but nothing to spend it on. One day off each week, but nothing to do. Plenty of training—thank God for the training. Keeps me busy, keeps me from sitting around and thinking.

Somebody said the 82d will head home once all the heavy forces arrive. I hope not. I didn't sign on just to clear the way for somebody else to get the medals. I got to have my chance to show what I can do, I got to prove myself.

Prove myself to who? I got nobody to impress. I got nobody back home. Truth is, I still want to prove myself to Kathryn. But why? So Kathryn will say Boy did I make a mistake, Boy did I get the wrong guy. Then she'll say Sorry Andy, I made a mistake, I got the wrong guy.

Sure she will.

November 3, 1990

Got a letter from Kathryn today. Not a fancy letter, not a good-smelling one, just a white envelope with white paper from the Ramada Inn Beaufort where Andy took her on their wedding night. So she sends it to me. Dear Jimmy, I'm married, how are you, I'm married. I bet Pete got one too. I wonder who else got one? Maybe she made copies for everybody.

November 21, 1990

I swear I'm going nuts. Nothing but tents everywhere like some kind of shantytown. No space, no room to breathe. Everybody keeps their stash under their cot. Cookies and cake and soap and toilet paper from home. From girlfriends and wives and lovers back home. But I got nobody back home, so I got nothing to stash. I keep empty boxes under my cot so nobody will ask.

November 28, 1990

No beer here because the Saudis want it that way. The Saudis want it! Somebody needs to tell the Saudis we came over here to keep the Iraqis from whipping them and taking their oil. Who's protecting who here? Why do we care what the Saudis want?

Some of the boys do a little snow from time to time. Put it in a nasal spray, mix it with a little vodka and water. Like they got allergies or something so nobody knows, nobody cares. They say it's like a couple cups of coffee. Doesn't sound so bad. One thing I know—a soldier got to kick back sometimes or he loses his edge.

What do they expect anyway? No beer!

Kathryn felt as though she were staring through the window of a burning building at a confused and frightened child. But there was no way into the building and no way out. All she could do was watch the flames grow higher and hotter, knowing how the story had to end.

December 16, 1990

More waiting. Four months in country and nobody knows what's going on. First we're supposed to be guarding marines, next we're guarding oil wells. Where are the bad guys?

Made a new friend—best one I've had for a while. Don't know what all the fuss is about. I hardly even feel it. Helps me relax a little, gives me a little lift—no big deal.

No more letters from Kathryn. Just as well—great girl, but I got a little shopping to do before I buy.

December 25, 1990

Andy called Kathryn today. Free phone calls, three minutes to anyone in the States. Who are they trying to fool? The line is bugged—somebody listens in the whole time. I told them to take their phone call and shove it.

Why are they after me? What do they want to know? Andy said it's no big deal, said I was acting crazy. No big deal for him, maybe. They don't care about a man with family—they think a family man can be trusted, they know he's got something to lose. They save their worry for grunts like me. We're the dangerous ones, we're the ones who got to be watched.

Why is Andy helping them? Can't trust anyone anymore.

She could trace the effect of the drug from entry to entry. Jimmy seemed to rise like a phoenix to heights of supreme confidence and then plummet into confusion and paranoia in the course of a single page. But gradually each high became a little less convincing, and each low brought him closer to the flames.

January 20, 1991

Saw Pete again today.

Kathryn stopped. *Saw Pete?* But didn't Peter say that he never saw Jimmy in the Gulf?

Saw Pete *again?* A single visit Peter might have forgotten—but more than one?

I was talking about Kathryn again, about how much I miss her—Pete blew up! Said I should stop whining, said I wasn't the only one who loved her, who wanted to marry her. Who else? I said.

Turns out Pete's got it worse than me. He's not just sorry about Kathryn, he's mad at Andy! He thinks Andy just got there first, thinks he took Pete's place. What about me? I said. I got there before Andy—before anybody. Doesn't matter, he said—it was HIS place, like Kathryn belonged to him or something. I told him he was nuts. I told him Kathryn would take me before she takes him. That's when he took a swing at me. Not a little poke, either—they had to pull us apart.

And all this time I thought I was the only one.

Kathryn read the words again and again: *Pete's got it worse than me...*

What made Peter angry enough to attack poor Jimmy—and what in the world did he mean that Andy had taken *his* place? The very idea should have enraged her—but it didn't.

It chilled her to the marrow of her bone.

February 18, 1991

I'm in trouble. I'm in big trouble.

Andy found my stuff. He was digging through the MRE boxes under my cot—said he was looking for something to eat. He found the mirror, the razor, the straws—everything. I thought he'd blow a gasket but he didn't. Said he understood. Said he wanted to help. Andy is a straight arrow. Andy is an okay guy.

But he told Pete.

Pete said he was going to turn me in! I asked him not to, I threatened him, finally I begged him. They'll discharge me, they'll wash me out. I'll miss the show! You should have thought of that he said. It's rules, it's regulations, it's the honor of the outfit. Don't do this to me, I said. This could mean court martial, this could mean jail. I'm on his heels, I'm begging, I'm running after him like some sniveling mutt. We got all the way to the door of the HHC before he stopped. Okay he said, I won't turn you in.

Not now anyway. Not NOW he said.

He was going to do it if I didn't stop him. What if he gets steamed at me again, what if we have another fight? Pete gets mean sometimes, he gets REAL mean. I won't beg anymore and I won't go licking his boots.

Not now he said—but maybe tomorrow or the next day...

I'm going nuts, I'm going nuts, I swear I am going nuts.

February 22, 1991

Word came down today, we're going in tomorrow. Thank God—anything but this waiting. Haven't seen Pete for three days. What is he doing? Who is he talking to? Had chow with Andy. Good luck tomorrow he says, good luck Jim. Yeah Andy you got the good luck. You got the girl, you got the good luck. Tomorrow I'm a hero and they give me the medal of honor—then Pete turns me in. I hope I take a bullet tomorrow, that's the only way out of this mess. That's MY luck Andy, you get the girl and I get a bullet.

Kathryn's hands shook so badly she could barely turn the page. She prayed that there would be no further entry, that the three boys simply went to war and Andy was lost and Pete and Jimmy came home. She thought she wanted to know everything, that there was nothing worse than the agonizing uncertainty of not knowing. But now she understood for the first time that there was something *infinitely* worse—learning what you wished you never knew and could never again forget. *The truth doesn't care,* Nick told her. Part of her still wanted to know—and part of her was sorry she had ever asked.

The boys she had loved since childhood, the boys who held her hand on the front porch swing, the boys with the bright, clean uniforms and the shining hair were dissolving before her eyes like wet sugar candy.

February 27, 1991

God have mercy on me a sinner. What have I done? I didn't know. God forgive me. I didn't know what I was doing.

We attacked Al Salman last night. We were with the French going in at night. We called in fire from the big 155 mms in back, then we huddled and waited till the smoke cleared. That's where we ran into Pete's unit, and there he was.

God what happened—what went wrong? We moved too fast, we got overextended. They warned us, they told us no heroes, but it went so fast. It was so dark, it was so easy. Andy ran forward and took a position behind a berm—then it all came apart. We thought they were all dead, we thought all we had to do was walk in and raise the flag. They were there all right—a whole brigade of the Iraqi 45th. There was a firefight. Man, what a show—tracers and shells everywhere like fireflies like the 4th of July. Andy got cut off, there was nothing we could do except duck for cover. We could see him fifty yards ahead, but we couldn't move, couldn't get to him.

I poke my gun up over the wall and start firing high, firing to keep them away from Andy. I'm firing and firing and I look over at Pete. He's aiming his gun but not firing. Now he's aiming low, he's adjusting his thermal site. He's aiming at Andy!

Andy is waving to us, waving us forward. Come on he says, it's okay now. I'll cover you. Come on, why don't you come? You can make it.

Pete fires.

I cover my head and I start to cry like a baby. I cry just like a little baby.

Pete looks at me. "I tell you what," he says. "You help me bury my problem and I'll help you bury yours."

Kathryn stumbled back from the table, sending the chair clattering across the floor. She stood struggling for breath, not knowing what to do next, not knowing what to think or feel.

He's aiming at Andy, the little words said, and *Pete fires*. Such simple words, such harmless words, but they tore through her soul like a bullet—like the bullet that killed Andy. Like the bullet from *Peter's gun* that killed Andy! And now she knew, now she knew what she longed to know for eight long years—and she would give anything in the world not to know again.

He lied to me about Andy and about Jimmy and about everything every day since. He held me, and he watched me cry, and he told me that he loved me. I could have married him and had children with him—the man who murdered my own husband.

The unfolding reality engulfed her like a series of thundering waves, each more powerful than the last, pounding her and tossing her about like flotsam and depositing her exhausted body at last on the cold kitchen floor. Kathryn drew a deep breath and prepared to weep, prepared to summon forth the keener's wail that comes from the blackest corner of the soul.

But before she could make a sound, the doorbell rang.

It was four o'clock.

The doorbell rang again.

Kathryn tried to struggle to her feet, but a wall of nausea slammed her down again. She forced herself up, gagging, and tried to straighten herself as best she could. Her legs would not support her the entire distance to the door; she stumbled to the sofa and collapsed. She quickly wiped her eyes and waited, staring silently at the door.

The doorbell rang a third time.

What do I say? What do I do?

The man she invited to her house a hundred times before was a faithful and trusted friend, a man she had known and loved for three decades. But that man was dead now, gone forever, destroyed just minutes ago by a handful of words scribbled in a soldier's diary. The man outside the door was a man she had never seen before, a liar and a murderer, a monster capable of unspeakable evil. Was she supposed to greet him with a kiss? Should she sit with him and hold his hand, the same hand that squeezed the trigger and casually put an end to her husband's life? Should she chat with him about the future—about *their* future—as though he had not single-handedly engineered the destruction of Kathryn's entire world?

A moment later she heard the sound of a key fumbling in the lock. The door swings slowly open.

"Didn't you hear the bell?" Peter said.

Kathryn said nothing. It was all she could do to keep her composure, to keep from vomiting or screaming or gasping for air. She felt like a child standing petrified in a dark room, overwhelmed by a sense of approaching evil. No, it was more than that.

She felt like a seven-year-old girl helplessly trapped in a '57 Chevy.

Peter stepped closer and looked at her—at the pallor of her face, the emptiness of her gaze, and the rigidity of her posture. He whistled softly.

"Hey," he said. "Who died?"

■

Nick watched the sheriff enter the house from a block away where he carefully hid his car behind a pair of rusting construction dumpsters. His '64 Dodge had become something of a landmark in Rayford, and this was one time he couldn't afford to be recognized. He waited several minutes before approaching on foot, sticking close to trees and shrubbery in case he had to make a last-minute dive for cover. He would only need a few minutes to raise the hood of the sheriff's car, take care of business, and be on his way. Five minutes had already elapsed. If Kathryn managed to keep the sheriff occupied for even half of the thirty minutes he asked for, he would still have time to spare.

The driveway rose sharply toward the house, and the black-and-white Crown Victoria was parked to the right of Kathryn's car. He approached almost casually from behind—but twenty yards away he suddenly recognized a second figure in the car, a hulking silhouette on the passenger side.

Nick took several quick steps back, afraid that the deputy might have already spotted his legs in the rearview mirror—but there was no sign of motion or recognition from the car.

Nick glanced at the patrol car, then at the house—then at his watch.

■

"I'm sorry I kicked your Bug Man friend, if that's what this is all about." Peter searched in vain for the cause of Kathryn's gloom. "But he had it coming."

By sheer force of will Kathryn raised her eyes and looked at a face she had never seen before. For the first time she noticed the barracudalike jut of his jaw, the awkward spacing of his empty gray eyes, the spatter of cratered pockmarks on his mottled skin, and the wiry coarseness of his sallow hair. It was evil. It was *all* evil. Why had she never seen it before?

"I know you must be upset about the shooting," he ventured. "You know, Dr. What's-his-name."

"Teddy," she managed a trembling whisper. "His name was Teddy."

"Whatever. That must have been tough for you. Sorry you had to see that."

Kathryn looked into his hollow, soulless eyes.

"Why, Peter? Why did anyone have to die?"

"It's a shame." He shook his head. "Sometimes it comes to that."

Kathryn stared at him. "What's it like? To kill a man, I mean."

"I don't like to talk about it."

"But I want to know. Do you look at his face, or do you avoid his eyes so you won't hesitate to pull the trigger? Do you try to think of him as just a target—like one of those big silhouettes at the firing range—or do you think about where he came from, who might love him, who he might be leaving behind?"

He looked at her. "Boy, you're in a mood today."

"I want to *know,*" she repeated, holding back her tears.

"There's no time to think. In my line of work, sometimes you have to make a split-second decision. There's no time to think about things like that."

"I'm not talking about your line of work—I'm talking about murder. What do you think about when there *is* time? What do you think about when you *know* you're going to kill someone?"

He hesitated. "I don't suppose a murderer thinks about any of those things."

"Sometimes killing is necessary," she said. "Sometimes it's your duty. You can always tell yourself later it was my job, I had to do it, he deserved to die. But what does a murderer think later? What does he tell himself? How does he explain it all away?"

A pause. "I suppose he tells himself he had to do it too."

"He had to do it," she repeated. "But of course he didn't have to. He *chose* to. It was just his selfish, stupid, cowardly way of trying to fix things—trying to make things go *his* way."

"I...I guess so..."

"Do you suppose a murderer thinks of himself as a good person who just had to do a bad thing? Because that's a lie, you know. But maybe it doesn't matter—maybe he's gotten so good at lying to himself that he can't tell the lies from the truth anymore."

He shifted uneasily. "How should I know?"

She stared into his eyes. "Don't you think about these things, Peter? I do. I think about them all the time."

■

"How would you guys like to make ten bucks?" Nick smiled at the three bored youngsters draped across a buckling swing set.

"You guys?" the first boy mocked. "Where you from, mister?"

Nick eyed him. "I'm from a place where the kids have got guts."

"What do we gotta do?" the second boy asked indignantly.

"You boys know Beanie? Beanie, the deputy sheriff?"

All three nodded.

"He's a friend of mine, and I want to play a little joke on him. He's sitting right over there in the squad car, see him? The sheriff told him to stay in the car, and I want to sneak up and surprise him. All you have to do is distract him—keep him occupied for, let's say, twenty minutes."

"How do we do that?"

"How should I know? Talk to him, tell him some jokes, show him your baseball cards. What am I paying you for? You think of something. But remember—*twenty minutes."*

The third boy cocked his head to one side. "Each. Ten bucks *each."*

"Ten bucks even," Nick replied, "and I'll give each of you a scorpion the size of your *hand."*

The three boys raced to Beanie's window.

"Hey, Beanie!" the first called out. The deputy turned to them, displaying a broad, white swatch of gauze plastered across the center of his face.

"Wow!" the second boy stopped. "What happened to your nose?"

"I got hit," Beanie sulked. "Go 'way."

"Is it broke?"

"Nope." Beanie brightened a bit. "Agnes says my head's too hard. But it sure did bleed! You shoulda seen it."

"You got two black eyes," the third boy joined in. "Cool!"

Nick swung to the left and approached the car obliquely, hoping to remain in Beanie's blind spot. When he reached the tail of Kathryn's car he ducked down and crawled forward along the left side, then right across the front of the car, staying low and tight against the bumper and grill. At the right front corner he paused, then dropped to the ground and rolled across the gap between the two cars, stopping on his back directly in front of the Crown Victoria.

He heard a sound. He glanced to the right to see one of the boys smiling and watching him. Nick jabbed at his wristwatch and then gestured angrily for the boy to move away. The boy shook his head, held up both hands and flashed the number "twenty."

Twenty, Nick nodded furiously, *and I'll put the scorpion in your bed.*

■

Peter leaned back and stretched his arms across the top of the sofa.

"This is all about Jimmy, isn't it?"

"What do you mean?" Kathryn could feel his eyes on the back of her head, and it made the hair stand up on her neck.

"I tried to warn you. You got your hopes up. You thought you could prove that Jim was the victim of some sinister plot, so you hired some fancy Bug Man—but it wasn't as easy as you thought."

"No," she whispered. "It turned out to be more complicated than I ever imagined."

"I should have stepped in. I asked the doc not to take your money, but he wouldn't listen. I knew he was the wrong sort from the beginning. I know it's hard when you trust someone and they let you down."

She turned and stared at him. "You have no idea."

"So you've had enough? You're willing to listen to reason now?"

Kathryn turned her head to one side and studied him thoughtfully.

"People commit suicide in different ways, don't they, Peter? Some people put a gun to their head and pull the trigger, and it's over in an instant. But others hang themselves, and I imagine that takes quite a bit longer. Some people poison themselves or even starve themselves, and then it could take weeks or months to die. But it's all still suicide, isn't it?"

"I suppose so," the sheriff shrugged.

"You can help someone commit suicide, can't you? What do they call it—'doctor-assisted' suicide? You aren't actually killing anyone, they can't convict you of anything, you're only *assisting*—but you still make the suicide possible. You don't pull the trigger, but you buy the gun. You don't make him take the poison, but you hand him the pills. There must be a thousand ways to help kill a man, and it's all still suicide."

The sheriff said nothing.

"It gets confusing, doesn't it, Peter—the question of who's to blame, I mean? One man ties the noose, another puts the rope around his neck, and someone else kicks the chair away. Who did the actual killing? It isn't necessarily the one who took the final step, you know—sometimes it's the one who was *thinking* the clearest or the one who had the most malice in his heart. It's strange, isn't it? You drive a man to depression, you take away all of his hopes and dreams, and then you hand him a gun and he pulls the trigger. It's suicide. But who really killed him?"

The sheriff glanced at his watch. So did Kathryn.

"You were right, Peter. I can see now that you were right all along. Jimmy was responsible for taking his own life—but I think someone helped him. I think someone handed him the gun. And I know who did it too."

She stared hard into the depths of the thick, gray ice.

"*I* did it," she said. "I killed Jimmy when I didn't love him enough to see how much he was hurting."

Kathryn studied Peter's eyes, praying for some telltale shift in the ice, some glimmer of guilt or remorse, some flickering recognition of the utter damnation of his own soul. But the ice remained immovable, impassable, and that's when Kathryn knew beyond all doubt that the soul of Peter St. Clair was beyond redemption.

He put his hand on her shoulder and squeezed. "Don't be too hard on yourself, kiddo. You didn't know."

A swell of revulsion and utter contempt heaved up from her stomach into her throat and she struggled to hold back the rage that surged up within her.

"I've had enough," she said through clenched teeth. "I'm ready to listen to reason now. I want you to give me a reason, Peter, just one reason..."

Kathryn rose from the sofa. "I want you to tell me the reason you murdered my husband."

CHAPTER 36

Nick lay with his head directly underneath the radiator of the Crown Victoria. It was darker than he had hoped. This would be a lot easier if he could simply raise the hood, but that was hardly something the deputy would consent to. He pulled a white handkerchief from his shirt pocket and spread it open on the ground by his right ear. He fumbled through his pockets for a pair of light-tension forceps, then squeezed his left forearm up into the narrow gap between the radiator and grill. He felt delicately along the surface of the radiator until his fingers arrived at the first tiny lump stubbornly wedged between the fragile metal fins. Then he brought his right hand up to the same location and maneuvered the forceps into position, carefully plucking out the specimen and dropping it onto the handkerchief to his right. He repeated the process again and again, as quickly as possible, until he could feel no more telltale projections at all.

"Show us your gun, Beanie!" one of the boys entreated.

"Yeah!" another chimed in. "Show us your gun!"

Beanie shook his head sadly. "Unca Pete took it. Says he gotta clean it real good. You got to have a clean gun."

Nick smiled. It didn't take the sheriff long to figure out the reason for his assault on Beanie at the picnic table. By now the Beretta was clean as a whistle—or gone entirely, and with it any chance of matching the blood in the barrel to Teddy's. "I'm not a fool, Doc," the sheriff had warned him.

No, Sheriff, I've got to hand it to you—you're no fool.

He rolled onto his right side and carefully pulled the dotted handkerchief up close. He quickly discarded a variety of Lepidoptera and various scarabaeid beetles—the moths and June bugs that abound in the thick summer skies, and the occasional honeybee that had drifted across the road on its way to gather pollen. All that remained on the handkerchief was a tiny pile of Diptera, an assortment of flies of various colors and sizes.

From his left pants pocket Nick removed a photographer's loupe. He raised his glasses and pressed the tiny magnifier tight against his right eye, then one by one began to pluck up the remains of each insect and examine it like a jeweler appraising a precious stone.

"Who hit you anyway?" one of the boys asked Beanie, staring at the white bandage plastered across his face.

"I dunno. A doctor. A doctor hit me."

"A doctor? Why would a *doctor* hit you?"

"I dunno," Beanie repeated irritably. "But he hit me—*hard.* And then he jumped on me, and he was gonna hit me again, but Unca Pete stopped him."

"What did he look like, this doctor that hit you?"

Beanie scrunched up his face and thought long and hard. "He didn't have no eyes."

"No *eyes?*" one of the boys laughed. "He was a blind doctor?"

"I mean *glasses.*" Beanie scowled at them. "Big, funny glasses."

The three boys looked at each other.

Large body, red eyes, gray-checkered abdomen—it's a sarcophagid.

Nick tossed it aside.

Broad head, flattened body, multicolored eyes—just a big old horse fly.

He quickly glanced at his watch—only five minutes left. He pulled his glasses back down and began to rapidly sort through the remaining specimens—the metallic green and blue calliphorids here, the common Muscidae over there—soon only two specimens remained and they appeared to be identical. He seized the most intact specimen with his forceps and held it up to the loupe.

Greenish blue with purple reflections. The lower squamae are brown, the posterior margins of the second and third abdominal segments are jet black—and it has anterior spiracles!

He rotated it forward and searched the bulbous, dome-shaped head for the final indicator. Sure enough, the upper eye facets were greatly enlarged. It was a *Chrysomya megacephala*—the same species that Noah identified from the puparium left by the fly on Jim McAllister's body. Jim McAllister was in southern Georgia or Florida just over a week ago—and so was this car.

Means, motive, and opportunity, Sheriff. Three strikes and you're out.

Nick was startled by the sound of a door closing and the scatter of children's feet. He quickly placed the two *megacephalae* in the center of the handkerchief, folded it carefully, and stuffed it into his shirt pocket. He reached up for the bumper and began to wriggle out from under the car when a pair of massive hands grabbed on to his belt and shirt and jerked upward. His body rose from the ground as if weightless. His forehead smashed against the bottom of the grill, stunning him, but the impact barely even slowed his upward ascent. He continued to rise up into the searing, blinding sun—and then an instant later came crashing back down onto the hood of the car, knocking the wind from his lungs. He felt the two massive hands release him for an instant and then fasten again on the front of his shirt, pinning him against the scalding metal.

Nick's mind was a blaze of fire, and he felt a trickle of blood run down into his left eye. He shook it out and looked upward into the smiling face of the deputy sheriff.

■

Peter sat in stunned silence.

Kathryn rose and walked to the kitchen. She returned a moment later holding Jimmy's journal in her hands. She held it open to him like a lectern, like the Book of Life revealing all that he had ever done or thought. Without a word she dropped it into his lap and backed away.

Peter began to flip slowly through the pages, and wave after wave of agonized realization swept across his face.

"Where did you—"

"He hid it inside the Bible—a place he knew you'd *never* look."

He read one entry and winced. He read another, then rubbed his neck and rolled his head in great circles.

"You coward!" she seethed. "You thought you had been cheated; you thought someone had taken something that was rightfully yours. But I was *never* yours, Peter. *I was never yours!*"

"I can explain—"

"So can I! I can explain *everything* now! You found out about Jimmy's drug habit, and you went to turn him in—but you didn't, did you? You realized there was a better way to use that little piece of information, didn't you?"

"Kath, wait—it wasn't like that—"

"Then when you ran into Jimmy and Andy at Al Salman you saw your chance. Andy got ahead of you, he got separated. It was dark, it was crazy, there were bullets flying everywhere—and Andy started waving to you. He wanted you to come to him, Peter, he wanted you to help him. He was calling you—he was calling his *friend*."

Tears were streaming down her face. Her voice trembled with rage, and her legs shook as if they might buckle at any moment. Peter started to rise from the sofa to reach for her.

"Don't!" She forced herself to stand erect. "Not *ever* again!"

He sat back again.

"Why did you have to bury him? Why didn't you just shoot him in the back and claim it was an accident? Why didn't you blame it on 'friendly fire?' I would have believed you—everyone would have!

"What was it like when you saw later that I couldn't let go of Andy? What did you feel when you realized that when you buried Andy, you buried any chance that I could ever love you? Did you wish you could go back? Did you wish you could do it all over again? You did it to yourself, you little coward! When you shot Andy in the back, you shot yourself too!"

Peter said nothing.

"And then you made poor Jimmy help you bury Andy. You got rid of Andy's body, but Jimmy could never get him out of his mind. Jimmy wasn't like you, Peter. He had a conscience—he had a *soul*. He remembered what he had done and it ate him alive."

She stopped abruptly. A sudden look of realization came over her face.

"*That's* why you overlooked Jimmy's drug habit all those years, isn't it? You didn't want him getting clean and straight and dealing with his conscience—you *wanted* him hooked. But Jimmy had no money for drugs.…But that means…you must have… You *supplied* him, didn't you?"

She shook her head in disgust. "You didn't kill one man at Al Salman, Peter, you killed *two*—and they were both better men than you'll ever be. Jimmy was right, you know," she said with utter contempt. "I would have taken *him* before I'd take *you*."

Peter sat quietly staring at the pages of the journal. He lifted a page, looked it over front and back, then slowly ripped it from the binding and lay it on the sofa beside him.

"Since the day he married you," he said without looking up.

"What?"

"Isn't that the question you were going to ask me next? 'How long did you think about killing Andy?' Since the day he married you."

Kathryn watched in horror as he tore away a second page. Nick said he hoped to bring back proof—but that proof, whatever it was, would only tie Peter to the death of Jimmy. The journal was the only thing on earth that linked Peter to the death of her husband—and Peter was shredding it before her eyes.

"Give me back my journal!"

"*Jimmy's* journal," he replied quietly.

He gathered the remaining handwritten pages together and removed them, then tossed the journal on the floor at her feet.

"There you go. All yours."

He collected the handful of scribbled pages and carefully folded them, placing them in his front shirt pocket.

"It doesn't matter," she choked. "You can destroy those pages if you want to—but *I* still know what you did. Maybe I can't have you arrested or send you to jail, but I can hate you for the rest of my life. You've lost, Peter. You did it all for nothing. You will never marry me, and I will never, ever love you. Take a good look—because I never want to see you again."

Peter rose slowly from the sofa. He bent over slightly, hooked his thumbs inside his trousers, and hitched them up an inch or two. Then he straightened, stretching his shirt front tight again.

"Do you believe everyone has a perfect match? I do. I think God made one perfect person for everyone, and your job is to search the world over until you find her—and then you get married. But what if there's a mistake—what if someone else marries *my* perfect person? Not on purpose, not out of meanness, but just because they didn't know any better. Then there's something wrong with the world—something that has to be fixed, don't you see? They can't be happy together, because there's someone better for both of them out there somewhere, and I can't be happy because they're keeping me from my perfect match."

He shook his head. "How can I make you understand? I didn't hate Andy, and I don't blame you for marrying him. You were just…confused, that's all, and I just had to straighten things out."

He began to step quietly toward her. Kathryn heard a buzzing sound slowly begin to rise. She started to tremble.

"I don't expect you to love me. Not right away. It's going to take time. There's been so much pain and disappointment, and we have so much to talk about…"

The angry buzz grew louder as he drew nearer. He held out one hand as he approached, like a rider trying to steady a skittish mare. He was only an arm's length away now, and the buzz in Kathryn's mind was almost deafening.

He took her gently by the shoulders.

"I told you before, Kath. I told you all along. *We were meant to be.*"

With every bit of strength left within her she swung her right foot up between his legs. He crumpled to the floor.

She stumbled back and stared wild-eyed at the figure writhing on the ground—and then she turned for the door and ran, ran as fast and as hard as she could run. She had to run, she had to get away, because the swirling black cloud was right behind her, and she knew that it would follow.

■

Nick could barely breathe under the weight of Beanie's hands. He had to break that grip; he had to get away. He knew he was in no immediate danger from the childlike deputy, but at any moment the sheriff would emerge from Kathryn's house, and then with a single word the harmless deputy could become the sheriff's executioner. Nick grabbed the pipelike wrists and strained, but he was no match for the deputy's incredible strength. He felt along the back of Beanie's right hand for the exact spot where the bones of the thumb and first finger joined in the base of the massive hand; he made a knuckle with his own right hand and drove it hard into Beanie's ulnar nerve. The deputy winced in pain and momentarily released his grip. Nick rolled hard to the left, pulling his right arm from his shirt, then his left. The startled and confused deputy stood motionless, still pinning an empty shirt to the hood of the patrol car.

The realization that his prisoner had escaped began to slowly dawn on him. He dropped the shirt and slowly started toward Nick with outstretched arms. Nick ducked his head into the patrol car for an instant, jerked the hood release, then began to backpedal quickly around the car until they faced each other from opposite sides. He continued to circle, Beanie slowly following, until he had maneuvered the deputy to the trunk of the car. Then with one quick motion he raised the hood, grabbed two spark plug wires and ripped them from the car.

At that moment the front door exploded open and Kathryn raced out. She saw the shirtless Nick with Beanie in frustrated pursuit, and Nick saw the look of absolute terror in Kathryn's eyes. They both knew that escape was the only thing that mattered now.

"We'll take yours!" He pointed to her car.

"The keys are in the house!" she shouted. "Where's yours?"

Nick pointed down the street toward the two rusting dumpsters. Kathryn spun to face the deputy.

"Beanie, Uncle Pete is hurt! He's in the house, Beanie, and he needs you! Do you understand? *Uncle Pete is hurt!*"

Beanie stared blankly, then he nodded slowly and lumbered off toward the open door. Kathryn and Nick raced across the driveway and down the street toward the waiting Dodge.

They scrambled into the car and slammed the doors. Nick fumbled for the keys.

"Go, go!" she shouted.

"What's your hurry?" He grinned as he tossed the two spark plug wires into her lap. "They're not going anywhere without these."

She held them up and then looked at him.

"Is this it? Is this all you got? Just *two?*"

"I thought I did pretty well, under the circumstances."

"Nick—don't you know *anything* about cars?"

Nick shrugged.

"A Crown Victoria has an eight cylinder engine! You can't just pull out *two* spark plug wires, you need three or four! The engine will run rough on six cylinders, but it will still run! All you did is make their car run as badly as *yours!* You bought us a few minutes, that's all—now get this pile of junk moving!"

They roared out from behind the dumpsters as the patrol car lurched down the driveway behind them.

I got it, Mrs. Guilford," Nick shouted over the roar of the engine. "I got all the proof you need."

"What proof?"

"When the sheriff released our specimen, he thought he had covered his tracks, but he was wrong. The fly left behind a puparial capsule, and from that capsule we were able to identify the species. The fly from Jimmy's body doesn't come from North Carolina, Mrs. Guilford—not anywhere in the state. It's found only in Florida and southern Georgia. Did you hear me?"

"Southern Georgia...Peter's hunting cabin!"

Nick nodded. "Sometimes a car is an entomologist's best friend. The radiator acts like a giant butterfly net, collecting specimens wherever it goes—and leaving a record of where it's been. I checked the radiator of the patrol car—guess what? I found the same species of fly. That means the sheriff spent his vacation in Georgia, not Myrtle Beach—and Jim McAllister was with him.

They drove back together—only your friend came back in the trunk with one leg propped up. A microsearch of the trunk will verify it. We've got all the proof we need, Mrs. Guilford, we've got—"

Suddenly Nick slammed his fist against the dashboard.

"What is it? What's wrong?"

"My *shirt!* I left the radiator samples in the pocket!"

Kathryn said nothing.

Nick glanced over at her. "Mrs. Guilford—you've got to believe me."

"I believe you," she said evenly. "I believe everything you've said all along. I believe he killed Jimmy. I believe he killed Teddy. I believe he killed poor old Mrs. Gallagher."

She turned and stared at him.

"I found Jimmy's war journal. It wasn't in the papers Amy gave me—Peter went through them himself. It was hidden inside that Bible. It told about the Gulf, about the drugs, about the conflict. It told about everything." She closed her eyes hard. "It told how Peter shot Andy in the back."

Nick said nothing. He knew he should reach out and comfort her; he knew he should take the time to express his outrage and sympathy—but his mind was too busy racing, fitting together the remaining pieces of this fascinating puzzle.

"Where is this journal?" he asked.

"He destroyed it," she said without emotion. "It doesn't matter."

Nick groaned. "It matters, Mrs. Guilford. Without the specimens from the radiator, we can't tie the sheriff to the death of your friend. And without that journal, we can't prove that he had anything to do with the disappearance of your husband. We know what happened, but we can't prove anything. We've got *nothing,* Mrs. Guilford, we've got—"

He stopped abruptly.

"The puparium!" he shouted. "It's at the lab—I dropped it off on the way back from the university. We've got to get it, Mrs.

Guilford, it's all we've got left. With that puparium I can at least prove that your friend didn't die in North Carolina. That's enough to convince the medical examiner to reopen the investigation, and anything can happen from there."

Nick raised the sagging rearview mirror and stared into the distance behind them. Through the billowing oil smoke he could see glints of black and white. The patrol car was gradually gaining on them—now less than two hundred yards away.

"They're right behind us—and they're getting closer. At this rate they'll catch us before we reach the lab."

Kathryn twisted the mirror and looked. "In this car we're about as hard to spot as a forest fire!"

"I thought I slowed them down more than *that.*"

"Part of the problem is the car," she said, "and part is the *driver.* Switch with me!"

"What?"

"Switch with me!" she shouted again, and without hesitation she grabbed for the wheel. Nick rolled to the right and dragged himself into the backseat, and Kathryn slid into the driver's seat after him.

"The fence with the razor wire," she shouted. "Does it have another gate?"

"On the west side. There's a service entrance."

"Then I know a shortcut. It should be right about...*here!*"

She jerked the wheel to the right, and the Dodge slammed into the curb. The car lurched crazily left and right, then once again as the rear wheels followed after. There was a bone-jarring clank of metal as the rims cut hard into the concrete through the aging tires, and Nick was slammed weightless into the ceiling. He came crashing down again beneath a hailstorm of paper, notebooks, and debris. Instantly there was a second clank, then a third and much louder one as the muffler tore away and did a rusted dance on the pavement behind them.

The hood of the car blasted into a thick screen of privet and viburnum and then nosed suddenly downward, careening down a steep bank and into a small fence. A single strand of barbed wire stretched across the windshield and snapped like an old guitar string. The car cratered hard in a dry red gully before nosing up again into a vast field of shimmering yellow-white and green.

"When you said *shortcut*"—Nick struggled up from the floor of the backseat—"I assumed you meant a road."

The car bounded across the open meadow like a charging water buffalo. A sea of roof-high reed and feather grass whipped and stripped across the windshield as they plunged ahead.

"How in the world can you see?"

"You just have to know where you're going," she shouted. "I know this field—I used to race here with the boys all the time when we were teenagers!"

"Who used to win?"

For an instant Kathryn actually smiled.

"Then the sheriff knows this field too?"

"He knows." She nodded. "Take a look behind you!"

Nick whirled around and saw the patrol car not more than thirty yards behind them, drafting in their wake like a stock car at Rockingham.

"He'll be even with us soon! He'll try to pass us, to cut us off!"

She shook her head. "He's gaining on us because the grass is slowing us down! If he pulls out from behind us he'll lose ground! He knows he doesn't have to catch us—he just has to stay with us until we finally have to stop!"

Suddenly Kathryn began to slow down, narrowing the gap between the two cars.

"What are you doing?"

She watched until the patrol car filled the rearview mirror with a thundering blur of black and white.

"Do you have anything valuable in the trunk?"

"Do I what?"

She jerked the wheel hard to the right and jammed the brake pedal to the floor. The Crown Victoria braked an instant late, slamming head-on into the Dart's right fender. The patrol car windshield blazed white as twin air bags exploded into the driver and passenger, and before the shock of impact could wear off she stomped on the gas again and spun away, spewing a cloud of red dust behind her. She veered hard right, dragging the crumpled remains of a fender as she disappeared into the tall grass.

Nick was thrown forward like a toy, hurtling almost into the front floor, then rebounded back once again amid the paper and debris.

"It would *help* if you told me what you were going to do *before* you did it."

"You'll get used to it," she said. "I did."

She steered the car in a wide circle until she was at a three o'clock position to the patrol car, no more than twenty yards away. She slammed the brakes down hard again, shoved the stick into reverse and looked back over her shoulder.

"I'm going to back up now," she said to Nick. "Just thought I'd let you know."

"You're going to *what?*"

"Didn't you ever go to the Demolition Derby when you were little? Oh, that's right...you're a *city* boy."

She jammed the accelerator to the floor. The car fishtailed left and right, and the grass behind them began to divide slowly, then faster and faster like an endless parting curtain. They both braced themselves...

A split second later they saw the black-and-white cruiser flash past them on their right. They had missed the front end by less than a foot.

As they raced past they saw that the hood was crumpled and bent down and back, and the grill and right headlight were shattered. They saw the face of the deputy frozen in shock and confusion.

But the driver's seat was empty.

Kathryn curved left away from the car and sped backward thirty yards or more. She braked hard and sat silently for a moment, the engine idling but her mind still racing. She felt a hand on her shoulder and heard a voice near her right ear.

"He's on foot, Mrs. Guilford. He can hear our engine—and he has a *gun*. For crying out loud let's get out of here!"

Kathryn stomped the gas and veered hard left—then slowly began to curve right again in a wide circle around the patrol car.

"The other way, the other way!" Nick jabbed frantically over his shoulder.

She shook her head furiously.

"Was their engine still running? I couldn't tell. We've got to make sure or they'll be on us again in no time!"

She circled wide, counting the hours off a mental clock as the car roared on.

Three o'clock…four o'clock…five o'clock…

She knew the chance she was taking. In her mind's eye she saw Peter crouching invisibly in the tall grass, waiting for her to pass again, waiting with gun in hand and shell in chamber for the moment of impact when the car stood still, waiting to rise up and rapid-fire into the backseat—and then into the front? Peter had already done the unimaginable—was *anything* beyond him?

Nick crawled into the front seat again.

"When you think you're lined up, let me know. I'll poke my head up and guide you in. We only get one shot at this."

"Better poke your head up fast," she warned. "Peter loves a turkey shoot."

Eight o'clock…nine o'clock…ten o'clock…

From the corner of her eye Kathryn caught a glimpse of khaki and steel flashing through the grass to her right. An instant later the sheriff stood motionless less than ten yards ahead of them, gun raised and ready, aiming directly at the driver of the car.

He raised his head from the line of sight with a look of shocked recognition, then jerked the gun aside and tried to steady his aim on the passenger's seat—but the car was almost on top of him now and he had to lunge to the left, firing two shots wildly as the right fender brushed past his leg. The first shot shattered the windshield into a mosaic of a thousand green and white tiles, and the second exploded into the backseat in a puff of grayish oatmeal.

Nick twisted to the right and hunched down into the seat, and with all of his strength shoved the passenger door open. It caught the sheriff full on, knocking him from his feet and sending him tumbling away—but the force of the impact slammed the door back on Nick. The crumbling door wobbled for a moment, then broke completely away from the car and bounded end over end into the tall grass.

Stunned and senseless, Nick lurched forward and rolled out of the car.

Kathryn screamed and lunged for him—too late! Twenty yards ahead she skidded to a stop and turned to the rear window. There was no sound, no motion in the tall reeds. Nothing. She reached for the horn—and then stopped.

She threw open the door and leaped up onto the searing hood. Her right foot punched through the shattered remains of the windshield as she scrambled up onto the roof. Thirty yards to the left she saw the gleaming white roof and red signal bar of the Crown Victoria. To the right, to the left, behind her—nothing. Then a single figure slowly staggered up out of the sea of green. It was Nick.

And he was wearing no glasses.

Kathryn started to shout and then caught herself. She waved her arms frantically—but what good would it do? What could Nick see without his glasses? Was she anything more than a blur to him, just a mysterious white smudge against the blue summer sky?

Then a second head rose up above the tall grass.

Peter turned slowly, dazed, still shaking off the effects of the collision—and he was limping. He stared toward the patrol car, then behind him, and finally turned to Kathryn, who seemed to be somehow standing on the very tips of the blades of long grass just thirty yards away. His mind began to clear. Kathryn looked in horror at Nick, still stunned, standing out like a tombstone on a prairie.

Peter followed her eyes. He raised his gun.

"Nick, get down!"

Nick disappeared into the grass like a trout with a captured fly. A gunshot echoed across the open meadow.

"Run!" she screamed. "But stay down!"

She watched the brush crumple and bend beneath the feet of an invisible figure, and she saw a path began to open—directly toward the sheriff.

"No, the *other* way!"

The grass stood still for an instant, then began to bend and open rapidly in the opposite direction. The sheriff limped forward, following, searching. Suddenly he stopped, dropped from sight for a moment, then straightened up again.

"Looky what I found," he said, holding up a pair of enormous spectacles. He dropped them at his feet. There was a crunching sound, and then he began to hobble in Nick's direction again.

Kathryn's heart leaped into her throat.

"Is *that* all you're looking for, Peter?" she shouted. "A blind Bug Man? Well, go ahead if that's what you want—but by the time you find him I'll be long gone!" She forced herself to laugh.

Peter stopped. He looked out across the vast, glistening meadow. Then he looked back at Kathryn.

He turned.

Kathryn took a last mental fix on Nick's speed and direction, then jumped down from the car. She threw open the door, stretched her right leg in, and revved the engine twice. Then she slammed the door hard and loud, doubled over, and vanished into the meadow. An instant later she reappeared, ducked into the car, and ripped out the keys.

She scrambled off into the thick grass, the blind in search of the blind.

CHAPTER 38

"Can you see the Quonset from here?" Nick whispered.

"It's about two hundred yards away," Kathryn whispered back. "I thought you were farsighted."

"I said I can see better at a distance—I didn't say I can see."

They lay exhausted at the outer edge of the meadow. They had scrambled and clambered a half-mile or more, Kathryn leading the way and Nick struggling to follow the blurred flurry of arms and legs ahead of him. They lay facedown, panting, the heavy feather grass bowing and tickling at their arms and necks.

"Okay." Nick hoisted himself up again. "Let's go for it."

"Nick, wait. It's open ground—we'll be sitting ducks. Maybe we should wait here until it gets dark."

Nick shook his head. "We have to get to the lab before he does. He knows we're going there for a reason. If he finds that puparium and destroys it, we're sunk."

"Nick—what if he destroys *us?*"

"He can't be far behind us. He's going to find us anyway. You said he was limping—our only advantage is to stay ahead of him."

She looked at him. "He may be limping, but you're blind."

He squeezed her arm. "But I've got eyes. Look, the sheriff had a chance to shoot you while you were driving and again when you were standing on the roof of the car. But he didn't. Don't you see? If we stay close together he won't take a chance on shooting and hitting *you*—not at a distance anyway. If we can get to the lab before he does, we can grab the puparium and head out into the woods. If we can make it to the woods we've got a chance."

Kathryn felt a wave of panic sweep over her.

"Let him have it. I don't want you to die. It's not fair. Let him *have* the evidence."

"I appreciate that," Nick said softly, "but I'm afraid it's a little late. You see, Mrs. Guilford, I *am* the evidence now."

They rose side by side, still cautiously doubled over, one arm wrapped around the other's waist like yoked oxen. Behind them in the distance they heard the sound of thrashing grass. They glanced at each other silently and took off running.

They ran frantically, desperately at first—then Nick tightened his grip on Kathryn's waist and reined her back.

"Easy. Pace yourself. Long way to go still."

Nick ran wide-eyed, feeling for the ground ahead of him with every step. Misty shapes and blurs of color streaked by on all sides.

He stumbled and fell headlong. Kathryn hurried him to his feet again, cursing herself for failing at her duty so badly. She looked back over her shoulder—no sign of a figure emerging from the meadow. She looked ahead to the Quonset—no more than fifty yards to go. She felt a sudden surge of energy.

"Come on! We're almost there!"

Only thirty yards to go, then twenty. They approached the

building from the side circled around toward the front. They rounded the corner with a sense of elation, exhausted but exuberant.

There on the front step stood the deputy.

They stumbled to a halt. Kathryn jerked Nick back abruptly.

"What is it?"

"It's Beanie," she said, panting. "Blocking the door!"

Kathryn released Nick and charged forward. "Beanie!" she waved her arms in a menacing arc. "Go away! Let us in!"

"Can't."

"Beanie, it's me!" she said almost in tears. "*Please* let us in!"

"Can't," he repeated. "Unca Pete said not to."

"What else?" Nick called out. "What else did Uncle Pete tell you to do?"

"Said I should catch you. Hold you till he comes."

"And if I don't want to be held?"

"Said I should *break* you."

Kathryn threw herself at him, pounding at his simian chest. "Beanie, this is Aunt Kathryn! *Aunt Kathryn* is telling you to go away and leave us alone!"

Beanie smiled down at her, oblivious to the tickling blows.

"It's no use," Nick said. "Rock beats scissors, Mrs. Guilford—*Uncle Pete* overrules *Aunt Kathryn.* Besides," he said, nodding toward a blur at the edge of the meadow, "I think we're out of time."

Two hundred yards away, just washing ashore from the rolling sea of green, the sheriff came limping toward the Quonset.

"We've got to separate," Nick said urgently.

"I won't leave you!"

"Listen to me!" he thundered. "He's not interested in me, he wants you! All he's *ever* wanted is you! He sent Pinocchio here to deal with me—to *hold* me, remember? That means he plans to go after you first, then come back for me. If we stay together they'll catch us both at once. Our only chance is to deal with them one at a time. We've got to separate!"

"What happens when he comes back for you?"

"One thing at a time, Mrs. Guilford. You've got to go!"

She took one faltering step away, then glanced back at the meadow. The sheriff was just a hundred yards away now. His left hand supported his wounded thigh, and his right hand rested on his holster. She turned in terror to Nick.

"But you can't *see,*" she pleaded.

"You can't help me now, and I'm afraid I can't help you either. But believe me, Kathryn," he said with a smile and a nod, "you're more than a match for any man *I* know. Now *go!*" he thundered again, and she turned and ran weeping toward the far meadow.

Nick watched for a moment, tormented by the thought that his final image of Kathryn Guilford might be nothing more than a streak of blue and a smear of dancing auburn.

He turned back to the building. He saw nothing but a blurry green semicircle, like a slice of lime beneath a sheet of waxed paper. He could make out the shadowy shapes of the windows on each side and a dark rectangle in the center dominated by an enormous, khaki-colored smudge. He had to get into the lab. Everything he knew, everything that might help him was inside.

"So, Deputy," he called out. "I thought you were supposed to *hold* me."

The khaki smudge shifted uneasily.

"You can't hold me from over there. You're not doing your job, Benjamin. Uncle Pete's gonna be awful mad!"

The shape began to stretch and grow until it covered the shadow of the door. Nick started to back away.

If he gets those hands on me again, I'm finished.

He dropped to his knees and began to feel the ground all around him. He scuttled back on all fours constantly reaching, searching, until he came upon a small branch about three feet long. He grabbed the very end, stood up, and pointed it at his approaching foe like Peter Pan attacking a pirate ship.

The khaki blur was almost on top of him now. Nick stood staring, blinking, sensing. Suddenly he saw a streak of pink and felt the branch swept aside. He jumped back a step and shoved the branch in the deputy's face again. Once more it was brushed aside, and once more he repeated the strange maneuver. The deputy grew impatient—this time he grabbed the branch, and at that instant Nick pulled hard. The childlike deputy instinctively joined this little game of tug of war and pulled back even harder, drawing Nick close—dangerously close. Nick jerked the branch again, this time with his full strength—and then he waited. He waited for that instant when the deputy would pull back again with *his* full strength.

And when he did, Nick let go.

The deputy toppled backward and sprawled in the gravel parking lot with a huff and a crunch. Nick turned toward the lab—he had bought himself thirty seconds, maybe less, and he would need all of it. He fixed his eyes on the blurry rectangle in the center of the Quonset and ran toward it, ran as fast as he possibly could with his arms extended straight ahead like a frantic sleepwalker.

I see the door—but how far away is it? Can't afford to slow down—and I sure don't have time to go searching for a doorknob.

An instant later his right ankle caught the edge of the wooden step, and he stumbled headlong into the screen door. His arms and head punched through the screen wire like tissue paper. The center strut caught him across the ribs, and the wooden frame shattered and folded inward like an umbrella. For an instant he lay trapped, surrounded in a tangle of wood and wire like a Lepidoptera in a butterfly net. He leaped to his feet thrashing, flailing, kicking himself free. He turned back to the door and saw the khaki blur rise from the ground, straighten, and then begin to grow larger once again.

Twenty seconds...I've got twenty seconds, no more.

He stumbled back against the glass cases. Nick whirled around and slapped his hands against the cool glass. He paused for a split second, thinking—then he stumbled to the left, feeling his way along the glass fronts until he came to the corner, to the last case on the bench, to the fragment of signboard he had once taped to the glass that cautioned unknowing visitors: BUTHIDAE—DO NOT REACH INTO TERRARIUM WITH REMAINING HAND.

He tore off the cover, grabbed the huge case by the lip, and dragged it over onto the floor. It landed in a thundering crash of glass and rock and sand, and then there was silence.

Except for the tiny, brittle sound of a hundred skittering legs.

Nick leaped backward, feeling rapidly along the glass cases to his right until he came to the case at the opposite end. He backed around the corner, positioning himself behind the massive terrarium.

"Sorry, Lord Vader, there's a disturbance in the Force."

The deputy arrived in the doorway, picking his way through the tangled wreckage of the screen door.

"Hello, Deputy," Nick said with a nod. "Welcome to *my* world."

The deputy started forward. Nick waited, seeing nothing, estimating the seconds required for the deputy to reach the corner—and then with one great shove smashed the terrarium onto the floor at his feet.

"Look out!" Nick pointed at the floor. A dozen glistening black-knuckled hands with bulbous claws and arcing tails reached out for the deputy's feet. Beanie staggered backward in terror, back toward the open doorway, stumbling blindly into the entangling heap of wood and wire and mesh.

He fell like a giant redwood on the shattered remains of the other terrarium.

He lay stunned for a moment, arms and legs wallowing in the debris—and then there was the skittering of legs again, the flash of slender pedipalps, and the lightning whip of needle-tipped metasomas.

"Ow," he said dully, and then "Ow!" again.

He raised himself to his elbows. "Ow!" He jerked his right elbow up and rolled onto his left side.

"Ouch! Ouch! Ow! Bees or sump'n!" He slowly rolled to his feet.

Nick felt his way down the aisle toward the office door, listening. If he counted correctly the deputy had just taken a half-dozen stings from the *Androctonus australis*—the north African fat tail scorpion—one of the deadliest scorpions in the world.

He found the door. He fumbled for the doorknob, slipped inside, and slammed it shut behind him. He turned to the lab.

The puparium. Got to find the puparium.

He had left it in a folded handkerchief resting in the center of the worktable—or was it by the microscope? He swept the room with his useless eyes. He saw wispy streaks of green and white, mounded blurs of black and chrome, and flashes of fluorescent blue and shadowy gray. How could he possibly hope to find a puparium the size of a grain of rice?

My extra pair of glasses!

He lunged forward and crashed into a rolling stool, sending it rocketing into the corner. He bumped blindly into the worktable and began to work his way to the right, patting his outstretched hands over the cluttered surface, his darting fingers detecting only textures of vinyl and paper and plastic.

They're in the desk drawer. Or on top of the bookshelf. No—they're in the filing cabinet with the hot plate. He began to slow down. *Or in the glove compartment of the Dodge. Or in my trailer. Or in Pittsburgh…*

He stopped. If he couldn't find his extra glasses when he had perfect vision, what were the chances of finding them now?

Behind him the office door burst open. Nick spun around. He could hear the sound of the deputy's shallow breathing and repeated swallowing. His footsteps seemed to shuffle, almost stumble into the room.

The deputy already had systemic effects; his adrenal gland was dumping catecholamines by the truckload. A single sting from a fat tail can kill an average-sized man in a few hours—how long would it take the venom of six to work its way through this mountain of flesh?

One thing's for sure—I can't wait around to find out.

"Beanie, listen to me. Those weren't bees that stung you, they were *scorpions.* Do you know what a scorpion is?"

Nick eased slowly to the left as he spoke, edging his way toward the exterior door. He stared wide-eyed at the blur before him, watching for the slightest change in shape or size.

"It's like a wasp, only worse—*much* worse. More like a *snake.*"

"Weren't no snake," said a whimpering voice.

"*Like* a snake. Like a copperhead, or a rattlesnake—even worse than that! You've got to sit down, Beanie; you've got to rest."

"Unca Pete said to catch you. Unca Pete said to *hold* you."

It's no use—whatever Uncle Pete wants, Uncle Pete gets. If I can't get him to slow down, then I've got to get him to speed up—I've got to speed the circulation of the venom through his system. I've got to make him run!

Nick whirled around and groped for the doorknob.

"Well, come on then, Deputy!" he called back over his shoulder. "Catch me if you can!"

He threw open the door and lunged out. He took two quick steps forward, caught the wooden deck rail across the groin, flipped head over heels and fell five feet to the ground below. He lay stunned, winded, the sky circling above him in screaming streaks of blue and white.

Suddenly a khaki thundercloud loomed overhead, and Nick heard the heavy clump of boots on the wooden stairs.

Can't breathe...no time...got to get up...got to get moving!

He struggled to his feet and started to run—but which way? The last time he ran, he was yoked to Kathryn; the last time he ran he had her eyes. This time he was on his own. He did a quick mental inventory of the hazards and barriers around the lab—the coils of razor wire, the half-buried posts, the rusted pump housings, the overgrown sinkholes. But there was no time, no time to plan a strategy, no time to chart a path or course. "One thing at a time," he had told Kathryn—and right now the thing was to *run.*

There was only one direction to go—wherever the deputy was not. He spun around until he spotted that imposing silhouette, then launched out in the opposite direction.

The deputy started after him. He ran slowly at first, toddling like a child, then lumbering like an awkward foal, then galloping like a Great Plains buffalo. Nick listened to the pounding footsteps behind him. They grew heavier and more erratic, and the breathing was increasingly labored—but the deputy was still matching him step for step, even *gaining* on him. With his sight he could have easily outdistanced the clumsy, plodding deputy—but now he was forced to run like a child himself, shortening his stride and checking each uncertain step. He felt like a circus clown jammed onto a tiny tricycle, his long legs jabbing up and down like pistons, pedaling furiously but going nowhere fast.

He looked up ahead. He could see no trees, no bushes, no details of any kind—but he could at least distinguish where the dark ground ended and the glowing sky began, and it rose sharply to the left.

If I can't beat him with speed, I have to beat him with endurance. I've got to make his heart pump; I've got to make his blood flow. I've got to go up!

He veered left and began to climb. The steep hill cut his own speed in half, but it slowed the struggling deputy even more. The upward climb forced Beanie's thundering heart to pump, to push, to strain…and with every gushing pulse the deadly neurotoxins spread.

Suddenly the footsteps behind him stopped. Nick turned, panting, listening. He heard the deputy double over and retch. He staggered forward, halting every few steps in crippling convulsions.

"Can you feel it, Deputy?" Nick called back. "Can you feel the poison spreading through your system? Does it hurt where they stung you? Are your arms and legs swelling yet? Are your eyes watering, does your tongue feel thick and fat, is your throat closing up? Next comes the cramping and then paralysis—that means you can't move, even if you want to. And then you die, Deputy, you *die*—just like Teddy died when you put a bullet in the back of his head!"

The deputy looked up, forced himself erect, and started toward Nick again.

Nick began to backpedal, easily maintaining the distance between them now. "Come on then," he shouted. "Come and get me, Beanie boy! Uncle Pete said to hold me, remember? Uncle Pete said to break me! Well come on then, *break* me! I dare you! Come on, Beanie, don't let Uncle Pete down!"

Nick turned to run again—he saw a horizontal flash of purplish brown and then an explosion of fire and light.

He ran head-on into the limb of a tree.

He lay on his back, nauseous from the impact. He felt his forehead—a jagged ravine lay open across the center, and blood poured into his eyes. He squeezed them shut, rubbed them with knotted fists, and forced them open again. He saw nothing but blotches of light through streaks and stains of red. He was blind now, *really* blind.

And he heard footsteps.

Heavy, dragging, desperate footsteps. And breathing like the sound of ripping canvas, like hissing steam and gurgling tar.

And it was close.

Nick rolled onto his stomach. He felt a tree root coursing under him like a vein. He felt his way along the root, crawling forward until he came to the trunk. He circled around to the opposite side, then reached up and felt for the lowest limb. He pulled himself up and stopped, his own stomach in convulsions, every heartbeat exploding in his head like mortar fire.

He reached up—he pulled—he rested. Waves of dizziness and nausea almost washed him from the tree.

He reached up—he pulled—he rested. He dragged himself up limb after limb—how far had he climbed? How high was high enough?

"Come on!" he shouted below him. "Come after me, you pathetic puppet! Climb! Work! Pull yourself up!"

Below him he heard the rattle of fluid-filled lungs and the crackle of crumbling twigs. The deputy was climbing after him.

An instant later a ham-sized hand clamped his left ankle in a grip of iron.

Nick reached up—he pulled…no more. He had nothing left. He threw his arms around the tree and held on.

Now the deputy began to pull—slowly, firmly, until it felt to Nick as though the deputy's entire weight was suspended from his ankle. Nick tried to kick his leg free—impossible.

Now Nick's own grip began to give way. He dug his fingers desperately into the trunk, but he continued to slide helplessly to the left. There was fire in his knee and left hip socket, and the coarse bark raked across his naked chest like burning coals.

The limb began to bend…

"Beanie!" Nick raged through grinding teeth. "Will—you—hurry—up—and—*die!*"

The huge hand began to tremble, then loosen, then slip away, taking Nick's tennis shoe with it. There was an instant of silence, then a great rustle of leaves, and a snap like the crack of a rifle—then silence again.

Nick looked down. Somewhere far below him a smear of brown and green and khaki lay perfectly still.

"Shoofly pie," Nick whispered.

He threw his arms around the tree again, and everything went black.

CHAPTER 39

The sheriff limped to the open doorway and glared in. He saw the twisted wreckage of the screen door and the floor littered with dirt and rock and shards of broken glass. The door to the blue-bright office stood open, and within the office one exterior door swung slowly on its hinges.

From seventy-five yards away he had watched Kathryn turn and flee toward the far side of the building. He hobbled forward, clutching his left thigh where the door handle caught him just below the hip. The impact had knocked him twenty feet and left a throbbing fist-sized knot of purple and green. He never lost consciousness, but it had been a full minute before he struggled to his feet and spotted the despectacled head of Dr. Polchak bobbing like a buoy above the sea of yellow-green. He drew his sidearm and leveled it—but Kathryn's shout made him rush his shot, and he fired harmlessly overhead, cursing himself for his lack of discipline.

He stopped and swept the field with eyes as dark as blood.

There.

A hundred yards away in the center of an open meadow Kathryn stood perfectly still. She faced away from him with her head slightly bowed, and her arms seemed to disappear at the elbow as though her hands might be folded in front of her. She looked to him like that goddess in the picture book at the Holcum County Library, majestic and holy and alabaster-pure, but without arms—because the goddess reaches out for no one, but waits eternally for someone worthy to reach for her.

But he was unworthy…he knew that now.

He limped forward. She heard him approach like the slink of a jackal.

Ten yards away he stopped.

"Kath," he said softly. "We got to talk."

She never moved—not a twitch, not a nod, not even a breath. She stood motionless, implacable, and mute. Her auburn ponytail hung down, tied by an artist into a thick sable brush, swaying from side to side and painting a masterpiece of soft curves and perfect forms—a masterpiece that he would never touch again. Her jeans were spotted and soiled but still crisp and tight. Her T-shirt draped between her shoulder blades with sweat.

And two white shoestrings met in a bow at the center of her back.

"Okay," he said. "Then just listen. I know you're mad at me—hey, I don't blame you. I'm not asking you to forgive me. I just want you to try to understand—about Andy, about Jimmy, about everything."

He took a step forward.

"Yes, I was mad when you married Andy. But what could I do? I knew Andy loved you. I knew Jimmy loved you too—we all did. But when I saw you and Andy together, I knew you loved him back. And that was okay—really. I figured it was just sort of his turn."

He stepped forward again.

"Remember what I told you? I always knew we were meant

to be together. I never knew when—I just knew it had to be. Finally, eventually, someday. And I figured lots of things would probably happen before that day. Like I might go off to the service or you might move away—but it didn't really matter, because I knew that someday, somehow, we would both end up together. It just had to be.

"I wish I could tell you why I'm so cocksure about it. Some things you don't just think with your head, it's something deeper—something way down inside. It's like when I hunt way back in the woods—you can blindfold me, you can spin me around, but when I take the blindfold off I can always find my way out. I got no map, I got no compass, but it doesn't matter—'cause I've got something inside that tells me which way the arrow points, that tells me which way is up. I see the sun, I see the stars, I can see the big picture in my head—and I know where I fit in the picture. I can't explain it, but that's how it works—and that's how it works with you too. I know how my life is supposed to go—I can see it—and you were supposed to be part of it."

Another step closer still.

"When you married Andy I figured, 'Okay. Not yet.' So I waited. I waited real patient. I waited like a gentleman because it wasn't my turn yet. But I knew that someday things would have to change—I could see it in my head.

"So every day I expected something to change, something to happen. Every time Andy crossed the street, I thought a truck might pop out of nowhere and run him down. Every time the 82d did a training jump, I thought his chute might not open, that he'd be the one we'd bring back in a bag. But it never happened. Things just kept going the way they were, all wrong and needing to be made right.

"Let me tell you, it wasn't easy to just sit and wait for things to straighten themselves out. It's like when you see old Mr. Jenks sleeping night after night on the bench outside the True Value. Don't you ever get tired of waiting for him to get sober, to straighten up and get himself a job? Sometimes the church gives him a new set of clothes or takes up a collection and gives him a few bucks—and then he goes and drinks it up again. They can't make him change, but they can help him change. Sometimes I got tired of waiting, sometimes I thought maybe I should help things change. Maybe I should be the one driving the truck, maybe I should help him pack his chute.

"But I never did. I just kept waiting, giving him his turn like a friend should do—but things kept going on all out of kilter. And then that day that Andy came to see me in the Gulf, he said, 'When we get back, me and Kath are gonna have kids. Time to start a family,' he said. And that's when I knew that things had to change right away. He wasn't being fair, don't you see? His turn was almost over, and he was planning to take what was mine. My turn. My kids. My family."

He spoke gently and calmly, and he moved constantly forward as he spoke.

"I'm still not sure what happened at Al Salman. I didn't plan it, that's for sure. Andy got ahead of us just like Jimmy said. Tryin' to be the first one across the line, I suppose; he was like that. He was backed up against a berm, and there were hostiles on the other side. Jimmy started firing over the berm, trying to hold them back. I stuck my head up too. I was planning to do the same, I really was. Jimmy was firing away, firing at nothing, wasting ammo like a fool. I played it smart, I sited across the top of the berm and waited for some dumb wog to stick his head up—and then my site crossed Andy's head…

"You want to know the truth, Kath? I'm not sure if I shot him on purpose or not. I thought about killing him—I don't deny that—but I don't remember ever saying to myself, *Do it, Pete. Pull the trigger. Kill him now.* It just…happened. But after it happened, I knew that the world was closer to the way it was supposed to be.

"I'm not saying it was right—but sometimes the world doesn't care if things are right, it just shakes things up and puts them back in order. You see a baby bird on the ground because the nest got too crowded and Mama kicked him out to let him die. Is that right? You see a little girl with no hair 'cause she's got some kind of gut-rotting cancer or something, is that right? It doesn't much matter, does it? The world has a path it follows, and when it gets off course it just fixes things and jumps back in line again. And if you're one of the things needs fixing—well, you're just out of luck, that's all."

He stood just behind Kathryn now, little more than an arm's length away. A bee buzzed by, and he dipped his head to let it pass.

"I don't think you're really mad at me," he said softly. "I think you're just scared. You're scared because no one has ever loved you like this before. No one else ever could—the kind of love where the whole world will change its course to make sure it happens. You know what, Kath? Sometimes it scares me too—knowing that no matter what I do, no matter what anybody does, we got to end up together. Together forever."

He flipped up the leather hasp on his holster and slid out the gun. The M9 Beretta held fifteen rounds.

He pulled on the slide and quietly ejected four shells.

"Now about Jimmy." He took a deep breath. "Yes, I found out he was using cocaine in the Gulf. And no, I wasn't going to turn him in—but I sure told him I was. I thought the threat of it might do him some good; I thought it might scare some sense into him. It didn't—because he was weak. Jim was always weak. That was his problem, and that's why I knew he could never have you.

"Sure he helped me bury Andy—why shouldn't he? He had just as much reason to want Andy dead as I did—maybe more. You think he didn't lie awake at night just like I did and think about accidents and things that might go wrong? You think when the three of us shipped out he didn't hope that only two of us would come back—or maybe only one? And that night at Al Salman, when Andy got cut off—you think he really wanted

Andy back safe and sound? He didn't go after Andy, you know. He just sat there safe and snug behind his little wall hoping and praying that some Iraqi bullet would do the job for him. And then he stuck his rifle over the wall and started firing—firing at what? You know what I think? I think he hoped one of his own stray shots might find the mark.

"But life doesn't work that way. You can't just hope for things, Kath, you got to make them happen; you got to be the man. Jim looked over at me, and he knew what I was thinking—he knew because he was thinking it too. The only difference was I was willing to do it. So I pulled the trigger. I did what he could never do; I did what he could only wish and whine and snivel about. And you know what he did then? He started to cry, he started to blubber like a baby—because he saw that I was strong and he was weak, that I did what he could never do, and that I was the only one who deserved to have you."

As he spoke he drew back the slide again and again. Four gleaming brass cylinders tumbled through the air and disappeared into the thick meadow grass.

"Who knows? Maybe I was weak too. Maybe I should have sent Jim after Andy and then finished both of them off. I didn't; now I wish I had. So we came home, Jim and me, and he was weaker than ever, he was hooked on that stuff for good. The only time he felt strong, the only time he felt good about himself was when he was flying high. He'd whimper and wail and moan about what we done, about what happened to 'poor Andy'—and then he'd do a little fluff, and all of a sudden he was strong; he was in control again. And then he'd always say, 'I'm going straight, I'm getting off this stuff. And when I do, I'm going to the authorities, I'm turning you in for what you done.'

"But I knew he never would, because he was a coward. Because the next day he'd be down at the bottom of the well again, and he'd be craving the stuff—just once more, just one line, just this last time, and then that's it. He knew that if he really went to the authorities they'd make him go straight, and we both knew he couldn't live without it.

"But I figured, what if he can't get the stuff? Then he'd have nothing to lose, then he just might turn me in. So when he ran out of money, I began to supply him. I struck a bargain with Ronny. Did you really think he made that kind of money just by selling burial polices to old ladies? Don't worry about Ronny—he won't be turning up in any meadow. He won't be turning up anywhere.

"And that's how it went for years. I looked the other way when Ronny did business in Holcum County, and Ronny kept Jimmy happy. I knew Jim would never turn me in. He needed me—he needed the stuff.

"Then a couple of weeks ago I was at my place in Valdosta, and one day Jim showed up—hitchhiked the whole way down. Said he had a change of mind, a change of heart. Said he had to clear his conscience; he had to come clean and make things right. I told him I would make things right just like I always did—that all he needed to do was keep his mouth shut—but he kept saying he was going to turn me in, that this time he really meant it. I didn't believe him at first—I thought it was just the cocaine talking again—but the longer I listened, the more I believed he just might do it this time. He really meant business; he even had his gun with him.

"So I hit him. Just once. Right between the eyes. Not hard enough to kill him, just hard enough to shut him up. I needed some quiet, I needed some time to think. And then I looked at him lying there on the ground, and I knew what I had to do. It was just like Al Salman again. I didn't plan it; I didn't want it to happen—life just gave me the chance to straighten things out again, and I had to choose. I couldn't just wish and hope that Jim would keep his big mouth shut, I had to make it happen. I had to be strong again.

"So I pulled out his gun, and I put it in his hand. And I was strong.

"But I didn't have a plan, so I had to think. I went back in the cabin, and I thought—I thought for a long time—and I figured it all out. I loaded him in the trunk of my car, and then I laid him in the meadow back here in Rayford. I knew some hunter would find him, and I knew they would call it a suicide. And I knew you would weep and wail and mourn, and then you would get over it. And then everything would finally be the way it was supposed to be."

Then, for the first time, the statue spoke. Without turning, without even moving, a tiny voice drifted up from Kathryn, half whisper and half-moan.

"Amy… You murdered Amy, didn't you?"

"That wasn't murder," he grumbled. "I just put her out of her misery like her old cat. I had to. I didn't know what Jimmy told her before he left; I didn't know what she might tell you."

"You killed Teddy too. And Mrs. Gallagher. Oh, Peter, *Mrs. Gallagher.*"

"You made me do that!" the sheriff snapped back. "You made me do it when you wouldn't listen to me, when you got that Bug Man involved in all this."

"You knew what that fly would prove," Kathryn said. "That Jimmy died in Georgia and not in North Carolina. Then it wouldn't be a suicide—then there would be questions."

The sheriff said nothing.

"Do you know why it didn't work, Peter? Because you were weak—weak in the mind, just like you've always been—weak in the mind and sick in the soul. When you went to the lab and let the fly escape, you thought you had fixed everything. But you didn't. The fly left behind a little capsule, a kind of cocoon, and from that Nick still figured out where the fly came from. And when you were at my house, guess what Nick was doing? He was checking the radiator of your car, looking for flies just like the one he found on Jimmy's body. He found them, Peter, he found them. And when he shows them to the authorities, there'll be all kinds of questions. You're going to have a lot of explaining to do."

"I wouldn't worry about the doc," he shrugged. "I don't think he'll be showing anything to anybody. I stopped in at the lab on the way over—quite a mess. I don't think Benjamin had a very hard time catching up with a blind man, do you?"

Kathryn began to tremble.

"You're right about one thing," he said. "After the doc's death there'll be a lot of questions asked around here—more than I'll be able to explain. That's why I can't go back. That's why it all has to end here."

The sheriff pulled the slide twice more. Now only two bullets remained.

"I'm not asking you to forgive me. I just want you to understand—all this has happened because I love you. Because I was willing to be strong, because I was willing to do the hard thing for both of us." He looked down at the gun. "And I'm going to do the hard thing again, Kath—for both of us."

"You can kill me," she trembled, "but we still won't be together. Because I'll be in heaven with Andy, and you'll be frying in hell.

"Don't know much about hell," he said. "But I figure there's no heaven if I can't be with you."

He reached out and stroked her hair. A pair of bees circled her head once and buzzed away.

"I would never hurt you, Kath. I know how to make this quick and easy. I hope you understand that I can't leave you behind. If I did someone else might have you—and that can never be. We were supposed to be together, Kath—and if we can't live together, then..."

He slowly raised the Beretta and placed it at the base of her skull.

"Let me turn around," she whispered. "Let me see you one last time."

He lowered the gun.

She slowly turned.

In front of her she held a small, square crate covered with fine wire mesh. It was a bee crate—and it was empty.

She dropped it. It bounced away at her feet.

Around her torso, suspended by two white shoestrings, was a piece of screen wire rolled into the shape of a small tube. Inside was a single honeybee with an abdomen twice the size of an ordinary bee.

It was the queen.

And on the queen, on the wire tube, on Kathryn's waist and breasts and arms and neck, three thousand honeybees swarmed in one buzzing, roiling mass of black and gold.

The sheriff gasped. His arms went limp, and the gun slipped unnoticed from his hand. He stared in utter disbelief—yet there she stood, her soft, pink skin swarming with thousands of wriggling, crawling creatures of her own private hell.

Kathryn slowly raised her arms above her head and then stopped. Her face was pale and rigid, her lips were pressed tight shut, and her eyes were fixed in a scream of terror and rage and indomitable will.

And Peter knew that she was right, that he was weak, and that he had never been worthy of this woman. He lowered his eyes and opened his mouth to speak, but nothing came out. There was nothing left to say.

An instant later Kathryn threw her arms around his neck and squeezed.

There was a muted roar.

There was a muffled crunch.

And there was an overwhelming odor of smashed bananas.

CHAPTER 40

Kathryn drifted in a velvet void. She turned without turning and looked about. It was black, everywhere black, nothing but black. She strained her eyes to stare deeper into the darkness, but she had no eyes to strain. She raised her hand to feel for her face, but she had no face, and no hand either. She was only a mind, floating free in the starless night of sleep—or was it death? There was no pain, there was no care, but she was somehow still aware. And somehow she knew that the darkness had an end, that if she had hands to reach out with she would find walls not far away—cool walls, smooth walls, curving up like a vaulted dome above her. And somehow she knew that she was staring at the inside of her own skull.

Then a buzzing sound whizzed by very close, a sound that some ancient instinct told her should evoke fear—but there was no fear, not here. There was a second buzz, then another, and each one struck the wall of her skull with a bright white spark and ricocheted back even louder and closer than before. The buzzing grew louder, and the sparks flashed brighter until it all blended together into one blinding, sizzling light. And suddenly the walls were gone, and the light came streaming in.

And the light brought back the pain.

Now a face appeared above her in the light. It was an odd face but nevertheless a strong and good face, and it was strangely familiar. The face began to soften and come into better focus. In the center was a pair of enormous spectacles.

She reached out her hand to touch the face, and she had hands again.

"Hello, Dorothy." Nick smiled down at her. "Welcome back to Kansas." He sat beside her on the edge of her hospital bed and cradled her right hand in his.

She looked up into the familiar brown orbs that bobbed and floated behind the glass—only now they floated in a storm of red and black that spiraled out from under his glasses like the fingers of a hurricane. Across his forehead was a long white bandage spotted with dots of scarlet.

She reached up and touched his cheek.

"Are you…alive?" she whispered, her lips barely moving.

"More or less—if you call this living."

"You look terrible."

"Look who's talking."

Her eyes drifted from his face, to her hand, to her arm. The hand looked normal enough, but on her forearm she saw a spatter of reddish spots and blisters that increased in size and number until her entire upper arm seemed to erupt in a cascade of fleshy bumps and moguls. She reached up and felt about her face and neck. Her neck was a continuous mass of lumps and welts. Her cheeks were puffed and bloated, and her bloodshot eyes peeked out from their swollen sockets like two cranberries from a muffin.

"How do I look?"

"*Lumpy* is the word that comes to mind. But on you it looks good." He leaned back for a moment, taking a better view. "You look like one of those Cabbage Patch Dolls, remember?"

She slowly rolled her eyes, then closed them.

"Those were very popular, you know."

"How long have I—"

"Been away? About three days. Not bad considering you took about a thousand stings, mostly to the torso. The doctors stopped counting at seven hundred, but I counted more."

She raised one eyebrow.

He shrugged. "I had some time to kill. A thousand stings is nowhere near the record, but still very impressive." He leaned forward and gently brushed a stray wisp of auburn from her forehead. "I'm afraid your friend the sheriff didn't fare as well."

"What happened?"

"Are you sure you want to know?"

She hesitated for an instant—only an instant—and then nodded.

"My guess would be he was unconscious before he hit the ground and dead within a minute—two at the most. You were very thorough. He took about as many stings as you did, but it didn't take a thousand to kill him, just two or three. I warned him to stay away from bees. I should have warned him to stay away from women who *wear* them."

She smiled, and it hurt.

For a minute he said nothing more. He just sat staring, slowly shaking his head. "Well," he said abruptly, "I'd say your entomophobia has improved *considerably.*"

Another smile, another shooting pain.

She touched his face again. "He told me you were dead."

"He told you that?"

"He saw the lab. He said it was a wreck."

"Well *that's* true. Of course, it was a wreck before. I think he was referring to the screen door. I had a little trouble finding the doorknob, so I had to run through it." He paused. "Or maybe he was talking about my scorpion collection. I'm still looking for a few of them."

Kathryn's eyes widened.

"I was a little careless on the way to the office," he said. "It seems I accidentally spilled my collection of north African fat tails on the floor—and I'm afraid the deputy had the unfortunate experience of falling down on them."

She winced.

"It was heart failure or possibly respiratory collapse—probably both. He lasted less than an hour, but it was a very *long* hour."

"Poor Beanie," she whispered.

"The deputy's cousins have already claimed his body."

"And Peter?"

Nick shrugged. "No wife, no family, and no friends left, either. Nobody seemed to want the sheriff's remains. Don't worry, it's all been taken care of."

She took a moment to close her eyes and rest.

"Ronny," she said suddenly. "Ronny was the supplier."

"I figured. If the deputy couldn't drive himself to Teddy's trailer, somebody else had to do it—somebody who also had an interest in seeing Teddy dead. The sheriff was occupied; that left only one other interested party: the supplier. After all, if the sheriff went down, he could take Ronny down with him. I'll bet Ronny was more than happy to drive. We'll have to see what we can do about Ronny."

"I don't think anyone's going to find Ronny."

"The sheriff?"

She nodded.

"Very thoughtful of him. Saved us a lot of trouble."

She pointed to Nick's bandaged forehead.

"This? I was attacked by a *Quercus falcata,*" he said solemnly. "That's a *red oak* to you. I ran into a tree—a very hard one.

Which reminds me... I passed out *in* the tree. They never would have found me if you hadn't made it back to the lab and given the police my general direction. After all you went through, you were still able to make a phone call?" Nick let out a whistle. "In Pittsburgh, you are what we call 'one tough chick.'"

Kathryn looked up at him. "So what happens now?"

"You mean the investigation? We take the evidence we have to the authorities—not the ice cream man this time, the *real* authorities. The puparium should still be in the lab, and I'm betting the sheriff didn't have time to dispose of my shirt, so we can recover the specimens I collected from his radiator, too. That should be enough to request an exhumation, and then the medical examiner's office in Chapel Hill will look for further evidence."

"So now I *know,*" she said sadly.

"So now you know. How does it feel?"

She said nothing.

"If it's any consolation," Nick said, "we proved that your friend didn't take his own life. It turns out your hunch was right after all."

"So was your sense of smell. About Peter, I mean."

"And you're off the hook. You may have hurt your friend's feelings, but you didn't drive him to an early grave. Too bad Amy's not around to hear that."

She paused. "And I found out something I thought I never would. I found out what happened to Andy."

He squeezed her hand.

"*Most* important," he said brightly, "you avoided a possible marriage to a deranged megalomaniac."

"What? Did *you* propose too?"

"Not likely." Nick smiled. "Proposing to *you* seems to be a definite health risk."

Kathryn looked thoughtfully at the ceiling. "All in all, it was a good week's work."

"We worked pretty well together," he nodded. "Which reminds me... Now that Teddy's gone I'll be needing a new assistant, and...well, I was just wondering..."

She blinked.

"...if you'll be *paying* me anytime soon. It takes a lot of money to hire a research assistant, you know."

She glared at him. "I'll pay you," she said crossly. "I said I'd pay you and I will. Twenty thousand dollars."

"Plus expenses," he reminded her.

"What expenses?"

"My car. Destroyed in the line of duty. Destroyed by you personally, I might add."

"I barely scratched it!"

"The windshield is gone. The right door fell off. The rear fender is missing. There's a bullet hole in the backseat. And after you left it, with the sheriff's assistance it burned to the ground."

She covered her face and let out a snort like a startled mare.

"I find your lack of respect for the dead alarming," Nick said. "I have no choice but to bill you for the full replacement value of the vehicle. That brings your current total to twenty thousand *and* thirty-seven dollars. That might seem a little high, but I had a half of a pizza in the backseat."

She laughed in spite of herself. It was agonizing, healing laughter.

"And I don't take checks," he frowned. "Not from *your* bank anyway."

They sat in silence for a minute.

"You called me Kathryn," she said quietly.

"What?"

"In front of the lab. When you said we had to separate, you called me *Kathryn*—not Mrs. Guilford."

"That's right, I did, didn't I?"

"I remember something Teddy taught me. The first principle of taxonomy is: Never mind what a thing appears to be, what is its true *nature?* Well now I know for sure that I'm not 'Mrs. Guilford' anymore. I'm Kathryn again. Just plain Kathryn."

"Kathryn," he repeated. "That will take some getting used to."

"Try it out from time to time. It'll grow on you."

He smiled again, and then he rose to leave.

"Do you have to go?" she said.

"I'm afraid so. I have another client who requires my attention."

"Another client? *Already?"*

■

On the extreme western boundary of Holcum County, in a remote area of old abandoned home fields, a pale green Quonset hut sits at the end of a winding gravel road. Behind the hut, across a short meadow, a dirt path disappears into the woods. Down the path, past the sagging hulk of a decomposing sow, past a mottled cadaver dressed in shreds of flannel, lies the burned-out skeleton of a '64 Dodge Dart.

The windshield is gone. The rear fender is missing. The right door gapes open. But the trunk remains closed.

And inside the trunk, flies buzz, eggs hatch, and a thousand wriggling maggots engorge themselves on a bloated figure still wearing a sheriff's star.

...TO BE CONTINUED

Where Your Faith Finds a Friend™

ISBN: 1-58229-314-7

Enjoyment Guarantee

If you are not totally satisfied with this book, simply return it to us along with your receipt, a statement of what you didn't like about the book, and your name and address within 60 days of purchase to Howard Publishing, 3117 North 7th Street, West Monroe, LA 71291-2227, and we will gladly reimburse you for the cost of the book.